CIRCLES OF TIME

"A powerful story . . . Rock recreate[s] another world of flesh and blood humanity that lives and breathes. . . . His characters feel and think in surroundings that are, in history, just the day before yesterday. There is love and hate and human misunderstanding, as well as joy and bitterness."　　　　—*San Diego Union*

"A first-class journey."
　　　　　—*Des Moines Sunday Register*

"The reality of time is what Rock's richly populated novel is about, the transition period between eras. . . . The reader comes to care about the Grevilles and [their] friends . . . But as one cheers their accommodation to life after the war, the novel moves on to Germany."
　　　　　—*The Washington Post*

"Rock is a master of the generational saga, a contemporary Galsworthy who creates characters we remember for their passions and loyalties and failings. . . . You simply won't want *Circles of Time* to end."—*West Coast Review of Books*

"A marvelous marriage of history and fiction that offers a vivid picture of what life was like in that era. . . . Rock's forte at creating breath-

ing characters is matched by his understanding of history. He captures the excitement of café society as well as the nightmares of virulent inflation in a Germany struggling to overcome the debts created by war. . . . It is wonderful to read about old friends from *The Passing Bells.*"
—*The Chattanooga Times*

"Some of the finest, most interesting and entertaining reading I've encountered for a long time."
—*The Jackson Daily News* and *Clarion Ledger*

"Impressive and thought-provoking."
—*The Sacramento Bee*

"Top entertainment . . . immensely energetic . . . crunchy with busy characters and situations."
—*Kirkus Reviews*

CIRCLES OF TIME

Phillip Rock

A DELL BOOK

Published by
Dell Publishing Co., Inc.
1 Dag Hammarskjold Plaza
New York, New York 10017

Dell ® TM 681510, Dell Publishing Co., Inc.

ISBN: 0-440-11320-2

Reprinted by arrangement with Seaview Books, a
division of Playboy Enterprises, Inc. Books

Printed in the United States of America

First Dell printing—August 1982

For Charlotte Wolfers
Death is a sleep.

CIRCLES OF TIME

Book One
PASSAGES
1921

With leaves and flowers do cover
The friendless bodies of unburied men.
Call unto his funeral dole
The ant, the field-mouse and the mole,
To rear him hillocks that shall keep him warm,
And, when gay tombs are robbed, sustain no harm;
But keep the wolf far hence, that's foe to men;
Or with his nails he'll dig them up again.

John Webster

I

He drove up to Flanders in the early summer of 1921 knowing that it would be for the last time. He had finally, after nearly four years, reconciled himself to the unalterable fact that she was dead.

He drove slowly from Paris along the dusty, poplar-lined road to Amiens. All of his belongings had been shipped the week before to London and he carried nothing but a few clean shirts, some underwear and socks in a battered leather bag. He felt a peculiar sense of freedom, as though the past had finally been left behind and all the ghosts that had haunted him for so long had been laid to rest. In Amiens, there were tourist buses lined up in front of the Cafe Flor waiting to take sightseers out to the old trenches along the Somme. He stopped for a sandwich and a glass of wine and watched the people—mostly middle-aged Americans and English—board the buses with their cameras and binoculars. He felt dispassionate about the sight. It had bothered him greatly in the past, but now it didn't matter. It was just a tourist attraction they were off to visit. No different, in a way, from any other ruin or relic of history.

That it *was* different, few people knew better than himself. He had witnessed the war almost from the first day, a lowly twenty-three-year-old theater reviewer for the Chicago *Express*, picked to be their war correspondent because fate had placed him in Europe when the German Army crossed into Belgium in the summer of 1914. The editor of the *Express* could have sent a more experienced man, but he believed the war would be over in six weeks—three months at the outside—and vacationing Martin Rilke was on the spot, and could speak French and German besides.

He took the road to Albert and then on to Arras and over the Vimy Ridge to Bethune. There were still belts of rusted barbed wire to be seen, and here and there the burned-out hull of a tank entombed in a grassy mound that had once been putrid mud. Woods of shell-splintered stumps were growing again. A greenness had crept over the land, a blanket of grass and vine, sapling and leaf, to hide the places where a generation had been butchered.

He was known at the Hotel Gaillard in Hazebrouck as a man who came at least three times a year to stay for a few days. It was not the most popular of towns, Hazebrouck. A place to stop on the road to Dunkerque, or Calais. No more than that. The little town had escaped the shells, but a million soldiers had tramped through its streets on the way from Saint Omer to the front. "*Boots and cannon wheels ground us down*," the mayor would say as he puttered helplessly in the ruined garden of his hotel, not to mention the vast dumps of shells and mountains of supplies, or the five thousand cavalry horses. The dumps and the horses were gone now, but their imprint remained on a bleak and trampled landscape.

From Hazebrouck the road went north over the slopes of Messines into Belgium and the Great Salient, past tortured earth still rank with rusted iron and death. Past the blasted sites of villages with names that rang like a dirge—Wytschaete and Hollebeke, Langemarck and Passchendaele. The lunar rubble of Ypres.

He had brought flowers, which he placed at the base of her cross, then ran a hand over her name, wiping dust from the black painted lettering. Ivy Thaxton Rilke—of the Imperial Military Nursing Service. Killed at the age of twenty by a shell.

"You knew her, then?"

Martin looked up. An elderly Englishman in well-tailored tweeds stood on the gravel path leaning on his walking stick.

"My wife."

"Ah," the man said with a sigh, as though a great mystery had been solved to his satisfaction. "I've passed often and wondered about her. There are so few women reposing here, you know. My sons are down the path a ways. John and Hubert."

"I'm sorry."

"It's very lovely here this time of year. The trees are growing wondrously well. Do you come often?"

"Several times a year."

"Really? Odd that we haven't met before. I try to come over once a month. I live near Dover."

Martin turned away from the grave and stepped off the well-clipped grass onto the path.

"This is my last visit," he said. "I realize now that she's gone."

The Englishman smiled slightly. "Totally, you mean? I've talked to others who feel the same way and no longer come. I can't share that belief. Death is a sleep, Swinburne said. My sons are in slumber."

No, Martin thought as he walked back to the car, they are dead as Ivy is dead. Not sleep but death. Death, not sweet repose. He had faced the reality of the war and cut the knot that bound him to the past.

He left the wheezing Renault with a friend in Saint Pol-sur-Mer, telling him to keep it, or sell it, and then took the channel steamer from Dunkerque to Folkestone. Standing in the stern of the little ship, he watched the coast of France blend into the sea haze and slowly fade from view. A part of his life fading with it. A moment in time over. Sailing toward another.

He was thirty, a man of average height and sturdy build. His hair was flaxen and parted loosely in the middle. His oval, square-jawed face just missed being handsome—the mouth a trifle too wide; the thin, high-bridged nose a shade too long. His most arresting feature was his eyes, which were blue and merry, a paradox for someone who had seen so much of the world's horrors.

He had a whiskey and soda in the station saloon and then took the 3:15 to London. It was an uncrowded train and there were only two other passengers in the first-class carriage. One of them, an elderly curate, went immediately to sleep, and the other, a large woman wearing a fox fur, sat as far from Martin as possible, as though she smelled the whiskey on his breath. He had forgotten to buy a newspaper, so there was nothing to do other than look out the window or write in his journal. The view was certainly worthwhile. England in June. The North Downs and the Kentish Weald. Soft, patchy sun on fields and woodland. Rain clouds to the east drifting slowly inland from the sea. He had seen England for the first time on just such a day. Both he and the world had changed drastically since that summer in 1914, but the English countryside appeared to have drowsed on, untouched by the past seven years. Heath and common, copse and hedgerows. Sheep, placid in the fields. Children gathering blackberries, waving at the train. But the pastorals of England, like the pastorals of France and Germany, were deceptive. Trees and pastures, gabled towns and thatched villages, implied an innocence and serenity that no longer existed.

"Do you mind if I smoke?"

The woman looked at him and stroked the black-button-eyed head of a silver fox.

"Not an odious cigarette, surely."

"Cigar," Martin said. "Havana, and very mild."

The woman nodded her approval. "I find nothing objectionable about a fine cigar." She continued to look at him, fondling the tiny, grinning head. "I took you for a German. You have that coloring."

He managed a polite smile. "I'm an American, of German ancestry."

"Oh," the woman said, and looked away.

He took a notebook and pen from his bag, lit a cigar, and settled back in the seat. He began to write in Pitman shorthand, the strokes and curls flowing across the page as fast as he could form his thoughts. . . .

Monday, June 20, 1921. Observations and reflections. By train from Folkestone to London.

How many times, I wonder, have I been on this train and taken a seat by the window and written in a journal? Times beyond count. A milk run in

1915 and '16. The carriage jammed then with men coming back to Blighty on leave. The mud of Flanders still on their boots, that glazed "trench look" in their eyes. Only half believing they were not in fact dead and being transported to hell.

"I took you for a German." That look of hate before she heard me speak in unbroken English. There had been that look during the war. The cold stare at my civilian clothes. The acid remark: "Been to France on holiday?" The atmosphere always warmed when I told them I was a newspaperman. They were well-informed men. They despised most war correspondents for good reason, but most had read my pieces and appreciated the honesty—even after the censors had chopped out the more unpleasant bits. They had raised reading between the lines to a fine art and knew what I was saying about the war.

"I took you for a German." The hate runs deep—here and everywhere. "I took you for a Frenchman . . . [the man on the train from Saarbrucken to Berlin, ignoring me coldly because he had heard me speaking French at the station; warming up after our passports were checked before leaving the occupied zone] . . . a damned frog bastard." We spoke German and I told him I was from Chicago. Second-generation German-American. "I have an uncle in Milwaukee," the man said. "You Yankee fellows backed the wrong side. You'll find out."

Who knows? As Jacob Golden used to say, there are no heroes anymore. We are all villains obsessed with the idea of kicking civilization to bits. The only animal on earth who fouls its own nest and makes a virtue out of slaughter.

The man at the cemetery pitied me. The faint smile, the glow in his eyes. The righteous look seen on the faces of the devout when told that one no longer believes in God. But I admit it took all the courage I had to walk away from her grave. It's easier to hang on. To return once a month, or three times a year, and "visit." I'm sure the man from Dover does just that. He visits, passing the time of day with his dead sons. The woman I saw once by the grave of her husband, seated in a little folding chair. "Talks a blue streak," the caretaker told me. "Comes across from London twice a year and tells him all the news of the family. They get a bit daft, poor souls." Hanging on. Blocking the reality of oblivion from the mind. A mere prolonging of pain. Like sawing off a leg with a pen-knife where one quick swing with a sharp blade would be more humane.

The war itself too painful to comprehend for most people. The statistics just starting to be printed. A million English dead. Twenty-seven percent of all young Frenchmen. God alone knows how many Germans, Russians, Austrians, Italians, Turks, and Serbs. And who can tally the continuing cost of the peace? How many dead from famine? Typhus? Influenza? The figures are meaningless anyway. No one can grasp them. Each digit a person. Ivy—slender, dark-haired, violet-eyed. Naked and loving in our bed. Reduced in importance to a single number on a list.

The old man's sons. John and Hubert. Who were
they? What did they do? Will we feel their loss?
Two more numbers added to the tally sheet. Nine
hundred thousand, nine hundred and ninety-
seven left to record, to personalize, to focus on a
once-living face.

He put notebook and pen on the seat beside him,
removed his reading glasses, and wiped them with a
handkerchief. Through the window he could see a
changing landscape, the greens and golds of the countryside blending into the smoky gray of towns, the
blistered fringes of London. He reached for the notebook, and as he picked it up, the letter from Arnold
Calthorpe slipped out from between the pages. No answer required, but he had to give it some thought.

CALTHORPE & CROFTS
Publishers
Bloomsbury Square
London

Dear Martin:

I trust this reaches you before you depart from
Paris. Both Jeremy and I congratulate you on
your new job. Very impressive. I wish your appointment had taken place before we printed the
jacket for the book, but that can't be helped.

Martin, as we discussed last year, *A Killing
Ground* is quite likely the best possible book at
the worst possible time. First reviews—or rather,
lack of them—appear to justify that prediction.
Only the most liberal, socialist, or pacifist press
has bothered to review it so far—and there aren't
many of those left in Britain these days! We are

anything but disappointed, as—also agreed between us—making money is not the object. We
feel pride in printing it, just as you feel pride in
having written it. However, we must face up to
the fact that the book may come in for criticism
designed to discredit it and you. A "muckraking"
charge as example. Give some thought to rebuttal—a thousand words or so on just why you
wrote such a savage exposé. Something we could
send out as a "letter of publication" to any Tory
paper that takes a swipe at you. This need not be
done at this moment, while you are so busy and
temporarily "uprooted." After you get settled,
drop by the office and we will discuss it.

Sincerely yours,
A. T. Calthorpe

He put the letter back in the notebook, then picked
up his pen and began to write.

Regarding Calthorpe. How he thinks I can
avoid charges of muckraking is beyond me. It is
muckraking in the purest meaning of the term.
But then I'm a Chicago boy, a town where muckraking is something of a fine art.

I wrote the book as my own personal catharsis,
a way to cleanse my soul of gall. All those months
covering the peace conferences at Versailles. Day
after day observing the haggling over spoils. The
fixing of blame and the establishment of costs—
the peacemakers like so many lawyers wrangling
over an accident case. And out there, along the
old trench line of the western front, lay the dead.

No one spoke for them. They were only mentioned as adjuncts to noble phrases—the "glorious dead". . . "not in vain". . . "fallen heroes" in "the war to save democracy" or "the war to end all wars." And there they were in the boneyards, the millions who could just as well have been strangled at birth for all the good they had done to *save* or *end* anything.

An observation through the window. Rows of dark brick houses. A factory flanking the railroad line. Men standing in front of locked gates carrying signs: "Not a Penny off the Wage." No pastorals here. A tiny glimpse of postwar England. Strikes and more strikes with over a million out of work. The pickets look shabby and ill fed. How many of them, I wonder, came back from the war believing Lloyd George's promise that they were returning to "a land fit for heroes"?

And so much for that.

Joe Johnson, editor in chief of the London office of the International News Agency, was waiting for him at Charing Cross, pacing up and down the platform, chain-smoking and anxious. As Martin left the carriage, Johnson spotted him and hurried over, grinning with relief.

"Jesus, I was starting to worry you might not have been on the train."

"Well, here I am," Martin said.

Johnson glanced at his watch. "Kingsford set up a cocktail party at the Cafe Royal. A meet-the-new-boss affair. If you hadn't shown up . . ." He left the implication of that unsaid. "You have about an hour and a half. Have you got a change of clothes? You look like you slept in that suit—in a field."

"I have the use of a flat in Soho. My trunks should be there by now. Don't worry, I won't disgrace myself, or Kingsford."

"Everyone is invited. Fifty, sixty people. You're really getting up in the world, Marty, and it couldn't happen to a better guy."

"Thanks, Joe, but they should have picked you."

"Like hell. I get enough Kingsford memos as it is. European bureau chief. Jesus Christ. I'll tell you the truth, Marty, Lou drank himself into a straitjacket because Kingsford was hounding him twenty-four hours a day with cables. Now it's your turn. I'm torn between patting you on the back or sending a note of sympathy."

"I can handle Kingsford. I didn't ask for the job; he asked me. I run the bureau my way and he can stay in New York and write all the cables he wants, but not to me."

Joe Johnson looked dubious. "Well, we'll see. Maybe you're a tougher sonofabitch than you look."

"You can bank on that, Joe. I don't mellow with age."

He squeezed into the older man's little Austin and had no sooner closed the door before they were gunning away from the curb, down Pall Mall and up Regent Street into Soho.

"Lower James Street," Martin said, wincing as they narrowly missed a pedestrian running to catch a bus. "The flat's above the Ristorante Velletri."

"Want me to wait for you?"

"No, that's okay. It's only a block or two to the Cafe Royal. I'll just clean up and walk over."

"Don't get sidetracked," Johnson said gloomily, "or Kingsford'll have my head on a plate."

Jacob Golden had bought the spacious six-room dwelling after being expelled from Balliol in 1911. It was, he had told Martin, his gift to himself for having shocked and dismayed every don at Oxford for two years. A Hungarian restaurant had occupied the ground floor of the two-story building; but when the war started, the Hungarian owner and his cooks and waiters had been marched off to an internment camp, and an Italian family had taken over the premises.

"Ah! Signor Rilke!" Marco Velletri, owner and chef, greeted Martin with a bear hug and a garlicky kiss on the cheek. "It has been—oh, too long, no?"

"Over three years too long, Marco." Here turned the *embrazzo*. "Did Signor Golden leave the key?"

It had been left as promised. His trunks and crates of books had arrived from Paris and were neatly stored in the spare bedroom. A note from Jacob was pinned to the mirror above the dresser.

Saturday

My dear Rilke:

Welcome back to jolly old Britain—although why anyone would give up a perfectly decent job in Paris is quite beyond my comprehension. Make yourself at home. Champagne in the kitchen—cold if Marco remembered to put ice in the box. I'm off to Macedonia to investigate starvation there. My chaps want full report on the reasons why. Told them that the reason for starvation is because there's no ruddy food. Not good enough for the jolly old League of (almost all) Nations, which has a penchant for quadruplicated reports on official forms. Mine will be a masterpiece—as always. And, as always, will be filed neatly away and forgotten while the Greeks continue to eat mud and straw. You may put that in your journal somewhere as an observation of despair.

I am, sir,
Yr. mo. Hble. St.
Jacob

There was no time to do more than remove some fresh clothing from one of the trunks, take a bath, shave, and search a trunk drawer for a missing black shoe. Ivy's photograph was in the drawer, under a loose pile of assorted socks, and he placed it on the dresser before leaving the apartment.

The INA cocktail party was being held in the Chelsea Room on the third floor of the Cafe Royal—a large gilt and red-plush room overlooking Regent Street. The party was in full swing when Martin arrived, a string quartet playing in a far corner drowned out by the babble of voices and the clink of glasses. Scott Kingsford spotted him and pushed his way through the crowd.

Scott Kingsford was more of a salesman than a journalist, a quality he would have been the first to admit. In ten years he had turned his International News Agency into the second most powerful news-gathering service in the world. He had done it by having an instinct for what newspapers would buy and what newspaper buyers wanted to read. That instinct had made him a millionaire at forty-five. But he wasn't content to sit back on his laurels. He wanted INA to be the biggest agency of all and was willing to spend money to see it happen. That meant hiring the best talent on the market, and spending money to experiment with less traditional froms of news gathering and dessemination, Marconi wireless transmission being his current project. To Europeans he was the epitome of the brash and obnoxious American, an image he did his best to uphold.

"Martin," he called out, coming at him like a bear. "This is your party, kiddo. Get a drink in your hand and I'll take you around."

He was proud of Martin Rilke. Acquiring a Pulitzer Prize winner as a bureau chief was a feather in his cap, a major coup. He introduced Martin to the staff of the London office, which would be his working base, and to the large number of British journalists who had been invited. Martin knew most of the people at the party and introductions had not been necessary, but it pleased Kingsford. After the circuit of the room had been made, Kingsford steered him to a relatively quiet corner of the bar.

"Damn, I'm happy. Getting a Martin Rilke was what this European operation needed."

Martin swallowed some scotch. "What is a 'Martin Rilke' exactly?"

"Hell, don't hide under a bushel basket with me. A Martin Rilke is the best damn reporter I know." He downed his gin cocktail and signaled the barman for a refill. "You have carte blanche over here, Marty, and I'm willing to put that in writing before I go back to New York. I'll only say one thing. I like balance. Know what I mean? Editors in the States are tired of grim news from this part of the world. They had a bellyful of it during the war, and all the brouhaha of Versailles, and Wilson and the League. Harding got elected on his return-to-normalcy crap, and that's the mood of the country right now. They want to know what's going on over here, of course, but not just the downright depressing stuff. Balance, Marty. Folks would like to read about Paris cafés, and what women will be wearing in the fall."

"I know what you mean."

"You have a reputation for hard news, so naturally I expect pieces from you on what's taking place in Germany and Italy and—well, hell, you know what I mean. But get your staffs to bear down on the lighter side, and beef up the photo departments, and the sports desk. A lot of American tourists will be coming over, so expand the travel-information coverage—the best hotels for the money, the best restaurants, the places that shouldn't be missed."

What Kingsford expected came as no surprise to Martin. INA's potpourri approach to news was the secret of its success, and he didn't have to handle any of it personally, just make sure that the various desk editors sent out their quotas of light and frothy material. Becoming head of the bureau gave him the freedom to go where he wanted, when he wanted, without having to convince anyone that his reason for going justified the expenses involved. It would be a heady new experience after seven years as a reporter on four different papers and two wire services. The chief now. The guy who called the shots.

After his third drink he began to feel euphoric, and when the party broke up he readily agreed to Kingsford's suggestion that they "tie one on" at a Soho night spot. Martin, unlike so many men he knew, did not consider heavy drinking to be a primary qualification for a career in journalism, but what the hell . . .

DORA IS A HARPY had been crudely painted on the wall of a building in Old Compton Street. It was not a graphic insult to a woman, but a nose-thumbing at the Defence of the Realm Act, passed in 1914 and still very much in effect. One of its numerous provisions had to do with the hours of sale of alcoholic beverages—which is to say that pubs closed early, and after-hours drinking was against the law. A large policeman walked slowly down the street with his hands folded behind his back, ignoring the graffiti utterly.

"Stop a minute," Kingsford said to the taxi driver. "I know the joint is around here someplace."

The driver spat out of the window. "They move about a bit, guv'nor, 'ere today and gone tomor'er as it were. Coppers keep 'em on the run. If you don't mind me suggestin', I knows of a club over in Gerrard Street that ain't been raided yet."

"Okay." He sat back with a sigh. "Christ, it's as damn silly as Prohibition. All this fuss to keep a few people from having a drink after ten-thirty at night. All it does is increase man's urge to sin."

There were a lot of people seeking to fulfill that urge. Rolls-Royces and Daimlers were parked along both sides of Gerrard Street, their chauffeurs standing in a huddle, smoking cigarettes and talking. Inside the small, nondescript building that had once been a rooming house was a press of people, most of them in evening clothes—the men in tails or dinner jackets; the women in long dresses, glittering with jewelry. Tobacco smoke hung in a blue haze, drifting from room to room like mist. Four tuxedoed black men stood on a narrow platform in the largest of the rooms playing jazz on cornet, trombone, bass, and drums. There was dancing—a swaying movement of bodies jammed in a tiny cleared area between small tables. The heat and the noise were a palpable force.

Martin and Kingsford elbowed and pushed their way through the crowd to the bar where three men in white mess jackets were serving the drinks. They ordered martini cocktails.

"More like Paris than London," Kingsford said, shouting to be heard over the noise. "Except in Paris they put ice in the gin."

A young woman, her breasts barely covered by the plunging neckline of her thin silk dress, stepped close and asked him to light her cigarette. Kingsford lit it with a solid gold lighter and watched her hips as she swayed back into the crowd.

"Flappers. That's a story angle, Martin. The new sexual morality. The ease of the postwar lay. Flaming youth in the fleshpots of London and Paris. Sex sells these days. But nothing tawdry, you understand."

The music became louder, the smoke denser, and the number of people in the club began to increase as the theaters along Shaftesbury Avenue began to let out. It was nearly impossible to find room enough to bend an elbow.

"Let's go," Kingsford bellowed. "To hell with this place."

The girl in the silk dress, who had returned to Kingsford half a dozen times for lights, put an arm about his waist as he shoved his way from the bar. He didn't object. When they got out to the street, he helped her into a taxi and held the door open for Martin.

"We'll go to the Savoy. Maybe she can line up a friend."

"I'm out on my feet and I've got a big day tomorrow."

Kingsford shrugged. "Suit yourself. I never tell a man how to spend his evenings." He held out his hand. "Put it there, kiddo. You're tops in my book. I'll be leaving for Southampton first thing in the morning. When I get back to New York I'll send you that data I was talking about. Go over it. Let me know what you think."

And then he was gone, the taxi rattling off toward Charing Cross Road.

"God, what an evening," Martin said under his breath. It was starting to rain. There were taxis lined up nose to tail halfway down the block, but he ignored them, turned up his coat collar, and started walking.

Kingsford's loudmouthed crudeness had been wearing, but the man had a touch of genius that would make working for him both exciting and a challenge. It had been impossible to carry on a conversation in the club, but he had heard enough of what Kingsford had been yelling in his ear to be intrigued. Wireless had been the subject, his personal project at the moment. Kingsford envisioned not only the radio-wave transmission of news from the city desks in Paris, Berlin, and Rome to London, and then retransmission of that news to the million or so people in the States who were tinkering around with crystal sets and headphones. He was prepared to spend a million dollars and had mentioned airily that someday there could be a great deal of money in a wireless-radio network. Martin couldn't see how, but that was Kingsford's problem.

He was soaked to the skin when he reached the apartment. He took off his clothes, put on a robe, and went into the kitchen to scrounge something to eat.

There was a vague, tantalizing odor from the kitchen below. The restaurant was closed, but the odors of pollo cacciatore and veal Florentine lingered on. It must have been disconcerting to Jacob, he thought, writing up his reports for the Council on World Hunger while suffering Marco's luxurious concoctions.

There was nothing in the ice chest except ten bottles of Moët & Chandon and a small pot of caviar, the lid sealed with red wax. He pulled out a bottle, found cheese and smoked sausage in the larder, biscuits in the cupboard, and took it all into the bedroom to eat.

Ivy's lovely face stared at him from the silver frame on the dresser, her lustrous black hair covered by a nurse's cap. She was not smiling, which he regretted, but she had been unused to cameras and had been terribly self-conscious and grave when he had posed her in the light from the window—the window in this very room. March 27, 1917. The date was written on the bottom of the picture. The last afternoon they had ever spent together. He had left for Salonika the next day, booted out of England—in a firm but civil way— for violations of the wartime censorship provision in the Defence of the Realm Act.

DORA IS A HARPY. A lean and wolfish bitch would have been closer to the truth. He hadn't thought it too much of a hardship at the time, as the war was in France and he would be back there when the Middle East assignment was completed. The war was in France, and Ivy would be there, too, and there would be time. Time for her to get a bit of leave and join him in Paris, time to shut out the war for a few days. But there hadn't been any time. Not for them. When he got to Paris in September, they told him she was dead. Killed at a casualty clearing station near Passchendaele. He took a swig of champagne and stared at her face.

Death is a sleep.

The INA offices occupied two floors of a venerable Victorian building near Fleet Street. The rooms had originally housed several firms of tea brokers, and the mahogany walls and brass fixtures reflected a more opulent past. The brass was now green with age and the mahogany paneling cracked from neglect. Long, narrow rooms where men in frock coats once spent their days poring over bills of lading or sampling tea from Darjeeling were now filled with men in shirt sleeves huddled over typewriters, or snatching copy from banks of chattering Teletype machines. The quarters were overcrowded and chaotic. The building being constructed around the corner in Fetter Lane would solve the overcrowding, but the chaos was a problem for the new bureau chief to solve.

It took Martin a week to make sense out of the disorder and to implement his own system and get rid of the deadwood. His predecessor had been a fine newsman but a rotten administrator. Martin gave a dozen key people the sack and sent out feelers to lure replacements from other wire services and several London papers. The bait was money. Scott Kingsford had given him a blank check.

"You're getting it straightened out," Joe Johnson said one evening, bringing a bottle of scotch into Martin's office. "For seven days he did labor, and, lo, the waters parted."

"Not much of a Bible scholar, are you, Joe?"

"I never read anything that tries to improve my soul—or my mind, for that matter." He poured whiskey into two water glasses. "I've got the National League box scores for you, hot off the wire. The Cubs lost to Brooklyn, four to two."

"To hell with it," Martin said. He sat back in his chair and swung his feet onto the desk. "Did that piece on D'Annunzio come in from Rome?"

"No, but we got a few hundred words from Talbot in Florence. A Communist labor organizer was gunned down by the Fascists. Pulled from his car on the Via San Georgio at high noon and shot in the head. Mussolini made a statement to the foreign press. He said the man had been paid by Trotsky to bomb a convent. Said they found the bomb in the car, and written instructions in Russian to blow up the nuns. That makes about the tenth murder in Florence in the past two weeks."

Martin sipped his drink. "Four to two, eh? Who pitched for the Dodgers?"

"Flanagan. Giffrow went for Chicago but got shelled in the sixth. Back-to-back homers. What about the wop shooting?"

"With the red scare and the Palmer raids, there are too many people in the States who'd applaud the shooting of a Communist. We're not doing Mussolini's propaganda for him. Cut the baloney about nuns and Trotsky and pin the story to Kermit's article on the continuing violence in Italy."

Johnson nodded, and then scowled at his drink. "I didn't mention it before, but I read your book. Small but mighty. You went at the brass hats like a terrier."

"As an editor, Joe?"

"Oh, cool, crisp prose. Nothing overwrought. Perfect use of understatement and irony. About as clean as a left jab to the jaw. One attack on one afternoon of war. A very clever way of symbolizing the whole bungled mess."

"Thanks."

"No thanks required. You asked my opinion—as an editor. If you'd asked me as a friend, I would have said you opened a can of worms. It's a lousy time to take a swipe at the late Great War. Jesus, they're still digging graves, and the mood in some quarters is edgy."

"Meaning?"

"Raw nerves protecting shaky reputations." He reached into his pocket and took out a folded piece of paper, which he tossed onto Martin's desk. "A drinking buddy of mine works on *The Times*. That's a copy of a letter that'll be printed in tomorrow's edition. The guns are leveled, Marty, and you're right in the sights."

Martin took his feet off the desk, reached out, and opened the piece of paper. The letter was signed by Major General Sir Bertram Dundas Sparrowfield, D.S.O., K.C.M.G. (retired). The address was The Willows, Arbury, Hants. He scanned the words:

> *A Killing Ground* by Mr. Martin Rilke, a book that was just recently brought to my attention . . . a damnable and malicious compendium of half-truths and gross conjectures compiled by a rank amateur with no military experience whatever. . . . Unlike some of our British war correspondents, many of whom had been army officers before turning to the practice of accurate

and responsible journalism, Mr. Rilke, a German-American from Chicago, is a callow reporter, no wiser in the art of military science than a Fleet Street stringer. . . . Mr. Rilke's press credentials were revoked by this government in 1917 . . . the writing of an antiwar tract in violation of DORA, which could well have afforded comfort to our German enemies . . .

Martin tossed the paper aside. "It doesn't sound like the general wrote it. I talked with him a dozen times during the war and he could barely put five coherent words together. I doubt if he could tell you what a 'Fleet Street stringer' is, under the threat of torture."

"Well, maybe he didn't write it, Marty, but he signed his name to it."

"No doubt of that—and didn't miss a dig. *German-American*, *callow* reporter as opposed to *responsible* journalism. My *loss of credentials* during the war . . . comfort to *German* enemies. A well-put-together smear."

"What are you going to do?"

Martin shrugged and reached for a cigar. "Ignore it, I guess. What *can* I do? Write a letter to *The Times* defending the book? Nothing I could say would ever convince the war apologists that I'm right and the general is wrong. Anyway, I'm seeing my publishers tomorrow and I'll sound them out about it."

Johnson finished his drink and stood up. "Back to the mines. I've got a thousand words from Salonika to blue-pencil. Turks and Greeks slaughtering each other under the olive trees. Wars go on and who the hell cares about the last one."

* * *

Calthorpe & Crofts was a small firm started before the war to publish the works of experimental poets and avant-garde writers. They had avoided the self-conscious precociousness common to that type of endeavor and had put out a dozen or more books that had been both critical and commercial successes. *A Killing Ground* was their first venture into nonfiction. Jeremy Crofts had been dubious about taking a book that most of the houses in London had turned down flat, but Arnold Calthorpe had argued so strongly for it that he had finally given in. To Calthorpe, publishing the slim manuscript was an almost holy duty. Unlike his partner, who suffered from partial blindness in one eye and had been medically unfit for service, Arnold Calthorpe, in a burst of patriotic fervor, had enlisted in 1914 at the advanced age of thirty-five. He became a captain in the Oxford and Bucks Light Infantry and served three years in the trenches. The experience had left him with chronic rheumatism and a deep, livid scar that nearly bisected his face. It had also left him with a deep rage at the war which had destroyed so many of his friends.

"Yes," he said, staring through his office window at the green of Bloomsbury Square below. "We were certain there would be letters to *The Times* from various military fossils. That was to be expected." It was starting to rain again, a brisk wind driving it against the glass. He rubbed his finger joints and turned into the room. "Going to be a beastly summer. If I had half a brain I'd chuck it all in and move to California."

Martin, seated in a leather armchair, smiled.

"Hardly your style, Arnold. Motion pictures and orange trees."

Calthorpe leaned against the edge of his desk and reached for a tin of cigarettes. "Care for a fag, Rilke?"

"No, thanks. I only smoke cigars."

"That's Jeremy's vice. He has some good ones in his office. I'll filch a few."

"Don't bother. I carry my own."

The publisher lit his cigarette and tossed the still-smoking match into a wastebasket.

"I don't believe for a moment that General Sparrowfield actually wrote that letter. Neither, I'm sure, do you. The fact is, your book not only condemns the way the generals handled the war, but makes a mockery out of the war reportage that was printed in every newspaper in Great Britain. It must be acutely embarrassing to certain correspondents who have just written books of their own. Their view of the fighting differs so drastically from yours, one can only wonder if they observed the same war."

"I know that. I can think of one or two men."

"And one or two newspaper publishers, if it comes to that. Northcliffe, Lord Crewe . . ."

"But there can't be many people left in England who aren't aware of the truth by now. Every man who came back from France told what went on there."

"Did they? My dear Rilke, most of the men who got demobbed never talked about the war at all and still don't—especially to civilians. It's just a hideous experience they keep to themselves. I know how they feel. I'm the same. I can't talk about the war, even to my wife. Not in any depth, anyway. She couldn't possibly take in the ghastliness of it. She chides me when I duck every time I hear a motorcar backfire—but then, Doris was never sniped at in Polygon Wood." He began to pace the room, leaving a trail of cigarette ash on the carpet. "An embarrassment, Rilke. No more than that. *A Killing Ground* will not incite mobs to storm Fleet Street and burn down the citadels of the Tory press, but it would please some people if it, and you, could be discredited."

"It'll take more than a letter from an ass like Sparrowfield to do that."

"Granted the chap's an ass, but he commanded a division on the Somme, fought with distinction during the Boer War, and is a crony of field marshals, lords of the realm, and other exalted pillars of the Empire. In other words, old boy, he could be a rather imposing adversary in court."

"Court?"

"We received a letter by special post about an hour before you arrived. It's from a firm of solicitors in Chancery Lane. The general is prepared to sue you for libel."

"That's ridiculous. Every line in the book is documented fact."

"Perhaps, but the libel laws in this country happen to be arcane, and any damn thing could happen."

It was silent in the room except for the faint hiss of rain against the windows and the desultory tapping of a typewriter in another part of the suite.

"What's your view of this?"

Calthorpe ambled over to his desk and plucked another cigarette from the tin. "It's really not up to me to say. Under our contract you absolve us from liability in cases of libel, slander, or plagiarism. The financial burden is on your shoulders, I'm afraid, and law-suits can be expensive, win or lose." He lit his cigarette and puffed moodily, eyes narrowed against the smoke. "The letter was terribly brief, so I tele-phoned the firm and talked to a rather cheery fellow, name of Ormsby. Wanted more facts before I talked to you. They offer a simple way out: Sparrowfield will drop the suit if you will compose a letter of apol-ogy for all the nasty little things you said about him and his staff and publish that letter in either *The Times* or the *Evening News*."

Martin stood up and walked over to the window. A simple letter of apology. That would be the end of it—until another "defamed" officer was dug up and convinced that he had cause to seek satisfaction. Apol-ogy after apology printed in the newspapers until his credibility as a critic of the war was damaged beyond repair.

A libel suit would be expensive and would take time. And there was one other factor to consider: Sparrowfield's letter had specifically drawn attention to the fact that he had violated censorship regulations during the war—*could well have afforded comfort to our German enemies*. The implication being that this *German*-American had a past history of being anti-English.

That was nonsense, but it would mean having to defend himself against malicious innuendo, explaining just what it was that he had written in 1917 that had caused his press credentials to be canceled. To do that, he would have to bring Charles Greville's name into the courtroom, and the so-called antiwar tract he and Jacob had printed as a protest to the mindless

butchery on the western front—Major the Honorable
Charles Greville's account of the horrors that had led
to his mental breakdown. He had felt it was his duty
at the time to publish his cousin's words, not because
Charles was a relative but because Charles was a kind
and gentle man who had been shattered by an obscenity. He was still shut away in a war hospital in Wales,
quietly forgotten except by his family and friends.
The Grevilles would not be happy at the idea of his
raking up the past in a court of law.

"Well, Rilke, what's your answer to the lawyers?"

Martin continued to stare out of the window. The
wind had shifted and the rain was no longer slanting
against the glass; it was now swirling toward the
buildings on the opposite side of the square. Four ragged men, driven from their shelter in a doorway, were
running across the little park, stumbling and sliding in
the wet. He remembered the way the Tommies had
stumbled and slid in the mud at Thiepval as they
pressed for the German trenches, and how they stumbled and fell when the machine guns caught them in
front of the wire.

"I shall tell them—very politely—to go to hell."

II

Anthony Greville, ninth earl of Stanmore, walked slowly across the gravel drive toward his car. The new Rolls-Royce, which had been covered with a patina of brick dust for the past few days, now gleamed like polished ebony as his chauffeur completed the task of washing it with buckets of water and a chamois-skin rag.

"Nicely done, Banes."

"Thank you, m'lord. A bit difficult, I must say. That brick don't 'alf stick."

The earl nodded, and wiped abstractedly at his old tweed jacket. "Gets into everything. Clothes, hair . . ."

"That's a fact, sir." The man rubbed a speck of dirt from the windscreen. "Is His Lordship ready to go?"

"Yes. You might just get my bag from the cottage."

"Very good, sir." The chauffeur put the chamois in the boot of the car and then walked off down the path toward the caretaker's cottage.

The earl lit a cigarette and gazed back at the house. The south wing was still covered with scaffolding, but all the brickwork had been completed—crumbled bricks replaced, stained ones wire-brushed good as new. The other wings of the great house were finished and gleamed in the sun. Two years of work coming to an end—God and the contractor willing.

There had been problems right from the start with a succession of indifferent or grossly incompetent contractors. The present one had been on the job for a year and had kept up nicely with the work schedule—so far. Hopefully, by the end of July it would all be finished and the landscape gardeners could move in and have the plantings completed before the winter frosts sealed the ground. Wishful thinking, he knew, but all things were possible.

The contractor, a burly ex-footballer from Leeds, stepped outside the metal-roofed shed he used as an office and waved cheerily. Lord Stanmore waved back. Their relationship had not been without strain, but they had finally seen eye to eye on the little things, the details that the contractor had thought nit-picking and the earl important. He had finally impressed upon the man the fact that Abingdon Pryory was an old house being restored, not reconstructed to conform with modern architectural trends. On their very first meeting the contractor had been so insensitive as to poke fun at the fact that "Pryory" was spelt with a "y" where the "i" should properly have been. He had remained amused even after the earl's explanation of the misspelling: that the structure originally built on the site had been so entered in the Domesday Book. Everything erected after the eleventh century had retained the name, poor spelling and all, as part of a continuing tradition.

"Tradition, is it!" The contractor had laughed. "Can't say I'm much for ruddy tradition!"

"Then perhaps you're not the man I'm looking for," Lord Stanmore had countered icily.

As a great deal of money was at stake, the contractor soon revised his opinion and began to treat the idea of "tradition" with the same respect as his employer.

The chauffeur put the car into gear and drove cautiously down the drive, past the mounds of sand, bags of bricks, and piled scaffolding that lined it. The earl sat in the back and stretched out his legs with a sigh. He had put in some taxing days with the contractor, but, by Harry, everything was on the proper course now. He could envision what the place would look like when all of the work had been completed—the clipped lawns rising gently toward the terrace, the rambling house of brick and stone, sun glinting off its hundreds of windows. Better even than before the war, when Abingdon Pryory had been judged the most beautiful house in Surrey by the editors of *Country Life.*

A pity the army hadn't read that laudation when he had turned the place over to them in 1915. It might have made them more deferential toward what they had been given—or rather loaned for the duration of the war. The army had used the house as a rest center for officers, a place where battle-wearied men might find strength and renewal before returning to the trenches. The concept had been noble enough, but, for whatever reason, the facilities had been grossly abused. Far from being grateful for the luxury of two weeks in a lovely manor house, many of the men had treated house, gardens, and outbuildings with an animosity better levied against the home of a Prussian general than an English earl. Walls had been defaced, balustrades broken, doors parted from their hinges, and the stables chopped up for firewood.

There had been even greater official desecration: Windows had been removed to get at the leading; iron gates and fencing torn down and shipped to the smelters.

"Lead for bullets, iron for shells," a brigadier general in Whitehall had explained after the war. A moderate sum had been offered in compensation for damages, but he had been expected to refuse it out of patriotism, and had.

"A small enough price to pay for victory, eh, Lord Stanmore?" the brigadier had said with the cheerfulness of a man who had paid no price at all.

He felt a twinge of anger as the car headed down the mile-long drive toward the Abingdon road. Ahead were two stone pillars, a gap between them where twenty-foot-high ornamental iron gates had once stood. He had purchased the gates for his wife on their honeymoon in Italy, from the duke of Fiori's villa in Urbino—and a pretty penny they had cost, too! Now they were gone, turned into cannon or barbed wire.

They stopped at Abingdon village for petrol, and the earl gazed toward the Norman tower of the church. The war memorial that he had commissioned and paid for stood in a small square facing the church and could be seen from anywhere along the High Street. It was a simple monument, beautiful and dignified. An obelisk of Carrara marble inscribed with the names of the twenty-five men and two women from Abingdon who had been killed in the war. Some, to be sure, had not been natives of the village; several had simply been employed at the Pryory, or other large estates in the area. It had been the earl's contention that those people, granted that they had been born and raised elsewhere, should be included with

Abingdon's glorious dead. The village council and the vicar had agreed.

The earl's first clear and lasting memory was of Abingdon—being taken to a funeral in the churchyard. A cold, wet day. The spaces between the gray headstones filled with black—black clothing and black umbrellas. He had been four years old. A winter afternoon in 1866. The day his grandfather, the seventh earl, had been buried in the family plot. Fifty-five years ago. The village had changed over the years, but never more so than during the past five or six.

As Banes pumped petro into the car's tank, Lord Stanmore watched the activity in the High Street. Market day. So many people, and so few that he recognized. The village had expanded greatly during the war, almost a small town now. An aircraft factory had been built near Leith Common, seven miles north of Abingdon, in 1915. The factory, Blackworth Aeroplane & Motor Co., Ltd., had built aero engines and reconnaissance planes for the Royal Flying Corps. They had expanded greatly and were still very much in business—for which the earl was grateful, as he owned several hundred shares of its stock. Executives, engineers, foremen, and key workers had bought or built houses in or near Abingdon and had created a new prosperity for the village. This growth had not been entirely welcomed by the older inhabitants, who resented the influx of "foreigners." The earl had mixed views on the subject. Thinking in practical terms, land values had increased substantially—and he owned a great deal of land. But growth had changed the look of the village and its atmosphere: Where once there had been only one pub, the Crown and Anchor, there were now three, one of them boasting that they served "cocktails in the American manner." To the villagers who frequented the Crown and Anchor for their daily pint and a game of darts, such things as American cocktails verged on the heretical.

Yes, the village had changed. There were all kinds of new shops and even a cinema, its marquee jutting out over the pavement . . .

TOM MIX
in
LAW OF THE SIX-SHOOTER

The vicar had complained vehemently about the cinema and had tried to block it from being built, but the council had voted against him. Had the earl been asked, he would have sided with the vicar. *Law of the Six-shooter,* indeed!

Beyond the village, the road meandered for seven miles through countryside so beautiful that merely looking at it brought a lump to the earl's throat. There was not a square foot of that land that he did not know, from the beech groves at Tipley's Green to the solitary oak on the crest of Burgate Hill. Not a field he had failed to ride across, not a hedge he had not jumped at one time or another. The Abingdon hunt had long been abandoned, but he would organize it again once he was back at the Pryory. Was there a finer sight in all the world than pink-coated huntsmen riding to hounds on a frosty December morning?

The narrow, twisting Abingdon road ended at Leith Common where it joined the highway from Guildford to London. The Blackworth factory could be seen, raw red brick buildings and iron-roofed sheds and hangars. There was an aerodome near the factory site, shared jointly by Blackworth and an RAF squadron. Low trees screened it from view, and as they turned onto the London road a lumbering biplane cleared the trees, banked sharply, and passed overhead with a stuttering roar.

"Brisfit," the chauffeur said, leaning his head out of the window to stare upward.

Even a man like Banes who had never set eyes on an airplane before he was forty could spot the difference between a Bristol fighter and a Sopwith Snipe.

"Kindly keep your eyes on the road."

A minor reflection of the war's broadening aspects. Brisfits, American cocktails, and Tom Mix. The horizons had been expanded. In the earl's youth he had measured the universe by the distance of a day's canter. All gone now. Changed utterly. He sat back in a corner of the seat feeling tired and immeasurably depressed. It wasn't age; he was a tall, strong, vigorous man who genuinely surprised people when they learned he was nearing sixty. Not growing old. He could cope with that by simply ignoring it. It was change that depressed him, the terrible feeling that the earth was spinning away at an uncontrollable speed toward an unknown destination. He pitied the youth who would enter this new world. What landmarks would be left for them to hold on to? What solid, imperishable guidelines remained? An age turned topsy-turvy. Bleak and valueless.

Hanna, his wife, had questioned the wisdom of rebuilding the Pryory, and from a practical point of view she had been correct. The expense was enormous (though money was hardly a factor) and what they would do with the place once it was finished was uncertain. Live in it, of course, but there were really

only the two of them now, and it would take at least
twenty servants, counting gardeners and grooms, to
maintain it even halfway properly. William might
come down for the occasional weekend, but he had to
stay in London and read for the bar. His daughter
might stay for a while with her baby, but Alexandra
was uncertain what to do with her life since returning
from Canada. She had talked vaguely about going
abroad.

In all likelihood, there would just be the two of
them, rattling around in a house larger than most hotels. The thought was worrying to Hanna, if not dis-
maying, but they would work out problems when they
reached them. The most important thing to him was
that Abingdon Pryory would exist again as a functioning, lived-in house. Lights would glow through its
windows and smoke rise from its chimneys. There
would be horses in the stables and hounds in the kennels. He would be resurrecting a manner of living that
most people thought had become as dead as the dodo
bird. Turning back time with money and a good contractor.

The Greville's London house was in Chester Mews,
overlooking Regent's Park. It was of moderate size,
requiring no more than ten servants, and had been
built in 1790 for the mistress of a royal duke. Their
previous London residence, a thirty-bedroom mansion in Park Lane, had been donated to the government during the war for use as a military hospital.
It was still being used for that purpose, a burn clinic,
and still filled with the charred victims of German
flamenwerfers and other random horrors of the Great
War.

He drove with Banes to the garage and entered at

the rear of the house, through the garden gate, so as not to track dried mud or brick dust across the polished floors of the entrance hall. It was 4:30, a rainless day for a change, and the sun was still warm. The nanny that Hanna had hired for Alexandra's baby was seated on an iron bench, reading a book, her free hand resting lightly on the handle of the pram. She looked up as she heard his footsteps on the brick path and put the book aside.

"Good afternoon, your lordship."

"Good afternoon." He had forgotten the woman's name. "Pleasant weather."

"Oh, it's ever so nice. Quite balmy, in fact."

"Yes." He paused for a second by the carriage and looked somberly at the baby. Chubby little fellow. Pink-faced and reddish-haired. A Scot's face—but then, his father had been Scottish. The baby stared up at him with equal gravity. "Must be time for his tea."

"Oh, he's had his tea, he has. Cup of milk and half a cream bun." She gave the pram a gentle shake. "Tell his lordship how you enjoyed it, that's the love."

"I've never heard him speak," he said, stepping back. "Surely—"

"Not in *words*, m'lord, not just yet, but he does chat away to his Mary, don't you, Colin love?"

Ten-month-old Colin Mackendric gave his grandfather a dour look and then closed his eyes.

Lord Stanmore had decidedly mixed feelings about the boy. He liked children. The happiest moments of his life had been when his own were growing up and Abingdon Pryory had swarmed with their friends. His attitude toward children was in marked contrast to that of his father, who had not only detested them but the entire process of their creation as well. His own

childhood had been so barren of love that he had
gone out of his way to indulge his sons and daughter
when they had been young: their nurseries bulging
with playthings, and a special stable built to house
their ponies. His natural inclination was to do the
same for his first grandchild, but Colin Mackendric
had been, as far as he was concerned, born under a
cloud. The Honorable Alexandra Greville, with head-
strong foolishness, had fallen in love with an army
surgeon who was not only a good deal older than she
but already married. They had met in France during
the war, where she had served as a nursing sister. No
amount of reasoning or pleading had been able to pre-
vent her from running off to Canada with him after
the armistice. In all fairness to Colonel Mackendric,
he had not been a bounder and had never ceased in
his efforts to get a divorce. It had finally been
granted and they had married—one month before
young Colin's birth in Toronto. Four months after
that, Mackendric had died of a heart attack while performing surgery at a veterans' hospital, and Alexandra
had come home to England with the baby. One tiny
tragedy in an era of catastrophes.

He entered the house through tall French doors that
led to his study, a sanctuary filled with his books and
a vast accumulation of hunting and riding cups and
trophies. He poured a stiff whiskey and sipped at it.
Seeing the child had only added to his depression. His
chilliness toward both Alexandra and her son was too
apparent, and Hanna had criticized him for it. He
could understand her reasons up to a point, but dash
it all, he was what he was. His strict schooling at Winchester had taught him firm values and beliefs and
had given him an intuitive feel for the rightness of

things. Living with a man out of wedlock and then giving birth to a child who was mere days from bastardy hardly fitted the Wykehamist ideal of womanhood—even if that particular woman was one's own daughter. Parenthood was not a valid reason for the suspension of judgment. She had been wrong, morally and socially wrong. He could not stone her for it, but neither could he forgive.

"Tony! You're back."

Hanna was seated at her dressing table wearing a green silk kimono, her arms raised behind her head as she struggled to fasten a strand of pearls. The sight of her drove a good deal of the darkness from the earl's thoughts. Stepping up behind her, he fastened the gold clasp and then bent to kiss her softly on the nape of the neck.

Hanna Rilke Greville, Countess Stanmore, was fifty-two and looked forty. The startling beauty of her youth had not changed radically with middle age. Her figure had thickened, as plumpness was a trait of the Rilkes, but the soft curve of her neck, the high cheekbones and oval face, the startling blue eyes, and her thick yellow hair were the same as when she had taken London by storm in the long-ago summer of 1888—the most talked-about debutante of that glittering social season.

She had come to England with her father as a first stop on a grand tour of Europe. Adolph Rilke, who had never learned to speak English properly, told reporters in his thick German-Chicago accent that he intended to see that his daughter had "der tea at Vinsor taken mit der queen." Press wags had a good deal of fun with Adolph Rilke and with what they dubbed "the beer king's daughter," but the ill-concealed contempt that society columnists felt toward American millionaires and their social pretensions turned to abashment when father and daughter did indeed go to Windsor Castle for tea with Queen Victoria. The press had overlooked the fact that the Rilkes of Chicago and Milwaukee were the American branch of the von Rilkes of Mecklenburg-Schwerin and that Hanna Rilke was a cousin to Princess Mary of Teck. Overnight she became a prime catch for any social event, most of which she mildly scandalized with her Yankee candor. There were those who thought her brash and those who found her refreshing. Among the latter had been young Anthony Greville, earl of Stanmore, whose late father had cast a chilling shadow of profligacy and deceit. The charming truths of Hanna Rilke had been like a blaze of light to him, a wondrous zephyr of fresh air. He had, in a moment of impulsiveness following a particularly enjoyable supper party in Belgravia, asked her to marry him. It was an impulse that he had never found cause to regret.

"You look very lovely tonight, Hanna."

"Thank you, dear. I thought you might have stayed at the Pryory until tomorrow."

"Not necessary. Tomkins is going great guns for a change. The south wing is completed and the scaffolding comes down in a day or two. Really marvelous progress. I can see no reason why we shouldn't be moving in by the end of August."

"That's nice." Her voice was flat. Bending forward, she opened a pot of lip rouge. "I invited Fenton and Winifred for dinner."

"Did you? Well then, I'd better bathe and dress. I reek like a navvy." He kissed her neck again, failing to see in the mirror the unhappiness in her eyes.

His own suite was down the hall—bedroom, dressing room, and bath—rooms that were almost Spartan compared to his wife's. Eagles, his valet for many years, had seen him arrive and anticipated his requirements. The bath was drawn and clothes for the evening laid out.

He stretched out in the steamy water with a sigh of gratitude. And then he heard it, pounding irritatingly through the wall, intruding on his privacy, that damned jazz music.

"Eagles!"

The valet popped his large, balding head around the partially open door. "Yes, m'lord."

"That blasted caterwauling!"

"A Victrola record, m'lord."

"I know what it is, man. Go tell Master William from me to turn the bloody thing off!"

"Very good, sir."

Eagles left his master's suite and walked sedately down the hall to William Greville's room. He gave a perfunctory knock on the door and then opened it and stepped inside. The earl's youngest son lounged on the bed in a dressing gown, smoking a cigarette and waving his hand in time to the music on the Victrola. Eagles walked slowly across the room, waited until the final blaring note had sounded, then lifted the needle arm.

"King Kornet and the Kansas City Kings. I never heard that number before."

"It's new. Chap I know brought it back from the States." William leaned across the bed and snuffed out his cigarette in a nearly overflowing ashtray on the nightstand. "It's called 'Storyville Stomp.' Bix Fletcher's on trombone instead of Eddy Williams. Makes for a hotter sound, don't you think?"

"Well, it made His Lordship hot enough."

"Christ." William sat up and ran a hand through his thick dark hair. "I didn't know he was back."

"Got in half an hour ago. He's in the bath, and the sound annoyed him—to put it mildly."

"You can tell his nibs the concert's over."

The valet started for the door, then paused and looked back. "Have you been to that new club in Tottenham Court Road, the Dixie?"

"No. How is it?"

"Bit of all right. Darky band from New Orleans. Leader plays piano like a bloody madman—and stands up to do it."

"I'll drop in for a look."

After Eagles had left the room, William sat up with a groan and swung his long legs off the bed, wincing at the sudden stab of pain in his right knee. His kneecap had been shattered by a bullet in 1917, and although a series of operations by two of the finest orthopedic surgeons in England and America had done wonders, he was still unable to bend the leg properly and the knee ached like a rotting tooth in cold or damp weather. He had learned to live with it. *A cane would help*, one of the doctors had advised him, but he despised the use of a cane as only a tall, strong, twenty-three-year-old man could despise such a symbol of infirmity.

Eagles served as his valet as well, but since William didn't care a fig for clothes, there wasn't much for the man to do except cluck his tongue whenever he opened the wardrobe and surveyed the motley collection of sagging tweeds and well-worn flannels that hung there. It had been Eagles, a onetime bandsman in the Rifle Brigade, who had introduced him to American jazz.

William selected a pair of gray flannel trousers and a dark blue blazer, frayed at the elbows. He dressed hastily, lit a cigarette, left his room, and walked down the hall to his sister's suite at the rear of the house. The door to her bedroom was ajar and he poked his head in. No one was there, but he could hear voices from the adjoining room, what would have been the sitting room had it not been turned into a nursery.

"Hello," he called out loudly. "May I come in, or is babykins doing something nasty?"

"He's just getting a wash."

He sauntered through the bedroom and leaned in the open doorway of the nursery. His sister stood by a window holding her naked son in her arms while the nursemaid patted his back with a towel.

"Madonna and child," William said. "By Caravaggio."

It was an aesthetically pleasing sight. The blonde and exquisitely beautiful Alexandra, the pink and ivory baby, the nursemaid in her crisp white cap and apron, a mellow glow of sun through the curtains. Yes, he thought, pure Renaissance Italian.

Alexandra was two years older than he. They had never been particularly close as children and there had been times, when she was growing up and had been mad for boys and parties, that he hadn't liked her at all. He loved her now. She was the one person he could talk to, the only person who understood him.

"You know the rule, Willie," she said. "No smoking in the nursery."

"Sorry." He stepped over to an open bedroom window, crushed out his cigarette on the sill, and flipped it down into the garden below. "Father's back."

"I know," she said, handing the baby to the nurse. "Mary told me."

"Which should put a damper on the evening. I was going to play my records for Fenton."

She came into the bedroom and closed the nursery door behind her.

"You can still play them. And teach Winnie and me a few new steps. Have you heard of the Charleston?"

"Can't say that I have, but there are all sorts of new dances. As for playing any records tonight, fat chance of that. The gaffer's on a tear. Sent Eagles hopping over to tell me my Victrola was ruining his tranquillity or something." He flopped onto her bed, hands folded behind his head. "Getting back to a more pleasant subject, don't be surprised if there's a new dance craze sweeping London by now. I went to a club last night in Sloane Square and this little flapper I was with seduced me into dancing with her. Well, as you know, I can teach but can't do, so there I was galumphing around the floor with my leg as stiff as a post. I must have looked like a lame crane. People watching me thought I was doing something terribly clever, and before you know it everyone in the place was dancing with one locked knee!"

Alexandra laughed and sat beside him, one hand resting on his bad leg. "You seem to be walking better lately. Have you been sticking to the exercises I taught you?"

"Yes, *sister*. I've been very diligent, but it hurts like bloody blazes when I do them."

"It's supposed to hurt. Take aspirin."

"Take aspirin! Christ, that's what comes from living

with a doctor!" He could see her tense and he sat up and placed an arm around her shoulders. "You know what I meant, Alex."

She turned her head and kissed his hand. "You're a lovely man, Willie."

"No," he said, touching her hair. "You're the lovely one in this family. If I'm ever asked to vote for a saint, I'll cast it for you."

"Oh, come now!"

"I'm serious. Only a saint would put up with the way Father treats you."

"That's enough, Willie," she said firmly. "Papa has been—well, *Papa*. What on earth did you expect him to do, dance a jig in the streets?"

He sat up and took a tin of Woodbines from his jacket. "No, but neither should he place you in virtual Coventry. His discourses seem limited to 'Kindly pass the salt,' or 'It looks like rain.' I'm sure the two of you could jump into deeper conversational waters if he'd only bend his blasted Victorian codes a bit."

"Papa *is* a Victorian. Try to understand him."

He stuck a cigarette between his lips and searched his pockets for a match. "I don't understand *you*. If I were twenty-five and had come into my share of the trust, I'd be out of here like a shot."

She took his hand into her own. "Please, Willie, don't make it any more difficult for me than it is. Everything will work out for the best, you'll see. It just takes time. And I can't bear seeing you moping about and feuding with Papa over petty things. There are enough young men drifting about in a fog these days without your joining their ranks."

"I'm not drifting."

"Of course you are. You drink too much, smoke too

much, have too many girls, and just go through the motions of reading for the bar."

He put the matches back in his pocket and plucked the unlit cigarette from his mouth. "I'm considering chucking that in, but, for God's sake, don't tell his nibs. I'm just not cut out to be a barrister. Don't have the brains for it. I'm not Charles. If Charles had wanted to be a lawyer, he would have ended up Lord Chief Justice in no time flat. Father expects me to take over Charlie's life and I can't do it, Alex."

"Of course you can't."

"But the bloody rub is I feel an obligation to do *something* worthwhile with my life to compensate for the waste of Charlie's. Something—oh, I don't know—*grand*."

She gave his hand a squeeze. "What is it that *you* want?"

His smile was wan. "Promise you won't laugh."

"I promise, Willie."

"I'd like to marry a simple, happy girl and live in a warm country—Australia, perhaps. Queensland. Raise—oh, I don't know—sheep or horses. I love animals, good soil, dirt on my hands. Trying to understand things like socage in fief, barratry and torts is just not my cup of tea."

"It's your life," she said quietly. "And you only get one."

Her thoughts drifted as she lay in the bath, idly soaping her breasts, a small tactile pleasure that always made her think of Robbie, his gentle hands on her body, his lips. Her loneliness was an ache—real, physical, as painful sometimes as her brother's splintered knee.

One life.

She had known Robbie would die. There had never been a morning when she hadn't wondered if she would see him that night. When the telephone had rung she had known he was dead, not needing the stumbling, hesitant words on the other end of the line to confirm it. She had watched him grow gaunt and hollow-eyed, driving himself with an inner fury he had never talked about, not even to her when she lay beside him in bed. A penny for your thoughts. But he had never told her. Not that it was necessary. She knew his rage at the war, a war that had been over for nearly three years but still filled his days with the mutilated victims of Vimy Ridge, Festubert, Ypres. The legless, armless, faceless survivors of that useless slaughter. He had bled with each case—and there had been cases without end. He could never, in good conscience, allow himself to relax until the last mangled creature from Armageddon had left his care. A dedication so close to zealotry that it had destroyed him in the end. Colonel Robin Mackendric, killed by the Great War just as surely as if he had been blown up by a shell.

"Robbie." She whispered his name, then rested her head against the hard porcelain pillow of the tub and closed her eyes. Oh, God, if only he were with her now, holding her tightly in a silky, liquid embrace . . . stroking her . . . loving her . . . ending the pain. . . .

* * *

Lieutenant Colonel Fenton Wood-Lacy, his mind on a hundred other matters, missed the turn into Chester Mews and had to turn the car around.

"Bugger all," he muttered.

"No need to swear," his wife said. Lady Winifred, only daughter of Lord Sutton, Marquess of Dexford, was used to rough language. Her father in his youth had served briefly with a regiment of hussars during the Zulu war and boasted of his salty "trooper's tongue." Being married to a professional soldier for five years, she had heard her full share of barracks talk, but she was five months pregnant, her nerves on edge, and little things irritated her.

"Sorry," he muttered; then, "Damn and blast . . ." as the front wheels of the Sunbeam bounced against the curb and he had to back up in the narrow street.

She gave him a disapproving look but said nothing. His nerves were as raw as her own and she felt a wave of sympathy for him—and love. "You can swear if it helps."

"It just blows off steam." He smiled at her in the darkness. "Don't worry. It'll all come out in the wash. Tomorrow will tell."

She caught a glimpse of his face in the glow of a streetlamp. The smile was gone as suddenly as it had appeared, replaced by a taut-mouthed grimness. He had long, sharp features, the nose prominent and the lips thin. A handsome yet forbidding profile that had earned him the sobriquet of "Hawk" in the army. It was an appropriate name for he looked like a cruel and predatory bird, but it was merely a mask, a parade-ground face.

"I wonder if it was wise to accept Hanna's invitation," she said. "If Anthony's there, we're in for one of *those* evenings again. I don't think I can bear it. I'm as edgy as a cat."

"If the old boy's there, he's there," Fenton muttered as he put the car in forward gear and completed his turn without mishap. "Grin and bear it, as the Yanks say."

"You're probably more capable of that than I am. I keep remembering Alex when we were at school and one had to practically sit on her to keep her from talking. Now she's so quiet, and Anthony's raised ignoring her presence to a fine art. I find it very upsetting, and I'm upset enough as it is."

He parked in front of the house and then helped her out of the car. She was in her middle twenties, tall and full-bodied. Small breasts and boyish figures were in vogue, but her Junoesque bearing caused heads to turn. Her light brown hair was neatly bobbed, complementing a round face, small, uptilted nose, and hazel eyes. An active, athletic girl, she resented having to be helped from the car, but her morning sickness had been extreme lately and left her weak in the knees.

The butler had seen them arrive and held the door open as they came up the front steps.

"Good evening, Coatsworth," Fenton said.

Coatsworth had been with the Greville family for over forty years and no one considered it strange that he wore carpet slippers with his livery. He was old and arthritic, but an institution—like the Tower of London or Big Ben.

"Good evening, Colonel—Lady Winifred."

"How are you feeling?" Winifred asked.

"Quite well, all things considered."

"Did you try that ointment I sent over?"

"I did indeed, Lady Winifred. Quite beneficial."

He led them toward the drawing room, walking slowly and stiffly down the marble-floored corridor. Fenton touched his arm gently. "You needn't bother, Coatsworth. We can show ourselves in."

"Oh, it's no bother, Colonel. One likes to feel useful."

If Winifred expected overtones of tension due to the earl's presence, none were apparent. Lord Stanmore was a good host, warmly affable and talkative. He supervised the mixing of a new cocktail he had been told about—a Manhattan: "Whiskey, sweet vermouth, dash of bitters, and a cherry garnish—ice optional, but why weaken the mixture with cold water, eh?" It was obvious, however, that he ignored Alexandra in subtle ways, by talking over her or around her. Not once did he ask her a direct question or refer to her in any way. She appeared to accept this and, in her turn, avoided talking directly to him. It was managed so artfully that a stranger would not have been aware of it.

The dinner conversation was light and airy. The women discussed the latest fashions and the varied upcoming events of the summer social season, while the men talked among themselves about cricket, racing at Ascot, and the effect of Prohibition in America on the Scotch whiskey distillers. Then Lord Stanmore shifted the discussion to Abingdon Pryory.

"By God, Fenton, how I wish your father were alive. Now *there* was an architect for you. He could draw the plans and, if need be, hew stone, lay brick, or pour cement. How old were you when he first brought you to see the place?"

"Eight or nine. He'd just been knighted for his work at Sandringham House."

"The queen should have raised him to the peerage, by George. What splendid work he did for her there, and at Balmoral. But nothing compared to what he did at the Pryory."

"It almost seems like yesterday," Hanna said. "Sir Harold and his two little boys. We sent a carriage to meet you at Godalming. Do you remember that, Fenton? The matched bays and the grooms in livery?"

Fenton smiled at her. "I do indeed. It makes me feel positively ancient. Can you imagine a phaeton and team driving into Godalming station these days?"

"Ah," she laughed, "but that was prewar—pre-*Boer* War. You have a right to feel ancient."

The earl cut a slice of roast lamb and popped it into his mouth.

"Old and decrepit at thirty-two, eh, Fenton? Lucky, I call it. You were blessed to have seen those times. Victoria on the throne—peace on earth—the very zenith of civilization."

"But the seeds had been planted, Papa. Wouldn't you say that?"

He paused in the act of loading his fork with peas and roast potato and looked down the table at his daughter. "What seeds are you referring to?"

"The ones that grew into monsters," Alexandra said. "The ones that burst upon us in nineteen fourteen. Beneath that heavenly zenith you refer to, there must have been something dark and ugly, something fundamentally wrong with the world."

"If there was," he replied coolly, "I for one was not aware of it."

"I don't suppose many people were. I imagine that's part of our English character—a tendency to ignore the unpleasant."

There was a moment of strained silence, and then Hanna looked across the table at Winifred and said brightly: "I forgot to ask about the twins. How are the darlings?"

Winifred choked down what was in her mouth. "Very well." She coughed discreetly and held a napkin to her lips.

"I'd not call them darlings," Fenton said quickly. "They're the most devilish four-year-old children in existence."

"Girls aren't supposed to be any trouble," Hanna said. "Perhaps you need a new nanny."

Alexandra dabbed at her plate with a fork, the food virtually untouched. "We avoid the unpleasant and condemn the truth. As an example of what I mean, there was a letter in today's *Times* from some retired general, harshly, and most unfairly, criticizing cousin Martin's book. Did you read it, Papa?"

"I did not. But I'm hardly surprised. Martin sent us a copy before publication." He gave Hanna a brief, apologetic smile. "Personally, I'm very fond of Martin and have always been proud to be his uncle, if only through marriage. However, I found the book to be unduly bitter in tone and excessively caustic. What on earth's the point of it? The war is behind us now, all over and done."

"Just bury the dead?"

"In a manner of speaking, yes."

"In Martin's view that's not possible, not until we grasp the reality of so many graves. The waste of it all."

"We can blame the Kaiser for that."

"Can we? The guilt's too enormous not to be

shared. English generals squandered lives as callously as German ones. I'm sure Fenton would agree."

"I'm in rather enough trouble with the brass as it is, Alex," said Fenton lightly. "The very walls have ears."

William laughed. "I shan't tell on you. I rarely see generals at the jazz clubs."

"Which reminds me, William," the earl said, anxious to change the subject. "Must you play those infernal records of yours half the night?"

"I'm sorry, sir. I wasn't aware you could hear them."

"Hear them! The house vibrates with the sound."

Alexandra wet her lips with wine and set the glass back on the table. Her hand was trembling and some of the wine spilled on the cloth.

"Are you really in trouble, Fenton?"

"Perhaps 'trouble' is too big a word to use."

"Your career is under a cloud, isn't it?"

"A slight shadow, let's say."

"Because of your involvement with Charles's court-martial?"

"Now look here, Alex," the earl said. "I don't like the drift of the conversation. We do not discuss the war at dinner, nor do I think it appropriate to discuss Charles at this time. I don't like to be dictatorial, but I must insist."

"I don't consider you to be dictatorial, just closed-minded. Whenever I've attempted to talk about Charles, at dinner or any other time, you've turned a deaf ear. Don't you understand, Papa? As long as Charles is shut away, the war will always be a presence in this house whether we discuss it or not. I used to talk with Robin about it. He was a fine doctor and had strong views on shell shock. One of the things he believed in . . ." She paused, her eyes meeting her father's cold stare. "But you're not interested in anything Robin Mackendric might have said, are you?"

"To be frank, no."

"That's a pity."

"It may be, but you live in my house. Kindly respect that fact, Alexandra."

The dinner finished quickly and in virtual silence. Then the after-dinner ritual was observed, the ladies going into the drawing room, the men remaining at the table while Coatsworth served port and cigars. William, squirming in his seat, glanced at his wristwatch.

"May I be excused, Father? I have some boning up to do—on criminal codes."

"Of course," the earl said listlessly. He toyed with his glass of port while William said his goodbyes to Fenton and hurriedly left the room.

"He'll be out the front door like a cannon shot. Be back after midnight, tipsy more than likely."

"Youth must have its fling," Fenton murmured before taking a sip of wine.

"I'm sorry about the dinner. Rather a waste of a damn fine saddle of lamb. I can't for the life of me understand what got into Alexandra."

"Can't you?"

The earl scowled at his glass as he turned it slowly between his fingers. "You couldn't be closer to me, Fenton, if you were my own son. I can talk to you with honesty. I—well, dash it all, I can't forgive the girl. I regret the day she came home and brought that child with her."

"*That* child has a name."

The earl glanced up sharply, then sat back in his chair. He looked drawn and tired. "Colin. There's never been a Greville with a Scot's name. Never been a Greville, as far as I know, born within an inch of the bar sinister. Call me what you will, but, damn it, sir, there are codes of behavior that one must live by or the world will revert to barbarism."

"With all respect, sir, we've just witnessed four years of barbarism. Alex's fall from grace seems rather puny in comparison. I won't presume to question the validity of your moral convictions, but if Alex has some fresh viewpoint regarding Charles—"

"The man is shell-shocked," the earl said firmly. "Damn it, Fenton, my son wouldn't have been committed to a hospital if he weren't. It may be a damn hard bullet to chew, but in all probability he'll be shut away for the rest of his life."

Fenton's right hand began to twitch. He put down his glass and placed the offending member under the table and slapped it against his leg. It was his own symptom of shell shock, a muscle spasm that would occur unexpectedly and cause the fingers to stiffen and the thumb to jerk. It often happened when he was reviewing the men, and he had solved the problem by shoving the hand in his pocket. It gave him a nonchalant air that always pleased the troops—*"The bloomin' ol' Hawk's a proper toff, he is!"*

The hand had first betrayed him one morning at Hill 60 when he had ordered D Company over in support of the Royal Warwicks, who were floundering in the German wire. The move had been anticipated, and when the men had gone fifty yards from the trench, nested machine guns had caught them in a crossfire and all he could do was watch them die. He had wanted to scream in horror and rage, but that would have been an unthinkable—and unpardonable—

thing to do in front of the men. His hand had done the screaming for him, as it still screamed from time to time in moments of stress.

"Shell shock is an odd thing," he said with forced calm. "It can destroy a man's mind or merely numb it. No one who spent any time at all in the line came away totally untouched. It's not a disease but a compound of ghastliness, an accumulated burden of horrors. Charles had more than his share of shocks and withdrew into a safe world of his own, but that doesn't mean he can never come out of it."

"I've been led to believe otherwise. He's been in this state since nineteen seventeen. At peace with himself, Fenton. Attempting to bring him back to reality could snap his mind completely. He functions—dresses and undresses himself, feeds himself, goes for walks. He seems blissfully content in his dreams and should be left alone. I will not tolerate interference from Alexandra in this matter."

Fenton's mouth felt dry as brass and he wet his lips with port.

"From what I can gather, Colonel Mackendric had some rather positive ideas for treatment of shell-shock cases. I imagine he passed those views on to Alex."

Lord Stanmore stood up with icy calm. "I know for certain of only one thing that Colonel Mackendric *passed* on to her. I'm not interested in any other. If you will excuse me, Fenton, I have work to do. Kindly extend my apologies to the ladies."

Fenton continued to sit at the table until the spasms in his hand began to ease; then, leaving the port—which always reminded him of blood—he went in search of a whiskey.

III

He let Winifred out in front of her father's house in Cadogan Square, waited at the curb until one of the footmen had hurried out to help her up the steps, then drove around the corner and parked his car in Pavillion Road. It was barely ten o'clock and he felt keyed up and edgy. It had been an unsettling evening, especially for Winifred, who had said nothing since leaving the Grevilles. She was in an emotional turmoil as it was, and the conversation at dinner hadn't helped her frame of mind.

He stood by the car and looked up at the sky. A pale, waxy moon hung above the city, partially obscured by drifting clouds. He hated London at the moment with an almost irrational passion and wished to God they were home in Suffolk spending a normal leave, just he and Winnie and the twins. Taking the boat out and sailing on the Deben, or hitching Rosie to the dogcart and rattling up the road into the village for cider and cheese at the Four Crowns. The colonel on well-deserved leave with his wife and children. Only he wasn't on leave, he was in limbo, caught in a trap designed by the army high command with Machiavellian thoroughness.

He had been called back from his post in Ireland
the previous November with orders to proceed to the
Middle East in January. That order had been canceled before he had even stepped off the boat from
Dublin. Instead, he was to report to Wellington Barracks, London, and remain there as a casual until further orders—a "casual" being nothing but a poor
bloody sod of an officer with nothing to do but sit
around waiting for the powers in Whitehall to have
pity and ship him elsewhere. Finally, after eight interminable months, he had been told to report to Horse
Guards for posting. Posting where? He had no idea,
but would find out at 0900 in the morning.

He leaned against the car and stared at the sky.
Great rifts in the clouds now. The stars beyond. He
was not a great believer in God, but surely there was
something that controlled the destinies of men, a di-
vine finger that reached down from the stars to stir
the trash heaps of the earth. That finger had touched
him as it had touched Charles Greville. They were
two men forever linked, sharing a common event and
perhaps doomed by it.

He entered Sutton House through the tradesmen's
entrance at the rear, going through the kitchens so as
to avoid his father-in-law and his cronies. It was Lord
Sutton's whist night, the gathering larger than usual
judging by the trays of food being prepared by Cook
and her helpers. The marquess still followed the Edwardian custom of dressing his footmen in eighteenth-
century livery, and one of them was leaning against a
wall in velvet doublet and satin knee breeches, his
powdered wig askew, smoking a cigarette and nursing
a bottle of beer. He made an attempt to hide both,

but Fenton just winked at him as he walked toward the servants' stairs.

Winifred was seated at her dressing table removing her makeup when he came into the bedroom.

"Did you see Father?"

"No. I came in the back way." He sat on the edge of the bed and took off his shoes. "That chap Fenworth is with the group tonight. I spotted his limousine and driver. I'm sure he was invited so that we could have a little chat at the mellow end of the evening."

"Why not go down and have it?"

"Because he'll press me for a decision on that job offer. Christ! Fenworth Building Society."

She stared fixedly at the mirror and rubbed cold cream from her cheeks with a soft cloth. "I thought it sounded interesting."

"I just can't see myself taking the early-morning train from Ipswich and strolling down Threadneedle Street in a black suit. Besides, I already have a job."

"You may or may not," she said tautly. "That's something you won't know for certain until tomorrow. It wouldn't hurt to have another string in your bow."

"I have strings—all in basic khaki. I'll have a job, it's a question of what kind."

She lay stiffly on her back, very much on her side of the bed. He sounded cheerful enough. She could hear him humming in his dressing room. Whistling in the dark. He was concerned and worried, but not nearly as concerned as she was. The past months had been a nightmare for her, not knowing from one day to the next when his orders would come through and he would be posted to a permanent command. Commuting twice a week to London to be with him, their house in the country in a state of chaos with most of their belongings packed away in crates since Christmas. Their plans had been so definite in that long-ago time—she and the twins and his mother to go east with him, to stay in a large rented house in Gezirha on the Nile. But she hadn't been pregnant then. It would be foolish to go to Egypt now. And there was the possibility that he wouldn't be ordered to that part of the world anyway. They could send him God knows where, to any spot where the Union Jack flew— Hong Kong, Sierra Leone, Malaya. Life could be so simple and pleasant if he resigned his commission. It wouldn't bother her in the least to see him go off to London every morning on the train. The Fenworth Building Society. Offices throughout Great Britain and Northern Ireland, their advertisements pasted on buses and boardings and the walls of the underground—"Build a Future—Invest in the Fenworth Society." What was wrong with that?

Fenton switched off the bedside lamp and opened the window drapes. Moonlight filtered into the room in an ivory glow. He stood by the window gazing out at the dark buildings across the square.

"My mind's racing like a bloody engine," he said.

"Not as quickly as my own."

"I could have Peterson send up a bottle of champagne. Nothing like the bubbly to make one drowsy."

"I associate champagne with celebrations. I hardly feel like celebrating anything at the moment."

He walked over to the bed and sat beside her. "We have a lot of things we could raise a glass to. Or, anyway, I do."

"Do you, Fenton?"

"I have you. That's worth a toast."

She reached out and touched his hand. "I've been lying here feeling sorry for myself. Prenatal collywobbles, I suppose. I'll get over it."

He bent down and kissed her. "I love you, Winnie, and I want you to be happy."

"It would make me happy to see you going off to work every day in the city, but only if it was what you wanted. I couldn't bear it if you were miserable."

"I'd get used to it."

"No you wouldn't. I was just being selfish."

"Beneath that wonderful exterior of yours is something even more wonderful."

He pulled the covers back and got into bed beside her. She sat up and slipped the silk nightgown over her head and then lay back, waiting for him. His lips glided across her breasts and then down over the swell of her belly where a new life pulsed—lingering, caressing, until she clasped him tightly in her arms and drew him to her with a soft cry.

He drove past the palace toward the Mall. A platoon of grenadiers was leaving Wellington Barracks and marching up Birdcage Walk to the tapping of the drum. They looked splendid in their red coats and bearskin hats, the morning sun glinting off brass buttons and shiny rifles, but he could not think of them as soldiers. They were actors in a pageant, relics of some dimly remembered play. He could not reconcile their scarlet ranks with his own vision of soldiers—dun-colored creatures in steel helmets, muddy and stained, seen through the smoke and haze of a daybreak in Flanders.

He parked the car near the War Office and checked his image in the window glass. He was wearing mufti and the sight made him smile. With his dark suit, bowler, and furled umbrella, he could have been taken for a director of the Fenworth Building Society—if he weren't so obviously an officer in the Guards.

"Good morning, *sir!*" The khaki-clad old sergeant in the foyer snapped to attention.

"Morning, Sergeant. I have a nine o'clock appointment with General Wood-Lacy." He glanced casually at his wristwatch. "A bit on the early side."

"Quite all right, sir. The general's in his office. Do you know the way up?"

"I do indeed."

He walked up two flights of stairs and along a dark, narrow corridor, its walls lined with engravings depicting forgotten campaigns. The building was a warren of corridors, but he followed the proper ones, which led him, like the passages of a maze, to the oak-paneled antechamber of the general's office. An elderly, white-haired lieutenant colonel rose from his desk with a smile.

"Fenton, dear chap. So good to see you again."

"How are you, Blythe?"

"As well as can be expected, I suppose. It's rather a sad day for me. I shall miss the old boy."

"As I'm sure he'll miss you. Always imagined the two of you retiring together."

"That had been my hope, but General Strathling talked me into staying on for another year or two and joining his staff in Delhi." He came out from behind the desk and placed a hand on the brass knob of the door he had guarded, in a sense, for a good many years. "I'm still trying to persuade your uncle to come east. Purchase a house in Simla. He always enjoyed the Kashmir. You might put that bee in his bonnet if you have the chance."

General Sir Julian Wood-Lacy, V.C., C.V.O., was standing by a window when Fenton entered the room. The large office was barren except for the desk and a couple of wood chairs. The bookcases and files had been emptied, and pictures and maps taken from the walls.

"Looks like you've closed shop."

"Half a bloody century is enough for any man." The general took a puff on his cigar and looked away from his view of St. James's Park. "You're on time for a change." The old general, whose face had once graced a recruiting poster because of its bulldog pugnacity, eyed his nephew from head to toe and back again. "You look prosperous, like one of those stocks-and-bloody-bonds wallahs."

Fenton smiled and brushed his sleeve across his bowler before placing it on a hat rack near the door. His umbrella went into a stand fashioned from the leg of an elephant.

"Now that you're almost in civvy street, General, I'll recommend a tailor. Purdy and Beame, Burlington Street."

The old man scowled and scattered cigar ash on the carpet. "Don't be so damn cheeky. Care for a brandy?"

"At nine in the morning? I have more respect for my liver."

"I stopped respecting mine years ago." He glanced about the room helplessly. "If I can only find the bloody bottle."

Fenton sat down in a chair facing the desk and pointed toward a row of shelves on the far wall. "Forlorn bottle and two lonely glasses in yon bit of shelf. And I change my mind. One drink to your glorious career."

The general snorted as he stumped across the room. "What's so bloody glorious about it, I'd like to know? Just one more crock who put in his time."

"Let's not be modest. Old Woody, the hero of Mons."

"Hero of Mons my arse." He made a guttural sound deep in his throat that sounded like a threat, then poured brandy into the glasses and carried them back toward his desk. He walked stiffly and with great care. "Getting lame. If I were a horse I'd be shot out of pity."

"You need sun. India, perhaps."

"*He* told you to say that, didn't he?" He handed Fenton a glass and then sat at his desk with a grateful sigh. "Bugger Blythe. I'm not going to spend my last years staring at the Himalayas. I've got that bit of rough shoot in Yorkshire and a sturdy little house to go with it." He drank some of the brandy and then toyed with the glass, rolling it between his thick strong hands. "I asked for the job of passing on your new orders. I'm sure you know why."

"I can guess."

"Blythe has prepared a letter I dictated. A letter ostensibly from you. I think it is a good letter, one that certain people in this building will be quite relieved to get. The letter states, in simple, soldier prose, your reluctant but necessary decision to retire from the

army as of today in order to devote yourself to your
family and business interests. The letter will be received with gratitude and your early retirement will
be honored with a full colonelship. A nice little gesture on their part. What do you say to that?"

"Ah," Fenton said.

"And what does that peculiar sound signify?"

"Relief. Rather like hearing the second shoe drop."

"Then I take it you intend to do the sensible thing
and sign the letter?"

"On the contrary. I intend to receive my orders and
comply with them."

"You bloody fool."

It was uttered with a quiet intensity, not untinged
with respect for the tall, hawk-faced man seated
across from him. Sir Julian had never married, and at
seventy was not likely to do so. His only living
nephew was the nearest thing he would ever get to a
son. He swallowed the rest of his brandy.

"How long have you been in the army?"

"Thirteen years."

"And you have no more idea how the system works
than some Oxford Street ribbon clerk!"

"May I beg to differ, sir?"

"You may not, sir!" He was speaking to just another
subordinate who needed a good dressing down, and,
by God, he was the man to do it. "You believe you've
served king and country for thirteen years, but that is
not true. As a professional army officer you have
served only the general staff. It's they who set the
standards, and one either complies with those standards or gets out. The staff has always had a horror of
the unorthodox and they have had more than enough
of it in the past few years, thank you very much!

They've had to contend with Colonel Lawrence dashing about like some Drury Lane fairy in a bloody soppy burnoose. They've had Trenchard pulling his flying corps out of the army and forming his own service—and they have Elles wanting to do the same with his tanks. They do not like it, sir. They do not like it one bit. And they sense the seeds of heresy in you, by gad. Your peculiar behavior in nineteen seventeen will never be understood or forgiven. Your insistence on having Major Greville court-martialed was bad enough, but the mysterious appearance of the hearing transcripts in the hands of that German fella—"

"Martin Rilke is not a *German fella.*"

"A Yank then, with a Boche name. A bleeding newspaper wallah. By all rights you should have been booted from the service if not bloody well shot!"

Fenton's expression was stone. "I followed the King's Regulations to the letter with Charles. As for my giving the transcript to Rilke, there was no proof of it."

"No proof of it," the general sighed. Slumping back in his chair, he struck a match and relit his cigar. "As if proof were needed. The Yank circulated that transcript as an antiwar tract—the prattle of a shell-shocked man, young Greville comdemning the war and Field Marshal Haig's handling of it."

"He *was* my friend, sir. I owed him that much."

The general snorted and puffed smoke like a dragon. "Greater love hath no man than to lay down his career for a friend! Greville's beliefs were the same as your own, I warrant, or you'd never have bound him over for court-martial so as to give him a public forum. It was a cheap dodge, and the War Office did not appreciate your actions. You talk about *proof*, by

God. The only thing that saved your neck was *me*, sir!"

"I'm suitably grateful, I assure you."

"But I can't save your career. You're a marked man. If you stay in the army you'll be handed every dog's job they can find. Nothing but bitter duty until they succeed in hounding you out."

He opened the drawer and removed an official War Office envelope. "Your orders, sir. You are to embark on the P&O steamer *City of Benares* leaving Southampton twelfth July. You will disembark at Aden and proceed to Basra, then by train to Baghdad. From there you will go, by whatever transport is available, to Bani el Abbas on the upper Tigris and assume command of the Twelfth Battalion of the Sixty-fifth Brigade—a mixed bag: one company of West Lancs, an armored-car detachment, and two companies of Punjabis. You will arrive in the hot season, one hundred twenty in the shade—if one can find any shade. Fever off the river. Marauding Arabs and Kurds in the wasteland. Pure hell on earth. I doubt if Winifred will be overjoyed at your assignment."

It was very quiet in the office, only the soft ticking of a wall clock and the distant hum of London's traffic. Fenton drained his glass and then leaned forward and placed it on the desk. He smiled wryly at his uncle, whose face seemed carved out of oak.

"You never told me the army would be an easy profession."

"No, I never told you that."

"And I never promised Winnie I'd leave it." He reached out a hand. "May I have my orders, sir?"

The general held the envelope tightly between his

fingers. "There's still time. Blythe has typed the letter."

Fenton shook his head and took the envelope from his uncle's hand. He slipped it into his coat pocket and stood up. "Twelfth July. Not much time, and I have at least one important thing to do. Goodbye, sir."

Sir Julian watched him leave the office and swore softly under his breath: "Damn fool." There was no malice in the words. No bite to them. It was what he would have done, of course. A matter of pride. His own career had been under a cloud once, long, long ago. He had openly criticized a doddering fool of a brigadier for gross incompetence during an expedition in the Sudan. He had saved his own small force from disaster and had marched them back to the Nile, fighting every step of the way. His quick tongue had earned him a court-martial, at which, with the peculiar logic of the army, he was recommended for the Victoria Cross and then severely reprimanded and ordered off to India for hard duty along the northwest frontier. He had served his penance with fortitude and then had thrust his way back up the ladder of command. He offered a silent prayer that Fenton might one day do the same.

A dispatch from Spanish Morocco was on his desk when he got to the office at 8:30—three thousand words, like a chapter from *War and Peace*. Martin eyed it dubiously and then checked his daily calendar. A full schedule. Miss Shaw brought in a cup of coffee and a handful of Huntley & Palmer biscuits on a plate. He lit a cigar and settled down to work, tackling the Moroccan report. It was all good, readable stuff, but there was no market for it. Filler material at best. His blue pencil zipped and slashed like a surgeon's blade.

Next on his calendar was a correspondent from the *Telegraph* who had condescended to offer his services to INA in return for a salary that could only be described as princely. Martin remembered him from the war. The man had never gone up to the line, preferring to write his battle reports from his room at the Hotel Ritz in Paris using secondhand information. So much for him.

The interview was cordial but brief and the man left feeling slightly bewildered that he hadn't been hired on the spot.

"There's a man to see you, Mr. Rilke." Miss Shaw's head around the door. "He has no appointment, but he claims to be a friend of yours."

"His name?"

"A Colonel Wood-Lacy."

He hadn't seen Fenton in over a year, but they kept in touch. He was not only an old friend but a source of matters military. Fenton had gone to France with the BEF in August 1914, a captain in the Coldstream Guards. He had survived Mons and the first battle of Ypres, Neuve Chapelle, Loos, and the Somme offensives. The deaths of so many regular army officers, plus his own competence, brought rapid promotion. By 1917 he was brevetted a brigadier general, a young thruster obviously destined for further honors, but then he had fallen from grace.

"Gosh it's good to see you, Fenton. How'd you know I was back in London?"

"I had dinner with Jacob before he left. He told me the happy news." He glanced around the office. "I hope I'm not intruding. Never seen such a busy place.

Something momentous happen that I haven't heard about?"

"No. Just a normal day in the world. Poles fighting Russians, Russians fighting starvation, Riffs slaughtering Spaniards, Greeks murdering Turks and vice versa. I'll be blue-penciling most of it as being of no consequence. A serene day, in fact. Drop by when there's a war on." He motioned toward a chair. "Get a load off your feet."

"Are you quite sure? I hate popping in on people."

Martin stole a glance at his watch. "I'm sending a feature writer off to Poland and I have a few things to talk over. Take about half an hour. Then I can leave and we can have a leisurely lunch. How does that sound?"

"Jolly good. Just find me a quiet corner and I'll stay out of the way."

Martin headed for the door. "There's only one quiet corner in the joint and you're seated in it."

During the thirty-five minutes that Fenton waited, a copyboy dashed in four times to deposit sheaves of Teletype messages. Having nothing else to do, he stood by the desk and read them. The events of the day, hot off the wire. It made depressing reading. He could envision a morning in which a report would end up on the desk telling of the ambush and massacre of British soldiers near Bani el Abbas on the Tigris. *The Gatling jammed and the colonel dead* . . . as the Victorian poem put it. Martin would probably scrawl a blue line across it as being of no consequence.

* * *

The pub in Magpie Alley was suitably dim and ancient, with black-oak tables and timbered walls. Its customers were divided equally between Fleet Street journalists and lawyers from the Temple, each group keeping strictly to its own side of the room. Martin ordered for them, whiskeys and the mixed grill.

"Now then," he said to Fenton, "bring me up to date. Are you still waiting around for orders?"

"I got them this morning, read to me in person by Uncle Julian. I've been posted to some ragtag battalion in Mesopotamia—or, rather, Iraq, as they now call it. Prefer *Mespot* myself as being more indicative of the bloody country."

"What will you be doing?"

"Keeping tribesmen from blowing up the pipelines. Guard duty for the Anglo-Persian oil company."

"A man of your talents should be at the staff college."

Fenton took a drink of his whiskey. "I'm not the sort of chap they want at Camberley—or even in the army, if it comes to that."

"Why don't you take the hint and quit?"

"I wish I could answer that, Martin. Stubbornness, I suppose. But it's what I do. I'm a soldier and that's all there is to it. I put up with the gaff just as you put up with it in your job. I read a few of those Teletype messages a boy kept dumping on your desk. How can you wade through all that misery day after day and still keep your sanity? Why don't *you* pack it in and go off to some quiet village and write books about talking rabbits?"

"Because I'm not a talking-rabbit sort of writer."

"And I'm not a country-gentleman sort of bloke. I

took the king's shilling and I don't feel like handing it back."

"Commendable but dumb."

He smiled wryly. "Winnie's sentiments exactly. She once thought I was only marrying her for her money. She wishes now that I had."

Martin signaled the barman for another round of drinks. He had a grudging respect for Fenton. The pressures on him to leave the army were enormous. Had his career been on the rise, it might have made sense, but it had taken quite a different course. His reasons for staying on could have been construed as a simple case of bull-headed pride, but Martin knew better. Fenton loved the British Army and felt intense pride in being one of its officers. It was as simple as that. To each his own.

"You're not taking Winifred to Baghdad, are you?"

"Christ, no. Not even to Cairo. She's with child again. You might pop up to Suffolk when you have a chance and see her while I'm gone. You have my permission to take the boat out for a sail." He shifted his drink from hand to hand, frowning at it. "I didn't drop by your office to talk about my problems, Martin. Have you seen the Grevilles lately?"

"No, but I've talked to Aunt Hanna on the phone. And Alex sent me a long letter after Mackendric died. Why?"

"Alex would like to have Charles removed from Llandinam. She and the gaffer are at loggerheads about it—hell, about *everything*, if it comes to that. I agree with Alex. I don't think Charles should be shut away. I think she could help him."

"What makes you think that? She was a nurse, not a psychiatrist."

The mixed grills arrived, sizzling on the plates—fat lamb chops, kidneys, sausage, tomatoes, and crusty brown chips.

"Ah," Martin murmured as he reached for knife and fork.

"I had a lengthy chat one day with our battalion MO," Fenton said after a few minutes of silent eating. "In Ireland. Nice chap. Typical regular army sawbones. Never set foot in Harley Street. Chop off a leg . . . hand out a blue pill . . . all in the day's work. Well, I always think of Charles, and I brought up the subject of shell shock one night in the mess. This chap told me that when he had been medical officer with the King's Own he had refused to diagnose it as a specific ailment—wouldn't dignify it with a name. If some quivering bloke stumbled into his dugout after a bombardment, he'd give the poor fellow a blue pill, a double tot of rum, and then send him back to his unit. The more severe breakdowns, the truly palsied and incoherent ones, he'd send down to the transport lines with a note pinned to their tunics asking the transport officer to give them a couple of days' rest and then put them to work unloading lorries or something like that. He figured they were better off doing physical labor than being shut away in a hospital—and of more use to the war effort. A few weeks out of reach of the shells did wonders for them, he said, and eventually most of them came back of their own accord."

"Kill or cure."

"Something like that, but it worked. Alex told me that Mackendric had a theory about shell shock, too. He wasn't a blue-pill-and-run doctor, of course, but he was dead set against shell-shocked men being stuck away in mental hospitals. He believed that if you tell a man he's ill, he will be ill; that mental hospitals only serve to impress upon their inmates the fact that they must belong there or they wouldn't be in one in the first place. He felt that eight out of ten would stand a better chance of recovery if they were sent home to their families."

"Interesting," Martin chewed thoughtfully on a grilled kidney. "Is that Alexandra's belief, too?"

"Yes, but, as it comes via Mackendric, his lordship won't listen to it. Probably considers the poor chap nothing but a seducer of fair English virgins."

"They were married, for Christ's sake!"

"It was a race between the stork and the parson. Hardly the type of wedding a peer of the realm expects for his daughter."

"Mack was a brave and honorable man, a legend in the Forty-third Division. I heard about him two years before I met him."

"Quite beside the point. He may have been a legend, but he was thirteen years older than Alex and a married man to boot." He pushed his plate to one side and lit a cigarette. "Alex said something last night at dinner that touched me deeply. She said that as long as Charles is shut away the war will always be a presence in the house. He casts a longer shadow than that, Martin. If there's any chance of his becoming even halfway normal again, I believe we're obligated to help him."

"I feel the same way, but what can we possibly do?"

"The first, and most important, step is to get his nibs to see eye to eye with Alex. That will take a bit of diplomacy and the finer arts of persuasion. It will also take time, which is something I simply do not have. I sail on the twelfth."

Martin stared at his friend for a moment and then swallowed hard. "Hold it. Are you hinting I should be the go-between?"

"Why not? You're capable of it. Family and all that."

"I may have some sway with Aunt Hanna, but Anthony's another matter. There's a slight chill in the air from that quarter."

"Because of *The Killing Ground* you mean? Granted he wasn't thrilled by the book, but he must know in his heart that you wrote the truth. I don't suppose anyone wants to be reminded that the 'Great' War was mere mindless butchery. Still, I suspect he admires your anger—in his own peculiar fashion."

Martin put down his knife and fork. The chops had a greasy taste and his stomach was rebelling.

"There's another matter. I might just be sued for libel by General Sparrowfield. Or have you heard that news along the military grapevine?"

"Yes, as a matter of fact. There was a slight discussion in the mess yesterday afternoon. Quite a few of us served under Sparrowfield on the Somme. He was affectionately known as 'Old Bird Drops' in those days."

Martin smiled and took out a cigar. "Maybe I can use that in my defense. Anyway, getting back to my point, if I go to court, Sparrowfield's lawyer is sure to bring up the hearing transcript as an example of my wartime perfidious defeatism—or some crap like that. Raking up those old coals will hardly please His Lordship."

Fenton blew a smoke ring toward the beamed ceil-

ing. "Let's take first things first, old boy. You're not in
the dock now, are you? It's my opinion the letter to
The Times and libel suits are just ploys to make you
get windy. Birdy Sparrowfield trembles on the brink
of senility. He'd start ranting about how he skewered
Brother Boer in the Transvaal and make an utter fool
of himself on the stand. Deal with one thing at a
time."

"I suppose you're right."

"And even if he actually does sue, noting the glacial
slowness of the judiciary process, it could be months,
even years, before it all came to a head. In the meantime, there's still Charlie up there in Wales. You're a
persuasive fellow. And a born diplomat to boot. If anyone could get Alex and his nibs to agree on anything,
it's you."

"Well," Martin said, lighting his cigar, "it's worth a
try."

"Yes," Fenton said with quiet intensity. "It bloody
well is."

Going home in the evening rush hour, the taxi immovable in the crush around Trafalgar Square, Martin
paid the driver, got out, and began walking up Hay-
market toward Piccadilly Circus. War-wounded ex-
servicemen stood in the gutters selling matches, some
with medals pinned to their threadbare coats.

"Lost me bleedin' arm at Wipers, guv'nor. . . ."

He gave the man a sixpence and hurried on. Most
people ignored the pleas, or tossed a copper without
looking. The war was over. Studiously forgotten. The
age of jazz dancing and pink gins. He was thinking of

Charles, whose mind was locked into another time and place. To a crippled soldier begging in the streets, that might have seemed a blessing.

He was thinking of Charles as he drew a slender pamphlet from Jacob's bookcase. It was well printed and bound in heavy buff paper. The title took up much of the cover.

AFTER THE SOMME

An inquiry into the advisability of court-martial of Major the Rt. Hon. Charles Greville, 2nd Royal Windsor Fusiliers, conducted at Llandinam War Hospital.

> With an introduction by
> Martin Rilke, Associated Press.

The date of the first and only printing was March 25, 1917.

He poured a glass of champagne and sat on the sofa. Between sips he turned the pages—the transcript of a hearing conducted by three officers from the adjutant general's office at Llandinam, Wales, in February 1917.

COL. BAKER: Is there a prisoner's friend?
MAJ. GREVILLE: I declined one, sir. I intend to speak for myself.
COL. BAKER: This panel has no objection.
CAPT. JONES: I believe it should be placed in the record at this time that the report of Captain Finchaven, RAMC, on the state of Major Greville's

mind on the afternoon of fifteenth January, has been read by all the members of this panel. Do you have a copy of that medical report, Major Greville?

MAJ. GREVILLE: I do.

COL. BAKER: May I ask the major if he disagrees with Finchaven's diagnosis of his mental health?

MAJ. GREVILLE: I do. I was not insane. It was a calculated act.

COL. BAKER: That is for us to determine, Major Greville. It is the purpose of this panel.

MAJ. GREVILLE: I understand.

COL. BAKER: What sort of doctor is Captain Finchaven? It doesn't say on the report. Is he a surgeon?

CAPT. JONES: He is a specialist in neurasthenic disorders, sir. A professor of neurology at London University before the war.

COL. BAKER: I see. Have you studied medicine, Major Greville? Specifically diseases of nervous origin?

MAJ. GREVILLE: No, sir.

COL. BAKER: Then wouldn't you say it would be fair to assume that his determination of your mental condition on fifteenth January is more accurate than your own?

MAJ. GREVILLE: Captain Finchaven examined me after the act, sir. I do not recall being examined. I am told that I was raving and incoherent. I do not dispute that, sir, nor do I dispute the doctor's analysis of my mental condition *at that time.* What I do dispute is the inference that I was deranged when I arrived at Wimbledon Training Center that morning. I was clearheaded, sir. I had come to Wimbledon Common for a specific purpose, achieved that purpose, and surrendered peacefully to authority. It was the deed of a rational man.

COL. BAKER: This would appear to be a case of disputed opinion as to the condition of mental stability—yours as a layman versus that of a medical specialist with many years of training and practice. I can see no point in prolonging the proceedings here. I can find no justification for your brigade commander's insistence that you be court-martialed. Are we all in agreement on that?

CAPT. THORN ⎱ Agreed.
CAPT. JONES ⎰

COL. BAKER: Then I make the motion that—

MAJ. GREVILLE: I'm entitled to a plea, sir. Under King's Regulations I have the right to take the stand in my own defense.

COL. BAKER: Dash it all, man. I'm about to make a motion to quash the charge brought against you by Brigadier General Fenton Wood-Lacy. Isn't that clear to you, sir?

MAJ. GREVILLE: It is, Colonel, but that hardly alters the fact that regulations bestow on me the opportunity, if I so desire, of addressing the panel.

COL. BAKER: I must say that I find these proceedings to be the most curious in all my twenty years with the judge advocate general's office. You may speak on your behalf, but try to be brief.

MAJ. GREVILLE: I thank the panel.

COL. BAKER: That is not necessary. Kindly proceed.

MAJ. GREVILLE: I entered this war with the highest of ideals and the

firmest of faith in the rightness and justness of my patriotism. . . .

Martin closed the pamphlet and set it aside. Charles's
speech was too painful to read, even now, after
all the years that had passed. It was like a cry of pain.
All the horrors of the Somme attacks were in his
words, the anguish of seeing his generation driven to
slaughter. The words as bleak as that long-ago day in
Wales during the darkest days of the war.

Nineteen seventeen.

A hopeless deadlock on the western front, the armies like bleeding, savage animals bogged in mud.
The Somme offensive over and nothing to show for it
but six miles of useless, shell-pitted, stinking ground.
Half a million British dead and wounded—all for
nothing.

Nineteen seventeen.

The armies massing again for another big push to
end the war. The British pouring fresh troops around
Arras, the French massing along the river Aisne—
General Nivelle's grandiose plan for one massive blow
to end it all in a day. A lunatic dream, but the generals saw victory shining on the horizon. The soldiers
saw only barbed wire, machine guns, and graves.

Nineteen seventeen.

Major Charles Greville on leave. Calm, soft-spoken
Charles Greville strolling the streets of London with a
bomb ticking softly in his head. Going to the Cafe
Royal, the Ritz Bar, and the Bond Street shops and
seeing only corpses. Seeing only muddy wastelands
and the men of his company rotting in the shell holes.

I've seen them, I've seen them,
Hangin' on the old barbed wire.

Nineteen seventeen.

Major Charles Greville on Wimbledon Common, walking into the HQ hut of the Public Schools Training Battalion to see his brother, Second Lieutenant William Greville, age eighteen, fresh from Eton, his training completed and ready to go over to France. A brave, eager, strong young man . . .

The bells of hell go ting-a-ling-a-ling

. . . who would have answered unwaveringly the order to go over the top, blowing his whistle, urging his men onward from the crest of the parapet . . .

O death where is thy sting-a-ling-a-ling?

. . . and who would have died where he stood from the machine-gun fire traversing the trench.

And seeing it all, the vision of it, Major Charles Greville removed an automatic pistol from the deep pocket of his Burberry and blew a hole in his brother's knee.

IV

Standing by the window of her dressing room, Hanna could see Alexandra and the nurse enter the park. The nurse was wheeling the pram, and little Colin was seated bolt upright, pointing at a flock of large crows that were stalking imperiously across the grass. A murder of crows, she remembered Anthony telling her once. An *exaltation* of larks—a *murder* of crows. The creatures fitted their collective descriptions: larks an exaltation of the spirits as they wheeled against the sky; crows like dark assassins stalking the lawns.

She turned away from the window, depressed by the sight. Her daughter and first grandchild. She had always dreamed of it. Alexandra being married— perhaps to an officer in the dragoons so that she would walk with her young husband beneath an arch of sabers between rows of men with plumed helmets and burnished cuirasses. And then, a year later, the child—the elaborate christening ceremony at Abingdon church followed by a glittering party at the Pryory. All those dreams gone. Blown to ashes like her dreams for Charles. The ache in her heart her own personal war wound.

"Would her ladyship prefer the green or brown this morning?"

Her maid held two dresses for her inspection.

"The brown, I think. No—green. But not that one. The eau de Nile crepe from Paris."

"Very good, m'lady. Most appropriate. It's ever such a warm day."

While the maid searched the closet for the dress, Hanna parted the window curtains again. Alexandra, nurse, and child could no longer be seen. They were somewhere on the gravel paths in the green tunnels of the trees, just one of many groups of mothers, nurse-maids, and prams.

"Oh, it's lovely!" the maid exclaimed, holding the silk dress up to a shaft of sunlight. "You will look a picture in it."

She looked beautiful, the pale green suiting her complexion, the new length and simplicity of design complimenting her figure. The earl, taking coffee in the morning room, was quick to remark on it as she walked in. He had just returned from his daily ride in Hyde Park and was in a euphoric mood after an hour's hard canter along Rotten Row.

"You certainly look radiant this morning, Hanna. New frock?"

"Yes. From Harcourt in Paris. Do you like it?"

"Stunning, I must say. Had your breakfast?"

"Tea and toast."

He made a clucking sound. "Tea and toast is hardly what I'd call a breakfast. Cook is preparing grilled kidneys, gammon, shirred eggs, and stewed tomatoes."

"Sounds intimidating. I have my figure to think of— or what's left of it."

"Nothing wrong with your figure, dear girl."

"You're just being gallant."

She opened the French doors and inhaled the subtle

perfume from the rose garden. The open doors flooded the room with light. It was the most pleasant room in the house, she was thinking as she turned back to face it. White and soft yellow gold. Golden-oak flooring, a blue saffron Persian carpet, pale blue and dusty rose upholstery. The four Renoirs on the wall accenting the colors. It seemed a sacrilege to feel unhappy in such an exquisite space.

"You slept badly last night," she said. "I could hear you pacing your room."

He cleared his throat and retrieved the newspaper, opening it and raising its folds like a shield. "Had a spot of indigestion. The lobster, I expect. Too warm for shellfish. You must have been sleeping poorly yourself to have heard me."

"I've been a bit restless the past few weeks."

"Oh? I'll give Merton a ring. He'll have the chemist send over something. A sleeping draft, perhaps."

"Yes. That might help."

"Bound to, my love. Bound to."

"Love" was not an idle word. They had loved one another from their first meeting. But a gulf had been growing between them. It had begun during the war when the first irrational hatred of Germany and the Boche had swept England like a plague. For the first time in their lives they had found it necessary to avoid touching on certain subjects so as to avoid rancor. By an unexpressed agreement she never mentioned her concern for her numerous, and much loved, relatives in Germany. And he did not verbalize his wish that *all* Germans, her cousins or otherwise, should be blown from the face of the earth by British shells.

As the war had progressed year by year into increasing frightfulness, as the casualty lists bloated past all human understanding, other differences had grown between them. She became sympathetic toward the pacifist movement and its goal to end the war at any price. He endorsed the more popular attitude of war to the knife. But these opposite beliefs were never discussed for fear of destroying that one constant value in a vortex of chaos—their love for each other. They had, unwittingly and foolishly, woven a habit of avoiding the unpleasant by discoursing on the superficial. It was a habit to which they still adhered. Alexandra's return from Canada had sent them retreating into private reflections on the matter, with only infrequent and brief clashes over its numerous ramifications. The morning sunlight streaming into the room could not penetrate their separate shells.

"There was a murder in Bournemouth, of all places," the earl said. "A sordid little affair involving a chauffeur and a rich widow."

"Who murdered whom?"

"He did her in—for forged gain in a will. He'll swing for it, I suppose. Waste of a good driver."

A footman brought in the mail, separated it on the hall table, and carried two round silver trays bearing envelopes into the breakfast room. The letters addressed to Lady Stanmore far outnumbered those for the earl. Early in 1919, Paul Rilke had written from Chicago to gleefully inform his sister that the net profits of various companies—which Paul controlled and in which she owned substantial shares—had come to several million dollars in fiscal 1918. The news had shocked her to the bone. Because most of the money had been earned by the manufacture of shell casings, cannon mounts, machine-gun barrels, and bomb racks for airplanes, she had suffered nightmares for a

week, seeing in her dreams ditches filled with the
bony cadavers of men who had died for no greater
purpose than to increase her bank account. Her impulse had been to give her share of the profits to
charity, but her fortune was not hers to control. Her
millions were managed by her husband, or locked into
a trust set up by her father before his death in 1902
and administered by a consortium of law firms and
banks in Chicago and London. The best she had been
able to do was to persuade Anthony and the trustees
to increase her personal allowance by thirty thousand
pounds a year. She gave this money to a variety of
organizations dedicated to the welfare of wounded
soldiers or to the destitute families of dead ones. As
the honorary chairwoman of half a dozen charities,
her daily mail was prodigious.

The earl finished a second helping of grilled kidney
and gammon rashers, poured himself another cup of
tea, and began to open his slight pile of envelopes.

"Note from Dick Bates. Wishes you well. Says he
saw a five-year-old jumper at Tattersall's that I might
be interested in. Thinks I could get him for sixty gui-
neas."

Hanna sifted through her mail, most of the envelopes bearing the imprints of various charities. She
put those to one side and opened the remainder.

"We've been invited to a cocktail party at Bouchard's on Thursday evening," she said.

"Bouchard's?"

"The gallery in Old Burlington Street. A showing of
contemporary art to raise money for the Slade."

"I'm not overly fond of contemporary art—or the
Slade School, for that matter. I don't know why we
should teach the artists of this country to paint like

Frenchmen. There hasn't been a decent painting out
of Paris since nineteen six."

"And a short letter from Martin," she said. "He's
been having trouble reaching us on the telephone. I
thought the damage to the cable had been fixed."

The earl snorted loudly. "Oh, it's been fixed, all
right! I ask for a number in the city and get connected
to a fishmonger in Clerkenwell! Of course it's just like
the Irish, isn't it? Sinn Feiners go through all that
bloody trouble and risk only to slash a cable serving
Marylebone and Regent's Park! Hardly a devastating
blow against the crown, I must say."

"Odd he should write. I was thinking of him last
night. I came across a snapshot in my dresser drawer."

"Of Martin?"

"No. A snap Alex sent us from France. She and Ivy
Thaxton in front of a hospital tent. They're both in
uniform and smart as paint. Ivy was such a pretty
girl."

"Yes," he murmured. "Quite so." Ivy Thaxton. He
recalled her vaguely—but then, he had only known
her when she had been one of the many housemaids
at the Pryory before the war. He had never seen her
again after she had left his service to become a nurse,
except in a photograph or two that Alex had enclosed
in letters. Never had the chance to know her in a different light. His daughter's servant in Abingdon, her
best friend in France. Martin's wife. All of those
events taking place in another world—the brief and
tragic democracy of the battle zone. "What does Martin have to say?"

"Oh, nothing very much. He apologizes for having
been too busy with his new job to call on us. Would

like to drop by this Sunday if we're home. I'll tell him to come for dinner."

"I might go down to the house on Friday."

"But you'd be back by Sunday noon, surely." Her tone implied that she expected him no later than that.

Coatsworth remembered him—but then, the old butler remembered every face he had ever seen.

"It's good to see you again, Mr. Rilke."

"As it is to see you, Coatsworth. It's been a few years."

"Nineteen seventeen, if I'm not mistaken, sir. At the Park Lane house."

"You have a good memory."

The butler smiled as he took Martin's panama hat and placed it on the side table in the hall. "My memory is about the only thing that functions properly these days."

"You look just fine to me."

"Appearances are deceiving, I'm sorry to say." He shuffled toward the finely etched glass doors that separated the marble-walled foyer from the main hallway. "His Lordship is expecting you in the study."

Martin found the earl measuring gin and French vermouth into a crystal and silver cocktail shaker. A small book lay open beside him on the oak sideboard.

"Hello, Martin," he said, glancing over his shoulder as Martin came into the room. "I hope I have this right. Three parts gin to one part French . . ." He peered down at the book. "Stir well with plenty of ice . . . serve in chilled glasses . . . add twist of lemon peel, and garnish with an olive before serving.

An olive? Whatever for? It's an American recipe, of course. Rather heavy-handed with ice, vegetables, and things."

He stirred the mixture with a long-handled silver spoon and then poured some into two small glasses, handing one to Martin.

"The new martini cocktail, the book says. Just good old gin and French as far as I can see, except heavier on the gin." He took a sip. "Not bad. Quite smooth, in fact. I can't for the life of me see how a chunk of ice would improve it. But if you'd prefer . . ."

"Oh, no," Martin said, raising his glass. "This is fine." He suppressed a smile as he thought of what the bartender at the American Bar in Paris would have said about lukewarm gin and vermouth. "To your health, sir."

"And to yours, Martin. It's been donkey's years since we had a drink together."

"It was down at Abingdon—and the drink was port."

"Yes, about all one drank in those days, except for a glass of Highland malt. Although, to tell the truth, I rather enjoy these new cocktails—I find them quite challenging to prepare." He savored another small swallow. "I never had the chance to congratulate you on winning that . . ."—he groped for the name of it— "Pulitzer thing."

"I was surprised to get it."

"I'm quite sure you deserved it, Martin. How do you like your new job?"

"Very much, so far. Quite a challenge."

"Yes, I'm sure it is, but then you're so bloody good at what you do. I read all of your Versailles sketches in the *Guardian*, by the way. Bang on the mark. The one on little Orlando still sticks in the mind. I suppose the poor fellow is out the back door now that this chap Mussolini is running things."

"Yes," Martin said, gazing down at his martini. "Yesterday's news."

"Fate trips up fools, doesn't it? What a Caesar he thought he was." He turned toward the French doors. "It's beastly hot in here. Might as well take our drinks into the garden and wait for your aunt to join us. We'll be dining alfresco, which should be pleasant. Do you know it was over eighty today? Think of that. It's more normal for an English July to be struck by hailstones than sun."

It was seven o'clock and the sun still had a bite to it. The roses seemed overblown and soggy with heat. Petals littered the ground, and the earl crushed their perfume into the warm soil with the toe of his shoe.

"Plays havoc with the gardening. I was down at Abingdon for a couple of days. The landscapers are there and all that rain we had has been baked out of the ground."

"Aunt Hanna told me you were rebuilding the place. How's it coming along?"

"Nearly complete," he said moodily. "Be fit for habitation in a month."

"And you'll be moving down there?"

"I suppose we will. Your aunt's not overjoyed at the idea. Did she mention that?"

"No."

He touched a rose, the petals flaking away in his hand. "She's—concerned about the size. It's a big house and we're not exactly the largest family in the world. Still, what with guests and all, we won't be rattling around in it like two peas in a colander as she fears. I'll be getting the stables and kennels up to snuff and reactivating the Abingdon hunt. The district's swarming with foxes. There's been no hunting since the war. Did you ever learn to ride, Martin?"

"Never had the chance." Again he suppressed a smile. "What with one thing or another."

"Pity. But the war's behind you now. Time to learn the pursuits of peace. There's a joy to riding to hounds that's difficult to explain. Still, whether you ride or not, you'll always find a room waiting for you at the Pryory." He drained his glass and reached for Martin's. "Let's have a smahan more, shall we?"

Martin watched him carry the glasses toward the house. The smell of the roses and the earl's mention of the Pryory sent his thoughts reeling backward. Abingdon in the summer of 1914, the kindness of his aunt as she told him there would always be a room for him at the house. He had come to stay for a few days, part of his vacation plans. A week in England, three weeks in Germany and Italy, and then home to Chicago and his job on the *Express*. A visiting relative. The son of Hanna's favorite; and long dead, brother William. Something of a curiosity to Charles and Alexandra. Their American cousin, and the only Rilke they had ever heard of without money. Something of a mystery, too. The scent of a skeleton in the Rilke closet. Half-remembered stories of how William Rilke had been disinherited long, long ago. Of how he had run off to become an artist and had eventually cut his wrists to the bone in a Paris atelier. A penniless failure.

Ivy had known nothing of that. She had thought Martin a millionaire, or the son of one—because all Americans were millionaires, that was a common fact. Coming shyly into his room that first day, neat as a pin in her starched uniform, bearing freshly cut roses in a vase. She had placed the roses carefully on a table by the open window and some petals had fallen softly to the polished surface of the wood. . . .

"Hello, Martin."

Alexandra was coming toward him along the path, blonde and voluptuous in a light silk dress. They embraced for a moment in silence, his arms holding her tightly.

"Hello, beauty," he said. "As we used to say in Chicago, you're a sight for sore eyes."

"You're more than that," she said, kissing his cheek. "You're a tonic." She stepped back. "Let me look at you. The same dear man."

"A bit more of the dear man." He let go of her hands and patted his abdomen. "About all I do these days is sit at a desk."

"And do it brilliantly. I follow your career."

"You could follow it more closely by coming to see me. We have a lot to talk about."

"I've been a bit of a recluse the past few months. Haven't been up to seeing anyone. I'm coming out of it now."

"I know the feeling. It takes time."

The earl came out of the house carrying the refilled glasses. He hesitated a moment when he saw his daughter, then walked up to them and handed a glass to Martin.

"We're having a gin concoction, Alex. Would you care for one?"

"No, thank you, Papa." She seemed to gaze past him. "It's rather too hot for alcohol."

"One of the great myths," the earl said. "Ask any old India hand about *that*. The sundown peg or two is what kept them going. It helps sweat the fever through the pores."

The conversation turned idle, and then Hanna emerged from the house and the servants began to bustle about the damask-clad table set up under an awning on the terrace.

The icy vichyssoise was being served when William arrived at the table, looking drawn and pale and muttering apologies for being late.

"You might check your watch from time to time," the earl remarked coldly. "Do you remember your cousin Martin?"

"Yes, I do indeed," William said, bending across the table to shake Martin's hand before taking his seat. "I was still in school when we met. The Harrow match at Lord's, if I'm not mistaken. You came with Fenton."

"That's right," Martin said with a laugh. "I never understood cricket then and I don't now."

"It's a jolly game," William said without much enthusiasm. He eyed his soup balefully.

"Don't you feel well?" Hanna asked him.

"No . . . not exactly. A bit squeamish. Must be something I ate."

"Or drank," the earl muttered.

"It's those clubs you go to," Hanna said. "I'm sure they serve vile food."

William toyed with his soup. "They don't serve food, actually."

"The music alone would make one bilious," the earl growled. "More than enough to turn one's stomach inside out."

"What music is that?" Martin asked.

William looked at him defensively. "Jazz."

Martin nodded. "King Oliver, Early Wiley, Kid Ory . . . I was always going down to the South Side to hear the latest band up from Memphis or New Orleans. The Rhythm Kings were my favorite, and then there was the Original Dixieland Jazz Band at the Dreamland Cafe."

"Oh, I say . . ." William was staring at him in awe. "King Oliver. Oh, I say . . . I have several of his records."

Lord Stanmore put on an expression of mock surprise. "You mean to tell me that the perpetrators of all that caterwauling have names? Difficult to believe."

"Do you go to any of the clubs here?" William, eyes fixed on his cousin, swallowed a spoonful of soup, gagged slightly, and sat back in his chair. A fine haze of sweat broke out on his face. "I—like the—Mardi Gras in Dean Street." He dabbed at his brow with his napkin and glanced despairingly around the table. "May I be excused? I—I don't feel at all well."

"You look positively ghastly," his father said. "By all means go."

William pushed back his chair and hurried into the house through open French doors. The suppressed retching sounds he made were ignored.

"You must have a chat with him," Hanna said evenly. "He stays out much too late. It can't be good for him."

The earl stared fixedly at his soup. "No, I don't imagine it is."

"It's only a hangover," Alexandra said. "I'll go up later and see what I can do for him."

The earl said nothing, and Hanna shifted the talk to the heat wave and to a new play with Aubrey Smith opening at the Royalty.

A breeze stirred at twilight and caused the candles on the table to flicker. A footman served coffee while Coatsworth shuffled onto the terrace with a bottle of 1910 Cognac from the wine cellar. The informality of the setting, the cobalt sky, and the last tracery of sun on a motionless cloud imparted a picnic atmosphere and precluded the ritual of the ladies leaving the table while the men had their cigars. After pouring the Cognac into small bell-shaped glasses, Coatsworth brought a rosewood humidor.

It was time, Martin was thinking as he turned the excellent Canary Island cigar between his fingers.

"I saw Charles today."

"I beg your pardon," the earl said after a moment of utter silence. "What did you say?"

"That I saw Charles. I went up to Llandinam this morning."

"This *morning?*" There was disbelief in his voice. "To north Wales? Surely—"

"I flew up. We keep a company plane at Hendon. I left at seven and was back in London by four. I saw him, and we had a very interesting talk."

Lord Stanmore lit his cigar. His fingers trembled as he held the match. "That's not possible."

"Please, Tony!" Hanna's words were like a cry.

"I'm sorry, my dear, I know how much it hurts you, but one does not hold interesting talks with Charles."

"I did," Martin said. "We found a common ground for discussion."

The earl drew slowly on his cigar in an effort to calm himself. He fixed his gaze on Martin as though he were the only one present.

"Charles is a badly shell-shocked man. He spends his days seated on a bench watching the woods in the valley. He sits there for hours at a time—staring—waiting for his men to come back, the men of his battalion he ordered over the top in France and who went to their deaths. One can only talk to Charles about—things. The shape of the valley . . . the contours of the woods . . . the patterns made by cloud shadows. One could ask till doomsday and Charles would never say what *he* sees out there. Had there been a radical change in his condition, the doctors at Llandinam would have informed me."

"I didn't say there had ben a change, radical or otherwise. Let's just say that I broke through to Charles and we had a normal discussion."

"About what?" the earl asked, his voice so low that it was difficult to hear.

"Thomas Hardy."

God in heaven," Hanna murmured. *"Lieber Gott."*

"There are no miracles," the earl said. "I'm certainly not calling you a liar, Martin. I'm sure there is an explanation for this—*discussion* you held with my son. However, doctors have assured me—"

"Doctors can be wrong," Alexandra said. "There's a good deal of disagreement about shell shock—causes *and* cures."

He eyed her stonily. "I'm aware of Colonel Mackendric's views. You've explained them before."

"And you've listened with a jaundiced ear. Do you find it so impossible to separate the doctor from the man? Robbie may have had his faults, but a lack of dedication to the wounded was not one of them. Their recovery, physical and mental, haunted his every hour and killed him in the end. So when we talk about Colonel Mackendric, let's do it in that light and no other. Is that too much to ask, Papa?"

"No, dash it all, but Colonel Mackendric never examined Charles. Other men have, men I have faith in, and trust."

"There are times, Papa, when one must only trust the heart."

The wind picked up, stirring the boxwood and the elms, blowing out the candles on the table.

"Perhaps we should go inside," Hanna said. "I feel chilled."

The earl stood up. "By all means."

He escorted her into the house, Martin and Alexandra lingering on the terrace.

"Did you really talk with Charles and get a rational response?"

"Yes," Martin said. "They're all wrong about him. Oh, he's a shell-shock case all right, but he doesn't sit on that hill waiting for his dead troops to come over the rise. There's a glimmer of something lying beneath the surface and it'll never come out if he stays in that place."

"I know. It's just a storage bin."

He bit angrily on his unlit cigar and spat the tip into the garden. "Jesus. Fenton called me a diplomat. Some diplomat! I stomped in with two left feet."

"Perhaps. But you've shaken Papa. I could see the look in his eyes. He wants desperately for Charles to be well again—or at least halfway whole. He just finds it so difficult to believe it's possible."

"It is, though," he said fiercely. "I know it is."

She sought his hand and squeezed it. "Don't give up, then."

The earl was in the drawing room, pacing slowly, brandy in one hand and cigar in the other. He gave

Alexandra an accusing look as she entered the room beside Martin.

"Your mother's come down with an awful headache. You might go up to her and see if she needs an aspirin or something."

"I don't think she has the type of headache an aspirin will cure, Papa."

"I suppose there's some deep meaning to that remark. She has a headache because she's upset. Quite frankly, she's upset because the two of you lurched into a subject that forced me to play the devil's advocate. Your mother had become reconciled to Charles's condition. And now . . . all of this reckless raising hope where there is no bloody hope."

"I'm sorry, sir," Martin said. "I have to differ."

"Do you?" he said icily. "Quite frankly, Martin, I feel I've been tricked. You could have told me earlier that you'd been up to the hospital. It would have saved your aunt a good deal of mental anguish."

"My intention was to tell all of you at the same time."

"The journalist's dodge of springing a surprise. Was that it?"

"Something on the order, perhaps. But what I said was true."

"I can't believe it."

"Then fly up to Llandinam with me tomorrow. Just the two of us. Judge for yourself."

Lord Stanmore had never so much as touched an airplane. The idea was sobering. He glanced away from his nephew and fixed his gaze on the portrait of Hanna that Auguste Renoir had done for him in the early spring of 1889. How beautiful she was. All misty gold and ivory. He suddenly felt old, and tired. "Fly, you say?"

"Have you ever been up before?"

"No . . . not exactly."

"We own a remarkable plane. A de Havilland Eighteen. Has a range of over four hundred miles at nearly one hundred and thirty miles per hour. And it's strong as a steel bridge. An extremely safe machine."

"I'm sure it is, but—"

"And our pilot's first-rate. An ex-squadron leader in the RAF."

"Where could one possibly land the thing? On the golf links, I suppose."

"There's a flying club at Glynn Ceiriog with an excellent field. Ten minutes by car from Llandinam."

He had been tossed a challenge, the glove flung at his feet.

"Oh, very well. If only to lay all this to rest once and for all."

"Shall I pick you up in the morning, or would you rather meet me at Hendon aerodrome?"

"I shall meet you. What time?"

"Seven—seven-thirty."

"Very well. And I would prefer no mention is made of this to your aunt. She'd only fret over the notion of my gadding about in the clouds. You know how women are."

He showed Martin to the door and then retired immediately to his study. The architect's plans for a summer pavilion he wanted built at the Pryory were on his desk, but he was in no mood to go over them. He fixed a whiskey and sat down in an armchair feeling worn, spent, and not a little angry.

"Blast him," he murmured. He didn't enjoy being pushed into things, like flying. And as for that nonsense of having an *interesting* conversation with Charles—well, dash it all, that was just plain foolishness. He finished his drink in a gulp and fixed himself another.

He assumed that Hanna would be asleep, or at least he hoped she would be, but he could see a fine line of light under her sitting-room door as he walked down the hall toward his own suite. He tapped lightly. There was no answer, but he opened it and looked in. The door leading into her bedroom was ajar and that room was lighted also.

"Hanna?" he called out softly, walking into the bedroom. "Are you awake?"

She was seated at her dressing table, still wearing her dinner dress, staring at the mirror as though in a trance. He walked up to her and placed his hands gently on her shoulders.

"What's the matter, Hanna? You should have been in bed hours ago."

She turned her head slowly and looked at him. "He's dead, Tony."

"What are you talking about?"

"Charles. He's dead to us, isn't he? Dead but not buried."

He gripped her shoulders tightly. "That's a ridiculous thing to say, Hanna. Whatever gave you that idea?"

"Then why is he in that place? Why isn't he with us?"

"Why?" He was stunned by the question. "Surely—*surely* you understand why."

"I thought I did—once. I'm not sure anymore. And I have no say in the matter. *My* son. That's how you always talk of him, Tony—*my* son. Never *our* son. But he is our son—yours and mine. I have a right to say what *I* think is best·for him."

"Of course you do, Hanna, but you've heard the doctors, you've been to Llandinam and listened to their opinions—"

"And never questioned them. Alex was right when she said one has to trust the heart sometimes. We haven't done that."

His knees semed to buckle and he stepped away from her and sat on the edge of her bed. "I've done what I thought was best. That psychiatrist chap two years ago. You were there. You heard what he had to say. Charles so calm, so much at peace with himself. Could all change, the chap said. Some horror of memory might shock him into screaming, and his screaming might never end. I don't think I could stand that, Hanna—hearing his pain."

"Oh, Tony," she whispered, sitting beside him and holding him tightly in her arms. "What of our own pain?"

He felt a twinge of apprehension as he watched the airplane being pushed from the hangar. It was a powerful-looking biplane with a windowed compartment for six passengers between the engine and the cockpit. The machine was a vivid orange color with the words INTERNATIONAL NEWS AGENCY painted in black letters along the length of the fuselage.

His sense of unease increased as he climbed into the plane, but the passenger compartment was surprisingly roomy. He sank into a low wicker seat and looked out through one of the windows. Three men in white coveralls were gripping the lower wing and turning the plane into the wind.

"Hold onto the arms of the chair," Martin told him. "It's a bit bumpy until we're airborne."

"Yes," he murmured. "Suppose it would be."

The pilot, seated in an open cockpit behind and above them, shouted, "Switch on! Contact!"

The engine coughed . . . ticked . . . then slammed into life. Dark gray smoke streamed past the windows and the sound of the engine hammered at them through the round bulkhead in the front of the compartment. Martin leaned close to the earl and shouted in his ear: "Won't be as loud in air!"

"Quite so," he mouthed, the words lost. He stared out of the window as the plane began to roll forward, gathering speed, bumping and rocking—faster and faster—engine thundering. He felt a momentary sensation of being thrust back against the seat and then a sense of weightlessness as the ground dropped away. The engine emitted an ear-throbbing howl, which then diminished slightly in volume. They banked sharply to the right and he could see the field below with toy men standing in front of toy buildings. They leveled out, then soared higher and higher. He looked down in fascination at the rooftops of Golders Green, the tumbled panorama of London beyond, the molten silver twistings of the river Thames.

"Quite a sight," Martin yelled.

The earl nodded, eyes riveted on the view. He was incapable of speech.

* * *

It would always be 1914–18 at Llandinam War Hospital. The grim brick building—built by a coal baron in the previous century to resemble a castle—stood on a hill overlooking a valley dotted with sheep. Beyond the valley rose the wooded slopes and rocky crags of Moel Sych. It would have been a good site for a country hotel, a place for rock climbers or bird watchers to stay, but the men who lived there cared nothing for the grandeur of the Welsh hills.

"It gets more terrible year by year," the earl said quietly as he and Martin emerged from the wheezing Austin taxi that had brought them up from Glynn Ceiriog. "Although, of course, Charles is oblivious to it all."

The place had been a hospital for the care and treatment of shell-shock cases only. Financial considerations since the end of the war had altered that. It now contained multiple amputees as well, and men so badly disfigured that any meaningful form of plastic surgery was impossible. It was not a place that encouraged visitors, as much by its inaccessibility in a remote corner of Wales as by the horrors to be found there.

"Well, Rilke, back again I see." Dr. Knowles, onetime major in the RAMC, met them on the path leading up to the main building. Four of his truncated patients were taking the sun on the lawn, their wheeled wicker baskets pushed there by orderlies. "And Lord Stanmore. Jolly good to see you again, sir."

"Now see here, Knowles," the earl said. "I understand from my nephew that there's been a change in my son's condition."

"Has there?" The doctor frowned. "Not that I'm

aware of. Although I imagine Gatewood would know more about it than I would. Still, he would have mentioned it in the mess, I'm sure. We're all frightfully fond of Major Greville."

"I told Dr. Gatewood of my conversation with Charles yesterday," Martin said.

"Oh, that. Thomas Hardy and all. He did say something about it at supper last night. But I don't think he gave it much importance. I say, I hope you didn't get too worked up. The major's quite the same today as he was yesterday." He pointed toward a hill half a mile from the hospital grounds. "Up there as usual."

Lord Stanmore made a barely audible groaning sound. Martin smiled. "Good. I'd have been worried if he hadn't been."

It was a hard climb up the hill, along a narrow path overgrown with nettles. They could see Charles as they topped the rise. He was seated on a sagging wood bench, leaning forward, elbows resting on his knees. In old corduroys and open shirt, he looked like a farmer taking a rest. He could hear them coming and turned his head to watch them. He was thirty, but looked younger: a tall, slender, dark-haired man with a high-domed forehead and a long, patrician face. His eyes had a childlike quality, wide and trusting.

"Hello," he said. "Taking a stroll?"

The earl sucked in his breath, then removed his hat and fanned his face with it.

"Horribly hot for Wales."

"Oh, yes," Charles said. "It is. Summer, you see." He pointed off toward the valley. "The sheep down there are quite immovable today. Their woolly coats. Although, in Australia . . . Well, one would imagine a sheep could bear extremes."

"One would think so," the earl said. "Do you mind if I share your bench?"

"By all means do. Your friend is welcome as well. It's far sturdier than it appears."

"I'll stand," Martin said. "It's a lovely view from here."

Charles nodded. "Yes. Very lovely indeed."

"We could see you admiring it as we came up. It made me think of something I read once."

"Oh? And what was that?"

"A line from a poem—'*And what does he see when he gazes so?*'"

Charles rubbed his hands along the top of his trousers and smiled wistfully. "'*They say he sees an instant thing . . . more clear than today . . . a sweet soft scene.*'" He paused, not aware of his father's sharp intake of breath. "I remember you now. You were here—before."

"That's right," Martin said quietly. "Before."

"And we played a game with old Hardy. You were very good at it. I think I could stump you, though. What is a great thing?"

"'*Sweet cyder.*'"

"And another?"

Martin looked toward the sky and closed his eyes for a second. "Dancing."

Charles laughed. "Not exactly, but close enough. '*The dance is a great thing.*' Name one more?"

"I'm sorry," Martin said after a long pause. "You beat me."

"Love. '*Love is, yea, a great thing.*'"

"Of course. I forgot that stanza."

"Most people do."

The earl blew his nose loudly into a handkerchief. "Dashed if I know what all this means, Martin. Damned if I do," he said.

Martin placed a hand on Charles's shoulder. "Do you mind if we continue our walk? My friend has never seen the view from the other side."

"Really? He should, you know. It's well worth the extra steps."

"We'll be back."

"I would enjoy that. I'll give you a clue and you return with the line. How runs the Roman road?"

The earl's face was the color of brick from the heat and an inner turmoil. He stumbled slightly as they walked away, and Martin took him firmly by the arm.

"Are you all right? Let's sit under that tree."

"No, no," he said impatiently. "I'm perfectly fine. I just want to know what all that palaver was about. He's never said anything like that before."

"No one broke through to his thoughts before. But, to be honest, only a few people knew Charles—the inner Charles. I did because he opened up to me once. Roger Wood-Lacy certainly did, but Roger's dead. He kept a good deal of himself hidden. Poetry was more of a joy to him than riding to hounds."

"I know that, blast you." He wiped his florid face with the handkerchief. "Surely Gatewood—"

"Dr. Gatewood is a psychiatrist, not a mind reader. And Charles is only one of fifty neurasthenic patients—and a tranquil, easy one to manage. He doesn't scream or get violent. He isn't suicidal, he doesn't huddle in terror under tables all day. He's not a challenge to Gatewood in any way. He sits peacefully up here and looks out over the valley. When he was asked why he sat here, he replied that he was waiting for the men to come back. Gatewood assumed Charles was referring to the men of his battalion who had been massacred on the Somme. But he was flat wrong."

"What in bloody hell *is* he waiting for then?"

"He's not *waiting* for anything. He was alluding to a poem."

The earl stared at him blankly. "I'm sorry, Martin. I'm totally at sea."

Martin leaned against a wind-twisted tree and took a crumpled cigar from his jacket pocket. "It came to me yesterday when I walked up here and sat beside him on the bench. There's always a wind blowing across those mountains and it's a rare day when there aren't clouds. As I watched the cloud shadows racing down the slopes and across the valley, it reminded me instantly of the imagery in a poem by Thomas Hardy. I knew that Charles—as I remembered him—would have been struck by the same thing, and so I said, 'Hardy would have enjoyed this spot.' "

"And how did he react?"

Martin delved into his trouser pocket for a box of matches and lit his cigar. "Nothing extreme. He simply nodded and smiled, but I knew I had touched a chord—a link to the past. Hardy's poetry was something we had shared in common. We had both discovered poetry on our own and at about the same age. I was in high school in Chicago and he was at Eton. Both of us had read a Hardy novel or two—*Tess, Jude the Obscure*—but our English teachers had never discussed his poems. We felt very proud of ourselves for having found them. We had a pleasant talk about it once at the Pryory before the war. Anyway, as I said, the cloud shadows reminded me of Hardy's imagery and I quoted a line from 'Souls of the Slain.' Have you read that poem, by the way?"

"No."

"Well, it's an allegory about finality, the unbridgeable gap between life and death. It's a sad poem but not morbid. In it, a host of shadowy beings—spirits of lost men—swoop down from the sky and alight on the earth of their homeland. There's an allusion in one stanza to men who have warred under Capricorn—perhaps a reference to the dead of the Boer War. Soldiers certainly, because they are met by another spirit, who is referred to as the General.

"After I had said the line—from the third stanza—Charles smiled at me and quoted the following line. We recited the poem together, each taking a line. Like a game. It's a long work and I'd forgotten a good deal of it. Charles hadn't. He knew it by heart, word for word. I believe that when he sits up here he thinks of that poem, actually gets inside it. The *men* he watches for are those men, Thomas Hardy's men, not his own. He may have escaped into poetry altogether. Into Arnold, Milton, Swinburne, Keats. The poets he loved the best. A safe world to be in. An ordered, beautiful world of rhyme and meter."

Lord Stanmore reached out for the tree as though to steady himself. "Perhaps I'll sit down after all. I feel a bit queer."

"Maybe we should go back. You don't look well."

"Let me sit in the shade for a moment. That's all I need. A chance to catch my breath."

He sat under the tree, loosened his collar, and undid his tie. "That's better. I'll be myself in a minute."

His sudden smile was bitter. "Not that *that's* any great attainment."

Martin blew a stream of smoke into the wind. "You're a good man, Anthony."

"If 'good' means intolerant, unbending, and short-sighted, then I am indeed a good man." He leaned back into the tall grass and looked at the sky. "I broke the bonds of earth today. I soared in the clouds. It's not possible to experience something like that and still retain one's narrowness of vision. I see certain events with clarity now. One summer in particular. I'm not sure exactly which summer—nineteen five or six it would have been. Charles was—oh—fourteen or fifteen. Still at Eton. He was a fine rider and loved horses as much as I did. I was looking forward to taking him with me up to Derbyshire for a few weeks of cross-country and point-to-points. The Thurlstone Moors and the Hallam Trials. Had bought him a proper horse as a surprise, a six-year-old chestnut—Hailaway—a beautiful creature, as fine as anything running at Aintree. But when he came home for the holidays he was a different boy. He'd lost all interest in riding. All he cared to do that summer was read. Poetry. My library lacked the books he wanted, and so he was always dashing into Guildford to buy this or that volume and he'd go off by himself to read it. I remember how irritated I was. Went to Derbyshire without him and deuced angry I was, too." He blew his nose loudly and stuffed the handkerchief back into the pocket of his heat-wrinkled linen blazer. "He's back there now, isn't he, Martin? Back in that summer."

"I don't know. It's possible."

"Oh, yes, he's back there all right. I'm sure of it. But he's had some less pleasant summers since, hasn't he? Gallipoli . . . Cape Helles . . . and then the Somme. Two summers in a row of pure hell. What happens if he suddenly remembers *them?*"

The cigar was dry, the smoke harsh. Martin dropped it on the ground and crushed it carefully with his foot.

"No one can answer that question. Dr. Knowles wasn't quite correct when he said Gatewood had attached no importance to what I told him. Gatewood thought it interesting, but it hardly changes anything. It really doesn't matter very much what Charles sees from this hill—or any other hill, for that matter. He could be taken away from this hospital. It's only *your* fear that keeps him here."

"Yes," the earl said. "But that fear is real, Martin."

"I'm sure it is. His memory of the war could come back and it might shatter him completely. That's the risk, isn't it? A risk you're afraid to take. It could happen at any time, I suppose, except that if it happened here you wouldn't have to witness it. But what if it doesn't happen? What if all you're doing is permitting Charles to grow old on that bench?"

Charles watched them intently as they walked slowly toward him through the sun-wilted grass.

"Do you have the answer?" he asked as they reached him.

"I wish to God I did."

"Oh, not you, sir. You're not in the game. Your friend. Do you? The question being 'How runs the Roman road?' "

" 'It runs straight and bare,' " Martin intoned softly.

"Jolly good for you." He squinted at the sun. "Must be nearly noon. They'll be blowing a bugle soon to summon everyone for lunch. Curious thing. So many chaps without arms and legs here. They have to be fed like babies and they resent it terribly. One can see a sort of hatred in their eyes."

"Now look here," the earl said gruffly, trying to disguise the trembling in his voice. "Do you recall the name Abingdon Pryory? Does it mean anything to you?"

Charles sighed. "I've been asked that question before."

"Yes. I'm sure you have. Doesn't matter, I suppose. I—I want to take you there in a couple of weeks. Would you mind?"

"I don't know." He gazed somberly at his father. "What is it exactly?"

"Home," he said. "It's home."

V

William lay in bed and listened to the rain drumming against the windows, an October rain bearing the first chill of winter. What day was it? he wondered. Friday? Saturday? Saturday, he realized. Not that it mattered much one way or the other; the days blended into each other. He got out of bed with a groan, lit a cigarette, and then padded across the room in his bare feet and placed a recording on the Victrola. The fire the maid had lit before he was awake was just starting to catch, the coals glowing but little heat emerging. He got back into bed, blew smoke rings toward the ceiling, and listened to the music. It was a new King Kornet release with a vocal by Lonnie "Sweet Memphis" Maxwell, who sang with a distinctive, high-pitched and sensual voice, crooning over some phrases and alternately moaning or shouting the rest:

> *My gal can shimmy, my gal can shake,*
> *Shake, honey honey, shimmy and shine. . . .*

The music blared through the tall, curved horn, filling the room with syncopated sound and lascivious lyrics.

Shake it, honey honey, show your stuff,
Shimmy, baby baby, can't get enough . . .

Being able to listen to jazz without fear of complaints or outright censure was something he still marveled at even after nearly two months of being alone in the house—except for the servants, of course, who enjoyed the music as much as he did. The family were all down at the Pryory—with Charles. His brother's release had been his own as well.

He popped two perfect rings in succession and watched them float upward and slowly dissolve into haze.

Lord God a'mighty how that gal can shake.
Honey babe, honey babe, that's the way!

Free. All care and anxiety put to rest, at least for a little while. A miracle of sorts coming when it did. He had been faced all summer with the gnawing awareness that he would have to tell his father that he had been sent down by the university and was no longer welcome there as a law student for the coming term. Booted out for, as one don had put it, "the most wretched collection of examination papers in the history of the college." Fair enough. He could not argue with the man. His grasp of English common law had been as thin and nebulous as the smoke rings. But telling that to *Father* would have meant having to make another choice instantly.

"*But what on earth are you going to do, William?*" his father would have asked in vexation, and he had no answer for that question. He knew only what he did not want to do. He had needed time by himself, time to just drift along and, perhaps, find a path he could follow. The return of Charles had given him the opportunity to do just that.

They had all gone down to Abingdon in August—a family again, even if Charles was in a world of his own, living apart in a suite of rooms in the west wing with a man trained to look after people who had mental or emotional problems. A family even if there was still a slight chill remaining in his father's attitude toward Alexandra and little Colin. But that had been thawing nicely by September. Colin's happy laughter at seeing horses and dogs had touched the old boy's heart even if he kept his emotions to himself. The time had been ripe to present him with a bald-faced lie, and he had done so without the slightest twinge of conscience.

"Father, I shall have to live in London during the school term, you know."

"Of course, lad, of course. You might as well stay at the house with the caretaking staff rather than go into digs. But I'll be cutting your allowance to the bone. I'll not tolerate your spending good money on vile musical recordings, and I refuse to aid your deplorable indulgences. Going to jazz clubs and drinking whiskey will not help you become a barrister."

"I'll give all that up. I promise."

"Now that Charles is home, everything will be different."

"I know that, Father—and I thank God for it."

Well, he had meant *that* all right. They had been the only honest words he had spoken. Charles at home, walking the fields of Abingdon. God, he had nearly wept at the sight of it. And that ass of a neurologist, or psychiatrist, or whatever he was, who had come down from London and had asked him if he felt any anger or resentment toward Charles, any deep-rooted animosity for what Charles had done. He had been so startled by the question, all he had been able to do was shake his head in the negative. Charlie had plucked him in the knee with a Colt automatic, and because Charlie had done that, he was now listening to King Kornet and the Kansas City Kings and not lying six feet under the mud at Arras or Passchendaele.

And that was fate for you.

He lit another cigarette as a footman brought in his tea and toast and the newspapers.

"Vile morning, Master William."

"Yes, Lester, seems rather foul."

"Cook says this will be a winter for the ruddy record books."

"Well, I've never seen her to fail."

He lived in easy familiarity with the servants. There were five of them, including a gardener, just enough to keep the house running and to look after his needs. He had known all of them since his boyhood.

"You might turn the record over before you leave."

"Very good, sir. Sounds like a new one."

"Yes. Bought it yesterday. Shame Eagles isn't here to listen to it."

The elderly footman laughed. "Poor Mr. Eagles. There be none of them jazz clubs down Abingdon, I warrant."

"No, but there will be, in time."

He read the sporting sections of the papers carefully while he drank tea and munched toast—an appetizer for the gargantuan breakfast Cook would be preparing for him. After he had digested every scrap of toast and all the information the newspapers offered, he swung out of bed and got dressed.

Most of the lower rooms had been closed up, their furnishings covered with white sheets. The only warm and comfortable places left in the house were his bedroom, the kitchen, and the servants' quarters. He took his breakfast in the servants' hall, seated alone at the long, plain wood table, his back to the fireplace. The newspapers were folded in front of him, propped against a teapot, and he turned from one to the other for a final scanning as he ate a breakfast of grilled kidneys, tomatoes, gammon rashers, and fried eggs.

"Ah," he murmured, staring hard at one of the papers. "Ah, yes, indeed."

Money had been a problem. Alexandra would have given him a hundred pounds, but he had been loath to ask her, to involve her in any way in his subterfuge. His allowance was nothing but a pittance, precluding even the mildest of debaucheries. One could not possibly seek—let alone find—pleasure in London on three pounds a week. He had solved that problem by forming the Biscuit Tin Society with Lester and the gardener, the three of them meeting briefly every morning after his breakfast and pooling their considerable skills for the benefit of all.

The gardener came into the dining room, after first removing his muddy boots, and sat down respectfully at the far end of the table.

"This here rain could figure, Master William. What'er it be."

"It could indeed."

The gardener drew a well-thumbed copy of *Ladburn's Sheet* from his back pocket and squinted at it.

When the footman came in with the biscuit tin, he sat next to the gardener and set the tin on the table in front of him.

"Well, Master William, what's it to be today?"

"Ainsworth, the fourth race. That's my vote, anyhow."

The gardener nodded quickly. "That well might be. You'd be thinkin' of Jason's Girl, I'm supposin', Master William."

"Not at those odds," William said. "It's a false favorite anyway. She'd never win at a mile and a half on sloppy wet grass."

"There's Rangers Spurs—or Wolverhampton at Leeds," the footman suggested. "Not that I've anything against Ainsworth. And I'd say you've Bonny Bell in mind, sir. What hasn't raced since Chester."

William grinned at him. "You've got the nose for it, too, don't you!"

The gardener turned a page of *Ladburn's Sheet & Gentleman's Racing Guide* and ran a thick thumb down one column. "Saw it meself, of course. She could be primed for a killin' and that's for sure. Then again . . ."

"Yes," the footman said knowingly. "They may have her in a bit too deep."

"Granted," William said. "But I don't think so. She's got the weights and they've put O'Grady on her. Do you remember O'Grady at Gatwick last April? That man's a demon with the rain in his face and his mount over the fetlocks in mud. I won't influence you fellows, but I like a tenner of my share on her to win. I know we can get ten—even twelve to one on her."

Lester and the gardener exchanged glances. Then the gardener nodded curtly, stuck his racing guide back into his pocket, and stood up. "Done. I'd best be off. There's a drain clogged out back. Punt a tenner for me, too, Les."

The footman opened the biscuit tin and removed a fat pile of pound notes held together with a twist of string. He also removed an account book and a stubby pencil. "Ten pounds each it is then. I'd best be gettin' over to Tybald's in Hampstead Road before the odds go down on her."

"They won't," said William. "If it weren't for the covenant, I'd say we punt the whole pile."

"Oh, no, Master William," Lester said solemnly. "The ten-pound limit stands."

"I quite agree, Lester, and a sound covenant it is, too. I'd like to draw five or six quid from my account."

"Very well, sir." Lester counted out thirty-six pounds from the stack and made two notations in the ledger book, his lips moving as he wrote out the transactions: "Tenner each—Bonny Bell—fourth—Ainsworth. Six pounds—Master William's account—debit." He placed the balance of the money back into the biscuit tin along with the ledger book and closed the lid. "Done is done, sir. And good luck to us all."

He could not drive a motorcar with any degree of safety or comfort. The strain of manipulating the pedal was too much for his knee. It was a minor price to pay. There were taxis and most of his friends had cars. He took a taxi at three o'clock in the afternoon to his club in St. James's Street. His father had sponsored him into the club—one of seven in which Lord Stanmore claimed life membership—on his seventeenth birthday. Heppleton's had held a reputation since 1790 for being a "young man's" club and been popular for over a century with Etonians and the more affluent subalterns in the Brigade of Guards who sought relief from the subdued atmosphere at the Guards' Club or the Marlborough. Heppleton's had been something of a "hellfire club" during the regency years and had scandalized London with lurid stories of beautiful young harlots draped naked across divans for the casual convenience of rakehell members. The tales may or may not have been true, but they were cherished to the present day as part of the Heppleton tradition. It was comforting to the membership to dwell on the distant past, for the immediate one did not bear thinking about. After the first battle of Ypres in 1914, the club secretary had made the solemn gesture of placing empty brandy goblets on the top shelf behind the bar as a memorial to members killed for king and country. By 1916 the shelf could hold no more and the custom was abandoned. The ranks of glasses still stood, and the club was just now emerging from their shadow.

William made his way into the oak-paneled and leather-chaired smoking room, past the bar where a small party of visiting Americans were noisily celebrating their release from Prohibition. In 1919, in a move to keep Heppleton's solvent, the Membership Committee had broken with tradition and spread welcoming arms to all members of the Yale, Harvard, and Princeton clubs. The Americans had responded by spreading a great deal of money around, to the satisfaction of everyone except a few diehards. To William, the Americans were anything but "a raucous intrusion of leatherstocking colonials," as one member had put it. They had a guilt-free capacity for enjoyment, which he found enviable.

He took a chair near the fire and stretched out his bad leg toward the warmth. When one of the green-jacketed servants hurried over, he ordered a large whiskey, asked for a copy of *Country Life*, and requested the result of the fourth race at Ainsworth when it came over the wire.

"We're not using the wire today, Mr. Greville," the servant said in a whisper. "Mr. Jukes has a *wireless*. Think of that! Can't get it away from him. Been sittin' in that little cubbyhole of his behind the desk and toyin' with it by the hour."

"And he gets the races and the football results on it?"

"Indeed he does, sir. I understand there's a broadcasting station at Writtle. Music mostly, but every hour or so they give the sports. Mr. Jukes has a license from the post office to listen in so it's all quite legal, Mr. Jukes says, although Mr. Abersworth does not take too kindly to a wireless aerial being run up the side of the building, sir. To the roof, sir, and coiled about a chimney pot."

"How curious."

"Indeed it is, sir—and a savage waste of a man's time, if you ask me."

He sipped his whiskey and thumbed through the pages of the magazine. Members came and went, and eventually two of his friends arrived, complaining of the cold rain and the deathly dullness of the day.

"What's on for tonight, Willie?" one of them asked.

"I don't know. Thought I might try the Mardi Gras in Dean Street again."

"Prettiest bints in London are down Chelsea way.

The Palais de Dance in Beaufort Street, near the bridge. Asked a daisy of a flapper there one night if I might hold her hand. Know what she said in reply? 'A fuck's as good as a handshake, Johnnie!' Would you believe it!"

"All too well," a young man named Osbert said dourly. "It's all part of the conspiracy I was telling you about, David. One can see it happening."

"What conspiracy is that?" William asked.

"Oh, don't pay any attention to Osbert."

"You don't have to take my word for it, old boy," Osbert said. "You can read it for yourself in Henry Ford's book, *The International Jew.*"

"That's just Jew baiting, pure and simple."

"Yes," William said. "I read a copy of the *Dearborn Independent* when I was in New York last year. Utter rot."

"Granted he gets a bit potty at times, but you can't deny that Jews control the Bolshevik world revolutionary movement and are determined to undermine the entire structure of democratic society."

"Oh, Lord," David Hadlock moaned, "what's that got to do with my being offered a fuck in Chelsea?"

"It shows a deterioration of moral standards—a cunningly planned erosion of social mores and codes. I saw it happen in Italy after the war, until the *fascisti* brought some sense of order and control back to the country."

"Mussolini!"

"A great man, David," Osbert said quietly. "And Umberto Pasella . . . D'Annunzio and the noble *Serenissima*—great men all."

William yawned. "Let me stand you chaps a drink."

Osbert checked his wristwatch. "Sorry. Promised to meet a fellow at Boodle's. But let's have a proper chat one evening, Greville."

David shook his head as he watched the man leave the room. "Old Ozzie has undergone a sea change since the Eton days, I can tell you. Altogether a sensible sort. Now he's caught up in the notion of forming the British League of Fascisti. Ever hear of such nonsense? Can you imagine an Englishman worth his salt joining something with a wop name!"

"He doesn't know what to do with himself."

"No. Hates Oxford like poison. No excitement to it. Misses the fun of flying over the Dolomites and dropping bombs on poor ruddy sods of Austrians."

"Yes—must have been a lark."

He could feel one of his depressions coming on, creeping over him the way the gray evening was creeping over the windowpanes. They rarely lasted more than a few minutes and he was incapable of doing anything about them. They came and went like a dark and dismal tide. No specific cause. What the Negro singers called "the blues." *Got the blues so bad I think I'm goin' to die. . . .* It was that kind of feeling. He lit a cigarette and stared fixedly ahead. David was talking, but he couldn't hear a word. *Been in that place, but I ain't goin' back no more. . . . Yes, been in that place, but I ain't goin' back no more. . . . Goin' to pack my bags, the train to Baltimore. . . .* That yearning to be someplace else, moving on—to Baltimore—to heaven or hell. Just the blues. The regrets that could find no other name. That inner bleakness of soul that the Negro jazzmen understood so well and could articulate better than an Eton "old boy." The jazzmen would have found a voice for night sliding in across wasted days, a trombone moan for nothingness.

"You're not smoking?"

"What?"

"Not smoking, old boy. Just holding your silly fag in front of your face."

William turned away and dropped his smoldering cigarette into an ashtray. The servant was hurrying toward him from across the room.

"Mr. Jukes apologizes, Mr. Greville, but there was a delay in the wireless transmission. He has the fourth at Ainsworth now." He glanced at a slip of paper in his hand. "Bonny Bell was the winner, sir, with O'Grady in the stirrups. Paid off at fourteen to one."

"What happened between Chelsea and Leicester?" David asked.

"One goal to nought, Leicester, Mr. Hadlock." The servant shuffled through some other slips of paper before hurrying away.

"Blast."

"I won a lot of money," William said dully. "Quite a bit."

"On the horse, you mean? How much did you have on it?"

"Ten pounds to win."

David whistled softly through his teeth. "Ten bloody quid at fourteen to one? I'd say let's go out and have a bang-up time, but I'm down to my last dollar till next week."

"I don't want your five bob. My treat." He felt shaky, but the depression was fading. He stood up and stretched his tall, powerful frame. "Let's start off with a double whiskey at the bar."

"It's really not fair, old chap."

"Oh, shut up, David. What's money for?" He tapped his pocket. "A fiver and change. Not enough to do it up brown. I'll give Jukes an IOU for thirty quid."

"*Thirty?* We could hit every ruddy club in London with that much!"

"We jolly well will, too, or die trying."

An' drive those blues away . . . oh, yeah, drive those blues away. . . .

Drinks at the bar with the Americans—fine fellows all—then off to Scott's for oysters and stout followed by a smashing dinner at Rules in Maiden Lane. They were feeling in top form as they sauntered out of Rules at 10:30 full of roast beef and Burgundy. A taxi idled at the curb as they stood beside it planning the night ahead.

"I say Chelsea," David insisted. "Pick up some girls, touch a few spots, and then go back to my digs. I have a gramophone and a few passable records."

"There are prettier girls at the Mardi Gras, or the Apollo in Greek Street—and bloody good Negro bands. Better class of girl than Battersea Bridge, anyhow. Might find a couple with a posh little flat in Mayfair."

"If we do, your thirty quid'll melt like snow."

"Don't be daft. These days they're more likely to pay us! *And* take us to the Savoy for breakfast."

Soho was crowded with a Saturday-night throng. As the taxi crawled along Frith Street, they could see half a dozen Black Marias parked nose-to-tail down an alleyway and what looked like a battalion of bobbies strolling two by two from Bateman Street to Soho Square and back again.

"What's up, driver?" William asked.

"Raidin' the Sixty-Six Club tonight, or so I 'eard."

"Let us off at the square."

"As you want, guv'nor."

"Poor old dim-witted coppers," David said as they got out of the taxi. "Look at the poor blighters, just strolling about, gazing into windows, pretending not to see the Sixty-Six Club's sign. It's too bloody marvelous. They'll bust in on the stroke of midnight waving their silly warrants and there won't be a living soul in the place."

William was not that sure of the dim-witted quality of the Metropolitan Police. They were within pouncing distance of the discreet little sign that marked the "66" Club's door, but their presence was too obvious to be taken seriously. DORA's target for the night could be any one of a dozen or more after-hours drinking and dancing clubs in the cluttered maze of Soho streets and alleyways. But which one? It could be the Mardi Gras. Dean Street was only a short walk—or a bobby's lumbering run—from where they were now congregated. Not that William cared. He had been through the inconvenience of more than one raid. Nothing much happened in them except that the customers were hustled out into the street and the owners, barmen, and any known criminals were hauled off to the police station.

The Mardi Gras was filled with girls waiting for the fun to begin. It was still a bit early for that, just a few minutes past the legal closing hour. The bandstand was empty, but a large gramophone blared out a one-step. A few girls were dancing with each other while most of the men in the place looked on in amusement. William and David checked their overcoats and strolled to the bar, leaned against the polished mahogany, ordered whiskeys, and watched the girls dancing.

"Jolly good crop tonight," David said. "Hot little flappers all."

There was a sameness to them, William thought, like a flock of small, excitable, flashy birds. Their hair was cropped, dresses short—garters revealed as they moved shapely silk-clad legs, bodies revealed also as they danced, buttocks and breasts wiggling under scant frocks.

Shake, honey honey, shimmy and shine. . . .

By midnight the crowds were pressing in. Men in cutaway coats and women in furs rubbed elbows and backsides with shopgirls and typists and young men on the loose. The musicians had arrived and the throbbing, frantic notes of jazz cut through the cigarette haze like a blade.

Shake it, honey honey, show 'em your stuff. . . .

They latched on to two devastatingly pretty girls and William bought champagne for them—inferior stuff at a pound a bottle—and then the girls, after whispering together, suggested they move on to the Paradise Club in St. Giles High Street. It was two in the morning and they bundled into a taxi, the girls climbing onto their laps. As the taxi roared off into the darkness of the street, William's girl took his hand and placed it inside her dress, pressing his palm against a small naked breast.

"You're full of fuck, aren't you?" she whispered in his ear. "And I'll do what the French girls do—I promise."

The Paradise Club was even more crowded than

the Mardi Gras had been, a smoky, jazz-throbbing cave of a room. The drinks were more expensive, too, and the champagne even worse. Anything could be bought at the Paradise and the girls wanted cocaine. "For later," they said. "A little snow draws out the pleasure—makes it last longer." That made another fiver. The thirty pounds were nearly gone.

"We'll go soon," he said thickly. He was a bit woozy from the whiskeys, champagne, and lack of fresh air. The girl sat close to him, idly stroking his thigh under the table.

"My rooms," David said. "We'll toss for the bed."

"All in together," his girl squealed. "It's ever so much fun that way!"

"Off!" William pushed back his chair and stood up. "Forward the troops!"

He led the way toward the door, forcing a path through the crowd, people still coming into the place. A suffocating odor of wet cloth and furs, stale perfume and cigar smoke. He could see the open door, rain slashing down through the doorway out of the wet—round black blobs, like seals.

"Coppers!" he yelled. "Oh, the rotters!"

The Chelsea raid had been a sham. They had patrolled Frith Street, biding their time, then had crossed Charing Cross Road into St. Giles.

"*Police!*" a sergeant shouted through a megaphone. "*Stay where you are, if you don't mind. No movin' about!*"

"This way!" William said. The girls and David held on to his coattails as he plunged back into the crowd and bulled his way toward the bar. There would be a door behind it leading to a cellar where they stored the beer, the crates of whiskey and wine. All clubs were the same in that respect. There would be a way up to the street from there.

"*Stop that man!*"

Police whistles shrilled and the girls let go of William with a scream and fell away into the crowd. David stumbled over someone's foot and fell. A policeman jumped to avoid stepping on his back.

"*Stop in the name of the law!*"

William was being propelled onward by his own burst of energy. Christ, he thought gleefully, what a bloody lark! He reached the bar and was prepared to vault it when one of the pursuing policemen grabbed him from the back.

"None of that!"

William shook the smaller man off and sent him flying into a table.

"*Grab the bugger, lads!*"

Two panting, cursing bobbies lunged at him and held on to his arms, pinning him back against the bartop.

"Come along easy, you bastard!"

"Oh, bugger off." Strength swelled in him, racing through nerve and muscle. A Viking—a berserker. . . . He was suddenly back at Eton playing the wall game in mud and rain—kicking, butting . . . "*Bugger off, I said!*" He hurled them away from him with a roar. No thought of escape now. He was drunk with the need to fight, the pure joy of performing a mindless physical act. He might run like a broken-kneed camel, but, by God, he had arms like anvils. He could fight like a lion. A sweating red face loomed up under a copper's helmet and he drove a hammer blow into the man's jaw—saw him reel back and drop like a wet sack of sand. He burst into laughter and was still laughing when they all came at him like dogs on a fox. A hard wet boot caught him in the stomach . . . a night stick rose and fell. He felt no pain. A roaring in his ears . . . and then silence—an odd sort of peace.

"In 'ere and mind your manners."

An elderly police sergeant led him into a cheerless office. A burly man in a badly fitting blue serge suit rose from behind a desk and pointed to a wood chair facing him.

"Sit down, Mr. Greville." The man's warmth matched the day. Through the barred and dingy windows a cold rain seethed into the cobblestoned inner courtyard of the Chancery Lane police station.

Willian sat down stiffly. His stomach ached where he had been kicked, and his head throbbed. He stared apathetically at the inspector, who was holding a small white card between his thick fingers.

"The *Hon.* William Greville," the inspector intoned. "Heppleton Club, St. James's." He let the card slip from his fingers and gave William a baleful look. "The 'Hon.' stands for *'honorable,'* I take it. You didn't look very *honorable* when you were carried in here Saturday night like something the cat dragged about. No other form of identification in your wallet, so the chief inspector rang up your club. Somebody there informed us who you were, and set the wheels in motion. A club like Heppleton's—well, they know how to look after a member who gets himself in trouble. Lord Stanmore's son, they said." He made a clucking sound.

"Pity. Don't know what's happening these days when the son of an earl gets himself netted in along with common prostitutes and spivs of every description. The lowest of the low, lad. The lowest of the low." He turned his blue bulk in the swivel chair and gazed morosely at the rain-blackened courtyard. "And two fine chaps of mine in hospital. Broken jaw, cracked ribs. Two servants of the law used cruelly by a man they're duty-bound to protect. Yes, lad, they'd give their very lives if need be."

"They called me a bastard," William said quietly, "and tried to throttle me."

"You *are* a bastard," the inspector whispered, his voice like a cold wind. "If I had my way I'd boot you into a cell and swallow the key. Packet of cocaine in your pocket—two years for that alone. Someplace terrible hard. Wormwood Scrubs picking oakum with your fucking bleeding fingers." He turned back to the table and drew a cigarette from a tin of Navy Cut. He lit it with a match and dribbled smoke from the corner of his mouth.

"Your family solicitor was rung up. Sir Humphrey Osgood. He'll smooth the waters, I expect. I just wanted you to know what I think of you."

"I don't really give much of a damn. About jail, I mean."

"Oh, no. Wouldn't do, would it? Just about anything short of murder. The upper classes. God help us all."

Sir Humphrey Osgood had posted bail and done all else that needed to be done. He sat in the back of his Daimler next to William and sorted fussily through the contents of his briefcase. He was a tiny man with a head too big for his body and was referred to by his fellow lawyers—but not out of malice—as "the dwarf."

There was nothing dwarflike about his intellect or legal shrewdness.

"Monday is always the very devil of a day, William, or I'd go with you and wait for your father."

William studied the raindrops meandering down the glass of the side window.

"You had to telephone him, I suppose."

"I'm surprised you need ask that, William. Of course I had to call him. This is no boyish prank you're charged with. You're in quite serious trouble. Quite serious indeed."

"Two years in Wormwood Scrubs," William muttered.

"What's that you say? The Scrubs? Well, hardly. We'll get you off with a payment of damages and a stern warning from a magistrate, more than likely. Won't be *that* simple, but we'll find a way, never you fear." He tapped on the glass that separated him from his chauffeur and the driver pulled into Bell Yard and stopped in front of the law courts. "I must leave you now. Sure your head's all right?"

"Quite sure. A police doctor looked me over. I've got a hard head."

"A thick skull is more like it. My man will take you to the office and you'll tell Mr. Daventry and Mr. Marble everything that took place Saturday night and early Sunday morning. *Everything.* Is that clear? Each word said, every thought that crossed your mind, every gesture made. No need to feel shy. It may all seem very sordid to you, but nothing shocks *us.* We happen to have a client at the moment who has been accused of doing the most dreadful things with a cricket bat upon the person of a young woman. No, lad, you'll hardly upset us."

* * *

They gave him tea and cigarettes and he told the whole sorry tale, holding nothing back.

"Ah," Mr. Daventry said after a glance at Mr. Marble. "Did it offend and upset you when the young lady intimated her willingness to commit an act of sodomy?"

"Did it? I don't think so."

"Meaning that you're not sure. The act being illegal and contrary to nature, you could well have been disturbed by the suggestion and, thus, far from your normal state of mind."

William puffed on a Woodbine and looked away. Through the tall windows of the office he could see the dome of St. Paul's through drifting plumes of rain. It was that sort of nonsense, he supposed, that would have made it impossible for him to have been a successful lawyer even if by some miracle he had passed the bar.

"That could be true. I certainly was not in my normal state of mind."

"Of course you weren't, dear boy," Mr. Daventry said, sounding pleased. "*We* know that."

His father had waited patiently in the anteroom, scorning the copies of *Tatler* and *Illustrated London News* that were stacked neatly on a table. He had dressed hurriedly, William could tell. Short boots, his oldest tweeds. He looked immeasurably tired.

"Hello, Father."

"William," he acknowledged curtly as he got to his feet.

"I'm very sorry about—"

The earl raised a hand. "Please, William. Spare me the apologies. There is really nothing you can say. Nothing at all. I went to the house first. Talked to the servants. I'd set none of them to spy on you, so I cannot fault them for failing to inform me of your activities over the past six weeks. Your lying about all day, staying out most of the night. I telephoned King's and was informed—rather unkindly, I must say—that you had been booted from college quite some time ago."

"Yes. I intended to tell you about that—when the time was propitious."

They were the same height. Two tall men standing eye to eye.

"That time is now, I presume, when the cat's out of the bag. How you managed to afford your pointless and tawdry pleasures I can't for the life of me imagine."

So the Biscuit Tin Society had not been exposed. He was grateful for that, for his partners' sakes if not his own.

"I have friends."

"Yes," the earl said bitterly. "I can imagine what kind. Roaring boys and Covent Garden nuns!"

There was nothing further to be said. They were silent in the taxi that took them to Waterloo, silent on the platform as they waited for the 4:12 to Godalming, and silent in the carriage as the train raced across the storm-swept Surrey landscape.

Banes was waiting at the station with the Rolls and they got in and sat on opposite sides of the back seat, as far from one another as it was possible to get.

"Does Mother know?"

"I thought it best not to tell her. She will have to know eventually, I imagine, unless Osgood can pull enough strings to keep it out of the press and out of a public court. As for your 'leaving' school, she will of course have to know that eventually. I told her I had to go up to London on business and that you were coming back with me—a half-holiday of some sort."

"I regret your having to lie on my behalf, Father."

The earl drummed his fingers on his knee. "Not on your behalf, William. Not on *your* behalf, I assure you. I wish to soften the blow to your mother as much as possible."

"You underestimate her, Father. She's a strong woman."

"Perhaps. But she's felt enough pain over the past few years."

"So have I."

The earl glanced at him sharply and then looked back at his knee and his restless fingers. The car stopped and Banes got out. The ornamental iron gates that had been shipped from Milan to replace the old were swung back. The Pryory could be seen in the distance, the chimneys rising above evergreens, gaunt birch, and oak. Lighted windows twinkled in the dusk.

The earl cleared his throat. "It's stopped raining. Are you up to a walk?"

"Yes."

"You're sure you can manage?"

"Quite sure."

They got out of the car and stepped to one side as Banes drove away, tires spraying gravel and muddy water.

"I should have this road tarred over, I suppose, but I like the gravel. I can remember the sound carriage wheels made on it."

They started walking toward the house, darkening fields stretching away on both sides of the road. A few shaggy-coated sheep gazed at them from a willow copse.

"It's precisely one mile from the house to the gate," William said. "Digby, the Manderson twins, Tom Baynard, and I paced it off one summer, then ran it—one of the grooms timing us with a watch. I forget what my time was, but I won by a long shot, although Digby pressed me hard for a while. They're all dead now. Half the boys I knew at school are dead. I've thought a lot about the dead the past few years."

"Yes," the earl murmured.

"I felt almost ashamed to be alive. Charlie was dead in a way, wasn't he? I mean as far as all your hopes for him were concerned. Not even *hopes*, actually—certainties. I just wasn't up to the task, Father. I couldn't become something I'm not."

"I know that now."

"Do you? I hope so. There have been times when I've wished Charlie had done a proper job of it and put that bullet in my head. He'd rescued me from the trenches, but I was never quite sure what I'd been rescued *for*. Just to live? That didn't seem reason enough. But it is, you know. I don't have to be important or do something grand in order to justify my existence to either you or the dead."

"What is it that you want?"

"I want to be happy."

"Is that so impossible to attain?"

"No. I've given it quite a bit of thought. Just a few thousand pounds—and your blessing. Your blessing more than anything. Your cutting away the knot that bound me to Charles."

The earl stopped walking and faced his son. "Tell me."

"That land up in Derbyshire. I could build a little house on it, and stables."

"And?"

"And but a couple of good broodmares at Tattersall's, and choose the proper stud—you could help me there . . . decent lines . . . fine heart. I could do something like that, Father. On my own. Doing something with my hands. I could build up a racing stable. I might not be able to ride well anymore, but I damn well know I could train."

They stood facing each other in the darkness and they could hear the oak trees creaking in the wind.

"Nothing very grand about that, is there, Willie?"

"No, sir. Just mud and manure."

"Well, now—well . . ." He reached out and patted his son clumsily on the shoulder. "Perhaps—well, dash it all—the Greville silks at Ascot one day."

William smiled. "No, sir. The Biscuit Tin silks—the Biscuit Tin."

VI

There were times when she felt sure he remembered; times when he would stand for long moments staring at the limbs of a tree, or a section of the old stone wall at the bottom of the kitchen gardens. He had climbed the tree often as a boy, and had taught William to climb it. And she could recall going with him to the old wall and picking gooseberries while he probed between the dark, mossy stones for fragments of musket balls.

"They call it the Battle of Abingdon, but it wasn't a proper sort of battle, Alex, just a skirmish really, but the king's troops fired a prodigious number of shots, most of which banged into our wall."

She could almost hear his voice as he told her that bit of history. She had been eight or nine, Charles about fourteen. Did he remember as well? Was that why he always paused so long by the wall as they took their morning walk?

"What are you looking at?"

"The wall," he said.

"It's centuries old."

"Oh, yes, I'm sure it must be."

"A company of Roundhead infantry were trapped nearby during the Civil Wars. The summer of sixteen forty-two, I believe it was. Cavalier cavalry jumped them while they were picking apples. They fought so bravely that Prince Rupert had their dead buried with full military honors. Their graves are supposed to be in the orchard somewhere."

She knew where because he had pointed out the spot years ago—a long, low grassy mound between rows of plum trees. She had been unable to eat a greengage from the orchard for months after that.

"There are dead Roundheads in it. . . ! Dead Roundheads. . . !"

Mama had been very cross with Charles for showing her the graves. Did he remember?

"Graves?"

"Yes, but I'm not sure where. Perhaps you could show me."

He looked at her blankly and walked on, hands clasped behind his back. A cloudless December morning. Cold and crisp with a whisper of frost on the grass.

There was no point in pressing him. Dr. Ford had explained the fruitlessness of that approach in dealing with amnesia. Everything that Dr. Ford had said on the subject had seemed composed of negatives: Don't do this or that—that won't work and neither will the other. But in fairness to the man, there was little that anyone knew about the malady. It came, sometimes it went, but usually it remained forever.

She sighed, turned up the collar of her fur coat, and walked after her brother. The Irish setters that had been sitting at her feet bounded ahead with little whimpers of pleasure.

Mr. Lassiter, Charles's "servant," came from the house to meet them as they walked back through the

Italian gardens. He was a burly, middle-aged man who had been in the RAMC for two decades and then a therapist at Guy's Hospital in London.

"How'd it go today, Mrs. Mackendric?"

"About the same as usual, John. Many long pauses and apparent reflections."

"That's to be expected. They remember images, you see, but they can't place them."

"I hope there's coffee made," Charles said, smiling at them. "And some really hot toast."

The walks depressed her, but she did her best to hide her feelings. There was no point in expressing her pessimism to her mother and father, who saw "signs" of recovery in almost everything Charles did. They were in the breakfast room when she came in, her face still flushed from the cold, and pressing questions on her before she even had a chance to sit down and have a cup of tea. It was the same every morning.

"But what exactly did he say when you passed Leith Woods?"

"Nothing, Mama."

"Nothing at all?"

"Something obscure about Thomas Gray—and a comment about the ravens wheeling above Burgate House."

"What sort of comment?" the earl asked. "When I went for a walk with him the other afternoon he said something, but I couldn't hear what."

"It was probably nothing pertinent," Alexandra said. "The birds, more than likely. They seem to fascinate him."

Hanna dabbed at her scrambled eggs. "That sounds encouraging to me."

Alexandra said nothing. It was childlike of Charles,

his fascination with creatures—the ravens, the hares and rabbits, the sheep and cattle in the fields. Childish and terribly sad. She poured a cup of tea and changed the subject.

"I got a letter from Winifred. She doubts if she can come down over New Year's. The baby has colic."

Hanna sighed. "Poor Winifred. She did so want a boy."

"Poor Fenton, you mean," the earl said. "Three girls!"

Hanna gave him a stiff look. "I can't work up any sympathy over Fenton. I think it's terrible that he has a new baby and hasn't even seen it."

The earl looked at her blankly. "How the devil could he? One can hardly commute from Mesopotamia."

"He doesn't have to be there, does he!"

"Doesn't he? Why ever not? It's his job, isn't it? He's a soldier." He wiped his lips on a napkin and stood up. "Must be off. I want to talk to the vicar about the Christmas fete."

"Who's playing Father Christmas?" Alexandra asked.

"I am, blast it. We all voted for Crispin—publican at the Star and Hounds, jolly round fat chap—but he had to go and break his arm, damn fool. Can't be helped, but I'm hardly the type."

"I'm sure Colin will see past your woolly beard."

"Do you think so? Well, he's a smart little tyke. He'll take it in stride."

Hanna smiled slightly as she watched him leave the room. "An odd man your father. He's really pleased as punch at being asked to dress up as Santa Claus, but red-hot irons couldn't draw *that* from him."

"It's going to be a good Christmas for a change. We've all had enough bad ones, God knows."

Hanna gazed abstractedly toward the windows. "So much yet to do. The guest list to complete . . . a thousand things to plan."

"Is Martin coming down?"

"He wasn't sure. Your father talked to him on the phone. He may have to go to Petrograd, of all places. I hope he doesn't. I've invited a girl I would like him to meet."

"Oh, Mama, please leave poor Martin alone. He's quite capable of finding his own women."

"Women?" she said with a frown. "I'm not *finding him women—a girl*, a very sweet and charming girl."

Alexandra looked skeptical. "Have you met her?"

"No, not exactly. She's a niece of Angela's. The girl is very clever, Angela told me. Writes poetry and little articles for the Sussex *Weekly Herald*. They'd have a lot in common, I'm sure."

"I'm sure. Fellow journalist. How old is this gem?"

Hanna fussed with the teapot. "Oh, late twentyish."

"Or early thirtyish? Really, Mama."

"I don't care what you say, Alex. There's no harm in trying."

"Heaven forbid. It might be the love match of the century." She reached across the table and touched her mother's hand. "You were born to be a matchmaker and your intentions are always good, but don't try to involve Martin in romantic weekends—not in this house anyway. I'm sure it must always remind him of Ivy."

"Perhaps you're right, dear. Besides, to be truthful, I usually take what Angela tells me with a grain of salt. I'm sure her niece is long in the tooth and heavy in the hips. I can't go back on the invitation at this late date, though, can I? Perhaps I can pair her off with Major Aterbury. I'm not that sure he was such a good choice anyway."

Alexandra looked quizzical. "Good choice for what?"

"Oh," Hanna replied vaguely, "bridge fours, I suppose."

Solutions to vexing problems always came to Hanna out of the blue, usually when she least expected to find one. She had despaired of finding a solution for the problem of Alex and baby Colin. That problem had, to a certain extent, taken care of itself. But still a shadow remained. Her affair with Dr. Mackendric, the marriage certificate issued only days before the certificate of birth, still cast its pall. Anthony's attitude toward her had changed for the better since Charles had come home, and he seemed to be genuinely fond of the baby in spite of himself, and yet she knew it still rankled him—as it rankled her. It was a loose end that needed tying up. But how?

And then she thought of the solution. It had come to her in, of all places, the Abingdon cinema palace, seated in the row of plush seats at the back of the darkened house, watching D. W. Griffith's heart-stopping production of *Way Down East*. Alexandra had been seated next to her, and she had groped almost blindly for her daughter's hand as she watched that poor child on the screen flounder across that raging, ice-choked river. Oh, the cruelty of it all! She had begun to cry, her sobs of pity mingled with all the other sobs and cries that swept the audience. And then it came like a vision. Clear. Correct. Almost absurdly simple. Find Alex a husband.

She had gone through the process of trying to find a husband for her daughter once before. The circumstances had been as different as the times—the London social season of 1914. And finding a husband for an eighteen-year-old virgin was not quite the same thing as finding one for a twenty-five-year-old widow—with a sixteen-month-old son. Any number of potential swains had been unearthed by Hanna in that long-ago summer, and only Alex's fickleness had stood between her and a wedding, or at least an engagement. There had been one young man that Alex had liked well enough to consider marrying, but then she had gone off to France in 1915 as a Red Cross aide and fate had brought Mackendric into her life and all thoughts of Carveth Saunders, Bart., had been driven from her mind forever.

Time to start the process again, but how to go about doing it was a puzzlement. One could not advertise in the newspapers. She had confided in some of her oldest and dearest friends, and two conclusions had been reached: one, that England was overloaded at the present with women of marriageable age—the natural balance of young men to young women having been kicked into the dust heap by the slaughter of the war; and, two, that Alexandra might indeed be a twenty-five-year-old widow with a child, but she was still the daughter of the Earl and Countess of Stanmore, and a woman of considerable wealth in her own right. "The child's a damn good catch" was how one friend had bluntly summarized the situation. That might have been a cold-blooded statement, but it had the hard ring of truth to it.

With the aid of her friends, a list had been drawn of

bachelors—even widowers—any one of whom would make a suitable husband for Alexandra, and, of equal importance, a son-in-law acceptable to Anthony. The list had been culled, refined, and then narrowed to five names. All of the men on the list would be invited to Abingdon Pryory—not en masse, but separately, at one time or another—during the fortnight of house parties, dinners, and dances that Hanna was planning in celebration of the Christmas season and the new year. The most intriguing prospect, the man that Hanna had given the highest marks, had been invited to spend five days, to come down after Boxing Day and stay through until the new year—the festivities of New Year's Eve being, to Hanna's mind, the best possible time for romance to flourish.

Noel Edward Allenby Rothwell, Esq. Age thirty-five. Nephew of Sir George Barking. Partner in London brokerage house. Tall. Good-looking. Fine war record in navy. Never married. Handled investments successfully for both Mary and Adelaide—their highest marks.

Hanna, in the privacy of her sitting room, looked at what she had written about Noel Rothwell in her diary in September. She had learned a good deal more about the man since then, all of it encouraging. He was an active sportsman and a member of the Tatton Hounds, which hunted in Cheshire—that would please Anthony considerably. Yes, no doubt about it, Rothwell, Esq., was the main choice and she drew a firm line under his name for emphasis. He was as good as a member of the family—if Alexandra would only cooperate by falling in love with him.

* * *

The thought of flying to Russia in the dead of winter had not been in any way appealing to Martin, and fortunately the trip fell through. It had been Scott Kingsford's notion that a wireless broadcast from Petrograd on New Year's Day—with Martin interviewing Leon Trotsky—would be first-rate publicity not only for INA but for his rapidly expanding radio interests in the United States. Kingsford was buying radio stations in New York, Philadelphia, Cleveland, and Detroit and had formed an organization, Consolidated Broadcasters Company, to manage them. The Trotsky interview was to have been sent through a complex system of relay stations, including two ships at sea in the Atlantic, and aired over CBC radio stations. An ambitious and expensive project that had to be canceled because of insurmountable technical problems and the growing uneasiness of the Russian Commissar for Propaganda as to just what Comrade Trotsky might say.

The on-again, off-again confusion of the project had caused Martin to miss Christmas at Abingdon, but he was now driving a hired car down for the New Year's weekend, the back of the car piled with gifts bought hastily at Harrod's. The weather reports told of heavy snow in Yorkshire and Scotland, but the skies were clear in Surrey. It was cold but windless and only a light frost covered the fields. As Martin drove through the village of Tipley's Green, he could see pink-coated horsemen on a distant hill galloping hard toward Leith Woods and he could hear the faint baying of the hounds. He supposed that Anthony was in the group somewhere, riding hell-for-leather and risking a broken neck in the leafless tangle of the wood. He shook his head at the thought. Chasing a fox

seemed a cruel and pointless thing to do for pleasure—
but to each his own.

"I'm happy you were able to make it," Alexandra
said, kissing him on the cheek. She had seen him drive
up and had come out of the house to meet him, two of
the footmen trailing her. "What on earth have you got
in the back?"

"A few little gifts—mostly for Colin."

"Oh, Martin. He's so little. He doesn't need many
toys. You look like you bought out the shop."

"Well, this and that—a steam engine, cricket bat. I
was going to buy him a hobby horse, but I had a feeling Aunt Hanna and Anthony would buy something
like that."

Alexandra was laughing. "A steam engine! You
don't know much about babies, do you?"

"Not a hell of a lot. Guess I should have told the
clerk Colin's age."

"Yes, I think you jolly well should have." She
hugged him and they began to walk back to the house
as the footmen unloaded the car. "But it was sweet of
you. I'll put the steam engine away for a few years."

"How's everything going?"

"Better," she said with a wan smile. "Papa and I are
no longer in warring camps. It's not a truce, sort of a
grudging acceptance. And I've seen him with Colin
when he thought no one was watching. I'm sure he
loves him, but heaven forbid he should unbend
enough to tell me he does."

"He will one day."

"I hope it won't be too late. Oh, one other thing is
happening. Mama is playing cupid and not being exactly subtle about it. She invited a certain Noel Roth-

well down for the week and contrives every possible opportunity for the two of us to be alone together."

"Do you like him?"

She shrugged noncommittally. "He's all right, I expect. Suave and handsome. All the social graces. Perhaps a bit too eager that I should become seriously interested in him." She pointed up at the house, her hand encompassing the sheer magnificence of the facade. "This place works its effect. The manner of living here can intoxicate strangers. He's out for a day's hunting. Rides extremely well, according to Papa. I have the feeling he does everything well and knows it, too." She paused before mounting the front steps. "Will I ever get Robbie out of my mind? Have you slept with a woman and not thought of Ivy?"

"Yes, but it took time."

"Robbie would have wanted me to get married. He had a horror of mourning—of black cloth and widow's weeds. He had such a respect for life and all the healthy functions of the human body. It's just me, I suppose. Still clinging to him. Willie played some foxtrot records on the gramophone last night after dinner and Noel and I danced together. I liked it, being in a man's arms—enjoyable. He sensed it, I'm sure, and later, when we were alone in the library, he kissed me, rather passionately. I went stiff as a board. Totally frigid. He must have thought he was kissing a block of marble."

Martin put his arm around her and led her up the steps. "You're not stone, Alex. You're warm and real and very lovely. No wonder he kissed you with passion. So would any man. Robbie's dead and it marks the end of something, but not the end of everything.

You have a whole lifetime ahead of you. It would be terribly wrong to turn away from someone just because they might like to share that life with you."

"I know," she said softly. "It's—difficult."

"Sure it is." He gave her hand a firm squeeze. "Toughest thing there is sometimes, just going on living. But it's worth it, Alex. You'll see."

Noel Edward Allenby Rothwell, Esq., scrutinized his naked image in the dresser mirror and found nothing wanting about it. A fine figure of a man, he thought objectively. There was nothing vain about him. He was quick to recognize both his faults and virtues with equal dispassion. He knew other men of his age who had allowed their bodies to go to seed. Too much drink and too much food, too little exercise—the good and decent habits of their youth all gone by the board. Fat. Sagging muscles and puffy jowls. Poor livers and malfunctioning ductless glands. He kept himself in shape by willpower and daily calisthenics, and at thirty-five had the physique of a twenty-year-old. When the pressures of his job in the city became too harrowing, he had the good sense to get away for a few days, to catch a train for Scotland for a bit of grouse shooting or salmon fishing; to drive to Norfolk and take his thirty-foot ketch for a sail; or ride with the Tatton Hounds.

He winced slightly at the very thought of riding and lifted his legs painfully to get into his white cotton drawers. He had never known a more furious horseman than Lord Stanmore. An absolute madman in the saddle: clearing impossible jumps, threading his horse through the woods with an abandon that

seemed suicidal until one realized with what calculated skill he read the pattern of the trees. He had
kept up with him, by God. Rode close behind and had
been the second rider to catch up with the hounds
and the kill—the others trailing in, exhausted and
slightly befuddled by the pace. The earl had patted
him on the back and congratulated him for his horse-
manship. But he was paying for it now. There wasn't
a bone or muscle in his body that did not ache. Even
putting on his patent-leather dress pumps made him
wince.

He scrutinized the clothed image in the mirror and
found nothing amiss. The starched white shirtfront
was faultless, the black tie perfectly formed and cen-
tered, the dinner jacket—thanks to the valet the earl
had sent up to see to his clothes—neatly pressed. He
made a minor adjustment to an ebony cuff link and
then left his room in the east wing of the house and
walked slowly along the corridor toward the main
stairway.

The house and its contents awed him. He was far
from being a poor man and, as a stockbroker and in-
vestment counselor, had been in many impressive
houses, but nothing had quite prepared him for the
splendor of Abingdon Pryory. Where, after all, could
one stroll down an ordinary corridor on the second
floor of a house and find sketches by Constable and
little watercolors by Turner dotted about the walls as
though they were no more important than five-
shilling prints? And in the main corridor, the Long
Gallery with its many Palladian windows overlooking
the courtyard, as many works of seventeenth- and
eighteenth-century masters as could be found in a
first-rate museum.

He paused before leaving the gallery and descending the broad, curving stairs to the lower floor. He sat down carefully on a bench beneath one of the tall windows—a seventeenth-century Italian bench, he decided, judging by the delicate carved legs and the pattern of the needlework on the seat. The portrait of a man, obviously painted by Sir Joshua Reynolds, and just as obviously a Greville ancestor, stared at him haughtily from the opposite wall.

He took out a silver cigarette case and lit an Egyptian Deity with a small silver lighter.

They approved of him—both mother and father. There was no misinterpreting their signals of acceptance. As for their daughter . . . a stunner if there ever was one. Soft in his arms, sensual when they danced—and then cold as a mackerel when he had kissed her. Puzzling.

He blew a thin stream of smoke toward the Reynolds. Curious. A curious situation.

He had avoided marriage adroitly. He thought of it simply as a loss of personal freedom, the giving up of one's right to come and go as one pleased, to dine where and when one wanted, to play cards at one's club to all hours of the morning, or dash off to the Continent on impulse and enjoy a few days in Paris or Monte Carlo. A man with a wife was expected to forgo those singular pleasures and live contentedly within the restrictions custom imposed on the domesticated male. He had balked at those restrictions in the past, but to marry the only daughter of the Earl and Countess of Stanmore offered prospects of compensation too heady to be ignored.

He inhaled deeply and blew smoke through his nose. To be a member of this household, part of this beautiful house—all within grasp. He had only to find a way through that chill barrier the young widow threw up to protect herself from intimacy. Caution was the word. A slow and careful approach. It was rather like grouse shooting, he thought as he stood up and walked toward the stairs. If one was too impetuous and blundered through the bracken, the bird would be long flown.

Beautiful lady, there in the moonlight,
You made my heart stand still. . . .

There were over a hundred guests for the New Year's Eve party. An orchestra had been hired in London, and the seldom-used ballroom was festooned with ribbons and gaily colored balloons. A young man in a white dinner jacket sang to the dancers through a megaphone.

"Bloody soppy song," William said. He stood by the refreshment table, sipping a drink and talking to Martin. "Mother should have let me choose the band."

Martin smiled. "I think she was wise not to."

"You may have a point." He drained his glass and set it on the table.

"Care for another?"

"God, no, thanks all the same. One ginger beer is one too many."

"Change of habits, Willie?"

"Well, not exactly from choice. The firm admonition of a London judge. I could disregard his warning to stay away from hard spirits, but that wouldn't be playing the game, would it? So ginger beer it is—or soda water. Can't say I mind, actually. I certainly feel better for it."

"How's Derbyshire?"

"Cold as charity. Always dreamed of a warm country, but it's lovely in a wild sort of way, and there's no better grass for horses."

"You have your stables now?"

"Lord, no. It'll be a year before everything's done. But I'm in no hurry. I live in a sort of shack with a coal stove and a phonograph. It's not quite as grand as the Pryory, but I'm content." He looked at his watch. "Thirty minutes before the witching hour. Anyone in particular you want to kiss on the stroke of midnight?"

"No. As a matter of fact, there's a woman I would like to avoid having to kiss."

"Miss Templeton, you mean? Auntie Angela dug her up someplace. She's a literary person. Writes sonnets or something about virtue. After you, is she?"

"She's supposedly with someone, but she keeps zeroing in."

"Let's have a game of billiards. I don't think I could bear hearing that poor sod croon 'Auld Lang Syne' through his blasted megaphone."

> *Zam-bo-anga-anga*
> *where the monkeys kiss,*
> *Zam-bo-anga-anga boy*
> *and monkey miss. . . .*

The older couples left the center of the floor as the band swung lustily into the latest craze tune from America and stood watching in amusement as the dancers gyrated and hopped.

> *Zam-bo-anga-anga . . .*
> *Zam-bo-anga-anga-anga-anga!*

"No more!" Alexandra laughed.

"I quite agree," Noel shouted over the music. Taking her by the hand, he escorted her off the dance floor and through the crowd to the refreshment table. "Jumping about like an ape is hardly my forte." He dabbed at his brow with a pocket handkerchief. "Although I must say you did it superbly. You have a marvelous sense of rhythm."

"I love to dance, but *Zam-bo-anga-anga* is a wee bit exhausting."

"They'll be playing a waltz next—to get everyone on the floor in time for midnight." He asked one of the barmen for two champagnes and handed Alexandra a glass. "I'm not very good at toasts. Let me just say that it's a privilege to be having my last drink of nineteen twenty-one with someone as nice as you."

"Thank you, Noel. That's very sweet."

"Not at all. It's the truth. And I hope we'll see each other again during the course of the new year."

"I'm quite certain we shall."

Their eyes held for a moment and then she raised her glass and drank. He couldn't be sure what it was that he had seen in her eyes, but it wasn't discouraging. He had seen a light there—an interest.

"Ladies and gentlemen. Will you join us by dancing to the lovely strains of 'Charmaine'? It is five minutes to midnight. Five minutes until nineteen hundred and twenty-two!"

Alexandra set her glass on the table. "I love the waltz."

"Yes," he said, placing his glass next to hers. "So do I. It's what I was taught in dancing school as a boy. That and the gavotte."

They stepped smoothly into the flow of dancers,

and then the lights in the room were dimmed by the servants and only the candles in the wall brackets glowed, light sparkling and shimmering from the dangling crystal reflectors behind them. Almost everyone was drawn into the gliding whirl of the dancers as they circled the shadowed room. The strains of the waltz ended, a drum rolled, and then the music . . . the man singing—

Should auld acquaintance be forgot . . .

Noel took Alexandra gently in his arms. "Happy New Year," he said, bending to her, kissing her with an almost brotherly regard on the cheek. No stiffening rejection this time, he realized. Slow and easy— one tiny step at a time. That was the way to go about it. That was certainly the way.

Martin sat in bed, smoking a cigar and nursing a large whiskey and soda. His journal was on the bedside table beside him, but he simply wasn't in the mood to make an entry. God knows he had enough to write about if he cared to be reflective. New Year's was a time for reflection anyway. That, plus being at Abingdon Pryory, was more than enough to set his thoughts racing backward in time. But he fought the urge. It would be too easy to slip into maudlin thoughts about Ivy.

He took a puff on his cigar and then a swallow of whiskey. There were more pertinent things to jot down if he cared to write. Major General Sir Bertram Dundas Sparrowfield, in spite of discreet pressure from friends who had sought to dissuade him, was pressing his libel case with renewed vigor—prompted, Martin knew for sure now, by two jingoist war correspondents whose reputations had suffered diastrously since the coming of peace. He almost felt sorry for poor old "Bird Drops," puttering about in his Hampshire garden and being manipulated by two rogues who hoped to change the verdict of history by getting the general a favorable judgment in court. It was all so pointless anyway. All that had been accomplished so far was a growing awareness that a libel suit was pending, and the hardening of attitudes between the war damners and the war apologists. Sales of *A Killing Ground* had zoomed. Hatchard's in Piccadilly couldn't put it on the shelves fast enough. And that vast, arcane, ponterous, exasperating, and incredibly efficient machine known as the British judicial system had been dragging its collective feet for months, wary, if not outright horrified, by the idea of a *cause célèbre* thrust into their midst. They viewed Sparrowfield's case the way they would have viewed a ticking bomb. But the ex-war correspondents urged and whispered and the old warrior pressed onward with the same verve that had carried his decimated force—in the face of harrowing Mauser fire—across the Tugela in the Boer War.

He drained half the glass and set it, with an audible sigh, on top of his journal. His thoughts drifted, the idle flow broken by a sharp knock on the door. Before he could say anything, the door opened and Anthony stepped into the room, grim-faced and pale, a dressing gown thrown across his shoulders.

"Sorry to burst in on you at three in the morning. But it's Charles. He's gone."

Mr. Lassiter had brought Charles a glass of hot milk

shortly before ten o'clock that night, as was his custom. Charles liked to sit in bed to drink it and then would go off to sleep. It was an unvarying routine. Mr. Lassiter would then go to his own room in the spacious apartment, read a detective novel until midnight or shortly thereafter, and look in on his charge before going to bed.

"I looked in on him about twelve-thirty," he said, standing in the front hall, telling his story to Martin and William. "He seemed to be sleeping, so I went down to the servants' hall, it being New Year's Eve, and joined in the bit of celebration there until about two, two-thirty. When I went up to bed I looked in on him again and saw the bed was empty. I thought he might have been in the w.c., but he wasn't. Then I went into the sitting room and noticed the door into the side corridor was ajar. Closed it myself earlier, so I knew he'd gone out."

"Where does that corridor lead to?" Martin asked him.

"To a short flight of stairs. There's a door at the bottom opening into the garden. That door was ajar, too."

"Has he ever done this before?"

"No, sir. Never. He'll take a walk by himself in the daytime once in a while, but he's never done it at night."

Lord Stanmore came into the hall followed by half a dozen of the male servants, all of them dressed for the cold. Some were carrying electric torches.

"We'll pick up more torches and lanterns at the stables," the earl said grimly. "The grooms have been woken and we'll fan out and search for him. Do you have any idea what he was wearing, Lassiter?"

"Not much, near as I can judge. I looked through his wardrobe and his winter coat's still hanging there. Robe and pajamas, I'd say . . . and carpet slippers."

"Good God," the earl muttered. "It must be freezing out there this time of morning." He turned to one of the servants. "Round up a couple of blankets, and don't forget to bring the brandy."

They stood out on the terrace and a sense of fear gripped all of them. Scud cloud raced across the moon and it was bitterly cold. The earl turned up the collar of his overcoat and glared off across the dark gardens toward the inky shadow line of Burgate Hill and the mass of Leith Woods.

"That's where he'd go. Leith Woods."

"I think so," Lassiter said. "We walked there this morning, sir, and he lingered a long time."

They moved off through the gardens and down to the stables where the grooms were waiting for them, their electric torches winking in the darkness.

"We'll spread out when we reach the woods," the earl told them. "Call his name loudly and search the undergrowth carefully with your torches."

He strode off, the others hurrying along behind him in silence. Down the bridle path and then over a stile and across the fields, the frosted grass crunching under their feet. The woods loomed in the distance, gray-black and sullen under the moon, skeletal branches of wintry trees ingrained against the sky. An owl hooted far away on Burgate Hill. And then they heard it, deep in the wood, the sound of it cutting to the heart, rooting every man in his tracks—the sharp crack and thudding echo of a gunshot.

* * *

It had been coming to him all day in brief, dis-
jointed flashes: images and words . . . the sounds of
voices. All dimly remembered for the briefest of moments. One image had been so vivid he had sat under
a tree in Leith Woods, holding his head in his hands,
struggling to keep the image alive, in focus—to sort it
out and give it meaning. But it had escaped him, as all
the images escaped him, and they had walked back to
the house for breakfast.

After breakfast the images had come again, quite
strongly and with increasing frequency. Walking
slowly around in the sitting room, he had touched the
covers of books on the shelves, feeling keenly that he
had touched the books many times . . . in some hazy
past. Here? In this place? He did not know. Scraps of
thought flooded him, but he could not make sense of
the patterns. A jumbled whirl that made his head
ache. He had spent most of the afternoon sleeping,
but even his dreams had been disturbing—a stream of
swiftly moving pictures, like motion-picture film running crazily through a projector . . . like the time at
the barracks when he had run a Broncho Billy cowboy
film as a treat for the men and something had gone
wrong with the machine—everything speeded up and
the men laughing and shouting . . . *What barracks?
What men?*

There had been music in the house tonight, and the
people who had come to visit him had been the people he had been seeing all day, moving in and out of
his thoughts. Lying in bed after drinking the warm
milk, he had remembered a tune. Lilting and beautiful; he had whispered its name—" 'Charmaine' . . .
'Charmaine.' " Lovely. A hunting sound played on
a gramophone in a farmhouse . . . and they had

marched to the tiny village in the summer, heat waves rising from the dusty road and the men singing . . .

> *Here we are, here we are, here are again. All good pals together and jolly good company.*

The voices of the men loud in his ears before fading away. But who were those men? . . . That village . . . where was it exactly?

He had lain in bed in the darkness staring into a void, searching for one solid thing to grasp on to.

"*I was . . .*" he had said, "*a soldier . . . in the farmhouse . . . and there was a gramophone . . . which we played . . . and then . . . we went up to the line . . . and . . . took over trenches near Fricourt.*"

But where did all that take place? And when? And who was he?

It was always quiet in the woods. One could think calmly there. One could, perhaps, by sitting very still, put all of the tiny pieces together and make sense of them. Draw all the fragments of image and sound into a cohesive whole.

In the woods—deep among the trees.

He sensed dimly that he was cold—colder than he had ever been before. He tried to tuck his naked, bleeding feet under the bramble-ripped fringes of his dressing gown. A ragged man, he was thinking, seated in the wilderness.

"But what man . . . who?"

Only the owls answered, calling from the branches far above his head.

"I am . . ." he whispered. "I am . . ."

He was called by a name. Charles . . . Charles Greville, or Major Greville. But the name meant nothing
to him. There was no solid person behind that name.
It was like being given a number, a depersonalized
string of digits. And yet . . . *someone* . . . a shape of
substance was rising from the murk.

A twig snapped not too far away. And then another.
He stiffened against the trunk of the tree and strained
to listen. Again—closer now—moving past. He dropped
silently to his hands and knees and began to crawl
with infinite care through the underbrush and the piles
of dead leaves.

*To make a sound was death because Thompson, out
on patrol one night in the wood, had sneezed and the
Fritz machine gun in Mild-and-Bitter sap had opened
up and four of his men had been killed and three others wounded, including Thompson with a nice Blighty
in the shoulder. Or one could touch a hidden wire
running to the Boche trench which would set a tin can
moving and old Fritz would toss stick grenades on
you. No . . . no . . . silent as the grave was the ticket
. . . slow movements of elbows and knees . . . feeling
ahead of you with your fingers as you went . . . cautious . . . cautious . . . never mind the barbed wire
that tore the flesh . . . never mind the slimy feel of a
dead man's face. . . .*

He had reached a clearing and lay flat in the icy
grass. Shadows and pale moonlight in the glade. The
shadows moved slowly, keeping together, gliding
soundlessly through the moonlight. He stared at them,
straining to hear . . . and then it came—a little whisper of death only a few yards off to his right, the click
of brass against oiled steel, the snap of a bolt. But not

France. Not no-man's land—Abingdon . . . Leith Woods . . .

He rose screaming to his feet—*"Bastard—you bastard!"*

A rifle cracked and a herd of deer scattered, hooves thundering on the hard ground, crashing off into the woods. He heard men cursing and running, two or three of them, blundering through the underbrush. He took a few faltering steps and shouted after them—*"Bastards . . . bastards!"*

His words echoed back and then faded. The sounds of running faded also and it was silent in the glade, so silent he could hear the beating of his heart. He stumbled on a few more paces and nearly tripped over the gunnysacks and ropes the men had left behind. He sank down beside them and began to wrap the stiff sacks around his feet and legs. He would die before morning if he didn't do it. His fingers were stiff as bone and they bled against the rough hemp but he wrapped himself in the sacks and sat quietly, waiting for the dawn. He was sitting there when a light flashed across him and someone began shouting. He was so cold—so terribly tired—but he managed to raise his head and smile into the rays of a torch.

"I'm Charles Greville . . . live at . . . the Pryory. Some . . . bastards tried to poach . . . my father's deer."

Book Two

JOURNEYING

1922

VII

It seemed strange to Ross to be back in England. He had never felt so much as a twinge of homesickness, had barely given the place a single thought in six years, but as the tugs pushed the big liner against the Mersey tide and eased her into the Cunard dock, he had felt a lump rise in his throat at the sight of the Union Jack fluttering atop one of the buildings.

Liverpool in February, sleet blowing in the wind, hissing into the dirty brown river. The buildings of gray stone and sooty black brick. A cheerless-looking place, old and tumbled together. Narrow, twisting streets. He remembered Liverpool and the country around it—Birkenhead across the channel, and Runcorn and Widnes further upriver. Had worked his itinerant trade along the Mersey a long time ago and could not think back on those particular times with much fondness. Still, it was the old flag. It was England.

He shared a taxi with Mr. Mayhew. He had met Mr. Mayhew on the second night out from New York, the ship rolling and pitching in a bitter northeaster. They had been just about the only passengers showing up for dinner and had joined company. Afterward, they had gone into the saloon for brandy and cigars.

Mr. Mayhew was a man in his sixties and owned a large gearworks in Bradford. He sold his gears to the Jordan Motor Car Company in Cleveland, and to the Apperson Brothers and Studebaker, among others, and so they had common ground for conversation. Ross had worked for Rolls-Royce and had been sent by them to America early in 1916 to oversee the building under license of their aircraft engines. He had worked for nearly three years at the Chambers Motor Factory in Cleveland, a concern that Mayhew knew well. A friendship developed between them that lasted the voyage—and beyond.

"Have you stayed at the Adelphi before, Ross?"

"No, I don't believe I have."

"My home whenever I'm in Liverpool—which is often. First-rate service, I can assure you. And if one has a taste for mutton chops—which I confess I certainly do—the Adelphi cooks them to a turn."

Ross suppressed a smile and looked out the window of the taxi at the early-evening traffic crush in Derby Square. *Have you stayed at the Adelphi before, Ross?* Not bloody likely.

It was as he imagined it would be—a marble and mahogany lobby, crystal chandelier hanging from the domed ceiling and reflecting tiny shards of light onto red carpeting. An orchestra was playing somewhere in the cavernous, gilded place. Muted sounds of violins. A tinkle of cutlery. Music with the mutton chops. No, he had never stayed at the Adelphi when in Liverpool. It had been sixpence a night for a hard bed in those days—and three pennyworth of rancid fish and chips for his supper.

He felt a momentary sense of ill ease as he approached the desk, wondering if the dapper, smiling clerk would see through the trappings of well-cut suit and topcoat, the expensive shoes and Stetson fedora and recognize instantly the lower-middle-class man wearing them. But the clerk only continued to smile and turn the registry book toward him.

"Welcome to the Adelphi Hotel, sir."

"Thank you." He signed: James A. Ross—Coronado, California, U.S.A.

The clerk glanced at the book. "I say, sir. Must be very nice *there* in February."

"Yes, it is."

"Will you be staying with us long, sir?"

"Just overnight, I'm sorry to say."

Well, that was a lie, but his room was comfortable and reasonably warm and the mutton chops were everything Mr. Mayhew had said they were. After dinner, the two men went into the bar for brandy.

Mr. Mayhew took out his cigar case and extended it to Ross. He had grown quite fond of the sturdy, sandy-haired, freckled young man.

"You seem a bit on the subdued side, lad. It's being back in England. Am I correct?"

"I'm not sure I understand what you mean."

Mr. Mayhew bent forward and offered the flame from his cigar lighter. "Oh, I think you do. I know America. God knows I've been there enough times, from Maine to California and most of the states in between. Know the land and know the people. Know Old Blighty for that matter, too. You're a bit—well, ill at ease in the Adelphi. I can tell."

Ross shifted slightly in his seat and looked down at his hands. His nails were well manicured but of a darkish color. His hands were scrupulously cleaned, washed with soap and rubbed with pumice, but there were minute black lines on the palms that would never be scrubbed away. They were the hands of a man who had worked more than half of his thirty years with oil, grease, and machines.

"I wouldn't say I was ill at ease exactly."

"A hotel like this . . ." Mayhew leaned back and waved his cigar at the room—the oak walls and leather chairs, the shiny glass behind the bar. "A place like this to have a drink. An establishment for *gentlemen*, Ross—for *toffs*."

Ross looked up, scowling, then saw the look of friendly amusement on the older man's face. He smiled shyly. "Is it so obvious I don't fit in?"

"Yes, it is—but only to you. I'm sure you wouldn't think twice of going to a fine hotel in New York, Detroit . . . San Diego, Ross. That hotel in Coronado. You've been there, surely."

"I live there. My room has a balcony and faces the ocean."

"Facing the blue Pacific." Mayhew sighed and puffed for a moment on his cigar. "Why, you live like a king in California, but feel like a navvy in dirty, smoky, freezing Liverpool."

"Hardly a king," Ross muttered, shaking his head. "I don't pay that much for the room."

"It's attitude, not price. You live in one of the most gracious hotels in the world and never question your right to live there. And no one else questions it either, even if you were to drop an 'h' or forget to sound your 'g's. I've known many an American millionaire who chewed tobacco and spat on the ground and never saw the inside of a schoolroom after the age of eleven. A land with a different set of values, Ross. Any man who has the talent for making money or getting things done ranks above a duke there. You're an American now, aren't you?"

"Yes. Got my citizenship papers just before I left California."

"Well, there you are, then. Lean back, dear boy, smoke your cigar, sip your brandy, and act like the *bloomin' toff* you are!"

Liverpool to London. A first-class carriage. He watched the towns flash past the windows. Stoke-on-Trent and Longton. Stafford and Birmingham. Slag heaps and mills. Row houses with slate roofs stretching away endlessly, street after street, featureless and drab.

He had grown up in one of those houses, raised by an aunt and uncle, long dead. His future had been set to everyone's satisfaction, including his own, the day he turned thirteen. It had been on that day that his uncle, a foreman at Lockhart & Whitby, had taken him to the sprawling engineworks in Wolverhampton to begin his years of apprenticeship at five shillings for a sixty-hour workweek. At the end of six years he had become a journeyman mechanic and brought home one pound eight shillings in his pay envelope, the money placed in his aunt's hand and seven shillings returned to him.

"You're a good lad, Jamie."

But then what was it? Spring? Riding his bike one Sunday afternoon in the golden country between the Severn and Wyre forest, from the top of a hill seeing westward the Shropshire dales and, over his shoulder, east by north, the haze of Birmingham, Sandwell, Wolverhampton staining the sky even on the sabbath.

Something had called to him, a wild gypsy voice, to make him pack his tools the next morning and tie the canvas bag to the tail of his bike and pedal off into the unknown.

"*The lad's an ass,*" had been his uncle's only comment.

He found that he could make more than one pound eight shillings in a week cycling through the west country, following the course of the Severn—Stourport and Worcester, Tewkesbury, Gloucester, and on into south Wales. Not a town, village, or farm that didn't contain something that wouldn't run properly or run at all. A tractor, a pumping engine at a mine, a doctor's Vauxhall . . .

"*Is it worth ten shillings to you to make it go?*"

A journeyman. Journeying. Free as a tinker. He slept under the stars if need be, but his merry good looks rarely went unnoticed if evening found him in a town. The number of women he had slept with from Hereford to Anglesey was beyond recall. He got rid of his bicycle that first winter on the road, purchased a secondhand motorbike, and worked his way along the Mersey and up through Manchester, Bradford, and Leeds. A Sheffield millionaire hired him as chauffeur and mechanic. He had taken the job partly to spend the winter in a warm house eating decent food for a change, but mainly because it gave him the chance to delve into the mysteries of the Rolls-Royce motorcar— the only type of motorcar he had never worked on.

A fine job, but he left it after a year and made his way to London, driven by a restlessness he could not explain. A chauffeur-mechanic had no trouble finding employment. He could pick and choose. In the spring of 1913 he entered the employ of the Earl of Stanmore.

Odd, he thought, how fate or circumstances worked. Here he sat in a first-class carriage with a letter of credit in his suitcase for fifty thousand dollars, on his way to meet with Sir Angus Blackworth at the Blackworth plant near Abingdon. He wondered idly if the Pryory was still lived in. As he lit a cigar he decided it would be worth going by there—if he had the time.

Two mechanics in white coveralls checked the bolts securing the engine to the test frame, then turned on the ignition switch and the propeller. The nine-cylinder radial kicked smoothly into life, the full-throttled roar muffled by the sound baffles in the testing shed. One of the Blackworth engineers scanned the flickering needle on the test panel.

"Three hundred," he shouted. "We can get her up to three hundred fifty easy enough."

Ross, his suit covered with a blue smock, leaned forward and scowled at the dials. "Not that easily. She's straining at three and a quarter. Blow a cork in a minute."

The engineer eased off on the throttle control and then cut the switch. "It's still the best aero engine on the market. Reliable as all get-out."

Ross nodded in agreement. "It's the engine we're looking for, all right, but we've got to have more horsepower. Our specs call for four hundred minimum."

The engineer lit a cigarette and eyed Ross through the smoke. He had been prepared to dislike the man when they had first met. Had put him down as just another Yank, cocky and overpaid. But after talking with him for a few minutes he had detected Birmingham in his speech and they had spent an hour over tea talking about their apprentice days, the engineer having served his at the Clybourne works in Coventry, Lockhart & Whitby's chief competitor.

"Why don't you use the Liberty or the Packard twelve? There must be hundreds of the ruddy things back in the States."

"Can't," Ross said. "The U.S. Navy wants a radial. It's what our contract calls for—an air-cooled, low-maintenance power plant. There's nothing being built in America that even comes close to the Blackworth Argo, but we must have more HP."

"Better see the old man then. He's under the impression you're here to buy what we've got."

"Did he tell you that? I made it clear to him we'd need changes."

The engineer laughed and puffed smoke. "The gaffer only hears what he wants to hear. The plain fact of the matter is we've got more engines than we can use or sell. The armistice caught us with a warehouse full. He was hoping to clear 'em all out with a fat Yank contract. You'd best hop over to number four hangar and set him straight."

Sir Angus Blackworth had earned his knighthood because of the exploits of one of his planes, the Blackworth BFC-3 scout-bomber. Two squadrons of the tough, fast two-seaters had raided the U-boat pens at Ostend and Zeebrugge early in 1918. Their light bombs had barely dented the ferroconcrete submarine shelters, but lucky hits had sunk two U-boats in the Brugge canal and a large fuel depot had been set aflame, the column of black smoke seen as far away as Ramsgate and Dover. The exploit had fired the public imagination as well, and Angus had been whisked from his workshop to Buckingham Palace to be touched on the shoulders by the king's sword. The honor proved to be of little worth in the postwar world. He was struggling against stiff competition to make it in the field of civil transport. His hopes rested with the Blackworth Atlas, a three-engine, high-winged biplane of metal and wood construction covered with duralumin and fabric and built to carry a crew of three and ten passengers. Aircraft Travel and Transport, Ltd., was interested in the plane for their London-Paris route, but the test flights of the prototype had been disappointing. Sir Angus now spent every waking moment in the hangar crawling over and through the big machine with a notebook and slide rule. He knew the solution to his problem even as James Andrew Ross of Corona Aircraft Company, San Diego, California, U.S.A., was explaining his own.

"Power," Sir Angus muttered, seated on the lower wing, his short legs dangling. "That's the bleeding ticket, isn't it? The ruddy secret to flight. Power and more power."

"It's always been the key. More so now. What does this brute weigh?"

"Near fourteen thousand pounds—unloaded."

"There you are, then. The ratio of weight to horsepower is out of kilter. Now, you take our plane. Three hundred HP was fine until the navy wanted more out of it than just scouting. We have to take off and land on this ruddy carrier they're building, carry a Vickers on the engine cowling and two Lewis guns on a Scarff ring for the gunner-observer, have a range of six hundred miles, and lug five hundred pounds of bombs if need be. We'd never get the beast off the ruddy deck at original specs. We had your Argo in mind from the start, but we'll need another hundred horsepower."

"I could use that myself."

"That's right. Well, the Argo's a good engine, trusty as a five-quid watch. I've got ideas for it. I could get her to four hundred fifty. Mean rebuilding it from the bearings up, but it would be bloody well worth the effort."

Sir Angus knew a braggart when he saw one. There were mechanics and engineers floating around who'd promise the blinking moon and deliver nothing but grief. He knew the type all right, and he knew he wasn't looking at one now. He'd taken the trouble to check up on J. A. Ross when he'd first received the letter from him on Corona Aircraft Company stationery inquiring whether he had thirty Argo radial engines for sale. A man at the American Board of Trade in London had sent him particulars. Corona Aircraft was a growing concern in San Diego with firm contracts from the U.S. Navy. Ross was chief engineer and partner.

Sir Angus extended his arms. "Help me down from here, lad." Once on the ground he looked up at the big plane. "She's a beauty. And she'll sell. I'll have two versions, one for passengers and one for freight. It's a good, honest machine. All she needs is more power. Of course, I didn't need you to tell me that. I was building engines before you were born. The truth is, I have all these Argo-135's left over from war contracts that were canceled. Thought I could use them on this aircraft—or, anyway, hoped I could but knew in my heart I couldn't. Oh, she flies well enough with them, but not with the number of passengers or pounds of freight I want her to carry."

"I understand."

"I'm sure you do." He rubbed a hand across his shaggy white eyebrows. "When do you need your engines?"

"The navy wants delivery when they launch their aircraft carrier. That could be a year, year and a half, maybe longer. They've been having problems with it. Changing designs all the time. It makes it hard on us. They still haven't settled on the type of arresting gear they'll use. We can't start building the frames until we know how they intend to slow the plane when it lands on the ruddy deck. A hook of some kind, but we have to know where to place it."

"And you people just sittin' around twirlin' your thumbs?"

"No. We're keeping our people busy building ten seaplanes for the navy with ten more on order from civilian companies. Using Liberty engines for those, so we've got no problems."

"Meanin' you don't have to rush back?"

Ross shivered slightly. The hangar doors were closed against the wind-driven sleet, but the great corrugated-iron building was colder than a well digger's arse. He thought of Coronado Island, people walking on the beach in the winter sunshine.

"I'd rush back tomorrow if you had a four-hundred-and-fifty-horsepower to sell me."

Sir Angus stamped his feet in frustration. He looked like an angry gnome. "I'd not even be botherin' to talk to you if I had that! It'd be hand over your money, haul away your bloody engines, and be quick about it!" He plucked a pencil from his pocket and chewed on it, calming himself down. "Now look here, Ross. I know a good deal about you. Solid little company in San Diego and all that. Mentioned your name to a fella I know. We were havin' a drink at my club in London. He was with Rolls-Royce during the war, engine designer, and told me they'd used seven of your carburetor patents. Said you was one of the cleverest chaps in the ruddy business. A natural-born engineer. Stopped a bit short of callin' you a bleedin' genius."

"Not very nice of him to stop there."

Sir Angus gripped Ross by the arm with a small, strong hand. "Now look 'ere. Two hands wash better than one, I always say. It's not just the piston displacement or compression ratios we're facin', it's a whole new carburetion system as well. There's higher-octane petrols coming on the market and a new system's needed to take advantage of them. If you could stay for six weeks or so and work with my lads, pool your bloody brains like, and come up with the design for what you need in an engine and *I* need in an engine, I'd be prepared to sell you the first thirty at twelve percent above cost, and give you the exclusive rights to build the ruddy thing in America under license—terms to be worked out to our mutual satisfaction. Does that sound fair enough?"

"Yes, of course."

"*And* I'll take care of all expenses while you're here—give you a car to use, a nice little cottage in Abingdon to rest your weary head in. Is it a bargain?" He stuck his hand out sharply and Ross took hold of it. "Good—good. It's been nice chattin' with you, lad. Now, if you'd just give me a boost up, I'll get back to checkin' the aileron linkage."

* * *

He could fault neither the car nor the cottage. The car, fittingly enough, was of American make—a Stearns-Knight Six coupe—and the cottage was far more comfortable and well furnished than he had expected. At the end of a quiet lane, it was one of seven cottages that the Blackworth Company had built in 1917 to house their chief engineers and families. Since those heady war years of rapid expansion and lucrative contracts, three of the cottages had stood empty. Ross had been handed the key to the last in line, the one whose side windows looked out on an unspoiled vista of fields and woods. It was like being in the middle of the country, a hundred miles from anywhere, but he was within easy walking distance of the little town.

He had rarely gone into Abingdon when he had been in service to the earl. The village had been too provincial for his tastes and he had spent his day off each week either in Guildford or London, racing off to those places on his motorbike. The only times he had gone into the village had been on Sundays when he had driven the family in for church service, and when Countess Stanmore had to attend a charity bazaar of some kind, usually at the vicarage. A sleepy sort of place in those days. One public house—the Crown and Anchor, more of an old codgers' home than a proper pub. Draughts and darts. It had all changed now.

He took a walk through Abingdon the afternoon of his fifth day of residence. It was a Saturday, the weather halfway pleasant for a change and the streets crowded with shoppers. He was amazed by the difference—the cinema palace, the variety of shops, the number of pubs, even two petrol stations and three garages. He had a fine lunch in a restaurant owned by three Italian brothers. The brothers pressed Chianti on him, eager to know more about America. They had spotted him by his clothes.

"Of course you are American. The hat, *che bueno!* The jacket! The way she nips the waist—*magnifico!*"

He told them what he knew. They had relatives in Cleveland. More wine. They had a cousin in California who never wrote. More wine for that. He felt light-headed when he left and walked it off, up the High Street and past the church. The war memorial sobered him.

FOR KING AND COUNTRY
1914–1918

And under that inscription twenty-seven names. He remembered four.

ALBERT DENNING
THOMAS HANES
SAMUEL MASTERWELL
IVY THAXTON RILKE

Hanes and Denning had been grooms at Abingdon Pryory—cheeky little chaps, envious of his motorbike and keen as mustard to learn how to ride it. He had taught them one long summer day, behind the stables, when the earl and countess were in France. Now they were dead in the Great War, all that patient teaching gone for nought. Sam Masterwell had been one of the footmen, an overgrown boy of a man who was always pinching the maids in servants' hall or trying to kiss them on the back stairs. The maids had hated him and called him an oaf. Now his name was carved in marble.

Ivy Thaxton. He had a dim memory of a girl by that name. One of the upstairs maids. Pretty. Dark-haired. They had talked a few times and he had offered to take her to the pictures in Guildford when she had an afternoon off, but never had. Ivy Thaxton *Rilke*. Lady Stanmore's maiden name had been Rilke. One of her nephews had stayed for a few weeks the summer of the war. Nice sort of fellow. Worked on a newspaper in Chicago. Picked him up at Southampton when he had arrived and had chauffeured him about London from time to time. It could be he was the one who had married Ivy Thaxton. From housemaid to the wife of a countess's nephew. Quite a boost up in the world. But the war had spoiled that future, as it had spoiled so many others.

He walked slowly back along the High Street. He had thought a lot about the war when he had been in America and had felt guilty about being safe in Cleveland, Ohio, while other chaps were dying in Flanders. All of the lads sent over by Rolls-Royce had felt the same way. The chief engineer on the project had given them a little talk about it, pointing out that what they were doing was helping to win the war, that the engines being turned out on the Yank assembly lines were powering the planes that were smashing the Boche good and proper—the giant Handley-Page bombers, the Bristol fighters and DH-4's. *"It's not bows and arrows that win wars these days, lads, it's machines. Every Falcon and Eagle engine turned out brings the war that much closer to a victorious end."*

It made sense. He was doing his bit even if his "trenches" were workbenches and lathes, his "western front" the shoreline of Lake Erie, but still he had experienced an odd feeling when reading about the Somme battles in the Cleveland *Plain-Dealer*. That had been in 1916, the year he had taken the big step to improve himself by enrolling in night classes at the Ohio Institute of Technology. The men he had met there over the next three years had expanded his horizons in a thousand directions. One of them, Harry Patterson, was now his partner in Ross-Patterson Motors and the Corona Aircraft Company.

"Nothing but blue skies," Harry had said when seeing him off at the railroad station in San Diego. Perhaps, but there would always be a chill in the blue from the shadows of monuments.

The Blackworth engineers and mechanics were clever, innovative, and hardworking. They also recognized the crucial nature of their work. The beautiful but woefully underpowered aircraft in hangar number four represented their futures, their pay envelopes, and the welfare of their wives and children. Rising unemployment in England was a frightening fact, and if they lost their jobs at Blackworth's they would all be hard put to find others. Twelve-hour days were normal. Sixteen hours not unusual. In three weeks the basic design for boosting the Argo radial to 450 HP at over 1800 rpm had been developed. It would take another three weeks or so of double shifts in the machine shop to prove the design correct. There was little for Ross to do now except wait for the testing.

He was drawn to the Pryory, passing the iron gates

daily on his way to and from the factory. The house itself, except for some of the chimneys, could not be seen from the road. He had been surprised to learn from Sir Angus that it was still inhabited.

"More money than sense, if you ask me," Sir Angus had scoffed. "One ruddy family in a house as big as a railroad station. Twenty servants if they have one. Still, if a man has money to burn, he might just as well go ahead and burn it, I always say."

Ross had no reason to go there except curiosity and a certain sentimental urge. He had been happy working for the earl. Lazy, almost indolent days at the Pryory or at Stanmore House in Park Lane. Nothing much to do except swagger about in his well-cut uniform dazzling the young maids. The memory of his former self made him smile—and made him grateful. Because he had had so much time on his hands, especially at night—the earl and countess rarely went anywhere in the evenings when they were staying at Abingdon—he had begun to dig deeper into the mechanical structure of the Rolls-Royce automobile. The earl's 1910 model Silver Ghost had its drawbacks and he had thought of ways to improve its performance. A fellow chauffeur, Lord Curzon's man, had talked him into taking out patents on his various carburetion devices and then into submitting his ideas and mechanical drawings to the Rolls-Royce company. They had found them of little use in motor cars, but of great practicality for their aero engines. When the war began, they had secured his patents and hired him, turning him into a starred man, a man exempt from military service. The substantial royalties they had paid after the war had made it possible for him to go into business with Harry Patterson. His entire life altered by what he had done in the garage at the Pryory. His tinkering with the Earl of Stanmore's car—if he cared to muse on the fatalistic implications of it—perhaps keeping his name from being chiseled on that memorial stone in Abingdon High Street.

It was impulse that made him stop his car in front of the gates one Saturday afternoon. He was on his way to Guildford to see a football match, but the gates beckoned and he pulled up and got out of the car. There was no lock on the gates, but he hesitated for some time before swinging them open and then driving through. What would he do when he got to the house? Knock on the front door and introduce himself? He wasn't anyone's servant now, but he just couldn't see himself doing that. When he reached sight of the Pryory, he slowed the car and thought of turning around and going back, but the sheer beauty of the house and gardens kept him moving forward in a state of wonder. Funny, he had worked in the place for nearly two years and had never given its magnificence a second thought. The gravel road branched off, one road curving away to the right to join a circular drive in front of the house, the other going toward the garages and the back. He turned the car to the left.

The footman who answered his ringing looked at him curiously. He knew quality clothing when he saw it and he sized up the well-tailored tweed trousers and Norfolk jacket at a glance.

"I beg your pardon, sir, but are you sure you want this entrance?"

"If this is the servants' entrance, it's what I'm looking for."

The footman looked blank. "It is, sir—but . . ."

"I used to work here at one time. Nineteen thirteen, fourteen."

The footman looked at Ross with frank curiosity. "You did? Here?"

"Look, do you mind if I step out of the cold?" He didn't wait for an answer and walked past the man into the pantry hallway.

"I'm not sure if there's anyone on the staff who would remember me. Is Mrs. Broome still here?"

"Broome?"

"She was the housekeeper."

The man shook his head. "No—sir. Come to think of it, I believe she died a few years back. Of the Spanish influenza. I heard them talkin' of it once."

"Heard who?"

"Why, them that knew the old dear. She was before my time, see. I've only been here six months."

"Who are *them?*" Ross asked patiently.

"Why, cook and Mr. Coatsworth. They've been here for ages."

He had never known the cook except by sight; her world and his had never meshed. But he'd known Coatsworth well enough. The old man had never been particularly friendly—but then, butlers were a stand-offish breed by nature.

"Would you tell Mr. Coatsworth that James—*Jamie* Ross is here? The chauffeur," he added as an afterthought.

"I will if he's about. He usually takes a bit of a nap this time of day. You can wait in servants' hall if you'd like. Follow me."

He remembered the way. The house had obviously been redone—he could smell paint, and the kitchen when they walked past it was larger and more modern than he remembered it—but the basic structure was the same. Servants' hall was in the same place it had been, and the same large size, but the furnishings were more comfortable. It was quite cozy, in fact, with chintz curtains and separate little tables where once there had been one long one.

"Care for a cuppa?" the footman asked.

"I'd prefer coffee."

"Right you are."

"No sugar—bit of cream."

He was finishing his coffee when Coatsworth came into the room, walking slowly. The old butler paused and looked long and hard before nodding his head slightly.

"Ross. Yes. It is Ross."

"You haven't changed a bit, sir," Ross said, standing up. "I'd have recognized you anywhere."

The butler's smile was thin. "You always were good at spouting the blarney. I'm not two steps from the grave, man."

"Oh, more than that, Mr. Coatsworth. I'd say three at least."

The butler eyed him dourly and sat stiffly on the edge of a chair. "You're Ross, all right. No doubt of that—the same twinkle in the eye. But you don't sound like the Ross I knew. Where have you been these past years?"

"America."

"America? Well, now, how about that? You're not one of those *gangsters*, I suppose, that we read about in the newspapers?"

"Not exactly. I'm an aeronautical engineer."

"An engineer, is it? Well, that doesn't surprise me.

You were always a clever lad when it came to machinery."

"I was sorry to hear about Mrs. Broome passing away. She was a nice woman."

"Yes, a very equitable woman, Mrs. Broome." He rubbed his hands across his knees, wincing slightly. "It was the influenza. It carried away a good many people. As many as died in the war, they say."

"It was very bad in America, too."

"Oh, I'm sure it was. Disease, I was reading in *The Times*, knows no boundaries. Missed *me*, though. I suppose God felt I had enough trouble with my arthritis." He stood up painfully. "I'll tell his lordship that you're here."

"Oh, no," Ross said quickly. "I wouldn't want to intrude."

"It's not intruding. His lordship still speaks of you as the best chauffeur he ever had. He's in his study having a postprandial cup of coffee. He would be most disappointed if I failed to tell him you were here."

It was apparent to Ross that the earl was genuinely glad to see him—which was heartening. He came striding across the study with one hand extended in greeting.

"By Jove! It *is* Ross. I said to Coatsworth, 'Not *our* Ross, surely,' but here you are. By Jove, here you are indeed." He shook hands with a good deal of force, then patted Ross on the back. "Come, lad—come sit down and tell me all about it. America, Coatsworth said—aeronautical engineer and all that. Yes, you must tell me all."

It took an hour or more, with the earl interrupting from time to time to ask a question or make a comment. Ross told him about being sent to Ohio to help the Americans construct Rolls engines, and of his enrolling in the institute and his three years of hard study, technical and cultural—elocution classes every Saturday, and a chautauqua program he had joined for two weeks every summer to study the classics. And he told of the company he had formed with his friend to purchase war-surplus Liberty and Packard airplane engines, and then of their decision to design and construct airplanes.

"Fascinating, Ross. Most interesting indeed," the earl said as he stood up and walked over to the cabinet where the whiskey was kept. "This Liberty engine you speak of—wouldn't that have done for your new aeroplane?"

"It's certainly powerful enough, sir, but not suited for the aircraft carrier. Experience on the English carrier, the *Argus*, proved that the hard landings a plane makes on a ship's deck causes problems with the radiators of liquid-cooled engines. Air-cooled radials are a must, and Blackworth's makes the best."

"I've met Sir Angus a couple of times—own stock in his company. Any way I can be of help?"

"That's very nice of you, m'lord, but everything's moving along smoothly now."

The earl poured whiskey into two glasses and carried them back to where Ross was seated in a leather chair by the fire.

"It seems like a millennium since you were last in this room, Ross. The first winter of the war, to be exact. You came to tell me you were leaving here to join the Rolls-Royce company at Enfield. I was quite put out about it as I recall. Leaving me with no one competent to replace you. I can remember your telling me to learn how to drive the car myself. That bit of advice only irritated me further. Well, there's been a good deal of water past the mill since then. I'm a damn good driver, I'll have you know—and I've even been up in an aeroplane."

"That's worth drinking to, m'lord."

"Times have changed so much. It seems a tragedy that it took a war to do it, but there you are. God's bitter jest, I suppose. But if it hadn't been for the war, you'd probably still be driving me around and not building aeroplanes in San Diego, California. Curious thought, it is not?" He raised his glass. "Let's drink to that instead, Ross. To your continued success."

"Thank you very much, m'lord."

"And no more calling me *m'lord*, Ross." He smiled wryly. "You're an American citizen now. You chaps fought a revolution to avoid calling chaps like me *m'lord*."

The earl walked with him along the terrace and around to the back of the house where he had parked his car.

"I'm sorry Charles isn't here, Ross, but he's up in Derbyshire staying with his brother. He mentioned your name just the other day on the way to the station. We had some trouble with the car, and Banes— do you remember Banes, by the way? He was Lord Gavin's driver, over at Newton Cross."

"I think so. Elderly man."

"A good deal more elderly now, I'm sorry to say, but it's difficult finding young chaps who are willing to go into domestic service. They'd rather drive taxis or live off the dole. Not a bad driver, Banes, but quite hopeless when faced with the mysteries of the internal-combustion engine. Anyway, we were driving Charles to the station when the car began to act up, stalling every time we stopped at a crossroad. It seemed to Charles and me like a simple matter of adjusting something or other, but Banes got all fluttery and said he'd have to call the Rolls people in London and have them send a man down. Charles turned to me and said, 'Ross would have fixed it in a minute.' So you see, we all remember you."

"I'm glad Mr. Charles is all right. I was afraid to ask."

"He's fine. Had some problems, but he's over them now."

They reached the car and the earl shook Ross by the hand. "I'm glad you decided to drop by. I enjoyed our chat very much."

"So did I." Ross paused by the car door. "Did they send a man down, by the way?"

"Rolls? I'm sure they will eventually, or we'll take the car into Guildford. There's a halfway decent mechanic there."

"Let me have a look at it, sir."

"Oh, no, my dear fellow. Wouldn't think of troubling you like that."

"It's no trouble. I'd enjoy it, as a matter of fact. Haven't tinkered with a Rolls car engine for years. Sounds like the idle is set too low—or the fuel-inlet needle is clogged—or—"

The earl laughed and held up his hand. "Why, you're positively straining at the bit, like an old warhorse hearing a bugle. Very well, if you insist. I'll go find Banes and have him give you the ignition key."

Ross swung open the garage doors so as to let out

the exhaust fumes, while Banes, unhappy at being dragged away from his tea, looked on morosely.

"There's nought much you can do with it."

"Oh, I think there is." He got into the car, turned on the engine, and sat listening to its uneven reverberations for a few minutes before switching it off and climbing out.

"Told you," Banes said gloomily. "Sounds like a major malfunction to me."

"Don't be daft, man. Where's the tool kit?"

The old chauffeur stared at him blankly. "I think there's one in the boot."

"Think?"

"Seems to me there is. I'm not much for tools. I'm a driver, not a bleedin' mechanic."

"Look, you can stand around and learn something or you can go back to the house and finish your tea."

"You don't need me, then?"

"Not really, no. But thanks for your help anyway."

"Think nothing of it," Banes said as he started out. "My pleasure, I'm sure."

Ross took off his jacket, undid his tie, and rolled up his shirt sleeves. He experienced a visceral pleasure when he opened the car bonnet and studied the great engine. There were some fine motorcars a man could buy in the States—Apperson and Duesenberg, Jordon and Stutz—but there was nothing built in the world to compare with the Rolls Silver Ghost.

He found the tool kit in the boot and began to remove the carburetor, working carefully, loosening each bolt a half-turn at a time. He was so intent on what he was doing that he did not hear someone calling until the name had been repeated twice.

"Banes—Banes—"

He straightened up with the spanner in his hand and looked toward the open end of the garage. A woman was standing there, silhouetted against the light. She took a step into the garage, and when she did he could see her face. There was no forgetting its loveliness.

"But you're not Banes," Alexandra said. "You're— Ross?"

"That's right."

"Good Lord, I don't believe it."

"Well, it's true," he said lamely.

"That's marvelous! I'm very happy to see you back, Ross. I'm glad Father has a proper chauffeur for a change."

"Well . . ."

"Is there anything the matter with the car?"

"The—carburetor needs some work."

She gave him a radiant smile. "I'm sure you'll fix it, then. Do you think it'll be done by five-thirty?"

"I don't see why not."

"Good. There's someone to pick up at Godalming station at six-fifteen. The London train." She turned to go. "It is nice having you back. Really like old times again, isn't it?"

And then she was gone. He stood staring after her, watching her walk toward the house, then he turned back to the carburetor and removed it from the engine.

Old times. He thought about the *old times* as he cleaned the choke-valve assembly with kerosene and a small brush. Driving young Lady Alexandra around London had been one of his chores. The summer season, the earl's daughter party-mad and dance-crazy.

Drive her here, drive her there—Chelsea to St. John's
Woods . . . Mayfair to Knightsbridge, all in one evening, the back of the car crowded with her friends.
The tango had been the craze the year of her seventeenth birthday and she'd danced it till dawn her
birthday night. He'd stood beside the car in a Chelsea
mews, gabbing sleepily with other chauffeurs while
tango music throbbed through the dark street.

Now he heard the click of her high-heeled shoes as
she came into the garage, and he looked toward her.
She hesitated a moment and then walked slowly toward him, looking slightly abashed.

"I just saw my father. I do apologize, Ross. I feel an
utter fool."

"Do you?" He grinned at her. "There are worse
things can happen to a man than being mistaken for a
chauffeur."

"I'm sure there are, but I—"

"Made an honest, and perfectly logical mistake." He
was holding the delicate mechanism of the step-up
piston and spring between his fingers. "You might do
me a favor. On the bench there—a very thin screwdriver."

She found the screwdriver and handed it to him. He
carefully transferred the tiny spring-lift piston to one
hand, tightened a small screw and set the mechanism
carefully inside the partially disassembled carburetor.

Alexandra watched him, intrigued by the proce-
dure. "Very delicately done, Ross. I always thought
mechanics just slammed things with hammers."

"That's one way."

"Father told me that you live in San Diego, California. It must be a beautiful place."

"It is. Actually, our factory is in San Diego and I

live across the bay, on Coronado Island. The navy has an air base on the north end of the island and we test our seaplanes there."

"Do you fly?"

"No. I don't like heights. I do all my testing with a slide rule. It's safer that way."

Her closeness was disturbing. The smell of her perfume mingled with the raw odor of petrol and kerosene. An unlikely mixture, he was thinking. About as unlikely as her standing next to him talking about San Diego. Out of the corner of his eye he could see the soft curve of her neck. He tried to shut his mind to it and concentrate on the ticklish job of putting the carburetor back together. He dropped a small screw into one of the vents and had to fish it out with a piece of wire.

"We'd considered going to California," she said. "My husband had been asked to spend a year at the American army hospital in San Francisco."

"He should go. It's an interesting city."

"He died a year and a half ago."

"I'm sorry."

"Thank you. Did you marry?"

"No. Haven't had the time to meet anyone. I will when things settle down. California's heaven for kids. Seems like a sin not to have any." He made one final adjustment and put the screwdriver down on the workbench. "There. That does it."

"Good as new?"

"Better, if I do say so."

She held out her hand. "I must go in and dress. It's been pleasant talking to you, Ross—and the best of luck."

He looked at her slim white hand and held up his

own, amber with kerosene. "I'll not shake hands or you'll smell of solvent for a week. But it's been good talking to you as well. I hope we see each other again before I go home."

It was the sort of thing one said in America. But why would they see each other again? What was there to see each other about? To talk of *old times?* He picked up the carburetor and took it back to the car.

"Perhaps we will," she said.

He tested the car by driving it around the long, circular drive in front of the house, stopping every few yards to satisfy himself that it wouldn't die again from lack of enough fuel. When he brought it back to the garage, the earl was waiting there with a stony-faced Banes. The chauffeur was now dressed in uniform, black cap and leather gaiters, black gloves. At least he *looked* like a proper driver of motorcars.

"Thank you most awfully, Ross," the earl said. "It sounds perfect now."

There was an offer of a drink—which Ross turned down as nicely as he could—and then he was back in his own car and grateful to be there. It had been a strange few hours.

Our Ross.

He had not been patronized in any way. It was all his own failings, not the Earl of Stanmore's or his daughter's. The problem with being at Abingdon Pryory was that he felt like *our Ross*. The servant who had come back.

"Damn," he muttered as he drove quickly down the long gravel road toward the gates. He hoped he would not see Alexandra Greville again. That wouldn't be her name now, of course—she had been married. But whatever her name was, he hoped he would not see her or be close enough to her to detect her perfume or notice the perfection of her face.

As he got out of the car to open the gates, he spotted the evening star, low and bright over the woods. A line of poetry popped into his head—a line learned at the chautauqua in Parma, Ohio. *She walks in beauty like the night* . . .

She walks in beauty. . . . He had never been able to associate that line with a living face before, but he could now.

VIII

"Hello, darling." Noel Edward Allenby Rothwell, Esq., got into the back of the car and planted a kiss on Alexandra's cheek. He sat beside her, holding her hand, while Banes saw to his luggage.

"And how was London all week?" Alexandra said.

"Lonely." He raised her hand to his lips. "Frightfully lonely."

She laughed. "But productive, I hope?"

"Oh, yes, but it was difficult to concentrate on the fruits of mammon. I found myself yearning for Saturday and four days of gracious living in company with a particularly beautiful lady." He kissed her hand again, let go of it, and patted her knee. "And lo, it came to pass."

"I think it was clever of you, Noel, to sneak four days."

"Not sneak, my dear—demand."

He settled back against the seat as the car pulled sedately away from the railway station. He felt blissfully content and very happy to be out of London. It had been a hectic week with signs of far more hectic ones to come. The financial world was in a state of flux that verged on the chaotic. Strikes in the Welsh coal mines, anarchy and civil war in Ireland, the crushing war debt were just a few of the ingredients in a pot that refused to stop boiling. And the French were not helping matters to simmer down. Their new premier, Poincaré, was determined to fly in the face of British and American opposition by tightening the screws on Germany another notch or two. Squeezing Germany until "the pips squeaked" was all very well when Lloyd George had said it during the heat of victory, but he had soon changed his mind. No one with a sense of history or a basic understanding of economics would deliberately drive a nation as large as Germany into bankruptcy and despair. International finance and trade were always in a perilous state of balance at the best of times. To destroy one country in order to bolster another, as Monsieur Poincaré appeared to be trying to do, could only result in wrecking that delicate balance beyond hope of recovery.

France felt justification, of course. The devastated land, the wrecked industry, the appalling loss of blood. But that blood could not be returned to France by trying to squeeze it out of German stones. Reparation payments had never made any sense. The draining away of German gold had only succeeded in turning the mark into a bitter joke, from twenty to the pound sterling to nearly four thousand to the pound—and inflating daily. Rubbishy bits of paper. The million and one wires that tied one nation to another through trade and finance were being cut away or tangled into a hopeless knot. What was happening in Hamburg and Cologne was starting to be felt in Glasgow and Coventry—and stocks reflected it. His week had been spent in trying to explain to bewildered clients why their portfolios were steadily shrinking in value. It was gratifying to be spending the next few days among people who, although they might have worries, certainly had no financial ones.

He looked through the window at the dark fields and hedgerows flashing past. Good English land. That's where the grand old families put the bulk of their wealth. Lord Stanmore as an example. Acres and acres of it, fields and farms and villages and more than just a few square blocks in London's West End. No sinking values there. He patted Alexandra gently on the knee again—an affectionate touch with a trace of crass familiarity.

"It's so *good* to be with you," he said—and meant every word of it.

Candlelight gleamed softly on the long, highly polished walnut dining table. The footmen made their rounds with the silver salvers. The roast was carved. The wine decanted and poured.

"Well, Noel," the earl said after the servants had left the room. "What do you think will happen in Ireland in this dogfight between the Republicans and the Dail?"

"No," Hanna said with mock severity. "I forbid political discussions at dinner, if you don't mind."

"But that's not politics, Hanna," the earl said. "It's more like war, if you ask me."

"Neither war *nor* politics has a place at the table." She smiled across at Noel. "Tell me, Noel, did your mother enjoy Spain?"

"Very much, Lady Hanna. Madrid was freezing, but Malaga was delightful."

"Yes, Andalusia is wonderful this time of year."

After dinner, there were port and cigars to be endured, and his opinion of the Irish situation to be aired and discussed, as well as other worldly matters, man to man—and then he was free to be alone with Alexandra.

They had demitasse and brandy in the library, seated side by side on a wide leather couch.

"I'm sure you must get rather bored down here in the country, Noel."

"Bored? How could anyone be bored being with you?"

"Is my company that exciting?"

"It most certainly is to me."

"Why exactly?"

He took a sip of brandy and then placed the glass on the table in front of them. "Because I feel such a sense of—*completeness* when I'm with you. It's as though a part of me has always been missing until now. A hollow man. I never knew what caused that desolation until we met. It was love, Alexandra. I fell in love with you—an emotion I'd never felt before for any woman." He turned to her and placed his hands on her shoulders. "It's a moment like this when I wish I were a poet—to tell you how I feel. All I can say is that I love you very much."

She smiled and touched the side of his face with her fingertips. "You do mean that, don't you, Noel?"

Bending his head, he brushed his lips across the back of her wrist. "You know I do."

They had kissed often during the past three months, but he felt a passion in her this time that surprised him. Her torso pressed against his and he eased her gently—oh, so gently—down on the couch. His fingers lightly touched the side of her right breast, a soft caress, the warmth of her flesh felt through the thin silk of her gown. Her mouth worked against his own and he fought against the urge to shift his hand to her legs. Gently . . . gently . . . He drew his head back and looked down at her closed eyes, her parted lips. He touched her eyelids.

"Dear Alexandra. If I only knew for certain."

She opened her eyes and studied his face. "Knew what, Noel?"

"That you would consent to marry me."

"You'd have to ask me to find out."

He got onto his knees before her, praying that she would find the gesture romantic and not slightly ridiculous.

"Will you marry me, my darling?"

"Yes." Her tone was thoughtful. "I think so, Noel."

And that was that. She looked gravely at her image in the dressing-table mirror as she unpinned her long hair, knowing in her heart that she had not so much made a decision as drifted into one. It had certainly made Noel happy. Her upper arms were sore where he had gripped her, and her lips tender from his kisses. In the morning he would go through the formality of asking for her father's permission and then they would be engaged. A June wedding, he felt, in London, Saint George's, Hanover Square, with the reception as Claridge's. A small wedding. Just family and a few friends.

She undressed and looked down at her body before slipping into her nightgown. Not exactly the perfect figure for 1922. More Peter Paul Rubens than John Held—the breasts too large, the hips too round. There were stretch marks across her abdomen from Colin. It had not been a difficult delivery, but he had been a large baby, over eight pounds. She had carried him high and had gained a great deal of weight. That weight was gone now, but it had left its marks—all to be revealed to Noel in June. And no one had ever held her naked except Robbie.

She awoke late after a deep, dreamless sleep and barely had time to dress and drink a cup of coffee before leaving for church service in Abingdon. She sat between her father and mother in the car, Noel on the jump seat facing her, smiling at her the whole way with a tiny we-share-a-secret smile. He own smile felt forced and lacking in joy.

After the service, Noel and her father strolled off by themselves in the rectory gardens and she stood with her mother in front of the church.

"Noel is acting a little oddly this morning, isn't he?" Hanna said.

"He has something to ask Papa."

"Oh?"

"I told Noel last night that I'd marry him."

Hanna's relief and happiness could not be expressed in words. She hugged her daughter to her, oblivious to the glances of the other worshipers who were leaving the church.

"I hope I'm doing the right thing," Alexandra said.

Hanna gave her a final hug and stepped back. "But of course you are, dear. How could you doubt it? He's a charming, exceedingly handsome man from a fine old Cheshire family. He'll make a perfect husband. I can't tell you how happy this makes me—and your father. We're not exactly blind, you know. We've discussed the possibilities. Noel's attraction to you has been obvious from the start."

"Yes, I suppose it has."

"Your father and I have even discussed the wedding gift. Something you could both enjoy. A London house, perhaps. In Belgravia or Mayfair."

"I'm sure Noel would like that."

"Nothing ostentatious. There are some charming smaller houses to be found near Belgrave Square or off South Audley Street."

The two men joined them, both smiling, her father with an arm draped across Noel's shoulder. All settled and done.

"So very pleased," her father was saying, bending to kiss her cheek. "So very pleased for both of you."

Going home in the car, the talk was of banns and announcements and the sheer mechanics of getting wed. She felt alien to the conversation. She had married Robbie in the front parlor of a justice's house outside Toronto, and after the ceremony the justice's wife had served them coffee and angel food cake. The justice's wife had been eight months along also and they had discussed their various discomforts and mutual joys without the slightest trace of embarrassment.

The earl cooled a bottle of Dom Perignon, performing the ceremony of twirling the bottle in the ice bucket and popping the cork himself while Coatsworth stood by. A father's privilege, he said, to pour champagne to bless his daughter's engagement.

"To happiness," he said, raising his glass.

"Happiness," Alexandra murmured.

After lunch she walked with Noel along the terrace and then down the curving stone steps into the Italian gardens, the wild March wind shaking the topiary-work and bending the cypress.

"You seem very subdued, Alexandra."

"Do I? Sorry. Just thinking, I suppose."

"Not second thoughts, I hope."

"No, of course not."

He stopped walking and pulled her close, hands buried in the deep fur of her coat collar. "Now look here. I know what you're thinking. But the past is over and done with. A clean slate from here on in. Mrs. Noel Rothwell. Although your father has made me the gracious offer of the family name. How does Mrs. Noel *Greville*-Rothwell sound to you?"

"Very nice. Quite melodic, in fact."

"Yes," he laughed, "it does trip lightly off the tongue. It will take me some time to get used to it. Noel Edward Allenby *Greville*-Rothwell. With a name like that I should stand for Parliament!" He kissed her impulsively on the lips. "Oh, Alexandra. I shall make you very, *very* happy."

"As happy as yourself, Noel?"

"Happier, my dearest—if such a thing is possible."

It had been, by any standard one cared to apply, a remarkable few days. From Sunday noon, when he had walked with her father into the rectory gardens, to Wednesday noon when she had seen him off to London at Godalming station, Noel had been thrust firmly into the bosom of the family with a gratitude that would have seemed puzzling to anyone not acquainted with the facts. She had made him aware of the facts—all of them—during a weekend in January. His second weekend stay at the house. They had walked down the drive to the gates and back, walking slowly while she talked. She had told him everything—

her affair with Robin Mackendric in France during the war, and then of her decision to live with him in Canada. Of Robin's efforts to get a divorce from his wife in Aberdeen, and of how the divorce had finally been granted and then made final shortly before Colin was born. Everything.

"I understand," he said, holding her hand tightly.

Of course he did. He was an intelligent and perceptive man. She was—at least by the code of her father—slightly damaged goods. Noel Edward Allenby Rothwell understood that code very well, even if he himself did not consider it applicable in this day and age, and certainly not in the present circumstances.

"I understand perfectly, Alexandra, and I admire you greatly for telling me. It doesn't lower my regard for you one iota. In fact, I must say, it makes me love you more."

Love you . . . love you . . . love you . . .

She had no doubt that he loved her. And why not? She would bring a great many things into his life, *Greville*-Rothwell being just one of them.

Did she love him?

She pondered the question on the drive back to the house as she tried to visualize the type of life they would lead together. Very social. Small dinner parties in their London house—Belgravia, Noel thought; so many parvenus in Mayfair these days—and long weekends at the Pryory. He would hunt and go shooting with his friends and she would go shopping and have tea with hers. There would be jaunts to Paris and the south of France. Winter cruises to Greece and Egypt. A boarding school for Colin when he was eight or nine. Children of their own, no doubt. Noel was a strong, virile man. He would probably give her more sexual enjoyment in bed than Robbie, his thoughts always on some trying case or other, had been capable of giving. But Robbie had given her *pleasure*— pleasure in a thousand little ways that would have been impossible to explain to anyone. She did not experience that kind of intangible gladness around Noel. Perhaps she would in time. Perhaps she would feel a regard for him that would pass for love, but she didn't love him now because she couldn't find anything about him to love.

But did it matter? She had been in love, and that emotion could never be recaptured. It was something she would hold in her heart forever, secret and inviolate. Noel would, as her mother had said, make a good husband. She would make him a good wife. Not a marriage made in heaven, perhaps, but certainly one that could not be faulted. And one that pleased her parents. The distressing past all forgotten now. Their happiness showed and she felt a kind of peace—a sense of atonement.

She filled her days by walking. Poor Mary, who suffered terribly from bunions, was not up to walking along country roads and across fields. The elegant, high-wheeled pram so suitable for the gravel paths of Regent's Park was totally useless at Abingdon, except on the terrace. And, besides, Colin balked at it now. He could walk along like a trooper on his sturdy little legs, flopping down when he was tired or holding up his arms to be carried. One of the grooms had devised a carrying sling for her from an old canvas rucksack. She could carry Colin in it, his legs dangling from the two holes in the bottom, the strap around her shoulder, and the baby riding comfortably against her hip.

She hiked to the top of Burgate Hill in that fashion, her son bouncing gently against her right hip, a light wicker basket in her left hand. When they reached the top, she put Colin down and let him wander among the daffodils and crocuses beginning to thrust up from the ground. She lay back in the grass to catch her breath and then opened the basket and took out the sandwiches and the vacuum bottle of milky tea that cook had prepared for them. They sat facing each other, eating the sandwiches and drinking the warm tea, and then Colin rolled onto his back with a cry and pointed toward the sky. "Mama! See! See! Mama, see! . . ."

She leaned back on her elbows, hearing it now, and saw the airplane sweep in and out of the great white clouds. It banked sharply—dived—looped—engine sound pulsing against the earth. Colin pressed his hands against his ears and squealed with delight. And then it was gone from overhead, flashing down toward the airfield at Blackworth's five miles away.

"By God," Sir Angus cried, "I'm not a drinkin' man, but, *by God*, I'm goin' to get drunk tonight!"

Ross grinned at him. "I might just join you."

The plane, a converted BFC-3, powered by the new Argo engine, taxied toward them, the pilot blipping the engine in triumph. When he cut the switch and the plane rolled to a stop, he jumped out, waved his arms like a madman, and ran toward them.

"Bloody fantastic! I can't tell you—simply *can't!*"

"Just simmer down, Gerald, and tell us all about it."

"It's a bloody marvel." The pilot took off his leather flying helmet and grinned foolishly at Sir Angus.

"Like being shot from a bloody cannon! I had her up to a hundred and sixty going over Guildford on the straight and level. Did you see me do that loop over Burgate Hill?"

"We did that," Sir Angus said.

"Not a cough—not a miss. Talk about smooth as bloody silk!"

"When she's refueled, take 'er up again. See how she does at twenty thousand feet."

"No need. I had her at twenty-two thousand over Farnborough." He tapped the notepad strapped to his leg. "Bloody fucking cold up there, but I'll decipher my notes."

"Good lad." Sir Angus clapped him on the shoulder. "Go get yourself a cup of tea and a tot of rum."

"Well," Sir Angus said, watching the pilot hurry off toward the hangars, "we did it, by God. We did it, lad."

"It looks like it."

"I have an ear, Ross. I closed my eyes when he took off and just listened. I could tell by the sound we'd done it. I didn't see him loop over the hill, I *heard* him loop. Not a beat lost—not a stroke. She's a blinkin' marvel, Ross."

They walked across the tarmac to the plane and stood in front of the engine, looking up at it, inhaling the odor of hot oil and burnt petrol. The mountings on the plane had been adapted to fit the big engine. With its oversize cylinders and large manifolds, the engine made the slender plane look overburdened and front-heavy—but it had flown like a dream.

Sir Angus reached out and touched the propeller. "The only way, Ross. I don't give dog turds for testin' on the frames. Take 'em up is my way. See what they'll do in the bleedin' air. We done it, Ross. May just be the best air-cooled engine in the world."

"I think so. Yes."

"The point now is—the blinkin' next problem is—gettin' these brutes rollin' off the line in quantity. I'll need the first three to put on the Atlas. When I fly that plane for buyers with these engines on her, I'll have more orders than I can fill. That means an extension of my credit line with Cox's Bank. And *that* means more engine workers on the payroll. I'll be able to have the first fifteen of your thirty crated for shipping by the end of August."

"That would be perfect."

"But if you could stay until May or early June—just to make bloody sure they're comin' off the line proper. Is that too much to ask of you, Ross?"

"I don't think so. I'll send a cablegram to my partner and explain the situation. We need these engines, Angus. Without them, we've got nothing."

"That puts us in the same boat, lad. But we *do* have somethin'. And that's why we're going to dent a bottle of Old Highlander and make bloody damn fools of ourselves!"

He worked longer hours in the engine plant than was necessary. The Blackworth foremen and assemblers had gotten the hang of the Argo-450's unique assembly problems and the engines were being completed, tested on the frame, and certified with gratifying efficiency. Every engine was then bolted onto the old BFC-3 scout-bomber and air-tested to make doubly sure there were no hidden flaws in the radial intake manifold and exhaust system that Ross had designed.

"We can stop air-testin' soon," Sir Angus said one morning. "She's as near perfect as we'll ever get 'er. You can be headin' back to San Diego in a week or two—that is, if you're satisfied."

"I'm satisfied now," Ross said. "But if anything starts to malfunction, I don't want it to be six thousand miles from here."

He continued to put in long hours, partly because he wanted the engines to be perfect, and partly because he didn't know what to do with himself if he wasn't working. Lying in bed at night, listening to the April wind splatter rain against the windows, he thought of San Diego . . . the Coronado Hotel . . . the palms rustling, the surf hissing across the sand. He yearned for the sun, the long bay of bright blue water, the slender strands of beach curving south toward the brown hills of Mexico. He was, by Jesus, *bloody homesick!*

They no longer worked on Saturday. It made a long two days for him. Nothing much to do on Saturday except take in a picture at the Abingdon cinema palace or drive into Guildford if there were a football match, and nothing at all to do on Sunday but stay home and read technical journals or sit at his drafting table and fool around with new designs.

It was on a Saturday afternoon, as he was walking along High Street toward the cinema, that he saw Alexandra again. She was walking slowly toward him, looking into the shop windows, a little boy beside her, tugging at her hand. She saw him and smiled.

"Well, hello—Mr. Ross."

Being called *Mr.* Ross by her startled him for a moment. He wasn't quite sure how to address her.

"Lovely afternoon, isn't it?" she continued. "I was sure it would rain."

"Yes—so was I."

The little boy was looking up at him, silent and curious. "And what's your name?" Ross asked, bending down to him.

"Colin," Alexandra said. "My son—Colin Mackendric."

"I like the name Colin. I had a friend called Colin," he said to the boy. "My best friend. We used to collect conkers, soak them in brine for a few days, drill holes in them, put them on strings, and have conker fights. Do you play with conkers?"

Colin stared at him.

"He's a bit young for that," Alexandra said.

"Yes, he is—for fighting with them. But they're fun to collect. Just find a big horse-chestnut tree and peel the seed out of the pod."

"He likes aeroplanes, don't you, Colin? Mr. Ross works at the place where the aeroplanes come from." She looked at Ross and smiled. "There's a plane that buzzes Burgate Hill sometimes when we're picnicking there. Colin loves it."

"So do I. We're testing our new engine in that plane. I'll tell the pilot to wave next time."

"That would make Colin happy. He waves at the pilot."

Colin had stopped tugging at her hand. He stood quietly beside her staring at Ross.

"Would you like to see the plane close up, Colin?" Ross asked him. "Perhaps your mama could bring you out to the aerodrome one day."

"Now," Colin said with an almost grim firmness. "*Now.*"

"Now?" Ross laughed a little uncomfortably. "Knows what he wants, doesn't he!"

"Oh, yes," Alexandra said. "Determination is his middle name." She touched her son lightly on top of his head. "But not today, dear. Mr. Ross doesn't have the time."

"Now," Colin said. "Now . . ."

"We'll have tea at that shop you like, Colin. You can have an ice and a gooseberry tart—or a jam roll. Would you like a jam roll?"

"Aero-plane," Colin muttered. "Want aero-plane."

"I think he's made up his mind," Ross said.

"I've never seen him quite this intractable before."

"Look," he said impulsively. "I'm not doing anything, Mrs. Mackendric. If you can spare an hour, we could drive out to Blackworth's in my car and give Colin a look at the plane."

Alexandra frowned, then looked at Colin, who was tugging at her hand impatiently.

"Well . . . if you're sure it's no trouble for you."

"None at all," he said a little too quickly. "I'd enjoy it. It's just a short walk to my house, Rose Lane."

"Very well," she said. "We'll go."

She sat beside him, Colin on her lap, and he did all the talking. Was almost afraid to stop—afraid that if he did stop, she would have nothing to say—afraid of silence. He talked about the engine and Sir Angus and about San Diego and the many things a person could do there on the weekends—the sailing . . . swimming in the ocean . . . the dances at the Coronado Hotel.

"You must be anxious to get back."

"I am, Mrs. Mackendric. I miss it."

"I wish you'd call me Alexandra. Your name's Jamie, isn't it?"

"James . . . Jim . . . Jamie. Jamie mostly. I used to spell my name J-a-*i*-m-i-e just to be different. Of course, it's pronounced the same. I don't know why I did it. Just an affectation, I suppose. People do things like that when they're young."

"I know. When I was at school I began to sign my name with an 'e' on the end instead of an 'a'—and put an accent on it as well. The mistresses soon put a stop to *that* nonsense."

"Yes, I'm sure they did. Well, I'm just plain Jamie now."

"And plain Alexandra."

"It's a lovely name."

"Do you think so?"

"Yes. Yes, I do."

"I was never that fond of it. There seemed to be so many girls at school with that name. I felt that children should be allowed to choose their own names. I would have chosen something exotic—like Francesca . . . or Consuela."

"I had an aunt named Florette, but everyone called her just plain Flo."

She laughed. "Of course. If I'd called myself Francesca, it would have turned into *Franny!*"

His hands felt sweaty on the wheel. Her perfume was subtle but intoxicating. Glancing at her as he drove, he marveled at the delicacy of her profile, the astonishing color of her hair, her skin and eyes. Staring ahead at the road he thought of a song the navy fliers would sing at the hotel bar in Coronado—no liquor served there now that Prohibition was in effect, but the fliers getting very happy on the "tea" they drank from plain china pots. The fliers in their white uniforms singing: *Down in Pensacola there's a blue-eyed blonde, a blue-eyed blonde, a blue-eyed blonde, and if I crash tomorrow I won't give a darn if that blue-eyed blonde loves me. . . .* Whoever wrote that song must have seen Alexandra Mackendric.

He parked the car near one of the Blackworth hangars. Across the field an RAF Bristol F.-2B fighter was being worked on and the stuttering howl of its engine could be heard plainly, causing Colin to jump up and down and clap his hands at the noise. Ross reached for him, afraid for a moment that he might decide to run off across the landing field toward it. There were three other Brisfits in the air, the pilots practicing takeoffs and landings. The squadron was Air Auxiliary, weekend fliers, and Saturday and Sunday were busy days. He lifted Colin up so that he could get a better view as one of the silver-painted planes came in over the low trees at the end of the runway and touched down. The boy screamed in a kind of ecstasy.

"Crazy about machines, isn't he?"

"He certainly seems to be," Alexandra said. "I don't know how he inherited that trait. His father was hopeless. We had a Moon coupe in Canada that was always on the blink. Robbie's only proven method of fixing it was a good kick."

"Sounds like a man after my own heart. Best thing you can do to some cars, just kick the hell out of them—if you'll excuse the language."

"You should have heard Robin Mackendric!"

He carried Colin into hangar number four on his

shoulder. There were men standing on the scaffolding erected around the three new engines on the Argus. Work on the transport plane was a seven-day-a-week business. One of the men glanced down and called out, "Mr. Ross, sir! Happy to see you."

"What's the matter, George? Having some problems?"

"There's something a bit odd about the intake manifold bolts on number two engine."

"Where's Sir Angus?"

"Went up to London, sir, with Mr. Haverman and Mr. Tess."

"Want me to have a look at it?"

"If you wouldn't mind, sir."

"All right." He put Colin down and started to take off his coat. "Are you up there, Mick?"

A young man in white coveralls peeked around one of the engines.

"Yes, Mr. Ross, sir."

"Hop down, will you?"

The man swung down from the scaffold and walked toward them, wiping his hands on a rag. "Mick, this is Mrs. Mackendric and her son, Colin. Would you mind showing them around? Young Colin here is potty about planes. Put him in the cockpit of the BFC, but watch the lad. He just might try and take her up for a spin!"

Later, she touched his arm as they walked back to the car, Colin walking between them in a kind of daze.

"He's never had such a wonderful afternoon. I wish you could have seen his face when that man—Mick—put him into the cockpit."

"I can imagine," Ross said. "I'm glad he enjoyed himself."

She glanced at him. "You really *are* glad, aren't you?"

"Why wouldn't I be? I like seeing kids have a good time."

"You look like you had a good time yourself. There's oil all over your shirt."

He looked down and dabbed futilely at a smear of dark grease across the front of his shirt.

"Hazard of the trade. And it won't wash out, I'm afraid. My fault for not putting on coveralls."

Colin reached up and touched the stain. "Bad Jamie. Got all dirty. Bad—*bad* Jamie."

Ross picked him up and put him into the car. "I'll get spanked for that."

The little boy put his hands on Ross's face. "No," he said solemnly. "Colin won't let."

Noel drove down from London and arrived late Saturday night, looking forward to a day's riding. But Sunday dawned in a torrent of rain and there was nothing much to do except play cards with Alexandra or shoot a few games of snooker with the earl. He'd purchased a stuffed animal from a large toy shop in Regent Street, but Colin seemed to disdain it. Seated on the floor in the nursery when he'd unwrapped it, the box and the wrappings occupied him more than the quite expensive bear.

"Thank Mr. Rothwell, Colin," Alexandra had said tightly.

"Thank you," he had repeated. Then he had done the most extraordinary thing. He had suddenly jumped up, thrust his arms out from his sides, and raced around the nursery making ugly slurping sounds—*Brrrrrrrrrr . . . brrrrrrrrrr . . . brrrrrrrrrr . . .*

"What on earth . . . ?" Noel had said.

"He thinks he's an aeroplane."

On one of Colin's frenzied passes around the nursery, he had kicked the bear into a far corner of the room and had kept on moving—*Brrrrrrrrrr . . . brrrrrrrrrr . . . brrrrrrrrrr . . .*

The child's behavior had rankled Noel all day and he brought up the subject late that night as he sat beside Alexandra in the library.

"Young Colin seemed a bit out of hand today, Alexandra."

"I wouldn't put it that way. He was utterly horrid." She took a sip of her brandy and stared at the fire. "It was being in the house all day. He wanted to go up Burgate Hill and see the aeroplane. I told him the plane didn't fly in the rain, but I don't think he believed me."

"Just temper, then?"

"Not temper so much as pure frustration. He's big for his age and simply bursting with energy. He wears poor Mary out."

"It's not my business, of course—not yet, anyway—but it appears to me that the boy requires stricter disciplining. You should hire a nanny who won't tolerate any nonsense."

"Mary's a good soul."

"It's not her soul that concerns me. The child must learn to be a gentleman. If he doesn't learn now, he's going to find himself in a great deal of trouble when he begins school. I don't believe this nanny is capable of giving him the type of early training he needs. With your permission, I'd be happy to interview some women when I get back to London."

"Leave it for a while, Noel. I'll have a long talk with Mary."

"Whatever you wish." He drained his glass and set it on the table. "He's really a fine little man. We can't permit him to turn into a larrikin, now can we?"

He sensed that he might have upset her, and when he took her in his arms he did so with particular tenderness. Her reaction surprised him. She clung to him fiercely.

"Darling . . ." he whispered.

She lay back on the couch while he kissed her throat and the deep hollow between her breasts. Turning her head, she watched the fire burning gently in the grate and heard the rain on the terrace stones. A feeling had come over her while Noel had been talking—an odd, elusive sensation that had nagged like a half-forgotten memory. It had come and gone in an instant, leaving her with a thought that stunned her. It was an image of Saturday afternoon, of Colin perched on the shoulders of Ross. The sensation she had felt at that time and only thought of now was . . . pleasure. The pleasure she had always felt with Robbie, a pleasure that went far beyond what Noel was attempting to give her with his lips—a pleasure of the heart.

* * *

Colin was a trial all day Monday as the rain continued to stream down. He drove his nanny to despair and
his mother to numbness. It was one of his "backward"
days. He would not walk forward—even the stairs had
to be climbed backward. He would not put things
into his toy box, only take things out. He insisted,
with shrieks of determination, that he must sleep
with his head toward the foot of the bed. When he
had won his battle to do that, he was as exhausted as
his nanny and dropped off to sleep as though hit on
the head—an action contemplated by many during the
long, wet day.

Tuesday dawned clear and fair, with only a few
ragged tails of cloud as reminders of the storm. Colin
was awake at cockcrow, stole silently out of the nursery, and then ran down the hall to his mother's room
and plopped noisily into bed beside her. She tried to
calm him back to sleep, but he teased and fretted until she had promised to take him up to Burgate Hill—
"But not one second before lunchtime." It satisfied
him. He lay quietly beside her while she slept on,
staring up at the sun-specked ceiling and making
barely audible motor sounds through pursed lips.

The plane came over twice during the two hours
they were on the hilltop. In both cases it flew very
low, circling the hill three times, the pilot waving at
them, his white silk scarf fluttering behind him in the
slipstream. Colin waved back with both hands, leap-
ing and screaming in a paroxysm of joy.

"Jamie! Jamie! See! See! Jamie! . . ."

"That's not Jamie," she told him. "Jamie doesn't fly
aeroplanes, he builds them."

"No, Mama—no! Jamie! Jamie!"

She let it go at that. When she brought him home he

was soaked to the skin from the wet grass and so tired and content that he fell asleep in the hot bath and Mary had to hold his head above water while she soaped him.

She waited until after six o'clock and then asked the Guildford exchange for his number—Abingdon 314. The phone rang six times before he picked up the receiver.

"Hello?" He sounded concerned.

"I'm sorry," she said. "Did I disturb you?"

There was a long pause. "Mrs. Mackendric?"

"Alexandra. I called to thank you for what you did. The pilot waved, Colin waved back—and a very happy boy is sound asleep."

Ross laughed softly. "I told Gerald to come in low over Burgate and, if he saw two dots, to wave. He enjoyed doing it. Came back on the second flight, I understand."

"Oh, yes. Two delightful performances. Colin was convinced it was you. I didn't have the heart to remind him you said you were afraid of heights."

"Tell him only people with feathers can fly."

"I don't think he would believe that."

"I *know* he wouldn't. A very clever lad, your son."

There was a sudden silence. Her hand began to tremble as it held the receiver. "Are you sure I'm not interrupting anything?"

"No . . . no. I was expecting a call from London and jumped out of the tub."

"I'd better hang up then."

"No," he said quickly. "If the line's busy, he'll ring back."

"You'll catch cold."

"I have a dry towel. I'm glad you called. I wasn't

sure if I told you how much I enjoyed the other day—
showing you and the nipper about. It—it was a pleasure."

"For—us, too."

"Good. Perhaps . . ."

"Yes, certainly," she said quickly.

"Saturday, then?"

"That would be difficult, I'm afraid. I have a guest
coming down from London for the weekend."

"Tomorrow? I'm at loose ends. We could make a
sort of day of it. Go by the field so Colin can watch
the plane take off, and then drive up to Dorking and
have lunch at Burford Bridge."

"That sounds wonderful. I'll have cook fix up a
hamper. Colin loves picnics."

He cleared his throat. "How—I mean to say—"

"We could come to your place about ten o'clock and
go on from there in your car. It would be—easier that
way."

"Yes—very much easier. Tomorrow, then."

"Yes. Tomorrow."

She hung up. Her heart was thumping and she
could do nothing for a moment but stare at the black
instrument as though in disbelief that she had actually
been speaking into it—to Jamie Ross of all people.

He had a good face—honest, open, easy to smile and
laugh. The freckles and sandy hair gave him a boyish
look. And he had a boy's enthusiasm for life, chatting
away as he drove the car, holding Colin spellbound
with stories about seaplanes, about kite-flying from
the cliffs at a place called La Jolla, about swimming
in the ocean at Christmastime, fiestas in Mexico. . . .

She looked away from him and gazed at the woods and meadows beyond Dorking, not really seeing anything. He was in no way similar to Robin Mackendric. Robbie had been outwardly grave and taciturn. Only she—and his patients—had known the warmth and compassion beneath the shell. And yet he reminded her strongly of Robbie. She felt at ease with him. She felt—happy.

They found a stand of horse-chestnut trees near the top of Boxs Hill—a long, hard climb up from the road. She rested, spreading a plaid blanket on the grass, while Colin and Jamie Ross searched for the spiny green pods which, when opened, revealed large shiny seeds.

"Lord," Ross said, flopping onto the grass near her, "that lad could wear a stevedore down to his knees."

"Yes," she said, sitting up and undoing the straps on the hamper. "And he can eat like one, too."

"So can I, if it comes to that." He watched her remove a cold roast chicken, hard-boiled eggs, celery, cheeses, and a bottle of cider. "The Grevilles always were good providers."

She gave him a thoughtful look. "Do I make you think of those days, Jamie—of servants' hall?"

He frowned and plucked at a piece of grass. "I'm not unaware of having been—your man Ross . . . but I'm not uncomfortable with you, if that's what you mean. I'm not the same bloke, am I? Or, anyway, I keep telling myself I'm not. But if I hadn't been his lordship's chauffeur, I wouldn't have thought twice about driving to the Pryory this morning and picking up you and Colin."

"Yes, I know."

"But I don't look at you and say, 'My God, I'm having a picnic in the woods with *Lady* Alexandra.' I just see you as—well, as a beautiful and charming woman who's easy to be with."

"Thank you, Jamie. That was a nice thing to say."

Colin saw the food and hurried over, his pockets filled with horse-chestnut seeds. After eating, he wanted to go for a walk, or a roll down the hill, or to climb a tree if Jamie would lift him up to the branches. But his frenetic burst of energy dissipated rapidly and he rolled onto his stomach on the blanket and fell instantly asleep. Ross covered him with his sweater.

"Out like a light."

"He likes you, Jamie. So do I."

He stared down at the boy for a moment and then looked at her. There was no mistaking what he saw in her eyes. As he took her in his arms—the softness of her body against him, her lips against his own—his thoughts whirled off in all directions. It wasn't possible—it wasn't *right*—and yet, in this world—topsy-turvy—upside down—everything changing, spinning toward unthought-of horizons—could he? Could she? And then he gave up thinking altogether, lost in the fever of their embrace.

IX

Jacob Golden bought a copy of the *Daily Post* outside Victoria Station and scanned through it as his taxi crawled through the West End traffic toward Soho. He found what he was looking for on page six, the editorial page, and was wryly amused by what he read there.

OUR VIEW

It is the opinion of the *Daily Post* that the libel action being brought by Major General Sir. B. D. Sparrowfield against Mr. M. Rilke, which will be heard before Mr. Justice Larch this coming Friday, 21st April, is a most unwelcome undertaking at this time. We fail to see what possible benefit the plaintiff can derive from such a suit. It will surely bring into sharp question the decisions the general and his staff made during an abortive attack against the German lines at Thiepval one fateful day in August 1916—a place and time in history that, we firmly believe, the overwhelming majority of Englishmen would as soon forget. . . .

Jacob smiled, folded the newspaper into a tight square, and slipped it into the pocket of his coat. He turned his head to look out of the window at Piccadilly.

"Hypocrites," he murmured.

He was thirty-two and looked much younger, a tall, thin, dark-haired man with a face of almost feminine delicacy. The female quality was enhanced by large, soft brown eyes, a complexion of olive-hued ivory, and his curly hair. The mouth saved him from prettiness. A taut slash, the lips usually curled in mockery.

He went up the stairs to his flat lugging a heavy leather suitcase. He smiled when he went inside and looked around. Martin's presence in the place was obvious by the neatness. After dumping his suitcase in his bedroom, he opened a cold bottle of champagne and stretched out on the parlor sofa. He was still there, drinking champagne, smoking cigarettes, and reading back issues of *The Times*, when Martin came home. Martin eyed the sea of tossed away newspapers littering the floor.

"Well, I can tell *you're* back."

Jacob raised himself and grinned. "Is that all the welcome I get, old boy? Sarcastic chastisement?"

"Of course not," Martin said wearily. "It's damn good to see you. Any champagne left?"

"Bottles and bottles. Do join."

Jacob Golden had few friends—his choice. People, he had once said to Martin, are too pathetic to be taken seriously and far too devious to be befriended. His caustic aphorisms tended to infuriate and had done so since he was a boy. His father had unwittingly placed him in a renowned and ancient preparatory school whose boys had dismissed Jacob instantly as "that thin Jew." A school of such stupefying snobbery and random cruelty that his only defense against it had been his withering tongue. He would have been in for severe physical reprisals by enraged peers if an upper-form boy, captain of his house and the school eleven, had not come to his defense and made it known that Jacob was to be left alone. Fenton Wood-Lacy had not so much befriended Jacob as he had placed him under the wings of his protection, the way he might have protected a wet and starving cat from mindless cruelty. That singular act had made Fenton a friend for life—an honor that, at times, Fenton could gladly have done without. Jacob's friendship with Martin was less easily explained. Their very oppositeness had something to do with it—light and shadow, mirth and grief, faith and despair. Martin viewed mankind with compassion, tolerance, and hope. Jacob viewed its dark underside and saw no hope for it at all.

"I was beginning to think you had departed forever," Martin said as he came back into the room unwinding the wire around a bottle's cork. "You could have dropped me a line from time to time."

"I could have, yes, but I knew you were staying abreast of my wanderings. I kept running into your lads in the most god-forsaken places."

"I know," Martin said dryly. "They kept mailing in your IOU's."

"Well, I'm sure you understand, dear chap. When one works for the League of Nations, one does so at considerable financial sacrifice. I was sent out to report on world hunger, not to become a part of it. Rest assured I shall pay back every penny."

The cork made a satisfactory pop. "All debts squared—by me. Call it rent. I love this dump."

"I know you do, dear old fellow. That's why I had no qualms about tapping your grossly overpaid correspondents for a fiver or two."

"How was the trip?"

"Interesting." He sat up and held out his empty glass for a refill. "Full of insoluble problems—and sobering revelations. I stayed out longer than I had to. Thrace . . . Bulgaria . . . followed the Black Sea into the Ukraine and on as far as the Don. The land of the Fisher King and Chapels Perilous—waste and barren. Even the crows eat stones." He took a sip of champagne. "I killed a man in the Ukraine, Martin. I thought you might like to know."

Martin sat in a chair facing the sofa and placed the bottle on the floor. "If you want to tell me."

"It's ironic, actually," Jacob said. "I mean, after all, I did go to prison for two years as a conscientious objector. Felt rather proud of my pacifism—almost smug, in fact. A Red Army commissar took a fancy to me—tall, strapping woman named Lyubov—but that's another story. Anyway, she sent two troopers with me as an escort when I left Berdichev for Kiev. We were jumped on the second day by a party of roving Whites. I had no arms and one of my Red trooper friends tossed me a pistol—a big heavy Mauser with a wood handle. Needed both hands to hold the damn thing. These bandits, or whatever they were, must have been half drunk, because they rode straight toward us swinging sabers above their heads. I rested the Mauser on my horse's neck and fired at a man with a yellow beard. Caught him flush and he must have been dead before he fell out of the saddle. The

Reds disposed of two more, and the others scattered. The one I hit lay on his back, a tiny dark hole in his forehead—like a cigarette burn in a blanket. So much for 'Thou shalt not kill.' "

"It was him or you."

"That's what the judge at my conscientious-objector hearing asked me, something about what I'd do if a ruddy big German was coming at me with a bayonet— *him or you?* Told him I'd reason with the bloke. Got a laugh from the gallery. Glib and witty Jacob Golden." He took a drink of champagne. "I've been somewhat of a fraud most of my life, Martin. The fact is, I killed him and felt damn good that he was dead and I wasn't dangling from the end of his sword."

"A fairly normal reaction, I would say."

"I suppose it is, but I've always taken the not-so-normal approach to things, haven't I? Always marched to a different drummer just for the sake of being out of step with others. It was a revelation, Martin."

"That you're just an ordinary man after all? Don't let it bother you. We are all ordinary men. You're alive. That's all that counts."

"Yes, I'm alive." He lit a cigarette. "The point now is, where do I go from here? I'm considered something of a hero in pacifist circles. I don't quite see how I can still march in those ranks after bumping off people like some later-day Billy the Kid."

"If you turned the other cheek, Jacob, that cossack would have sliced it right off your face. Even the most ardent pacifist would understand that."

"I'm sure you're right. Still, it does make one think a bit. How easy it is to justify murder if one's own skin is in jeopardy. It's made me view war in a rather different light. And speaking of war, are you as amused as I am by the *Post*'s pious turnabout?"

"Not particularly. They sniff a trend. After all, they didn't achieve the largest circulation in the world by swimming *against* the tide."

"Did you know they were going to jump onto your side?"

"No. It was a complete surprise. But I'm grateful for it."

"I knew. The Guv'nor told me. He telephoned me in Geneva last week."

"Oh? The two of you are talking again, I take it."

"If one conversation can be considered *talking*. He wants to see me about something important. Wouldn't say what it was."

"Is that why you came back?"

"Partly. I also came back because I quit my job with the League. Need a good reporter who speaks five languages and works cheap?"

"Anytime."

"Thanks, old chap, but I wouldn't allow you to burden yourself. No, I think I'll just knock about for a bit and try to get my jangled senses back in tune."

"Did you ever get my letter about Charles, by the way?"

"Yes. It was forwarded on to me in Bucharest. Made me jolly glad, I can tell you. The Guv'nor brought that up, too. Told me he found a picture in the morgue. Me the day I was arrested—astride the barrel of that howitzer in Trafalgar Square, tossing those pamphlets of Charlie's court-martial hearing into the crowd. I don't imagine anyone bothered to read a copy. Not the sort of stuff people were interested in, was it? I suppose they are now, though. Your book was selling like mad in Paris."

"Here as well."

Jacob smiled wryly and drained his glass. "And the jolly old *Daily Post* is aware of it, too. I think they want to ride on the bandwagon." He looked at his watch. "Now's as good a time as any to see the Gov-'nor. I wish you'd come with me. I'm substantially fortified with bubbly, but not quite up to facing the old boy alone."

The *Daily Post* building loomed over Fleet Street, its myriad glass windows and thin, fluted stone columns giving it the appearance of some vast Victorian railway station. Broad stone steps flanked by two cast-iron lions led to cathedral-size doors of gray-green bronze. Fleet Street wags called the place "The Golden temple." And it was. Harry Golden's monument to his journalism. Harry Golden—the great Lord Crewe.

"I'm just a Hebrew lad from Whitechapel who made his way in the world" was how Lord Crewe had described himself once to a magazine writer. There was no one who would dispute that claim, although the impression of a barefoot lad roaming the streets of the East End was far from the truth. Only the highly profitable family printing business had been in Whitechapel. Young Harry had grown up in a pleasant suburban house in Hampstead. But he had definitely made his way in the world, taking over, in 1885 at the age of thirty, a near-moribund newspaper called the *London and Provinces Daily Post and Times Register*, shorten-

ing its name and turning it by 1900 into the largest daily paper in England. He had done it by copying the style of journalism as practiced so successfully in America by Pulitzer and Hearst. He had pleased the masses with lurid stories of murders and love nests and had delighted the Tories by bolstering their vision of imperialism and empire. His jingoistic editorial policy regarding the rebuilding of the Royal Navy, the take-over of the Sudan, and outrage at the Boers had earned him a peerage. As a yachtsman of unsurpassed skill, Lord Crewe always knew which way the wind was blowing.

There was no day or night in the *Daily Post* building. Lights burned constantly and the giant presses in the cavernous basement rumbled on unceasingly. A uniformed page boy met Jacob and Martin in the foyer and escorted them to the private elevator that whisked them to the building's top floor.

"Brings back a few memories," Jacob said as they walked down a marble corridor toward the private suite of Lord Crewe—known within the building simply as "the Guv'nor."

"Yes," Martin said quietly.

It did indeed. Nineteen fourteen. Jacob had been a reporter on the paper, a specialist on the Byzantine complexities of Balkan politics. Jacob had liked some of Martin's humorous travel sketches of England and had persuaded his father to give Martin a job as a feature writer. A year later Martin had been sent to Gallipoli as a war correspondent, but his association with the paper had ended when he had returned to London from the Middle East. He had been angered by the fact that none of his pieces criticizing the Dardanelles compaign had been printed. He had not known then to what extent the press barons of both England and America would subdue the grim truths of war. As he walked down the corridor now, past Lord Crewe's vast collection of Italian Renaissance paintings, he could almost hear the Guv'nor's booming sailor's voice telling him that England's faith in its military leaders and the conduct of the war must not be shaken. *"It's victory, Rilke, and only victory that concerns this newspaper."* Lord Crewe moving briskly with the wind—but now the winds had changed.

"He will see you now." Lord Crewe's private secretary reentered the anteroom. He was a thin, stoop-shouldered man who looked and spoke like an Oxford don—and had been, until lured away by a salary far above what he had received at Balliol College.

Lord Crewe sat in a Biedermeier chair behind a long oak dining table that he used as a desk. He was a burly, barrel-chested man with a back as straight as a capstan bar—as different from his son as day from night.

"Hello, Jacob. Rilke—glad you came along, too."

"It's good to see you again, Guv'nor," Martin said as they approached the desk. "Been a long time."

"A coon's age, as they say in America. But I follow your career."

"So I notice—by today's editorial."

"Oh, that. I'm sure it surprised you, but a successful newspaper must swim with the stream. The war could not be told in nineteen sixteen, but it can be told now. We're planning a three-week series of articles, including many of your dispatches for us that were turned down by the censors—the army censors and my censors. We believe the time is right and we expect to create some furor."

"Furor sells papers," Jacob said quietly.

His father fixed him with an iron glance. "It does indeed. But then, that's what I'm in business for." He looked back at Martin. "We come out with the first part of the series on Wednesday. It should do much to influence Sir Edmund Larch's thinking when he starts composing his instructions to the jury—if indeed he decides to address the jury at all."

"I won't thank you, Guv'nor," Martin said. "You know me better than that. But I'm gratified by your change in policy, whatever your reason."

Lord Crewe laughed softly. "By God, Rilke, if I wanted the *Daily Post* to be a truly decent and up-standing newspaper, I'd turn it over to you. It would go bankrupt in a year, but what a year it would be! I regret you never went sailing with me. I am, as they say on blue water, an honest man at the helm. Now, if you'll excuse me, I must have a few words with my son in private. You can wait in the side room. There's some damn fine whiskey in the cabinet. Pour from the yellow jug. An exceptional malt that Harry Lauder sent me from a distillery in Strathbraan."

Martin stood in a room off the office that, like all of the rooms in Lord Crewe's suite, blended priceless antiquities with the practicalities of his profession. Egyptian artifacts from Luxor dwelt side by side with intermittently chattering Teletype machines. He stood by the windows, glass of whiskey in hand, and looked down into the gloom of Bouverie Street. The whiskey was exceptional and he was in the act of pouring himself another when Jacob came into the room.

"You might pour me one, too, Martin."

Martin grinned at him. "You do look a bit shaky. How'd it go?"

"Rather badly. He's dying, Martin."

Martin stared at him, the crock of whiskey in his hand. "What did you say?"

"Dying. Our secret—under oath."

"Of course."

"A cancer—in the blood. He's leaving for America next week. A clinic in Minnesota. Mayo Brothers, I believe he said. I don't think he expects to come back." Martin poured him a whiskey and he took the glass with a trembling hand. "Not that he gives much of a damn. A very fatalistic man, my father. But he has a fear of—wasting away. He went through that with my mother. I don't know, Martin. I have a terrible feeling he'll never reach Minnesota."

"Is it that far advanced?"

Jacob shook his head and then took a big drink of whiskey. "Not outwardly, no. But it's an insidious disease and he knows it. I think he'll shortcut the inevitable pain and misery. I think he'll slip over the ship's rail. That's an awful thing to say. But I think that's what he'll do. He—he has no fear of the sea."

They stared at each other in silence. They could hear and feel the muted thunder of the presses far below them.

"I'd get that thought right out of my head if I were you," Martin said hollowly. "Right out."

Jacob glared at his glass and swished the remaining whiskey around and around.

"If he dies—if he goes—he's leaving his share of the *Post* to me. Fifty-one percent of the stock. He told me, 'Jacob, I trust you to do what's right.' That's a bloody terrible thing to say. What in the name of God does he expect of me?"

"Don't you know?"

"No. What?"

"Only your best, Jacob. Only your very best."

Lord Stanmore fretted as he tried to secure a taxi in front of Waterloo Station. He finally stopped being a gentleman and stepped off the curb into the street, pointing his furled umbrella like a lance at an approaching cab.

"Taxi! Here!"

There were muttered grumblings from a few commuters standing in the queue, but the earl ignored them as he climbed quickly into the taxi and slammed the door.

"Strand," he said. "Royal Courts of Justice."

He settled back with a sigh as the taxi racketed away from the station and onto the approaches to Waterloo Bridge. It was a clear, bright morning, the Thames placid and olive green in color. A lovely day— or at least he hoped it would be a lovely day for Martin.

He had been strongly advised by Martin not to come. It was, his nephew stated over the telephone, a tedious journey at that early hour of the morning—the London train jammed with commuters—and the trial, he had felt, would attract some highly partisan spectators. Win or lose, there might be some nasty incidents following the verdict. The earl had dismissed the arguments, but had told Hanna and Alexandra that the trial date had been postponed and that he was going up to London on business. So much for that. A little white lie.

He felt justified in having told it when the taxi neared the law courts. There were policemen, mounted and on foot, patrolling both sides of the Strand from Aldwych to Chancery Lane. A most extraordinary collection of people could be seen on opposite sides of the wide street, shouting across at one another with highly vocal malevolence. On one side were a large number of men, many of them middle-aged to elderly, carrying small Union Jacks in their hands. Some of them carried well-printed banners reading: BRITISH LEGION—HONOR HAIG—RULE BRITANNIA. They appeared better dressed than the majority of their opposite numbers, who seemed a motley collection of young men of the lower classes, women, and crippled ex-soldiers, all of the latter wearing at least one piece of old uniform. They carried crudely painted banners that expressed a bewildering variety of slogans. NO WAR—EVER AGAIN . . . RED IS BLOOD, RED IS HOPE were two that caught his eye. The longest of these signs was held aloft by at least thirty women and it read: NO MORE WAR INTERNATIONAL—LAMBETH CHAPTER.

It was most curious. A tall, striking-looking woman stood in the street facing this monster banner and directing a chant of some kind, the words only dimly heard above the general noise. The woman, he realized with a dull shock, was Winifred Wood-Lacy.

The police kept the traffic moving steadily and the taxi pulled up in front of the law courts. The earl walked quickly into the grim, Gothic building and asked a uniformed man for courtroom "D."

"Not a chance, sir. Filled up 'arf an hour ago."

He drew himself to his full imperial height. "I am Greville, Earl of Stanmore. I believe there is a space reserved."

There wasn't, but it got him into the courtroom. He

stood with a dozen others against the back wall. Scanning the seats, he saw Charles, William, and Fenton's friend, Jacob Golden, seated in the third row. Well, he thought, at least they had a comfortable view of things.

The jurymen filed in and took their places. There was a long wait and then the King's Court judge in his ermine robes entered his court, walking slowly, eyes on the floor as though lost in deep thought. The ritual of his entrance was proclaimed and the man sat in his thronelike chair for a full five minutes, still deep in thought, and then summarily dismissed the jury. There was a rolling wave of comment from the spectators. A gavel pounded wood until the sound stopped.

"I have dismissed the jury," Mr. Justice Larch said in a flat monotone, "because it is my opinion, after reading most carefully through the evidence, that this case should rightly have been heard in chambers. Major General Sir Bertram Dundas Sparrowfield, through counsel, accuses Mr. Martin Rilke of defaming his name and honorable military reputation in a book written by Mr. Rilke and entitled *The Killing Ground*. The plaintiff charges Mr. Rilke with libeling both him and his staff. I do not, however, see the staff represented by counsel."

Major General Sir Bertram Dundas Sparrowfield, despite a blurted caution from his bewigged counsel, lurched to his feet.

What an. *ordinary* little man, Lord Stanmore thought. More like a village postman in appearance than a major general.

"I protest!" the general cried out in a high, squeaky voice. "I have always spoken for my staff—I speak for my staff now."

The judge gave him a brief, baleful glance. "You may *speak* for them all you wish, Sir Betram, but you may not *represent* them in this courtroom. Kindly resume your seat."

The general sat down slowly.

"The facts of the case are clear enough," the judge continued. "Mr. Rilke, a war correspondent then employed by the Associated Press, witnessed an attack against heavily fortified German positions in and around the village of Thiepval on the Somme on the morning and afternoon of fourteen August, nineteen sixteen, and, four years after the event, using his own notes, battalion log books, and the personal accounts of survivors of that attack, wrote a book on the subject. It is the veracity of that book's contents that form the basis of this suit for libel, specifically pages two hundred twenty through two hundred fifty-five—the summing up, as it were. I have read that section over half a dozen times. It is critical of many actions performed, or not performed, by General Sparrowfield and his staff on that day. It is especially critical of the fact that the general and his staff were headquartered in a château nine miles from the battle without any reliable means of communication with those battalions committed to the assault . . ."

The general popped up again, red-faced and blustering. "I do protest, sir! My battalion commanders had been most thoroughly briefed—most *thoroughly* briefed—all *aspects*."

The gavel pounded. "I must warn the plaintiff," the judge said, not unkindly, "that any further outbursts of this nature will not be tolerated. I must so advice plaintiff's counsel."

Both of the general's barristers rose to their feet. "It will not occur again, m'lud," they said in bleak unison.

"I trust not. It is most distracting. Now—where was I? Yes—critical of . . ."

Lord Stanmore had merely skimmed through the copy of the book Martin had sent him. It had annoyed him at the time. The past was the past. The war was over and should be laid to rest and forgotten like some hellish nightmare. He knew now that he had been wrong. The squalor . . . the horror of it . . . the gross, criminal mishandling of it . . . all needed to be burned into the very brains of people so that they would never, *ever*, think of war as a glorious national venture again.

". . . Mr. Rilke criticizes the use of pigeons as a means of communications between the line battalion commanders and the general's headquarters. This proved most unwise as the pigeons died when the wind shifted and the gas, which should have drifted into the German trenches, blew back onto the attackers. He also criticizes the decision to use gas in the first place after meteorologists had warned General Sparrowfield's staff that they could expect unpredictable wind patterns on the day of the attack. They chose to ignore that advice, with disastrous results."

The judge set aside his notes and leaned back in his chair. "Mr. Rilke, in my opinion, did not single out General Sparrowfield for censure nor hold him up to derision and ridicule. The attack of which he writes turned out to be a fiasco with an extraordinarily high percentage of fatalities and wounds among the battalions involved. Mr. Rilke did not invent that fiasco, nor did he picture it as being worse than it actually was.

He does, in fact, state in his foreward that this particular attack was typical for the period, that it was but one of many hundreds that occurred with similar results. Mr. Rilke wrote an entire book of some three hundred pages about this one sanguinary event, and yet the official communiqué for that day reduced it to a mere six lines. Defeats and massacres were not extensively documented for public dissemination. A veil, as it were, was drawn over those melancholy times. Now that it has been lifted, one can easily understand why some people might well be discomforted by the light. It is such with General Sparrowfield, I believe. One can feel a degree of compassion for the plaintiff for being, one might go so far as to say, a victim of history, but the plaintiff's suit for libel must be disallowed. This case is now dismissed."

There was polite applause in the courtroom. The cheering began when the decision was made known in the street—cheering from one side of the street and angry exclamations from the other. The police moved majestically between the two factions, thin lines of blue and the stationary, patient horses.

"Father! Sir!" William pushed his way through the crush in the corridor as the courtroom emptied. Trailing along in his wake came Charles, Martin, and Jacob Golden. Lord Stanmore spotted them and stepped to one side of the doorway as the crowd poured out to mill about on the pavement in excited groups.

"Congratulations, Martin," the earl said.

"Thank you, sir," and then he was being dragged off into the crowd and borne triumphantly toward the peace advocates who were forming like a small army around the Strand island of Saint Clement's Dane Church.

"There's to be a peace march," William said. "Along the Strand . . . the Mall . . . then through Green Park to Hyde Park. I don't advise your joining it, sir. Tempers are a bit edgy in some quarters."

"I can see that," the earl said. "Not that I had any intention of joining a march—for war *or* peace."

A small, angry knot of men passed by clenching rumpled copies of the *Daily Post* in their hands. A banner waved over them—HONOR FIELD MARSHAL HAIG. They were chanting: "Two, four, five, and six, tear the *Daily Post* to bits. . . ."

They moved off up the street toward the pacifists. A mounted policeman trailed after them.

"Yes," the earl said. "Rather a good deal of anger about."

"Are you going back to Abingdon, Father?" Charles asked.

"If I can find a taxi in this snarl."

"I'll go with you. I get a bit uneasy in crowds."

"Coming back to stay for a while?"

"Yes. Willie's going over to Ireland to look at a horse."

William was following the crowd, walking side by side with Jacob. "No More War International" had called for a demonstration on this day no matter what the verdict of the Rilke trial. A thousand or more people, the majority of them women, had come from all parts of England, Scotland, and Wales. They marched under their own banners: LEEDS CHAPTER—SHEFFIELD & BARNSLEY—BIRMINGHAM—CARDIFF. There was a sprinkling from France and Belgium, a lone Portuguese couple from Lisbon who had lost their son at Ypres. And mixed up among them were small groups of Socialists and Communists wearing red armbands. The staunch, bitter groups with their HONOR FIELD MARSHAL HAIG and BRITISH LEGION banners stood on the pavements and jeered.

There was no violence. The antipacifist crowd did not follow. The police controlled the traffic on the Strand and shepherded the marchers past Admiralty Arch into the Mall and on across Green Park toward Hyde Park Corner.

William pointed ahead. "I say, isn't that Winifred up there with the Lambeth group?"

Jacob, eyes downcast, thinking of other things, looked in the direction William was pointing. "Yes, it is. Why *Lambeth* of all places?"

"I haven't the slightest idea. Probably because there isn't a chapter from Cadogan Square!"

"I'll just pop on ahead and say hello."

"By all means," William said. "Give her my fond regards."

She was not surprised to see him. "I thought you'd be about somewhere—if you were back in England."

"Got back first of the week. How are you, Winnie?"

"Fine. A mother of three now, or had you heard?"

"No. A boy?"

"Girl. I called her Kate. Not Katherine—*Kate*. I like good, blunt, positive names that can't be messed about with. What on earth's the point of calling a child *Winnifred* if everyone is bound to call her *Winnie?*"

"I quite agree." He smiled at her and she glanced at him.

"What are you grinning about, Jacob?"

"Your strident positiveness, I suppose. I was thinking of when we first met. You must have been—oh, fifteen or sixteen. No older than that."

She frowned. "I don't remember."

"Don't you? I came to the Cadogan Square house with my father for dinner. Sir Henry Campbell-Bannerman, our most beloved ex-prime minister, was your father's guest. I'd just come back from the Balkans and was surlier than usual. We talked for about a minute. You were, in my opinion, too plump, too mousy, and too boring to be tolerated for longer than that. How little one knows."

She took his hand and squeezed it. "You're a lovely man, Jacob."

They were waiting in Hyde Park: thirty young men in dark clothes—black shirts and black ties. A few wore trench coats although the day was sunny. There was something ominous about their brooding silence, the way they stood watching, flanking the gravel path the tired marchers were taking toward Speakers Corner and Marble Arch.

"Reds . . . Reds . . . look at the Reds." A chanting, rhythmic, unnerving in its orchestrated hate. "Yids . . . Yids . . . see all the Yids."

A group of mounted policemen eyed them warily, but the dark-clothed men were not doing anything, not intimidating anyone.

"Reds . . . Reds . . . look at the Reds."

A few of them suddenly detached themselves from the group and walked alongside the marchers. They carried bundles of crudely duplicated copies of the *Dearborn Independent, The International Jew,* and pamphlets with Benito Mussolini's picture on the front. They tried to press their literature into the hands of the marchers.

"Read this, sir . . . read this, ma'am . . . the truth . . . the Jewish-Communist conspiracy subversion of Christian ethics and decency . . . the bulwark of fascist morality. Read it, sir. Read it, ma'am. . . ."

A gangly young man in a raincoat tried to press some pamphlets into Jacob's hand. "Read it, sir."

"Buzz off," Jacob said quietly.

The young man fell into step beside him. He stared at Jacob for a moment and then said, "You're an Ikey, aren't you?"

"I said buzz off. You're not wanted here."

"Yes," Winifred said sharply, taking a firm hold of Jacob's hand. "Go away."

The man noticed the gesture and sneered. "I wouldn't sleep with an oily Jew if I were you, miss. Get slippery kiddies that way."

Jacob jerked his hand from Winifred's grasp and sent a straight-arm punch into the side of the man's face. The man reeled off the path and fell clumsily in the grass, his broadsides and pamphlets scattering across the ground.

"You bastard!" Jacob said as he stepped out of the line of march and kicked the material. The papers flew into the air, sheets of newsprint flying off in the wind. "Bloody rotten filth!"

The small knot of Fascists surged forward, most of them screening Jacob from the peace marchers while half a dozen others waded into him with flying fists.

William came running as fast as his stiff leg would permit. He had anticipated the action as soon as he had seen Jacob send the man in the raincoat flying. Two young Fascists tried to stop him by grabbing at his arms. He shook them away like flies. Out of the corner of his eye he saw the pale, tense face of Osbert—the leader—Osbert's British League of Fascisti a reality after all.

"Don't be a damn fool, Greville!" Osbert called out.

But he was beyond stopping now. He burst through the screen of dark-clothed men like a runaway bull. A man turned away from punching Jacob in the ribs and aimed a blow at William. He took it gleefully on the forearm and then backhanded the man into insensibility.

Police whistles shrilled. Two mounted policemen spurred their horses forward. The ordered ranks of the peace march began to dissolve into confused and frightened groups of screaming women and small, angry knots of men. Banners and signs littered the pathway. William planted his feet and threw punches until he saw Jacob roll free and get up on one knee. There was blood coming from his nose but he looked all right and Winifred had run up and was kneeling in front of him, pressing a handkerchief to his face.

William turned and slammed his fist into the jaw of one Fascist and kicked at another—but they were scattering, running off across the park. The men lumbering toward him now were bobbies—half a dozen or more, blowing whistles, wielding truncheons. He thought of the grim-faced inspector at Chancery Lane police station . . . the cold cells with their iron doors. His knee felt on fire after being kicked and he hobbled toward a milling group of women.

"*Stop that man!*"

Several of the women clapped as he reached them. They formed a wall around him and raised a tattered banner as though to shield him from view with it. NO MORE WAR INTERNATIONAL—SUSSEX CHAPTER.

"*That man! Hold that man!*"

"Why don't you go after those bullies!" a woman screamed at the police.

A girl tugged frantically at William's sleeve. "Duck down, for heaven's sake! You're much too tall!"

He bent down to the level of the girl. She was red-haired and slender and wore a blue mackintosh and a black beret. She slipped quickly out of the mackintosh and draped it over William's shoulders like a shawl.

"Come with me," she said. "Quickly!"

The marchers were re-forming with some confusion. The girl, holding William by the hand, ducked through the milling crowd and then back along the line of march toward Hyde Park Corner.

"The police didn't see us," she said, glancing over her shoulder. "Keep walking slowly, and bent like that. You'll look like an old man from the back."

He certainly felt like one. His knee ached, and assorted other places on his body and face were starting to smart and throb. He'd punched quite a few men, but quite a few had punched him.

"Be careful," she whispered. "Coppers." She tugged at his hand. "Quickly—down here."

They descended the steps of the Hyde Park Corner tube station. The girl placed some coins on the ticket counter and they went deeper, down to the trains and onto one of them.

They sat facing each other. She smiled happily as the train began to move. "There! We made it. Sanctuary!"

"Where are we going?"

"I have no idea. I don't know London too well. It doesn't matter. The only important thing is that you're safe. You were magnificent! The way you bored into them—totally without fear. I suppose that comes from

long experience—crossing frontiers . . . border guards
. . . the *cordon sanitaire.*"

He could only stare at her. She had the most beautiful eyes he had ever seen. The palest of green.

"Where are you from?" he asked.

She straightened her beret, which had tipped askew. "Tunbridge Wells."

"And what do you do in Tunbridge Wells?"

"Do?" She shrugged. "Study history and economics
at Southborough College. Live with my parents, but
surely—"

"And what does your father do?"

"Father? He's in the church. A bishop, actually. But
let's not talk about me. I'm frightfully dull. I want to
know about *you.* You must have had all sorts of thrill-
ing adventures. Have you crossed swords with the
Fascisti in Italy?"

"Italy? No—not in Italy." He stared at her for a long
time and then leaned toward her. "Tell me something," he asked earnestly. "Do you like—*horses?*"

"You must lie down," Winifred said. "I'll ring for a
doctor."

"No, I'm fine," Jacob said. Keeping his head tilted
back, the handkerchief—now crimson—pressed to his
nose, he stretched out on the sofa. "Nothing broken. I
can tell."

"You took a frightful beating. Oh, those rotters!"

"You can't blame them, Winnie. They were only
doing their job."

"Job!"

"Jew-bashing. An ancient if not exactly honorable
profession."

"You're making a joke of it," she said, an edge to her voice.

"No, I'm not. I assure you I'm not. You might go in the kitchen and chip off some ice—and bring a bottle of bubbly while you're at it. The nineteen thirteen Clicquot will do."

"I hope Martin was all right," she said as she came back into the room with the ice wrapped in a towel. "I didn't see him."

"He was at the head of the parade. Quite safe and sound. He'll have a few choice words to write about *that*."

Winifred knelt beside the sofa and replaced the bloody handkerchief with the cold towel. "That should stop the bleeding."

"You're a good woman, Winnie."

"Forgoing modesty, I quite agree."

"Even if you did forget the champagne."

"You can have a drink later. Alcohol stops the blood from clotting."

He sat up, pressing the towel to his nose. "I think it's stopped." He removed the towel tentatively. "Yes. The tap is off."

"Keep your head back—just in case it isn't."

He smiled at her, reached out and touched her hair. "It's been quite a day for you, hasn't it, Winnie?"

"A bit hectic."

"I find the paradox amusing. The colonel's lady marching in a peace parade."

She eyed him gravely. "I told Fenton I was a pacifist before he married me. It didn't matter to him."

"God, no. It wouldn't have mattered to old Fenton if you'd been a cannibal."

She stood up. "I'll get the champagne. I could stand a drink myself."

"Is there anything troubling you, Winnie?"

"Why do you ask?"

"I'm a perceptive sort of bloke. I feel—vibrations."

She put a hand to her throat and toyed with the top button of her blouse. "Fenton's been gone for ten months now. They can keep him there for years, can't they? They might grant him some leave in another year—and then again, they might not. Their whole point is to drive him out of the army, isn't it?"

"Yes. I'm afraid it is."

"And he'll never break. He'll never give in."

"I can't see him doing it, no."

"I love him very much, but I'm human—just as Fenton is human. Did he tell you that he had an affair when he was stationed in Ireland?"

"Yes, as a matter of fact. It didn't mean anything, though."

"Not to him, perhaps. It meant a great deal to the girl. She sent him letters, which I inadvertently opened. It was quite a shock. But I couldn't really blame him. He must have been horribly lonely in Shannon. It gave him—comfort. For a little while."

"I suppose it did."

"It took me some time to get over it, but I can understand now."

"You're a woman of great compassion—and tolerance."

She gave him a quizzical look. "I detect the barest shadow of mockery in your tone."

"That's hardly surprising." He stood up with a groan and dropped the icy towel on the carpet. "I

view almost everything with a degree of amusement—
bitter amusement most of the time. Perhaps it's because I'm quicker than most people. I grasp the heart
of things while others are still fumbling around the
edges."

He was standing very close to her and she could
feel her breath catch. She put her hand to her throat
again, fingers playing with the blouse button.

He smiled, almost sadly. "You want very much to
undo that button, don't you, Winnie? Almost as much
as I want you to undo it. But something blocks the
act. That terrible word 'morality.' Your husband—my
oldest friend. And if I asked you to go to bed with me,
would the sky collapse on our heads? Would we burn
eternally in hell? Or would we just, as dear friends,
comfort one another—for a little while?"

He stroked her breasts and then kissed her nipples—
a kiss for each. When he rested his cheek against hers,
he could taste the salt of tears.

"Not regret, I hope?"

She shook her head and raised herself on one elbow. A little sun still filtered into the bedroom, falling across her nakedness like a pale spotlight.

"No, Jacob. I feel—very happy. You're a wonderful
lover."

"It's my female qualities, I imagine. I understand
women."

"Yes, you do. Do you understand why I'm crying?"

"Of course. You miss Fenton more than ever. Being
held . . . being loved . . ." He sat up and turned to
her, easing her down on her back. "I love you,

Winnie. God help me, but I do. I have a regret. I know that when you leave this bed you'll never come back to it. It doesn't matter. I had you for a fraction of time. 'Twill suffice. And I give you a promise. I'll get that thickheaded colonel back to you. I don't know how just yet—it'll take some thought—but I'll do it, Winnie. I swear on your loveliness, I'll do it."

X

There were times when he was almost overwhelmed by the sadness of memory. He felt it most keenly at Abingdon Pryory, when walking through Leith Woods or while crossing the meadows near Burgate House. The feeling of loss would fade in time, he was certain of that. All wounds healed eventually. It was a question of facing up to the reality of time. It was the spring of 1922, not the happy springs of 1913 or 1914. Those years were gone. Utterly past—and so many things with them.

"Bad Scoot! . . . Bad, bad Scoot! . . ."

He smiled down at Colin who was scolding one of the terriers which had run back after a fruitless pursuit of rabbits.

"You can't blame him, Colin. He's just doing what he likes to do best."

"No, Uncle Charles . . . no . . . bad Scoot!"

Charles sat down in the grass with his back against a fence post and took out his pipe and tobacco pouch. He patted the grass beside him. "Come, sit down. I think I have a toffee in my pocket somewhere." He fished it out and handed it to the little boy. "Can you take the paper off? It's quite sticky."

"Yes," Colin muttered. He flopped down beside his

uncle and began the studious task of unwrapping the square of toffee.

Charles lit his pipe and gazed off across the meadow toward the Gothic spires and dark limestone facade of Burgate House. Crows wheeled and cawed above the chimneys or stalked the derelict gardens. His sharpest pangs of memory came from looking at that empty house, and he knew that he would not be truly whole until he had reconciled himself to the fact that the woman who had lived there was living a quite different life now.

"Apples," Colin said as he chewed on the toffee. "Apples, Uncle Charles . . . apples."

It was part of the ritual of their morning walks together—the unpruned apple trees drawing Colin to the house as surely as memory drew him.

"All right. Piggyback?"

"Piggyback! Piggyback! . . ." He clambered onto Charles and locked his arms around his neck. "Giddy-up . . . giddy-up!"

Being on Charles's shoulders was the only way he could reach the apple boughs. The apples were small and green and not to be eaten, but he enjoyed plucking them from the stems and throwing them against the tree trunk or into the tall grass. On one of their walks Colin had seen the small, wild ponies that lived in the woods and meadows near Burgate Hill foraging for fallen apples under the trees. He threw the apples down for them.

"Here, horsey! Here, horsey!" he shouted. But the ponies never came.

"They're very shy."

"Why?"

"I don't know, Colin. They just are. But they'll come after we're gone and find the apples."

The sound of a car coming up the long drive startled Charles. He lifted Colin down and looked toward the house. The car came into view and then stopped in front of the house. A man and a woman got out and stood looking up at its soaring towers and spires for a few moments before slowly walking toward the front steps.

"Hello!" Charles called out.

The couple turned and looked at him curiously as he walked toward them out of the orchard holding Colin by the hand. They were middle-aged, the man tall and burly, the woman nearly as tall but very slender. The man held out a beefy hand as Charles reached them.

"Good morning. Mastwick's my name—John Mastwick—and this is my wife, Virginia."

"Charles Greville. And this is my nephew, Colin."

"Pleased to meet you," Mastwick said. He shook Charles's hand and then pointed up at the looming house. "Bit of a monstrosity, isn't it?"

Charles smiled. "I'm afraid it is, yes. A mad duke built it during the reign of Queen Anne. His only son was killed in the French wars and he wanted the house to look like a cathedral—or a tomb. I'm not sure which."

"He succeeded on both counts, if you ask me. Still, beggars can't be choosers. Lord Foxe has just given us the place—a ninety-nine-year lease at one pound per annum."

"We're not exactly being overcharged," Virginia Mastwick said with a thin little smile. "But, oh, Lord, it's going to take some doing to make it livable for the children."

"How many children do you have?" Charles asked.

"Twenty-eight," she said, "but we're expecting another twenty." She saw the expression on his face and laughed. "We're turning the place into a school."

"Moving our school here, to be more precise," Mastwick said gloomily. "We have a wretched, crowded little place at present near Spilsby in Lincolnshire. Lord Foxe heard of our school and our plight and made us this gesture. One could hardly refuse. Still . . ."

"Oh, I don't know," his wife said with a kind of forced cheerfulness. "A bit of paint and tidying up . . . We'll manage, John."

"Yes, I suppose we will."

"Is this the first time you've seen it?"

"No," Mastwick said. "We were here yesterday afternoon with Lord Foxe's agent. He took us through the place and tried to explain its peculiarities. First-rate plumbing—I'll say that much."

"What sort of school do you have?"

The Mastwicks exchanged glances. "It's a *different* sort of school," Mrs. Mastwick replied. "A coeducational school for—well . . ."

"The type of child who doesn't fit into a conventional school," her husband said. "Not disturbed children so much as unhappy ones. A school without uniforms, old ties, old ideas or rote. The children have as much to say about the rules and curriculum as we do. We've found that when children decide on their own codes they are less likely to break them, and when they study what interests them they're more likely to learn something. Classes are not compulsory, but after the novelty of *that* wears off we never have atten-

dance problems. Children want to learn, you know.
They're naturally curious and intrigued by knowledge.
They are given no grades as such—and no punish-
ment. Ignorance, we stress, is punishment enough."

"It sounds fascinating," Charles said. "It's certainly—
different."

"It's a concept that intrigued us for many years. An
idea, actually, that I first had when I was a boy at
Marlborough and had quite forgotten about until the
war. I was captured at Aubers Ridge in 'fifteen and
had a few years in prison camp to think about it."

"My husband ran a school for fellow prisoners of
war."

"Yes, most of them were quite uneducated, and
unorthodox methods were required to teach them anything. I enlisted in the army as a private, by the way.
I'd never been in the cadet corps at either Marlborough or Oxford and didn't feel that being an old Marl-
burian or Oxonian automatically qualified me as a
leader of men in battle. In fact, I found that most
young officers who came direct to the battalion from
public schools had nothing at all to qualify them for
the task except an extraordinary, quite useless, and
pathetic bravery. But we're drifting far afield. I take
it you live near here, Mr. Greville?"

"Yes, just across the hill. I used to visit here often
before the war."

"A friend of Lord Foxe?"

"He was just plain Archie Foxe in those days. But,
yes, I knew him well. I was married to his daughter."

"You must drop by when we're truly settled in—
although the Lord knows when that will be." He
reached down and patted Colin on the head. "And
bring your young nephew as well."

"By all means," Mrs. Mastwick said. "We'll be more hospitable by then—jam tarts and tea."

Charles started to turn away, and then impulsively looked back at John Mastwick and said, "We were divorced. Quite a long time ago. I'd been rather badly shell-shocked, you see."

The schoolmaster stared at him for a long moment, searching his face. Then he nodded knowingly. "Virginia and I will be moving some of our gear in on Saturday. Drop by. We'll have a nice long chat."

"I would like that."

"Yes," Mastwick said gently, "I can see that you would."

Alexandra parked her little two-seater Vauxhall in a lane off High Street, puffed nervously on a cigarette, and kept glancing into the rearview mirror. When she saw his car enter the lane, she got out and waited for him.

"Good morning," Ross said, leaning across and opening the door for her.

"Hello, Jamie." She got in beside him and snuffed out her cigarette in the ashtray.

"Where's His Nibs?"

"With my brother today."

"I'd thought we might go for a drive to the RAF field at Farnborough. He would have enjoyed that. There's an engineer I want to see. Chap's been experimenting with high-altitude blowers—superchargers, we call them. Sounds interesting."

"Must it be today?"

"No." He looked away from her and stared miserably ahead. "But I must see him before I—go back."

"California," she said dully.

"I can't stay much longer, Alex. I mean, the engines are coming off the line without any hitches. My partner—I told you about him, Harry Patterson—sent me a cablegram. I got it yesterday. They're having one or two problems."

"What kind of problems?"

"Technical. The new engine weighs a good deal more than our plans had called for. That means shifting things about a bit to maintain the center of balance. Find a new spot for the fuel tanks, or even set the wings back a foot. Nothing that can't be solved, but he'd like me in San Diego as soon as I can get there."

"When are you planning to leave?"

"A week from today," he said quietly. "I booked passage on the *Mauretania*. Sails from Southampton next Wednesday."

"I see."

"There's not much I can do about it."

"No, of course not."

Her hand, gloved in pale yellow kid, was beside him on the seat. He took hold of it in his strong grip.

"And that will be the end of it. But I suppose it's all for the best." Only his misery was convincing. "Just something that happened."

She sat stiffly, looking down at his hand holding her own. "Take me to your house, Jamie."

"Is that wise, Alex? It's going to make it that much more difficult—at least for me."

"I know it isn't wise, Jamie, but it's what I want."

It was what he wanted, too. Their lovemaking had been intense since that afternoon in the tall grass of Box Hill when reason had totally fled and only a

blind need had controlled them. It seemed incredible
to both of them that it had happened with Colin only
a few feet away, sound asleep under the warm
sweater. An almost savage coupling with both of them
nearly fully clothed. Fucking, she had thought wildly
at the moment, like two inflamed animals. Afterward,
they had lain spent, staring at the sky, their senses
sharpened, hearing the distant call of birds and Colin's gentle breathing. They had said nothing to each
other—for which they had both been grateful.

It was different now.

He stroked her thigh with a hard, callused hand
and she kissed the lean, flat muscles of his chest.

"I'm sorry, Jamie."

"Sorry for what?"

"For any pain this might cause."

"I'll live through it. It couldn't go on forever, could
it? I mean, I couldn't just pop around when whatsis-
name was off to the office, now could I?"

She kissed a nipple. "Couldn't you?"

"Be serious, Alex. I'm not that type of man."

"I know you're not. You're a very decent—*sort of
bloke*."

"People have love affairs. I read about them all the
time in penny-dreadful newspapers. Emancipated
women. Vamps and sheikhs. High jinks in Paris."

"You've never read a penny-dreadful newspaper in
your life."

"Christ! Today's morality. Read about it in the bleedin' *Times!*"

"Is that us, Jamie?" she asked quietly. "Just two sex-
crazed people? A flapper and her sheikh?"

He was silent for a moment, looking down at her—

white and pink and nakedly lovely cradled against him.

"Oh, God, Alex. I wish I knew what we were."

Hanna sensed something wrong, but was unable to fathom what it could be. A feeling—an intuition.

"I don't think Alex looks well," she said over mid-morning coffee on the terrace.

"Looks perfectly fine to me," the earl said, eyes on his newspaper. "Damnedest thing about Lord Crewe. Surely a man can't simply disappear on the *Aquitania*—unless, of course . . ."

"She seems—oh, I don't know exactly—so quiet lately —so terribly introspective."

"Prenuptial daydreaming, I expect. All women go through it. But hardly ill. Always dashing about in her little car—or walking all over the countryside. I wouldn't concern myself if I were you."

"You don't suppose she's had a tiff with Noel, do you?"

The earl cleared his throat loudly and stood up. "I don't think it would be possible to have a tiff with Noel. He's the most *accommodating* fellow I've ever known."

She stayed on the terrace, sipping coffee and look-ing out across the gardens. Charles and Colin could be seen, coming across the lawns from the direction of the stables, Colin running ahead, weaving in and out between plots of marigolds and daffodils. Playing at being an airplane, his tiny arms jutting out like wings.

The child's incredible energy made her smile. To see him was to see William at the same age—and to see him reminded her so much of her adored brother Willie. She could only remember Willie when he had been much older than Colin, but the same energy applied. He had always been doing something—hitting a ball, rolling an iron hoop furiously down Prairie Avenue, climbing a tree. She had envied his boy's freedom and had always wondered why her brother Paul had never joined him but had preferred to sit in his rooms reading books.

Now Paul was a tycoon—a multimillionaire—and poor Willie was decades dead and buried in a pauper's grave. Would things have turned out differently for him, she wondered, if Papa had made even the slightest effort to understand him? If he hadn't demanded that both of his sons follow the same path into the business? Breweries and real estate had bored Willie to tears. He had wanted to study art, to paint or sculpt, to create things with his hands and discover new forms of expression. Papa had never understood him—not one bit. Such a terrible choice poor Willie had to make— into the office with Paul or get out of the house.

She could remember as if it were yesterday the morning he had left—walking jauntily down the path, a suitcase in his hand, his straw boater tilted to one side of his head. Walking toward the streetcar. Whistling. Not knowing then that papa would disown him. Not knowing then that the bright red streetcar which would take him to the train—which would take him to the boat—which would take him to Paris, France— would carry him to failure, despair, and death.

A chill went up her spine, and when Colin came running up to her along the terrace she clasped him to her, hugging him so hard that he winced.

"Lord," Charles said, slumping into a chair across the table from his mother, "that boy could wear out a machine."

"Yes, bless him."

"We walked for miles. Some very interesting people have taken over Burgate House."

"Archie sold the place?"

"Leased. One quid a year. A philanthropic gesture. It's to be a school."

"What sort of school?"

He shrugged. "I don't know exactly. An experimental school of some sort. Sounds quite interesting."

Colin, curled in Hanna's lap, looked up at her. "What's school, Gran'mama?"

"School's where you'll be in a few years." She touched his nose. "A school for little monkeys."

"I could do something like that," Charles said softly. "Teach. Poetry . . . or history."

"I'm sure you could do better than that, dear," Hanna said in an offhand manner. "Your father was talking about you to Lord Buxton yesterday. There might just be something in the Foreign Office."

Charles looked down at his hands, folded tightly in his lap. "Foreign Office? I don't know . . . I don't really know about that."

"You'd be splendid there."

"I think—I could only do—what I might love to do."

Colin reached up and touched Hanna's nose. "I love Gran'mama."

"And Grandmama loves you, Colin," she said.

"An' I love Uncle Charles—an' Mary—an' . . ."

"And Mama," Hanna said, pinching him on the cheek. "And Mr. Rothwell . . ."

"An' Scoot . . ."

"Yes, dear, all the dogs—and the horses . . ."

"An' Jamie, Gran'mama. I love Jamie best."

She took a bath before dinner, lying for a long time in the warm water, her thoughts drifting as idly as the soap bubbles on the placid surface of the tub. The affair was over now and there was no point in even trying to examine it in any detail, nor in trying to explain it to herself. It was past, but no matter how hard she tried to keep her mind on other things, on meaningless things, she kept seeing his room—the yellow painted bureau, the wallpaper with its muted pattern of buttercups and daisies intertwined, the flecks of sunlight on the ceiling. She touched her body under the water and felt his touch. Remembered it—as she had remembered Robbie's.

"Oh, God," she murmured. "What a mess."

She was in her dressing room when her maid tapped lightly on the door and then stepped inside. "Your mother's in the sitting room, your ladyship."

"Oh? Tell her to come in here, Fran."

"Very well, m'lady."

She was straightening the seams in her silk hose when Hanna entered the room and closed the door behind her.

"I can't seem to get this pair to fit properly." She glanced at her mother and smiled. "Sit down, Mama. Would you care for a glass of sherry?"

"No, thank you," Hanna said, standing stiffly with her back to the door. "I only dropped in to ask you a question. May I do so?"

"Of course."

"May I ask why Colin would *love* a person named Jamie?"

Alexandra closed her eyes for a second and thought—well, someone was bound to find out about it sooner or later.

"He told you that?"

"Yes," Hanna said icily. "To Charles and me. I couldn't recall a *Jamie,* and then Charles mentioned Ross. When has Colin been in contact with Ross?"

"He took us both to the airfield at Blackworth's—to see the planes."

"And that's all?"

"No, Mama. Not quite."

"Meaning?"

"We've gone on picnics—little trips."

Hanna placed a hand to her throat and stared long and hard at her daughter.

"I haven't spent my life in a convent, Alex. Have you seen Ross when Colin was not with you?" She could see the answer in Alexandra's eyes. "Have you been having—intimate relations with this man?"

"Yes, Mama."

Hanna leaned back against the door as though barring it from entry.

"Good Father in heaven, how could you!"

"How could I? Because I found him attractive. Because I like him very much. He's a good man. A very sweet, dear person. A decent, warm human being."

"Decent!" The word was like a cry.

"Yes, Mama, decent. He didn't ply me with drink and seduce me. I seduced *him* if you want to know the whole truth."

"Are you so starved for sex that you have to—

rut about with a—a *chauffeur!* If you needed it so badly, why didn't you give yourself to Noel? I'm sure he wouldn't have refused you a little premarital copulation!"

"Please don't be bitter, Mama." She sat down wearily on the edge of her dressing-table bench. "I don't really expect you to understand how desperately I've missed Robin—how lonely I've been. Jamie, somehow . . . Oh, I can't explain. . . . They're not at all alike—and yet—being with him, I feel the same sense of—*comfort*."

Hanna toyed with her pearls, looping the long triple strands around and around her fingers. "It must stop," she whispered. "It must stop at once."

"It's over now. We ended it this afternoon."

"Is that the truth?"

"I've never lied to you, Mama, and never would."

"No. You've never lied to me. Very well. We shall say no more about it. What's done is done. You're a grown woman. I have no right to tell you what you should or should not do with your own body. But an affair like *this*. If your father were aware of it, I think it would kill him. I mean to say, *Ross*, of all people!"

"He's more honest and loving than Noel could ever be," Alexandra said, a hard edge of anger in her tone. "Have you ever, even once, seen Noel show any real affection for my son? And why do you say Ross *of all people?* He's not quite the same person you remember, Mama. If, in fact, you ever knew the man—he was just someone in a uniform opening the car door. He was more than that then and he is, I assure you, a great deal more than that now!"

Hanna took a deep breath to compose herself.

"There's no point in our screaming at one another like two fishwives at Billingsgate. I apologize if I've slandered the man. But surely you know what I mean. It's a question of *class*."

Alexandra's smile was wan. "I never thought of that word once in the past few weeks. The only word that crossed my mind was—'happiness.'"

Hanna walked slowly across the room and placed an arm gently around her daughter's shoulders. "You'll find happiness with Noel. You'll see."

"I wonder."

"You will, dear. After you're married and settled in your own house. Perhaps it would be better if you saw Noel more often. Not just on the weekends. You could go back to London with him on Sunday and stay thère until the wedding. Then your lovely honeymoon in Italy . . ."

Alexandra rested her head against her mother. "Oh, Mama, how simple you make it sound to be happy."

Charles woke early on Saturday morning, dressed hurriedly, and walked down to the stables where he asked one of the grooms to saddle a nine-year-old cob named Ginger. He then rode the placid animal into the vale and across the meadows to Burgate House. A thin plume of smoke rose from one of the dozens of chimneys and a large, battered van was parked in the drive near the Mastwicks' black Austin. The sound of the horse's hooves on the gravel caused two boys to pop their heads out from the rear of the van. Charles judged them to be thirteen or fourteen—strong, cheery-looking fellows.

"Hello," one of them called out. "Mind if we have a ride on old Dobbin?"

"What?" Charles said with a smile as he dismounted. "Both of you? I don't think Ginger would like that."

"Oh, no, sir," the other boy said. "Take turns." He jumped down from the lowered tailgate and walked up to the horse to pat its muzzle. "You're a nice old fellow, aren't you? Got very kind eyes, doesn't he?"

"He's a kind horse," Charles said. "You can take him for a ride if you'd like."

The boy glanced toward the house. "Can't just yet, but thanks all the same, sir. Danny and I have to unload the van for Father John first."

"Father John? Do you mean Mr. Mastwick?"

"That's right, sir—Mr. Mastwick—though we all call him Father John. I mean, he isn't a priest or anything like that. It's just what we call him."

"You're with the school, I take it."

"That's right. First contingent, so to speak. Drove down with old Hillary and Mr. Wallis, sir."

John Mastwick stepped out of the house carrying a mug of tea. He was wearing a heavy wool sweater that made him look even burlier.

"Good morning, Greville. Glad you came by. Tea's hot and Virginia's made some scones."

"Shall I tie up your horse, sir?" the boy asked.

"Oh, no. He won't wander away."

It was an odd feeling to go into the house again after so many years. Odder yet to realize that the only woman he had ever loved was no longer in any of the rooms. He had once felt that if he ever did walk into the house he would sense her presence like a palpable force, would hear her laughter drifting to him from the upper landing, through the great stone corridors. But there was nothing now—only silence, only empty rooms and slants of sunlight falling on dust.

"As you can see, Greville, we have our work cut out for us. But the kitchen is cozy enough—and wonderfully functional. By the end of summer we'll have a proper sort of place here."

"I'm sure you will. If there's any way I can be of help . . ."

"Very decent of you, very decent indeed. But half our children elected to spend their holidays here. All strong lads and lassies."

"The two out front seemed decent sorts."

"Yes. Danny and Gerald. Good lads. Danny's a bit shy around strangers—you notice he didn't get out of the lorry. He came to us from Harrow last year. His father was killed at Jutland. His mother stuck him away in a boarding school for which he was not fitted, and then into Harrow, for which experience he was fitted even less. He had a nervous breakdown there and tried to kill himself, poor boy, by drinking *ink*. Thought it must be deadly because, as he told me, death is black."

"Do many of your students come from the public schools?"

"Oh, yes. The majority, I would say. But we take any child we feel would benefit by being with us. Our fees vary according to the ability of each family to pay. We have five boys and two girls who pay nothing."

"And teachers?"

Mastwick paused by the kitchen door. "Well, that's still a bit of a problem. My wife and I, of course . . . Wallis . . . Sinclair . . . they came to us from Balliol.

We had a Miss Johnson who taught Latin and Greek—and botany. But she couldn't cope with our system and had to leave us for a more conventional position at Roedean. Pity. She was highly accomplished on the flageolet and we shall miss her music."

He had tea and scones and met Wallis, a man of his own age who had been slightly gassed at Festubert while serving with the Royal Engineers. He, and his friend Sinclair, had found the stultifying pedagoguery of Oxford impossible to deal with and had, short of giving up teaching altogether, fled to Mastwick and his radical approach to learning. He looked, lounging in a chair in wilted corduroys and tattered sweater, like a happy man.

Later, Charles walked with Mastwick through the derelict rose garden at the back of the house.

"Greville. You'd be Lord Stanmore's son, then."

"Yes."

"Eldest?"

"Yes."

"A viscount. And, if I'm not mistaken in my signals from you, a man looking for a position."

Charles laughed. "How terribly perceptive you are! I have toyed with the idea—yes."

"We don't pay very much. And the hours are long. Twenty-four in a day, I'm afraid. What could you teach our young charges?"

"Poetry. A love of language and imagery. History. I took a first in that at King's."

"Splendid! That would help us enormously." He stopped walking and turned to face Charles. "We could perhaps help you as well. I sense a most discontented man."

Charles looked past him, at the stalky rosebushes and the house, most of its many windows still shuttered. A bird wheeled out of the apple trees and settled under the eaves.

"I married the girl who lived here," he said quietly. "Lydia Foxe. It was a bad marriage from the start. I was—quite impotent. I don't know why. Fear, I expect. A dollop of ignorance to compound the matter. I was, I suppose, too finely tuned to ethereal romance to deal with the realities of sex. I'm sure we would have worked that out in time if it hadn't been for the war. That was another reality I had trouble dealing with."

"Didn't we all," Mastwick said softly.

"Had I been more emotional, capable of venting my feelings, I might have come out of it all right—if I'd been spared a bullet, of course. Other men would get drunk and blow off steam when the pressures became intolerable, or spend a night in a brothel. I kept everything inside and let it fester behind a shield of sangfroid. I broke, of course. Broke badly. I'm out of it now, but every day is a struggle."

"I understand perfectly. The first thing you must realize, Greville, is that you're hardly unique. Not singled out. I spent three days in a shell hole with bits and pieces of men I had known well. I shall never forget those three days if I live forever, but the images no longer trouble me. There's too much in my life now for that melancholy scene to warp."

"I find you very easy to talk to, Mastwick."

"The children say the same. I think that's why they call me Father John. It helps greatly to talk. As fine a purge as castor oil!" He plucked a dessicated rose pod from a bush and crumpled it between his fingers. "As for your wanting to teach here—don't rush into a decision. There's all summer to think it over."

Charles gazed back at the house. "I'm better off if I don't think too much. One has a tendency to brood."

"Did you live in this house?"

"No. We lived in London. But I courted her here. In this very garden."

"And where is she now?"

"Very much in tune with the age. Married to a Russian prince. A *genuine* Russian prince, I should add. From what I can gather reading *Tatler,* they divide their time between Paris and the upper reaches of paradise."

"Does that make you bitter?"

"Oh, Lord, no. Me and Lydia—it seems like a thousand years ago. I did have a fear that if I walked into this house it would open old wounds, but that didn't happen. It's just an empty house. Walls . . . rooms . . . a sprinkling of dust."

Noel had taken an early train from London, and then a taxi from Godalming station. He was having breakfast with Lord Stanmore when Charles got back to the house and strolled into the breakfast room.

"I say, how are you, Charles?" Noel asked, pausing in the act of slicing into a broiled kidney.

"Quite well, Noel. And yourself?"

"Topping, old fellow. Absolutely topping. I must say, you do *look* well. Quite exhilarated, in fact."

"I just came back from a ride." He crossed to the sideboard, ignored the silver warming dishes filled with a variety of foods, and poured out a cup of coffee. "I took Ginger for an outing."

The earl raised an eyebrow. "Ginger? That must have surprised the old dear. One doesn't usually saddle a cob, Charlie."

"I do, Father. I prefer to just—plod along."

"Time to change that," Noel said cheerily. "You'll soon be galloping with the rest of us."

The earl lingered over his tea while Noel went up to his room to change into his riding habit. He puffed on a cigarette and watched Charles, who was staring thoughtfully into a cup of cold coffee.

"Woolgathering?"

Charles looked up with a smile. "In a way."

"I had a talk with your mother last night. She told me about this—school? Is that correct?"

"Yes. At Burgate House."

"She said you were toying with the idea of teaching there."

"I might give it a try."

The earl drew smoke into his mouth and blew it out again. He did not inhale.

"I can get you a position at the Foreign Office. Buxton's one of my oldest friends—we were at Winchester together. No trouble at all. Undersecretary of something or other. Would you like that?"

"In all honesty, no. I'm not prepared—as Noel would put it—to *gallop* quite yet."

"Very well. I won't press you." He crushed out his cigarette and stood up. "And I do mean that, Charlie. Find your own way—at your own pace." He patted his son lightly on the shoulder as he walked from the table. "Ginger may be the slowest horse in the shire, but he gets where you want him to go."

The more Charles thought about it, the more right it felt. It would bring him out into the world a bit

more than he was at present, but among people who
would understand any doubts or insecurities that he
might have about himself. He felt comfortable with
Mastwick and his wife—and the chap Wallis, and the
two boys. They all had been hurt in one way or another and were now banded together. That one boy—
seeking death in a bottle of ink. Unloading a lorry
now. Functioning among people who had been able
to grasp his despair. Yes, he thought firmly, it was the
proper place for him.

Alexandra was not in her suite and he walked down
the corridor to the nursery. She was having a cup of
tea and talking to Mary while Colin ate his breakfast.

"May I intrude?"

"By all means," Alexandra said. "Care for some
tea?"

"Yes, I would—thanks. Good morning, Colin."

The child only scowled at him and then glowered at
his porridge.

It was a spacious nursery—a playroom filled with
assorted toys, and two bedrooms, one for Colin and
the other for his nanny. Tall windows filled the room
with light.

"It's a lovely room," he said. "Much nicer than your
old playroom, Alex, which had rather depressing yellow walls, as I remember."

"Jaundice yellow," Alexandra said. She poured a
cup of tea, added some milk, and handed it to her
brother. "Don't mind Colin," she whispered. "He's in a
terrible sulk this morning. I'm not sure over what."

"Aren't you? He gets sulky every weekend." He
walked to a far corner of the room and sat in a window seat. "Bring your tea and join me, Alex."

She sat stiffly beside him. "You're a perceptive man, Charles."

"To be candid about it, Noel affects me in a similar way. I don't sulk exactly, but neither do I cheer."

"Any specific reason for not liking him?"

"I didn't say I didn't like the man. I simply find him—shallow."

"He loves me," she said without emotion.

"I daresay he does. Yet I sense other factors besides your obvious charms. Son-in-law to a peer—*Greville* hyphenated to his name—Abingdon Pryory. Reminds me somewhat of Lydia. All of Archie's wealth never disguising the fact that it came from hundreds of tea shops and millions of tuppenny buns. She aspired to greater things than mere money. The prospect of becoming the future Countess of Stanmore."

"That's not entirely fair, Charles. She loved you. I know she did."

"She loved me in her fashion. And she was faithful—in her fashion. I hope I'm not sounding bitter, because I don't mean to be. Our marriage was wrong from the start. Fortunately for both of us, it was short-lived. I hope she's happy now. I know I am—in *my* fashion. It's your happiness I worry about. Or, rather, lack of it. Do you love Noel Edward Allenby Rothwell—*Esquire?*"

She took a sip of her tea and watched Colin struggling with his breakfast, fretting and whiny.

"No."

"Then for God's sake—"

"It doesn't matter, Charles. It really doesn't. I've been in love. I don't ever expect to be in love again."

"How dashed clever of you, Alex. But may I ask why your hands are trembling? You can barely hold on to the cup and saucer." He took them from her and placed them on the wide sill behind them. "Now look here. Something's wrong. I know it is. I felt it yesterday when little Colin blurted out that he loved Jamie—*best of all.* 'Who's *Jamie?*' Mother asked, looking slightly nonplussed. Only Jamie I could think of was Ross. Father had told me he was in Abingdon, an engineer, back from America and highly successful. Father sounded pleased as punch about it."

She gazed steadily at him. When she spoke, her voice was low and intense. "Would he be pleased as punch if he knew that I'd been going to bed with Jamie almost every afternoon for the past two weeks?"

Charles looked away from her, finished his tea, and then placed his cup on the windowsill. "I think that would depend greatly on why you've been going to bed with him. Frankly, Alex, the reason escapes me. I would imagine it's no more than the *prurigo copulandi,* simple venery in the classic manner. It seems to be the only explanation—the confession coming as it does from a woman who claims she could *never* fall in love again."

It seemed incredible to Ross that he had accumulated so much in such a short time. The parlor room, which he had used as a study, overflowed with mechanical drawings, technical papers, and journals of all kinds. Each scrap of paper seemed of vital importance in some way, but to take them all back with him would have filled trunks. He had only one, and it was jammed with his clothing. His leather suitcase was al-

ready filled to the bursting point with the blueprints
and test data on the new engine. He recalled seeing a
small luggage shop on High Street with two cheap
but sturdy metal trunks in the window. Getting into
his car, he drove into the village to buy them.

She was parked in front of the house when he returned. He turned into the gravel drive and was so
shaken by the sight of her that he almost forgot to
step on the brake and came within inches of demolish-
ing part of the house.

He waited by the car as she walked up the drive to
him.

"Hello, Jamie."

She wore a silk dress of the palest shade of lavender
and a small cloche that framed her face. She looked so
exquisite and so desirable that he had to turn away
and fumble with the trunks in the back of the car.

"I thought we—had agreed . . ." he mumbled.

"I had to talk to you."

He extricated one of the trunks and set it on its end.
"What is there to talk about, Alex?"

She gave him an imploring look. "Can't we go inside?"

"Why . . . yes, of course."

He led the way, leaving the trunk in the driveway.
She took notice of his packed steamer trunk and suitcase in the narrow hall.

"You're already packed?"

"Yes—except for half a ton of books and papers. I
have a man with a lorry coming by this afternoon. I—
decided to move into a hotel in Southampton until
Wednesday."

She stood close to him and touched his face. "Why,
Jamie?"

"You know why," he whispered. His throat felt tight and it was suddenly difficult to breathe. The closeness of her. The warm wash of her perfume in the narrow hall.

"Why?" she persisted.

He turned away from her again, almost in anger this time. "Because, blast it to hell, I'm in love with you!"

She trailed slowly after him into the parlor. He was scowling at the chaos on the floor.

"That's a bit of a laugh, isn't it?" he said bitterly. "Bit of a screaming farce!"

"Is that what you think it is?"

He stared at her in anguish. "No. Not really. It's more like having a knife jammed into my heart—and twisted. Screaming, yes, but not funny."

She walked over to the sofa and sat on the edge of it. "Yesterday—in bed—I asked a question. I wanted to know what we were. Two people in a sexual frenzy? What exactly? You didn't know—or, rather, pretended not to know. I was pretending, too. I knew in my heart what we were. What we are."

"And that is?"

"*Two* people in love, Jamie."

He walked slowly over to her and sat stiffly at the opposite end of the sofa.

"That just makes it worse, doesn't it? I mean to say, it's so bloody hopeless."

"From whose viewpoint? Ours? There's a registry office in Southampton. We could be married before the ship sails on Wednesday. Or we could be married at sea by the captain."

"God, Alex, it's not as simple as all that."

"You don't want to marry me? Is that it?"

"Christ," he groaned. "I'd give my right arm. You—Colin—but it wouldn't be right for either of you. Not fair. Not in the long run. Giving up—all *this*—the type of life. For what? A small house in Coronado or La Jolla. A husband who comes home every night with grease all over his shirt cuffs!"

"For a man both Colin and I love."

"Colin's a baby. He loves the airplanes."

"Not just the airplanes. He's a baby, yes, but babies have instincts. They sense love, warmth, and real affection. Babies *know*. Colin was wiser than his mother. I should have known that day on Burgate Hill."

"I knew," he said, staring down at his hands. "It terrified me."

"And you're frightened now, aren't you? Is it fear of going with me to see Father?"

He shook his head. "I'd walk through a furnace. His Lordship—we've always—even when I was his driver—talked man to man. He's—well, he's a bit like your son, you see. A man with instincts. I could talk to him all right. That doesn't frighten me one bit. What frightens me, Alex, is your waking up one morning in California and saying to yourself: 'God in heaven, what am I doing *here?*'"

She moved across the sofa to him and kissed his cheek softly. "I'd never say that, Jamie. Not if I always wake up beside you."

* * *

It was infuriating to Lord Stanmore, and he was quick to set the man in his place.

"I don't give a damn what the regulations are, I am seeing my daughter off to America and neither my wife nor I intend running half a mile to do so!"

The gatekeeper at the Cunard dock gave in to the tirade and swung open the barrier. It was a section of the long dock used only for delivery of supplies and freight by lorry and rail. The soaring black and white bulk of the S.S. *Mauretania* could be seen in the distance, white feathers of steam rising into the wind from her giant funnels.

"Drive as fast as you can, Banes," the earl said into the voice tube. He sat rigidly beside Hanna, palms resting on the bamboo handle of his furled umbrella. "It would be wrong not to wave them goodbye—despite our innermost feelings on the matter."

"What *are* our innermost feelings, Tony?" Hanna asked, staring ahead. Dark smoke began to rise from the funnels and they could hear distinctly the hoot of the great liner's steam whistle. "We shall miss seeing them after all."

"Nonsense. There's plenty of time." He tapped the umbrella handle impatiently against the glass separating them from the chauffeur. Banes pressed down on the pedal and the big car picked up speed, lurching and rocking over the maze of railway tracks and uneven asphalt roadway.

"You didn't answer my question," Hanna said, removing a handkerchief from her purse and wadding it in her hand.

"Well—dash it—after all . . ."

"After all *what*, Tony? You can be quite—*incoherent* at times."

"Bit of a stunner. Quite knocked me for six. Thought she was madly in love with Noel—although for the life of me I couldn't see why."

Hanna's smile was faint. "I thought you liked Noel."

"Good man on a horse and all that, but—oh, I don't know, not *quite* a gentleman."

"Jamie Ross is not *any* sort of a gentleman. He's just in the American sense, a good man."

He looked at her with some annoyance. "If you felt he was such a good man, Hanna, then why in the name of blazes did you shut yourself up in your room for three days weeping buckets? And why did *I* have to suggest that we come see them off? And why have you sat like a stone for the entire drive and not said a blessed word until now?"

"Because I'm a mother," she cried, dabbing at her eyes with the handkerchief, "and you couldn't begin to understand *that!*"

"No, thank God! Fathers are less devious!" He lowered the glass partition. "Over there, Banes—past those empty railroad cars. You won't be able to drive much further than that."

They were level with the soaring knife-edge of the prow. Banes coasted for a few more feet and then stopped and hurried out to open the rear doors.

"If I'd been aware of your feelings," said the earl with some bitterness as he took Hanna's arm, "we could have come down for the wedding."

She said nothing in reply. Explaining her feelings could wait. And they were not that easily explained. It had been too much of a shock—the suddenness of it, and the unpleasantness of it all—with a distraught and bewildered Noel racing about the house on Saturday seeking to understand the unexplainable, refusing until Sunday night to face the fact that the wedding was off—that Alexandra Mackendric and her son had departed, quite suddenly, for Southampton with a man by the name of James Andrew Ross, from Coronado, California, U.S.A.

But who in Christ's name is he?

Hanna had shut, and locked, her door against the anguish and the storm, feeling, for some time, as outraged as Noel Edward Allenby Rothwell.

A state of shock that took some time to pass. She had refused to open her door to Alexandra, and when her daughter had slipped an envelope under it she had come within a split second of tearing the envelope and the letter it contained into a thousand pieces. Instead, she had wadded it into a ball as she stood by her sitting-room window and watched them leave the house and get into Jamie Ross's automobile. What she had seen did not fully register on her mind for two full days. When it did, she sat on a chaise longue and opened the envelope, carefully smoothing out the contents . . .

> *My dearest Mama,*
> *I do not expect you to fully understand either my actions or reasons. I'm not totally sure I understand them myself—not quite yet, in any case. But I do know that what I've done will be for the best. I once told Papa he must learn to think with his heart. And that is what I have done. I love Jamie for many reasons, not the least of which is that he's a man Robin would have liked, a man to*

whom he would have gladly entrusted the welfare of his son. Open your heart to me, Mama, and bless us.

Alex

Hanna had folded the wrinkled sheet of paper and put it carefully aside. She was thinking at that moment of Colin, the glimpse of him she had seen from her window. He had been in the arms of Jamie Ross as they left the house and went to the car. Colin had been clinging to the man's neck—and he had been laughing.

"There they are " the earl shouted, pointing upward with his umbrella. "They're waving at someone in the crowd. Must be Charles."

They stood alone on the dock between the looming side of the ship and a towering, open-sided structure crowded with people who were waving to the ship's passengers. A blast from the ship's horn—answering toots from tugboats. The liner began to drift away from the dockside and out into the broad stretch of Southampton water.

"They've spotted us, by God!" the earl shouted again, waving his umbrella furiously.

Hanna could see them now—small figures standing at the rail. Colin was waving his arms. She waved back. And then the great ship turned slowly and they were lost to view.

"Ten days," the earl said in a kind of wonder. "Do you realize that, Hanna? We could be in California in a mere ten days. Quite possibly less. Something to think about this winter. Yes, indeed. Something to think about."

Hanna nodded, but could say nothing. The ship steaming majestically now toward the Solent and the open sea. Leaving the old world for the new. She whispered something to the wind that sounded to the earl very much like a blessing.

Book Three

SHADOWS

1923

XI

It was an honor to be invited to dine at Wipple's. The old club in Queen Victoria Street frowned on the casual guest. It had been founded by journalists in the eighteenth century as a club for journalists. The view from the upper windows of the embankment and the river had not changed over the years, but the membership had. No Grub Street hacks or Fleet Street stringers belonged to Wipple's any longer. Its membership was small and composed exclusively of newspaper or wire-service owners and editors whose opinions either bolstered or damned the day-to-day events of the nation—if not the world. Guests, by tradition, were limited to those men and women who were, at least at the time of their arrival, considered newsworthy. The "official" guest for the night of March 3 was the Honorable Andrew Bonar Law, who, after the recent downfall of David Lloyd George, found himself an unlikely prime minister at the age of sixty-five, struggling with ill health and a rising and vociferous Labor party that held one hundred and forty-two seats in Parliament.

Another guest of the evening—sponsored by Jacob Golden, although no one could quite understand why—was a Major Archibald P. Truex, a minor functionary at the War Office. There were some whispered speculations about that, for it was noticed by several sharp-eyed editors that Golden and Martin Rilke totally ignored the prime minister and spent the evening in huddled conversations with Major Truex, who was, to be kind, no more than a Whitehall drone. They also noticed the transfer of a manila envelope from the major's hand to those of Jacob Golden.

"What's the blighter up to?" Thornberry of the *Telegraph* remarked to his companion, a senior editor of the *Guardian*.

"Damned if I know. Some sort of *scoop*, I would imagine. That chap Golden. Like father like son—*de mortuis* and all that."

Major Truex, in consideration for an evening at Wipple's and a chance of ingratiating himself with a press lord, had ferreted through the filing cabinets at the War Office and had made copies of all correspondence pertaining to Lieutenant Colonel Fenton Wood-Lacy, Twelfth Battalion, Sixty-fifth Brigade, Iraq. It made depressing reading—except to Jacob Golden, who had discovered the first glimmer of light in it. He sat in the back of his Daimler, smoking a cigarette and humming softly to himself while Martin sat beside him, elbows resting on the fold-down table, scanning through the documents under the pinpoint glare of the reading lamp.

"They have him in a box—or so it seems to me," Martin said.

"Oh, yes," Jacob said cheerfully. "And a very tight little box it is. And Fenton, with characteristic style, keeps making the box stronger. Note the memorandum from RAF command, Baghdad, complaining to the army commander of Fenton's 'interference' and 'unorthodoxy.'"

"I just read it. That sort of criticism certainly won't do him any good."

"My dear chap, it's that sort of criticism that will get him home and assigned to the staff college."

"Your logic escapes me."

"It's simple, really—one merely has to understand the workings of the military mind at the higher levels of command. The more Fenton irritates them with his so-called unorthodoxy, the harder they'll bear down on the poor blighter and try to force his resignation from the service of king and country."

"That would be the best thing that could happen, it seems to me."

"To you perhaps, but not to Fenton. If he were hounded out of the army, it would destroy him—and everyone close to him. It's my opinion—and the opinion of my newspaper, which is one and the same thing—that little Britain might well be in dire straits one day unless the leadership of her armed forces is composed of men of imagination and vision. Do you know where the vast majority of our future military leaders are? They're buried in French and Belgian mud, that's where they are. And the type of ossified thinking that put them there still permeates the marble corridors of Whitehall. And furthermore—"

Martin raised a protesting hand. "Please, Jacob, don't try out your editorials on me." He removed his eyeglasses and polished them with a handkerchief. "You seem to be in fine jingo voice tonight."

"I happen to be a person who abhors war—as do the

readers of the *Post*. We made a survey—one of those man-in-the-street things—"

"I read it," Martin said dryly.

"And your conclusions?"

"That everyone wants the abolition of war—but that they want Britannia to rule the waves."

Jacob laughed and flicked cigarette ash on the carpeting. "Quite so. And rule the land and air as well. They don't, of course, want to pay for the honor with increased taxes. Thus the appeal of the budding Royal Air Force. Trenchard has sold his service very well. Why have vast, expensive armies—armies led by Boer War fossils—when one can achieve the same purpose with a few dashing lads in flying machines? The RAF is being sold like biscuits or bootblacking. Everything is young—daring—new. Trenchard points to the fact that it's the RAF who are holding the lid down in Iraq, keeping Faisal on the throne, and protecting the flow of oil from Abadan, not to mention the drilling at Mosul. And doing it all for the cost of a few bombs dropped on Arab villages.

"Stuff and nonsense. A false illusion. The only thing an airplane will ever conquer is another airplane. Read Fenton's report in rebuttal to the RAF wing commander's complaint. It's damned interesting. I intend to have a dozen copies made of it."

"I'll read it when I get home. I'm getting slightly sick."

"It was that final drink, old lad. I warned you about mixing gin and champagne. Stop off at my place and read it. I'll have Dunsford fix you a stomach settler."

* * *

Home to Jacob was now a four-story house in Berkeley Square, with large offices, a conference room, Teletype machines, and batteries of telephones on the ground floor. It had been his father's London residence and was still filled with Lord Crewe's furnishings and artworks. Jacob had simply moved in and hung up his clothes. The Teletype machines had not missed a beat. The news did not pause in mourning.

"Feeling better?"

Martin had downed the fizzy concoction prepared by Jacob's butler and belched in response to the question.

"Excuse me—and thanks."

"You know what the cockneys call gin, don't you?" Jacob said. "Blue ruin—because the face turns blue if one drinks enough of it. You're almost cerulean with your damned martinis."

They were seated in the billiard room on the third floor, a solid room of mahogany, leather, and green baize.

"May I ask a question, Jacob—before I read this?"

"Fire away."

"You've become obsessive about Fenton's problems during the past eight or nine months. Why?"

Jacob's expression was blank. "He's a friend of mine."

"He's my friend as well, but he's not a child in the clutches of wicked guardians. He isn't even being singled out for special treatment, just handed a particularly rotten post. He has two choices. He can turn in his commission and come back to Civvy Street, or he can have Winifred and the kids move to Baghdad where he can see them at least occasionally."

"Quite true, Martin. But in the first case, he will never hand in his commission—you know that as well as I do. And as for the second, there's a special cemetery in Baghdad for Europeans—mostly filled with women and children. Cholera and typhus are as common there as chilblains in an English winter. No, Martin. Fenton would never allow Winnie to go there. And neither would I."

"I see." Martin took out his glasses and settled back in his chair to read the report.

"Your utterance of *I see* had a peculiar tone to it," Jacob said as he stepped to the liquor cabinet and reached for a decanter. "I don't think you see anything at all."

"No. Nothing. I was given the Pulitzer because I'm stupid."

Jacob poured some whiskey into a glass and downed it neat. "You see what, exactly?"

"A man in love with a married woman."

"Is it that apparent?"

"It is to me. I also see a man in an agony of determination not to play David to a certain warrior's Uriah. You should have stuck to chorus girls—or lusty Russian Amazons—and not tangled yourself up in triangles."

"I'm not 'tangled up,' as you put it. Winnie and I have been having an affair—a love affair, at least from my point of view. Rather more of a *comfort* affair from hers. There's only one man she'll ever truly love, and it isn't me." He poured another whiskey. "I thought on the day this whole thing started it would be the only day. I was wrong. We see each other whenever she gets down to London. There are only two ways it can end: if Fenton comes back to England, or if he dies in Iraq. In either case I lose. Give her up if he comes back, or, if he should be killed out there, I'll be faced with a pall of guilt so impenetrable that all the love in the world couldn't sweep it away. Bit of a do, isn't it?"

"Yes," Martin said. "Bit of a do. How does whiskey mix with Bromo-Seltzer?"

"Quite well, actually." He reached for decanter and glass. "I'll give you a dollop of good Highland malt and then, *please*, read that bloody report."

The report was long and detailed. It was dated October 17, 1922, from F. Wood-Lacy, Lt. Col., 12 Batt., Bani el Abbas, to Officer Commanding 65th Brigade, Baghdad. Written in stiff, soldierly prose, it was an explanation of events that had occurred during an expedition against marauding Jangalis tribesmen between the 9th and the 23rd of September. Fenton's force had consisted of one troop of Indian cavalry, four Rolls-Royce armored cars, and two companies of soldiers, half on foot and the rest in Ford trucks. What had irritated the RAF command in Baghdad was the fact that Fenton had somehow—"in a devious manner," the RAF referred to it—talked the RAF squadron commander at Tikrit out of a strictly punitive bombing of Jangalis villages in the Jebel Hamrin and into joining the army expedition. Two Bristol fighters had been modified—"severely altered without official sanction"—to hold radiotelegraph transmitters and receivers. Another radiotelegraph transmitter-receiver was installed in one of the Ford trucks, and a combined operation, controlled by Fenton on the ground, was then undertaken which succeeded in rounding up the tribesmen and disarming them with only a few casualties on either side. It was the "coordination of forces" that had infuriated RAF Baghdad.

"Seems damned clever to me," Martin said, rubbing his eyes and putting his glasses in their case.

"Ah, yes. But too clever by half. You see, Martin, the RAF is the RAF and not the bloody army. They see themselves as the sole instrument for pacifying Iraq—that was Trenchard's promise to Whitehall: a few, relatively cheap squadrons of fighter-bombers to patrol the country and punish any tribes who revolt against King Faisal's quite unpopular regime. They consider the army to be mere guards along the railway pipelines and roads. The result being that the RAF punishes from the air by dropping bombs on villages and machine-gunning goat herds and camel herds and bedouin tents, but they're not achieving any permanent results. They're punishing, all right, but not pacifying. It takes troops to do that, and intelligent troop commanders who can sit down with the tribal leaders and work out truces and peace pacts.

"I think what Fenton did—and if I know Fenton, is still doing—warrants press exposure. It's novel—exciting—modern. I know that your boss would go for it—like a ton of bricks, as you Yanks say. Think of it, Martin. Radiotelegraphy—crude by current equipment, but still *radio*, old boy. Your man Kingsford's obsession. Bloody good publicity."

Martin nodded and sipped his whiskey. "How will this help Fenton?"

"Well, I see it this way. Could backfire, of course,

but that's the risk. Supposing INA—a totally objective news source—released a long article about a certain British colonel's novel methods in Iraq—dashing, yet sound; bold, innovative, up-to-the-minute, and, above all, successful. The *Daily Post* would print the article along with photographs and an editorial pleading for increased unity between the services, and for experimentation and freshness in military thinking. We would say that men on the order of Colonel Wood-Lacy could better serve their country by working on new ideas at the staff college, so that if, God forbid, we should ever have another war, our future generals wouldn't fight it like the last one."

Jacob took a hefty drink and refilled his glass. "I think it might work. The timing is perfect. The government needs all the help it can get. I've had old Bonar Law and Stanley Baldwin on the phone several times in the past few weeks asking me to please go soft on this or play down that or boost the other thing. They need me on their side. The article, the editorial, and a little quiet nudging from me will get a few telephones ringing in the War Office and Fenton will get new orders—in appreciation for a job well done. You'll see."

"I hope you're right. Now all I have to do is convince Scott Kingsford that sending a reporter to Iraq is worth the expense."

"Oh," Jacob said airily, "I already cabled him and got an affirmative answer. I'll supply the transport and Kingsford will provide his best man—*you*, old chap."

* * *

The twin-engine Felixstowe F.5 flying boat, its graceful hull painted yellow, its nose adorned with discreet lettering—*London Daily Post*—cut the dark gray waters of the Medway, bounced gently, and then soared to the somber skies and headed for the English Channel. There were five passengers, half the maximum number, and the uniformed cabin attendant had no problem keeping everyone supplied with food and drink. Two of the passengers, a *Daily Post* reporter and a photographer, would disembark at the plane's first stop, Geneva. The rest would go on, with landings at Taranto and Crete for rest and refueling, then on to the Nile and Cairo.

Martin fell asleep on take-off and only awoke when the large plane touched down on the icy waters of Lake Geneva. When the flight resumed in the morning he still felt tired and realized, as he looked down at the snow-covered Alps, what a blessing this trip was for him. He had not argued against Jacob's rather crazy scheme—had not volunteered to tell him that if he wanted seven or eight thousand words praising Fenton to the skies he could write them without bothering to leave his office in Fleet Street.

An inner voice—a tired, played-out voice—had urged him to go. He was worn down by the day-to-day routine of running the bureau. Of days filled with hiring and firing, of slashing a blue pencil across miles of typewritten copy. Tired to the bone of sending off reams of trivia to the world's newspapers—fashion news from Paris; travel bargains in England, France, Spain, and Italy; gushing accounts of the activities of theatrical, motion-picture, and literary figures, sporting events; heartwarming tales of human interest and titillating crimes of passion. His vision of the world had been reduced to what came over the teleprinters, and was being molded and directed by the vision of Scott Kingsford. As he gazed down at the blue-green Adriatic and the Italian coastline, he knew that he had reached a point of decision. When the plane landed in the Gulf of Taranto and taxied slowly toward the seaplane base at Cape San Vito, he had made up his mind. This was his last job for the International News Agency.

The air service to Iraq was controlled by the British. There were two flights a month from Cairo to Baghdad via Amman in Trans-Jordania, a seven-and-a-half-hour flight in a converted Vickers Vimy bomber, lumbering and noisy. None of Martin's fellow passengers, mostly high-ranking army officers or civil servants, seemed overjoyed when Baghdad appeared out of the wastes of the desert below. A mud-brown city straddling the yellow flood of the Tigris. A frieze of date palms and the peacock hues of mosques and minarets provided the only dots of brightness in the dun-colored landscape.

"You're fortunate not to be arriving in June or July," a man seated next to Martin remarked. He had something to do with the operation of the Baghdad-to-Basra railway, but Martin had forgotten his name.

"Oh, my, yes," the man continued. "One simply cannot comprehend the heat unless one has spent a summer here. One hundred twelve degrees is not uncommon in the middle of the night. And I've seen it reach one hundred twenty-five degrees in New Street at two o'clock in the afternoon when a simoon was blowing. My poor wife spent only one summer here, spending her days deep in the *serdah* beneath the house and her nights on the roof being eaten alive by mosqui-

toes. And then our youngest died—from drinking un-
boiled milk. Cholera, you see. And so I sent them all
packing back to Egypt. Alexandria is such a pleasant
place."

The builders of empire, Martin was thinking as he
was being driven through the streets of the city after
crossing the Maude Bridge. Making the railways run
and drilling for oil in the sands. Young army and RAF
officers with pink cheeks strolled through the streets
on their way to their clubs, as cool and well dressed as
though they were strolling along Piccadilly, barely
glancing at the hordes of Kurds, Parsees, turbaned
Moslems and Turks, Negro slaves, Armenians. Hebrew women covered from head to toe in silken robes,
Chaldeans and Persians. The whole polyglot stew of
the Middle East. The red-black-white-and-green flag
of the kingdom of Iraq flew over the palace by the
river, but the Union Jack hanging limply above the
British Residency was the only flag that mattered.

North of the city there was only the desert and the
winding river. Standing on the deck of the little river
steamer, Martin could see an occasional camel train
plodding slowly southward in the dust and a few
mud-walled villages along the crest of the riverbank.
A machine gun in the bow of the ship, manned by
turbaned Marathas, waved lazily back and forth
above the sandbags stacked around it. Sniping at the
boats was more of a sport than an expression of anger
among the Arabs and wandering Buddhoos, but the
bullets could kill and the superstructure of the
steamer was pockmarked.

At Bani el Abbas the flag of England whipped in
the wind over the military cantonment at the edge of

the ramshackle town. Martin scanned the shoreline with binoculars. The troops were under canvas, but there were a few corrugated-iron sheds and Nissen huts—a lorry park—a row of armored cars. Belts of barbed wire surrounded the outpost like a thorn fence. Shifting his view toward the town, he spotted Fenton standing on the jetty—a tall, slim, khaki-clad figure, his face shadowed by the broad rim of his topee.

"Well," he said, standing motionless on the jetty as Martin came down the gangplank, "look what the ruddy wind blew in."

"Just happened to be in the neighborhood," Martin said. "Lovely little garden spot you have here."

"Pure heaven on earth, old boy." He looked down at Martin's leather suitcase. "Is that all your luggage?"

"Yes, I'm not planning on staying long."

"Wise decision."

Fenton pointed to the suitcase, said something in Hindustani, and an Indian soldier walked over, picked up the suitcase, and carried it off.

"I suppose you were surprised to get my radiogram."

"Surprised is hardly the word, Martin. For the life of me, I can't see what brings you here. Nothing happens along the Tigris except the meanest forms of death."

The town was a warren of mud houses and narrow, twisting streets and alleys. Kurds and Arabs filled the bazaar or sat in small groups under the awnings of the coffeehouses, watching with smoldering eyes the strutting gendarmerie in kaffiyehs and khaki, spurs, bandoliers and pistols.

"They hate everyone," Fenton said, lounging back in the car. "This bloody country is a real devil of a place. They hated the Turks and they hate us for getting the mandate and putting Emir Faisal on the throne. They don't want a Hejaz Arab, they just want to be independent and fight it out among themselves. And now Sheikh Mahmud has the Kurds in open revolt. I had to put the town off-limits to the troops. We had a corporal get his throat cut last week. Right in the bazaar."

"At least the weather's decent," Martin said.

"Not bad. The rains are over. In another month or two the heat starts and it comes down on you like a hammer all through September."

"Maybe you'll be out of here by then."

"Not bloddy likely. All I'll get is two weeks' leave in Baghdad. Have a few drinks at the Sports Club and play some polo." He stared hopelessly ahead. "I hope to God you brought some mail from Winnie."

"Mounds of it."

"Marvelous. I'll wallow in it before dinner. You'll dine with us in the mess and then we'll hole up in my quarters and you can bring me up to date. It's like living on the far side of the moon here."

The mess was an open-sided tent with mosquito netting hanging down like tent flaps. The service was suitably civilized with the mess attendants scurrying about in white jackets and serving chilled wines and beer and lukewarm whiskey sodas. The English officers were mostly young and on their first tour abroad, but several had fought in Mesopotamia during the war, as had the three Indian risaldars from the cavalry troop. The atmosphere in the mess was subdued, as a company of Lancashires and the cavalry had just returned to camp that morning after a ten-day search for an RAF plane that had run out of fuel. They had found the plane fifty miles from the river, its pilot and observer spread-eagled on the sand with their throats cut and their severed genitals stuffed in their mouths.

"It's rough on the new lads," Fenton said as he poured whiskey in his quarters—one of the Nissen huts. "They've never seen violent death before, only read about it in books. They can accept a clean bullet hole in a chap's head, but to find chaps their own age tortured and mutilated just shakes them to the ruddy core."

"Does that sort of thing happen often?" Martin asked, his notebook beside him on the seat.

"Not every day in the week, no. But once is too often." He handed Martin a whiskey. "And the terrible fact is it will keep on happening every time a plane goes down unless troops can get to the crew in time. Poor blighters don't get much time, though. The Buddhoos always get to them first."

"What the hell are Buddhoos?"

"Any roaming group of Persian or Arab bandits. The country's infested with them. They like to capture the air crews alive, strip them, and then turn them over to the women for torture. If the lads knew what they were in for, they'd shoot themselves first, but the English are not a suicidal race."

He took a hefty swallow of whiskey and began to pace the narrow room. "I've tried to discuss the folly of these air strikes against remote villages with the RAF brass in Baghdad and Mosul, but they only half-listen. Polite, you know, but they really want me to shut up and mind my own bloody business. I have more luck with the local boys, the squadron leaders who have to do the nasty work. They fly these missions in squadron strength and stick together to keep from straying, but they still have chaps crash-landing in the desert or the hills. Not shot up, you understand; the poor bloody sods of Arabs never do get the satisfaction of bringing down a Brisfit with a rifle. It's mechanical problems—engines conk out from sand and dust in the air intakes, or there's too much grit in the oil and the bearings burn out. A thousand and one things can happen to a piece of machinery in this climate.

"Anyway, down they go, with nine out of ten men surviving the crash—and there's not a damn thing the men in the air can do for their pals on the ground. Bloody *nothing*. Just circle them for a while and wave goodbye. As soon as the planes have flown off, the Buddhoos close in. If not right away, soon enough. And then the butchering begins."

"It sounds pretty grim."

"It *is* grim. The Buddhoo women know what to do to a man with their goat-skinning knives. But enough gruesome stories. The point is that it shouldn't happen. Planes should only go out in conjunction with either motorized infantry or the cavalry, with the entire operation controlled and coordinated via radiotelegraph. The ruddy equipment is here, tons of it. Shiploads of American supplies were dumped in this country during the last year of the war. There must be ten thousand Ford trucks, and warehouses in Basra filled with radio sets. I grabbed half a dozen of the radios—U.S. Army Signal Corps-type SCR-49s. Lovely, compact little beauties—work off storage batteries for ground use and off the plane's generator, with some rewiring."

"You're in trouble over that, aren't you, Fenton?"

"Yes, but I don't give a damn. What more can they do to me? Besides, HQ in Baghdad thought it amusing that RAF command was in a tizzy, so that was one up for my side. The jealousy—no, outright animosity between the services is highly obvious here among the brass. It doesn't filter down to the men in the field, thank God. Number Fourteen Squadron at Tikrit has three radio-equipped planes and they won't fly a mission without informing me. Before they take off, I send out some cavalry and a company in Ford lorries, with a radio and two signalmen in one of them. If anything goes wrong during the flight, we can be on the scene pretty damn quickly. The plane the chaps found the other day was from Number Six Squadron in Samarrah. They have an ass of a commander who thinks radiotelegraph is a toy. If he thought differently, two fine chaps would still have their balls." He rubbed the back of his hand across his brow. "Jesus, let's talk about England and get quietly sloshed. Did you see Winnie up in Suffolk?"

"Yes—Jacob and I drove up there just before I left."

"Bloody awful about old Crewe. Heard about it, and then Jacob sent me a long letter. How's he bearing up as head of a newspaper empire?"

"Quite well."

"Well, he's adaptable, isn't he?"

"Yes—and more competent than he realizes."

Fenton sat on the edge of his desk and nursed his whiskey. "So you went up to my little corner of the world. Did you take my boat out?"

"God, no. It was blowing up a storm."

"Bosh, dear chap. I've sailed the Deben in raging

January gales." He stared down into his glass for a moment. "And the twins—and little Kate?"

"Three beautiful girls. You'll be proud of them, Fenton."

"Will? I am now. Bloody army. They were smarter in Victoria's time. No officer below the rank of brigadier general got married. It's too damn hard on a man—and a woman, if it comes to that."

"Still not ready to cash in your chips?"

"No. I won't be bluffed out of the game. They can keep me here until it hurts like hell, but they can't keep me here forever."

Martin got little sleep. He sat up in his bed in the visiting officers' quarters—a fancy name for a wood-and-canvas hut—writing in his journal until well past midnight. Then, when he did turn out the kerosene lamp, the sounds of the big camp disturbed him. He could hear the braying of mules and the whinnying of horses, the moan of the wind and the flapping of canvas, the crunch of boots in the sandy ground. He thought of lean, wolfish Buddhoos, their womenfolk trailing them like mad cats. And then the darkness was rent by a Stokes gun firing star shell, followed by the distant crack of a rifle. Sentries getting nervous, he reasoned. Driving off the darkness and firing at shadows. It reminded him of Gallipoli—the British and French lines at Cape Helles. He drifted in and out of an uneasy sleep and was grateful for the dawn and the bugle blowing reveille.

"Sleep well, sir?" a young second lieutenant asked as Martin sat down for breakfast in the mess tent.

"No. All that shooting last night."

"Oh, that's quite normal, sir. Just keeps the Bud-dhoos honest. They're sneaky little buggers. Some of them slipped under the wire one night to steal a horse. Tied all four legs and were dragging it out *under* the wire when a sentry spotted them."

"I hate to think what they planned for the poor beast."

The lieutenant looked shocked. "Oh, no, sir. They're *very* kind to animals."

There was a morning parade, as much in Martin's honor as to keep the men on their toes and feeling "regimental." There was a band of sorts—two drum-mers and three men with fifes—and they played "The Bonnie English Rose" and "The British Grenadiers" as the Lancashires and the Punjabis lined up in ordered ranks and the troop of lancers rode slowly across the parade ground in front of the armored cars. Fenton looked every inch a Coldstream Guards' officer re-viewing his men at Buckingham Palace, until he shoved his right hand into his pocket. The noncha-lance seemed perfectly in keeping with his ragtag bat-talion stationed on the edge of nowhere. When the battalion was dismissed, a corporal of the Lancs stepped out of the line, raised his sun helmet high above his head, and shouted: "Three cheers for ol' Hawk! Hip, hip . . ." The cheering was loud—and genuine.

"It's what keeps you in, isn't it?" Martin said quietly as he had a midmorning whiskey with Fenton in the mess. "The whole bull, brass, and comrade part of it. Old Hawk being cheered by his men."

Fenton frowned slightly and reached for the bottle of scotch. "It must be part of the reason, Martin. I've often asked myself that. I know it's deeply personal. Nothing to do with patriotism or King and Country. I suppose it's all tied in with my childhood, when Uncle Julian dropped by on his rare leaves. My father was such an ordered man—an architect and builder. One brick carefully laid on another. Uncle Julian had seen the other side of man's nature and was a part of it. The sword-bearers as distinct from the trowel-bearers. His tales—Christ, his tales: Chinese Gordon and the Sudan, crushing the Ashanti at Coomassie, high deeds and perils on the northwest frontier. Heady brew. When I left Sandhurst I expected to die in six months leading a forlorn hope in some exotic part of the world. Instead I was a subaltern in the Coldstreams banging debutantes all over Mayfair. It was a bit of a shock, but I took it in stride. I take everything in stride, Martin, even seventy-percent casualties on the Somme. I never broke down. Never turned into a two-bottle-a-day man. I'm a professional."

The Bristol fighter came low over the camp shortly before noon, circled the flagpole to check which way the wind was blowing, and then landed on a stretch of flat ground and taxied toward the barbed wire and the gate. A thin, gangly man in his late twenties climbed out of the front cockpit, the two thick stripes and one thin one on his sleeves proclaiming him a squadron leader in the Royal Air Force. He came cheerily into the mess and downed a cool bottle of beer without pausing for breath. Fenton introduced him to Martin as F.A.M. Weedlock.

"I've known old Fam here since the retreat from Mons."

"*Before* the glorious retreat," Weedlock corrected. "I was flying reconnaissance and spotted the Boche pouring through Belgium. Flying a rickety old Avro. What a bloody lark!" He signaled the mess attendant for another beer and then grinned at Fenton. "Well, you old cock sparrow, got orders today from Wing to pay a visit to Sheikh Ali Gharbi. Intelligence—if one can call it that with a straight face—says the old bastard's been running guns down from Kurdistan and has them stockpiled in those villages of his along the Shatt el Adhaim.

"When are you to take off?"

"In three days—dawn on the twenty-first."

"There'll be more than guns in those villages," Fenton said grimly. "Your bloody bombs can't tell the difference between a crate of rifles and a tent full of kids."

"I have noticed that," Weedlock said dryly.

Fenton glanced at his wristwatch. "I'll see if I can get through to Baghdad on the blower—if the Buddhoos haven't cut the wires again."

The flying officer watched him stride out of the mess and then smiled at Martin. "Bloody fucking genius that man. You known him long?"

"Since before the war."

"And what do you do?"

"I'm a journalist."

"Right. Of course you are. Rilke. The name sinks home now. Have you read the paper Hawk's written?"

"What paper?"

"Have him show it to you. As a war correspondent you'd be interested. Two hundred pages entitled *The Integration of Divisional Striking Forces in Combined*

Operations—with aircraft data courtesy of F.A.M. Weedlock."

"What is it about?"

"Just about everything the army and air force is against at the moment. Left to the belly and right to the jaw, as the pugilist chaps would say. The old one-two. Hawk's theory is that every division in the field would be highly mobile and totally integrated—planes, tanks or armored cars, motorized infantry and artillery. One general in charge of the whole kit and caboodle. Radios in every plane, tank, and lorry. It's complex and technical, but I think you'd enjoy it."

"What does he intend doing with it?"

"Christ knows. I don't think it's the sort of thing the War Office would go for these days. Too bloody expensive, for one thing, and steps on too many toes, for another. Can't see the chaps at the Air Ministry putting any of their precious planes back under army control—and the Tank Corps has the quaint notion it's above any control. Oh, well, so it goes."

Fenton came back into the mess and leaned against the bar. "Bloody line's been cut somewhere below Kasarin. Some Iraqi cavalry are looking for the break now. Anyway, what Baghdad doesn't know can't upset them. We'll follow plan B, Fam—same sort of operation as Sharaban. Grab a beer and come over to the office. We'll study the maps and work out the timetable."

"Can I witness this show?" Martin asked.

"By all means," Fenton replied. "You might as well earn your keep."

* * *

There was a road of sorts, graded by the Turks a long time ago, running from Bani el Abbas eastward toward the cliff faces and high plateau of the Persian frontier. The motorized force made fast progress for sixty miles, the armored cars roaring along in front and the Ford trucks following along in their dust, the troops they contained holding on as best they could as the trucks bounced and swayed over the ruts and potholes. The road finally ended, sliced by wadis, and Fenton, riding in the lead armored car, turned the column off the road across the flat, hard, windswept desert.

Nightfall found them on the edge of a plain strewn with boulders and fragments of rock, as though some violent explosion in eons past had destroyed a mountain and scattered its pieces across the sand. The column pulled up and troops climbed out of the trucks and sprawled wearily on the ground until the British NCO's and the Punjabi havildars brought their men to their feet and set them to pitching shelter tents and digging latrines. Martin, wearing clothes lent to him by a captain in the Lancs, and a sun helmet and quilted spine pad supplied by the quartermaster, walked stiffly to the armored car where Fenton was standing, studying a map by the glow of an electric torch.

"That was one hell of a ride, colonel."

Fenton's smile was wicked. "Wasn't it just! Four days hard march before lorries and balloon tires. Any irreparable damage, old sport?"

"Not if my testicles drop back into place. Where are we exactly?"

"Close to where we want to be." He pointed off across the boulder-strewn waste. "The sheikh's villages are about ten miles due north of here. We'll march off before dawn. The armored cars will skirt this mess by going east and blocking the loop of the Shatt in case our friends try to bolt for Persia."

"The Shatt being a river, I take it."

"Well, a river in the wet season—a nice, flat, dry bed now. We'll be at the main village by nine in the morning, just in time to have the area surrounded before the planes come over."

"And then what?"

"My dear Rilke, that's a question only tomorrow will answer."

Ten men were left behind with a machine gun to guard the trucks. The rest, Lancs and Punjabis, moved off into the predawn wastes carrying nothing but their rifles, a bandolier of ammunition, and two cloth-covered canteens of chlorinated water per man. The five men of the signals section brought the radiotelegraphy set, the storage batteries, and the twenty-foot bamboo pole to raise the aerial wire. They moved quickly and in silence and reached the steep banks of the dry river shortly after 8:30. They all knew, from long experience, that it was the best possible time. Dawn, to the Arabs, was the traditional moment of attack. When the sun was well up they tended to relax their guard and start going about the day's business. Fenton, lying flat in the scrub grass, scanned the main village of Sheikh Ali Gharbi, then handed the powerful binoculars to Martin who lay stiffly beside him.

"Tell me what you see."

Martin saw the village: black tents and mud huts scattered for a quarter of a mile along the riverbank; two hundred or more hobbled camels; a thousand sheep and goats; swarms of half-naked children;

women in dark robes clustered about the well or tend-
ing the numerous fires. The men, many of them with
rifles slung across their backs, strolled together in
small groups or stood clustered in front of the largest
tent.

"Just a lot of village activity." He handed the
glasses back to Fenton. "Anything unusual going on?"

"Yes. There are half a dozen Kurds down there. I
spotted their headgear—*kolas*. They wouldn't be hanging about here unless they had brought something the
sheikh needed. There are guns down there. No doubt
about it. The question is where." He looked at his
watch. "Fam should be here in exactly fifteen minutes. Time for us to get started."

Fenton drew a brass whistle from his pocket, stood
up, and blew three shrill blasts. Activity in the village
became momentarily paralyzed as the British and Indian troops rose to their feet and showed themselves
clearly against the skyline. The Punjabi *subadar-major*
stepped onto the path leading down to the village and
waved a white cloth tied to the end of a rifle.

"Coming down with us?" Fenton asked.

Martin nodded. "That's where the story is."

The Indian officer led the way, followed by Fenton, Martin, and the signalers with the radio gear. The
Arabs made way for them, staring at them with a mixture of fear and hate. When they reached the tent of
the sheikh, Fenton told the signalers to set up the radio.

The Indian officer lowered his rifle. "Well, colonel,
sahib?"

Fenton looked sternly at the Arabs blocking the entrance to the tent. "Tell him I wish to speak with
Sheikh Ali Gharbi. Tell him I am calling in the flying

machines on the telegraph box and they'd better get the sheikh out here pretty damn quick."

He turned away as the *subadar* started talking in Arabic. He watched the signalers attach the radio to the batteries in their leather carrying cases and wind the antenna wire around the bamboo pole. One of the men sat on the ground in front of the set, headphones on, testing the key.

Fenton tapped the man on the shoulder. "Send out code HQS and MBT."

The Arabs knew the significance of the clicking telegraph key from as far back as their years under the Turks. The clicking brought troops down among them. They knew how to stop it by climbing the poles and cutting the wires, but the radiotelegraph dismayed them. They watched closely as the British soldier worked the key. There were no wires to cut. The wire on the bamboo pole stuck in the sand went nowhere. And yet, even as they stared, they could hear the distant hum of engines.

The sheikh protested. He was an old man, crippled in one leg from an ancient wound. His small black eyes burned like coals in the leathery seams of his face.

"He says they have done nothing," the *subadar* said. "He says they have lived up to the treaty in every word and deed."

"Tell him he lies like a Buddhoo," Fenton said. "Tell him I know there are more guns and ammunition in the village than allowed by the treaty. Tell him if he doesn't show us where they are I'll have the flying machines drop bombs."

A panic was spreading through the village now as

the silver biplanes came into view, nine of them in three V-shaped waves coming low over the sand hills.

"Message from the planes, sir," the radio operator called out. "Codes HGL and KDS."

Fenton removed a slim notebook from the top pocket of his jacket and glanced at the code lists.

"Send affirmative—and code QLP."

"What does that mean?" Martin asked.

"QLP is circle and fire into the wilderness. Just to let these rogues know we mean business." He glowered at the sheikh and then said to the *subadar*: "You can tell the chief I've ordered the planes to test their machine guns. Tell him he knows what will happen to his people if they swing the guns on the villages."

The Bristol fighters swung into a line ahead formation and began to circle, banking sharply so that the rear gunners could swing their twin Lewis guns toward the barren ground beyond the dry riverbed. Only the lead plane, bearing a radio operator in place of a gunner, did not fire. The others cut loose and tracer slashed downward, churning yellow plumes of dust and sending clots of bullet-chewed earth into the air. Empty shell cases spewed downward like a brass rain.

The old sheikh stared at the sight like a man in a trance. Then he moaned and sat down limply on the ground and began to speak in a low, choked voice.

"The guns and cartridges are buried in the sand," the Indian officer said, smiling. "They're in the center of the riverbed—between those two white boulders."

"Good," Fenton said crisply. "Send code WQT." He stepped away from the tent and blew three notes on his whistle. A squad of Lancs came running down from the slopes, rifles slung over their shoulders.

"See those white boulders about three hundred yards up the bed?" he said as a corporal ran up to him. "Mark the spot between them with smoke and then get the hell out of the way."

The planes continued to circle, like lazy silver hawks against the vivid blue sky. When the smoke canisters had been set alight and the squad had dispersed, the planes dipped into shallow dives and dropped their two-hundred-pound bombs with great precision on top of the smoke. Geysers of sand and the shattered fragments of wooden crates and rifles spewed upward in the scarlet-and-black explosions. And while Martin took pictures with his little folding Kodak, ten thousand rounds of Mauser ammunition went up as well, popping and cracking, turning the riverbed into a churning maelstrom of whipped sand.

Fenton looked at his notebook. "What the hell's the code for 'job well done' and 'hurry on home'?"

"VLK and PVW," the radio operator said.

"Send it—and then call Lieutenant Baxter and tell him to withdraw the armored cars." He draped an arm about Martin's shoulders. "And that's just about that, old boy. We'll poke about in the riverbed and make sure all the guns have been destroyed, then hightail it for barracks, beer, and bed. I hope you got a little something out of all this to write about."

"A little."

"You might remember to note in your story that we left a lot of angry Arabs here, but no dead ones. Some of your more gentle readers might like to know that."

"Yes," Martin said quietly. "I think they would at that."

* * *

The *Daily Post* seaplane cut the turgid waters of the Nile and soared over the rooftops of Cairo. There were only four other passengers—the *Post*'s Egyptian-affairs correspondent and his family on their way back to England on holiday—so Martin could stretch out in comfort across four of the wicker seats and read through his shorthand notes. It would be a good, exciting article, he felt sure. One that would please Kingsford, especially if the photographs of the soldiers using the radio came out. It would help soften Kingsford's annoyance when he received the letter of resignation along with it. The article, and a carbon copy of Fenton's theory on modern warfare, should provide Jacob with the kind of material he needed to convince the War Office that Lieutenant Colonel Wood-Lacy might be a thorn in the side, even a pain in the arse, but was too original a thinker to be wasted in a desert.

"VLK," he whispered. "A job well done." He tried to give some thought to his own future, but the engines droned and the clear Mediterranean sun streamed through the round windows and he fell into a deep, untroubled sleep.

XII

Paul Rilke stood on the promenade deck of the Cunard liner, one pudgy hand resting on the top of his homburg to keep it from blowing away in the wind. It was a brilliant May morning, the Hampshire hills and New Forest bathed in sun, the waters of the Solent a deep, almost painful blue. He breathed deeply a few times, expanding his broad chest, then walked briskly around the deck before going into the saloon lounge for a morning bracer of Cognac and seltzer water.

He was a man that people noticed. Not so much for his looks—a fat, bald man of average height—but for the air of success and self-confidence that flowed from him like an electric charge. He was sixty years of age and looked exactly like a man who was worth fifty million dollars and who had every intention of making fifty million more. As he sipped his drink in the lounge he felt a fleeting regret that the voyage was nearly over. But there was always the return trip to look forward to. He loved ocean travel—the freedom and the fun of it, the abundance of good food and liquor, the long, pleasant nights of poker, and the inevitable—and sought-after—adventure. His wife of thirty-three years never accompanied him on his twice-yearly trips to Europe. She suffered from totally incapacitating seasickness, an affliction for which he thanked the Almighty.

When he entered his stateroom the woman was still there. She was only partially dressed, in a provocative black lace garter belt and a short, flimsy chemise, over the top of which peeked one large, firm, mauve-tipped breast. She was no more than twenty-five and claimed to be the wife of a Portuguese diplomat, but she had all the sexual refinements of a professional adventuress plying her first-class trade on the trans-atlantic run. He had an eye for the type and had never slept one night of an ocean crossing alone.

"I am so sorry to see land," the woman said, pouting. "So sorry it is over."

"So am I, honeybunch." He sat on the edge of the bed and motioned to her. She came with the eagerness of a spaniel and sat on his lap. He stroked her naked breast and tweaked the nipple.

"There's a little something in my coat pocket, honeybunch. Call it a gift."

After the woman had gone, he went into the bath-room, washed lip rouge from his face, and straight-ened his clothing. It had been a fine trip and he felt a wondrous sense of contentment. He was by nature a faithful husband; unlike many men he knew at the Union Club in Chicago, he had no sugar baby stuck away in an apartment. But he excluded the high seas from his moral conscience.

He spotted Martin in the crowd as he came down the gangway.

"It was damn good of you to meet me."

"No trouble, Uncle Paul."

Paul traveled light—a steamer trunk and a suitcase.

Banes, with the aid of a Cunard porter, secured the luggage to the rack at the rear of the car.

"I saw Hanna and Tony in Chicago," Paul said as he squeezed his bulk into the back of the Rolls. "California-bound. I understand Alexandra's in the family way."

"That's right," Martin said as he got in beside him. "Six months along."

"Are you caretaking at the Pryory?"

"Houseguesting. I'm writing another book, and it's more peaceful here than in London. And I enjoy Charles's company."

Paul bit the tip off a cigar and spat it out the window. "I saw your ex-boss in New York. I'm a heavy investor in his Consolidated Broadcasters setup. He still can't figure out why you quit. Why did you?"

"I'm not sure. Just got tired of it, I guess."

"What do you do for money?"

"I had enough saved—and I sell a few articles."

"Why don't you work for me? I need an agent in Germany I can trust."

"Thanks, but no. Sounds like a good job for Karl."

Paul snorted and lit his cigar. "I wouldn't trust that son of mine to go out and buy me a newspaper. A Yale man! Jesus Christ. I stuck him in the advertising department of Rilke Metals—kitchen stove division." He puffed on the cigar and squinted at Martin. "You don't give a damn about money, do you?"

"No."

"Like father like son. Willie was the same. When we were kids, Papa gave us fifty cents a week. I'd put aside a quarter and when I had five dollars I'd buy a share on margin from Papa's broker. Willie'd blow his half-buck in a day."

"Well," Martin said lamely, "that's how it goes."

The problem with being around Uncle Paul was that he was always dredging up the past. A reminder here, a remembrance there. Martin gazed out of the window as the car rolled out of Southampton. Happy-go-lucky William Frederick Rilke—a myth shared by both Paul and Hanna. The bohemian brother who had tossed away his inheritance to run off to Paris and become a painter. Martin's only memories of his father were of a morose, yellow-bearded man who had slipped in and out of their apartment in the rue Lepic like shadow and smoke. He was buried in the *cimetière* de Montmartre in a walled-off section reserved for suicides.

It was difficult to equate Uncle Paul now with the slender man who had come to Paris in the winter of that year of death, the winter of 1898, and had offered to take his brother's wife and son back to Chicago with him. His mother, speaking painful English, had agreed, and back they had gone. Paul had been kind and generous, buying a little house for them and paying a monthly allowance even after his mother had built up a modest business as Madame René, Modiste. It had been Paul's money that had sent him through the University of Chicago, and he had lived in his uncle's North Side mansion after his mother's death. He had many reasons to be grateful and he genuinely liked the man even though they disagreed on practically everything.

Banes turned off the highway at Godalming and down a narrow twisting road toward Abingdon.

"Abingdon Pryory," Paul said. "I remember the first time I ever saw this place. Came over with the old man for Hanna's wedding. Jessie and I had only been married a year. That was Jessie's first and last sea voyage. She was sicker than a hound.

"Well, let me tell you, Martin, there was no man on God's sweet earth tighter with a penny than your grandfather. I worked for him, of course—managed two of the breweries—and all he paid me was fifty dollars a week. Jessie and I lived with him, in the big old house on Prairie Avenue that was torn down before you were born. He deducted twenty-five dollars from my pay for room and board. Oh, he was something, the old man. They broke the mold after he came into the world. The only person he was ever generous with was Hanna. She just had to hold out her hand and he'd plunk a ten-dollar gold piece into it. That sure burned your Aunt Jessie, I can tell you.

"So, anyway, here we were in England, coming down this very road in a coach and pair—a victoria, I guess it was—the grooms in the Greville livery and Jessie just fuming inside. I mean, here she was, married to a man bringing in fifty dollars a week—and handing half of that back—and here was her sister-in-law, who she had never liked anyway, about to be married to a bona-fide English lord who had grooms in livery and matched grays. She burned even more when she caught sight of the house. Back home we lived in three rooms. Three *small* rooms in that ramshackle barn of a house—and here was Hanna about to be the mistress of a goddamn castle!

"Anyway . . . the old man pointed to the house and said in his crazy katzenjammer English how happy he was that his Hanna was marrying a nobleman, but that it was a pity the old earl had squandered so much of the estate before he died. 'You mean he's *broke?*' Jessie asked—sounding a bit pleased. 'Oh, ja, ja,' the old man said, then shouted proudly: "But vun million dollars cash I haf for der dowry given!'

"Martin, I swear to God, I thought Jessie was about to drop dead right there on the seat. And let me tell you, a million dollars was a million *dollars* in those days. Poor Jessie. She never got over the shock. I think that's why she has fourteen fur coats and seven cars and solid gold plumbing in every bathroom in the house. It just unhinged her mind."

Charles made a spectacular carom shot and then leaned on his cue as though oblivious to what he had done.

"You know, Martin, I like Uncle Paul. He has such a zest for life—and is absolutely unabashed about his love of money. I find that refreshing. So many of the men who make fortunes these days try to atone for it in good deeds. Homes for impregnated mill girls or something. I can't imagine Paul *giving* anything away."

Martin studied the table and tried to work out a shot. "Well, he's owned the losingest team in the American League for the past twenty years. I suppose that's a form of charity—at least to the players. That's baseball, by the way—an American game."

"I have heard of it," Charles said laconically, watching Martin miss his shot by a wide margin. "Obviously billiards is not."

"I used to be damned good. The eye has lost . . . whatever an eye loses."

Charles chalked his cue. "He wants you to work for him."

"I know. What did he say to you?"

"He offered a five-thousand-dollar donation to the school—if I could convince you that joining the old family firm was in your best interest. I rather like the proposition. Not a whiff of charity. Something for something."

"I suppose the school could use the money."

"Oh, yes, but we can survive very well without it. Why does he want you?"

Martin racked his stick and ambled over to the sideboard to pour a whiskey.

"Paul's thinking is about as devious as a straight ruler. He's always had a twinge of conscience about me. It's the inheritance. I was—oh, I don't know, five or six, when Grandfather Rilke died. I never knew I had an American grandfather. My father never spoke of his family. Anyway, according to what my mother told me later, the reality of being disowned came to my father when he received a check from a Chicago law firm in the amount of one dollar. He cashed it and got drunk. I imagine one could get very drunk in Paris on one dollar in those days.

"Paul gained a good deal by my father's disownment. When old Rilke died, he got what would have been his brother's share. It gave him two-thirds of the Rilke estate and Hanna one-third. That was fair enough, I suppose, because Paul had been running the business for several years. He could have ignored my mother and me—except for token money orders—but he came to France and brought us back. Looked after us very well and gave me everything but a share of the profits."

"And now he wants you to sign on. Potential heir apparent, do you think?"

"I don't know. Something on that order perhaps.

Karl's a washout. A pompous prig with a brain like a vacuum tube."

"I remember him vaguely. Dropped in on us one summer before the war on his way to Germany. Smoked a pipe and wore a Yale sweater. That's all I can recall of him."

Martin splashed some soda in his drink and leaned against the sideboard. "I'm not a businessman and Paul knows it."

"You may not be a businessman, old boy, but you're a first-rate organizer and an intelligent man. A Pulitzer Prize winner, a top executive in the second-largest news agency in the world."

"Ex-top executive."

"Your choice, though, Martin. You weren't sacked for juggling the old books or pinching secretaries' bottoms. Any corporation with interests on the Continent would hire you like a shot. One of your problems, if you don't mind my saying so, is that you tend to hide your light under a basket."

Martin drank reflectively and looked at Charles over the rim of the glass. He then finished the drink in a swallow and set the glass on the table.

"Speak for yourself, John—as the saying goes. I watch you riding off to Burgate every morning on your knobby-kneed horse. A canvas sack of books over your shoulder. Dressed in scruffy corduroys and an old sweater. *You*—a viscount, scholar, and gentleman, not off to great fame in Whitehall but on your way to teach a bunch of kids. And you know what you look like when you ride off? You look contented. And I'm contented. I have no burning ambition to make money or to be head of the Rilke empire after Uncle Paul kicks the bucket."

"Then I would make that plain to him, Martin. I don't think he quite believes there are people in this world who don't hunger for money and power."

"I have told him, but he only stares into space and says, 'Like father, like son.' It's a nagging conscience, if you ask me. The ghost of Willie Rilke grinning at him."

Paul looked far from ghost-ridden as he sat in bed, cigars and a brandy decanter handy. A bed tray spanning his short legs overflowed with papers. He peered at Martin over his eyeglasses as he came into the room.

"Saw the light under your door," Martin said. "Thought I'd wish you a good night."

"You already did. But come and sit down. Have a cigar and a glass of Cognac. I'll say one thing for Tony, he has the best damned wine cellar of anyone I know."

Martin smiled as he drew a chair toward the side of the bed. "I'm surprised you were able to get old Coatsworth to part with a bottle of the really good stuff."

"Oh, we see eye to eye. Coatsworth only hates to uncork a bottle for people who don't know the difference between good and superb." He lit a cigar and watched his nephew pour himself a brandy. "I know what's top-rate in wines—and people. I'm not offering you a job out of charity, Martin. You're the type of man I need. The world is about to explode with new technocracy, and Rilke will be a part of it, making and selling everything from radio sets to refrigerated railway cars. Work for me and I'll make you a millionaire in five years. I guarantee it."

"I wouldn't doubt it for a minute. But to be truthful, Uncle Paul, I'm not that anxious to become a millionaire."

"That's a lot of baloney and you know it. Everyone wants to be rich."

"Not necessarily in your sense of the term. Most people are content to be successful in whatever it is they do, be it painting a house or writing a daily column for the London *Times*. I've achieved that kind of success, Uncle Paul. I know that anytime I want to go back to work I can join any newspaper or wire service I want to."

"And in the meantime you can loaf."

"Well, hardly that. Writing a book isn't loafing."

"What's your book about?"

"The political turmoil of post-Versailles. The rise of fascism and communism in western Europe and the effect of these movements on democratic principles of government."

"How long will it take you to finish?"

"About a year."

"Can you hold out financially for that long?"

"Yes—with a little generosity from friends."

Paul scowled at the tip of his cigar and then flicked ash on the bedspread and swept it away with his hand.

"I'll make a deal with you. I'd like you to come to Germany with me. This is a very important trip. I won't explain now what's at stake—it's complicated and would take too long. Suffice it to say it's worth a great deal of money to me—to the Rilke companies. You've seen the German Rilkes since the war, I haven't. I know that cousin Frederick had a stroke, I know that his son Werner is running things now. That's about all that I know. You and Werner are friends, I understand from Hanna."

"I feel sorry for Werner and he respects me. That's about the extent of our friendship."

"When did you see him last?"

"About two and a half years ago. He'd finally been released from the hospital in Berlin. I drove him and his wife, Carin, to Altenburg."

"A pleasant trip?"

"Lovely scenery. Werner was in pain."

"What exactly is the matter with him?"

"He was hit in the belly during the fighting around Amiens in nineteen eighteen. They took out most of his intestines."

"How bitter is he about that?"

Martin's smile was a shadow as he poured himself another glass of Cognac. "Not overjoyed at having a grenade explode next to him."

"Naturally. But I didn't mean that. Does he feel much bitterness toward *us*? The Americans . . . the Allies?"

"As soldiers? No. Men rarely feel bitterness toward the men they face in battle. I wouldn't know his feelings about the peace treaties—we never discussed them."

Paul leaned back against the pillows and blew smoke toward the ceiling.

"Good enough. I'll assume he's like most Germans, not overjoyed by Versailles. But then neither were you—if I judged your articles correctly."

"That's right."

"And Werner probably read them."

"If he read the *Vossische Zeitung* in nineteen nineteen."

"We'll say he did—or at least heard about your criticism of the terms. I think it would make him inclined to trust you—and your motives."

"Exactly what motives are you talking about?"

"Business motives. Pure business, Martin." He waved his cigar at his paper-strewn tray. "Rough proposals I've been working on. I want to buy a variety of patents and manufacturing rights from the Rilkes and the Grunewalds. I'll pay good, sound Yankee dollars. Do you know what one dollar means in Germany today, Martin? It means over two hundred thousand marks." He blew a stream of smoke and stared at it for a moment. "Sweet Jesus. Before the war, one dollar bought *four* marks and a few pfennigs. Now it's two hundred thousand and will go to half a million by summer if the slide continues—and I can't see what can stop it. I'm offering our German cousins a chance to keep from going bankrupt. My proposal is fair—five million dollars deposited in any bank they wish—but I'm a little afraid they might turn me down . . . might think me a carpetbagger."

"Aren't you?"

Paul grunted and flipped ash onto the bed. "You're damn right. But I'm a rich carpetbagger paying in hard coin. And between you, me, and the gatepost, I'll go as high as eight million. And that's not highway robbery, Martin."

"No, I don't imagine it is."

"And if you can help me swing the deal—just pave my way with those damned Junkers on the Rilkeswerke board—I'll hand you fifty grand. Think it over—and goodnight."

* * *

Martin thought of Werner von Rilke as he lay in the darkness and watched the delicate tracery of shadows and moonlight on the walls. He had met most of the German branch of the family on his first trip to Germany in August and September of 1914—as war correspondent for the Chicago *Express*. There were so many German-American readers of the *Express* that the editor had wanted coverage of the war from the German side of the fence. Werner and his brother Otto had met him at the railroad station in Berlin and had taken him to meet their great-aunt, the ninety-four-year-old Lousie, Baroness Seebach, in her huge house in the Grunewald forest with its magnificent view of the Havel. Then back to Berlin the next day. Dinner at the Adlon and then on to the Winter Garden of Friedrichstrasse. Werner a happy-go-lucky guy of his own age. Otto a year or two older, studious and shy. Otto gloomy and pessimistic about the war and unhappy about being called up by the artillery reserve. Werner a lieutenant in the Lübeck grenadier regiment, hoping to see a little action before the war should end—Christmas at the latest. So long ago. Otto killed at Verdun, and Werner not so happy-go-lucky anymore.

They went by sea, a north German Lloyd steamer from Folkstone to Hamburg, Paul Rilke moody for a day, feeling somehow insulted that Martin had agreed to come with him—but not for money. But Paul had shrugged it off—'Like father, like son'—and he was in an expansive mood as they took the train from Hamburg to Berlin, smoking his corona-coronas and telling anecdotes about the German Rilkes and their varied family branches, the Seebachs and Grunewalds and Hoffman-Schusters. Martin only half-listened as he looked through the window of the carriage at the lush farmland, woods, and lakes of Mecklenburg. A white horse plodded slowly across a meadow, led by a young woman with flowers in her hair who did not look toward the train nor wave.

> *Ich liebe vergessene Flurmadonnen*
> *und Mädchen, die an einsamen Bronnen,*
> *Blumen im Blondhaar, träumen gehn . . .*

"What's that you said, Martin?"

"Just part of a poem, Uncle Paul—about the melancholy of young girls with flowers in their hair. This is a sad country."

Paul grunted and rolled the cigar between his lips. "They'd be happy enough if they'd won the war. It's the price they paid for marching into Belgium."

The Berliners looked happy enough viewed from inside a taxi rolling down Unter den Linden. The cafés were filled and the smart shops crowded. And there was no sign of unhappiness or poverty in the gilded lobby of the Bristol Hotel. But it was all thin icing on a sour cake. Martin was aware of that, even if Paul chose to ignore it.

The cold sweat of poverty lay beyond the bright lights and the verdant linden trees, behind the facade of elegant bars and restaurants along Kurfürstendamm, in the rotting stucco tenements of Nollendorfplatz and Neukölln. The great gray stone sprawling city with its hideous Hohenzollern monuments. But it was not all granite, bronze, and iron. Past the

Doric columns and mammoth horses and chariot atop the Brandenburg Gate stretched the chestnut trees of the Tiergarten. And there was the clean, brisk air and high, pale sky of spring. The chattering of birds and, from somewhere along Mauerstrasse, the tinkling hurdy-gurdy notes of Strauss.

Not all defeat, Martin thought as he stood by his window on the fourth floor of the hotel. Berliners knew how to roll with the punches and turn inevitable disaster into a gallows jest. The New Yorkers of Europe, proud, cocky, openly derisive of Germans who had the misfortune to live elsewhere—the great melting pot of people and ideas. Below him in Unter den Linden, shabbily dressed young men in blue workers' caps peddled copies of the communist newspaper *Die Rote Fahne* elbow-to-elbow with young men in faded army uniforms trying to sell copies of the *Volkischer Beobachter*, a crudely written weekly printed in Munich and grandly subtitled "Battle Organ of the National Socialist Movement of Greater Germany." The police did their best to hustle them away from the entrances of the hotels and restaurants, ignoring the street urchins who darted about like sparrows, peddling mimeographed sheets advertising the clubs and bars where every known sexual preference of man or woman could find satisfaction.

Berlin!

Martin stepped out of the elevator in the lobby and spotted Werner von Rilke seated stiffly in a high-backed chair next to a potted palm. He was wearing evening clothes, the black suit and white shirt enhancing his air of spectral frailness. His thin, handsome, sharp-featured face had a waxen pallor. He saw Martin coming toward him and got to his feet.

"It's good to see you, Martin." He smiled warmly. "I really do mean that."

Martin took his cousin's outstretched hand. "And it's wonderful to see you."

Werner scanned the lobby. "Where's Paul?"

"Still struggling with his shirt studs, I think. He'll be down soon. Can I buy you a drink?"

"I would like nothing better, old fellow, but I am no longer permitted to touch alcohol in any of its delightful forms. I think at times of my father's wine cellar and weep."

"How are you feeling?"

Werner reached down and touched the wooden arm of the chair. "No more pain, thank God. But I look like a rail."

"Well, you're thin, but you'll put on weight again."

"I don't see how. I have the intestines of a canary bird." A shadow crossed his face and then he smiled again. "But enough of talking about me. I was surprised and delighted when Paul cabled that you were coming, too. Not strictly business, I hope?"

"No. But to be truthful, Paul asked for my help."

"I thought as much. I told Father and Uncle Theodor. I said, 'Cousin Paul is bringing along an ambassador of goodwill.'"

"I hope you don't resent it."

"Why should I? Frankly, I'm all in favor of a deal— Paul needn't have worried. Things here have gone from bad to worse since he left Chicago. French and Belgian troops squatting in our factories in Essen and Duisburg . . . the mark going under like a drowning man. I don't envision any problems with Father or my uncle as long as Paul's check is good."

"Looks like I came for nothing."

"Are you working for Paul now?"

"No. He wanted some help and I felt I owed it to him."

Werner put an arm about Martin's shoulder and gave him a quick hug. "God! That's one of the things I admire about you, Martin. If the family tales are true, *he* owes *you*. But you live by your own codes, don't you? Your own unique sense of honor and duty. What a true German you are!"

There was no sign of hard times in the palatial home of Frederick Ernst. The baroque house of pale yellow stone set amid woods and formal gardens sparkled with light from every window. Uniformed servants stood on the gravel drive to escort the arriving guests into the house. It was a large party this night, in honor of Paul Rilke, although fully half of the guests had come out of a desire to meet Martin. His battle reports had been printed in many German newspapers even after America's entry into the war in 1917, picked up from Dutch or Swedish papers and run without the official permission of Associated Press. After the war, his articles on Versailles had been widely circulated. The *Berliner Tageblatt* had called him "An honorable and impartial man . . . a compassionate friend of the German people in this, our hour of despair."

Frederick Ernst was a large man, much like his cousin Paul, but the stroke he had suffered in the last year of the war had shrunk him. He was confined to a wheelchair now, the left side of his body paralyzed. It was difficult for him to speak; and when he did talk, saliva dripped from the frozen corner of his mouth. He dutifully met his guests in the long marbled hallway, and then a white-jacketed attendant wheeled him to an elevator and took him to his quarters on the second floor.

"I shall play host for Father," Werner said, taking Martin by the arm. "Just as I play at being chairman of the board—only the former is more pleasant than the latter. I find business to be boring, especially now when there is no business. There is only *speculation* now. It is a great game for the rich. I warn you, all you will hear tonight from most of the guests is how much they have prospered by the inflation. Hardly a man or woman here who hasn't paid off old debts with bloated, worthless marks—or bought this building or that good piece of property for virtually nothing by having had the foresight to speculate on inflation. How they paid so many thousands of solid marks down a year ago, the balance to be paid now. Clever, you see. Very clever. They exchange many hundreds of thousands of inflated marks for a trust deed in the property—and the poor seller can take all that money he has received and buy a sandwich with it and maybe, if he's lucky, a cup of coffee as well. And it's all so legal—to the letter of the contract. We Germans abide by the law."

"But surely, Werner, even the rich—"

"Suffer from inflation? They can weather the present while acquiring goods and property for the future. They have only to sell something—a painting, some Dresden statuary or other artifacts for Swiss francs, pounds, or dollars. I can show you an office building in Leipzigerstrasse—directly across from Wertheim's department store—which you could purchase tonight for one thousand English pounds. That's worth selling a painting or two to some war-rich manufacturer from Birmingham, isn't it?"

"And what of the people who have nothing to sell?" Werner's smile was faint and bitter. "They starve."

There were platters of roast goose and half a dozen different meat dishes. Servants in blue jackets with large brass buttons hurried in and out with steaming plates and tureens and an endless variety of fine wines. Martin ate slowly, barely listening to what a large blond woman seated next to him was saying. She was talking of inflation, as Werner had predicted, of how she had sold one of her Benz cars to a Dutch businessman for gulden and had exchanged that good money for a fine piece of property in Wilmersdorf "for a fraction of its real worth."

But what is *real worth*, Martin was thinking, in a nation gone insane?

"Things will stabilize soon," a man across the table was saying in a loud voice. "You'll see. The treasury will soon run out of paper to print and the inflation will be over!"

A tall, austere man with a gray vandyke beard took exception to the jest. "My dear Helmut, it's not less paper we need printed just now, it is *more*."

"That's all very well for you to say, my dear Lieventhal. It keeps your clerks at the ministry busy stamping extra zeroes on thousand-mark notes!"

Martin looked down the table at the minister. Erich Lieventhal, one of the industrial giants of prewar Germany, now doing his best as a public servant in the Republic to deal with the harsh reparations policy of the victors. He had interviewed Lieventhal more than a year ago in London and he had hinted then to Martin that only some dramatic, near catastrophic occurrence within Germany would ever drive home to the Allies the futility of draining the conquered nation of its gold, coal, goods, and timber. The French and Belgian invasion of the Ruhr to assure delivery of telegraph poles and lumber had coincided with the fall of the mark. The French couldn't force the German people to cut down their forests. Let them then be content with money. They could have as much as they wished, carloads of the stuff, the war debt paid just as quickly as the printing presses could spew out new million-mark notes. It was crazy, but in the madness of it all there was a method.

Martin continued to stare down the table, only to realize with a dull shock that he wasn't looking at Lieventhal at all, but at a young woman seated between the minister and Uncle Paul. Odd that he hadn't noticed her before—Werner had introduced him to everyone. And then he knew why. He had not noticed her because subconsciously he had not wanted to notice her. But he had no choice in the matter now. She was looking directly at him and smiling. And it was Ivy's smile he saw. The resemblance was a shock. The same slender neck and elfin face. The same black hair, creamy skin, and pale violet eyes.

He tore his gaze away and scrutinized the slices of roast goose on his plate. Seeing the woman brought back to him that terrible year after Ivy's death, the year in Paris when he had seen Ivy everywhere, had followed her a score of times through the Bois or along the Champs-Elysées, or gazed at her across the crowded tables in Montparnasse bars. Fate had conspired at that time to flood Paris with slender, beautiful, dark-haired girls. And now here was another! He sliced into a piece of goose and chewed on it as though it were a hunk of rubber.

A servant entered the room and bent low over the minister's chair to whisper into his ear. Lieventhal nodded, stood up, and left the room. He was back in a few minutes.

"I am most sorry," he said, "but the president just telephoned and wishes me to come to Weimar at once. Amelia and I regret having to leave your delightful party, Werner, but it cannot be helped. Kindly extend our regrets to your father." He then shook hands with Paul and escorted the girl from the room. Martin did not watch them go.

The party broke up early. There was a feeling of apprehension among most of the guests about driving along the dark suburban roads too late at night. A stream of chauffeur-driven limousines rolled away from the house, following the winding drive through the woods like a military convoy.

"You're welcome to spend the night here, Martin," Werner said after the last guest had departed. "Paul will be closeted in the library to all hours with Uncle Theodor and the Grunewalds—thrashing out terms. I doubt if they'll get the better of Paul."

"Shouldn't you be with them?"

Werner shrugged. "My role in the business is largely ceremonial. Besides, I told them my views—take the money, make the deal. It's only common sense, isn't it?

Tying ourselves to Rilke, U.S.A., gives us an immediate foreign market and access to dollars. We might make far less profit than we would have made under happier circumstances, but that's life, isn't it? Paul has our testicles in a firm hold, but he isn't squeezing too hard. We may lose some pride in the library tonight, but not our manhood."

Martin laughed softly and lit a cigar. "I must say, Werner, I admire your philosophy. You're a pragmatic man."

"Your William James influenced me greatly. I read all of his lectures when I was at Heidelberg, and in the course of my one delightful year at Oxford. So much more in tune with modern man than, say, Nietzsche." He closed his eyes for a moment and inhaled deeply. "I miss a good cigar—or a cigarette."

Martin looked about for an ashtray. "I'll snuff it out."

"Oh, no—no, dear chap. I enjoy seeing others do what I cannot. Please smoke—and if you have a glass of Cognac, smack your lips." He glanced at his gold wristwatch. "Barely eleven. If you'd prefer going back to your hotel, we could take in a sampling of Berlin night life. Would you like that?"

"Yes, I would."

"So would I. These formal dinner parties, with the men dressed like penguins and the women as divas, bore me to the very soul."

The dark forests of the Grunewald gave way to the bright lights of Wilmersdorf and the gaudy cafés and bars along Kurfürstendamm. The great, pulsing heart of Berlin lay ahead across the Landwehr Canal.

"I know of a place on Charlottenstrasse," Werner said. "Not far, appropriately enough, from the Comic

Opera. Naughty but not vulgar. No young men totter-
ing about in high-heeled shoes and lip rouge like the
places along Kurfürstendamm. I think you will be
amused."

Martin said nothing for a minute, and then: "That
girl with Lieventhal. Who is she?"

"His daughter. Amelia. Came late in life. Only
eighteen and the old boy is at least sixty-five. The
birth killed his poor wife, which is a pity. She was a
fine woman. Had a sense of humor Erich lacks."

"Does he need a sense of humor—in these times?"

"Now more than ever, I would think. Chaos breeds
comedians. One needs a talent for ridicule in order to
survive—at least politically. Erich tries sober reasoning
and lucid arguments with critics of the Republic
where savage ridicule would serve him better. How
else could he answer the taunts of the Freikorps fanat-
ics when they stomp through the streets in jackboots
and army uniforms chanting, 'Shoot the foulest Jew of
all, murder Erich Lieventhal'? The joke being that the
old boy is not a Jew and everyone knows it.

"Erich Kluge is his real name—son of a Prussian
army officer who died in a riding accident when Erich
was a year old. Every schoolboy knows the story
of how the young widow of the soldier married the
young scientist who would solve the problems of
bringing the miracle of electric light to Germany. The
immortal Sigmund Lieventhal—and even he was only
half Jewish! Ah, how Erich could savage the ignorant
if he only had the tongue for it."

The streets were crowded, a frenetic gaiety spilling
out from the restaurants, theaters, and cabarets. Men
in top hats and women swathed in furs mingled with
the gray, threadbare poor.

"Carin detests Berlin," Werner said, looking gloomily through the side window of the chauffeur-driven Benz. "She refuses to come here anymore."

"Where are you living now?"

"I bought a villa at Bad Isar—about ten miles from Munich. It's very lovely there—in the woods overlooking the river. I utilize one of the company planes to fly back and forth. I wanted Carin to come on this trip—she's fond of you, Martin—but nothing would induce her to leave Bavaria."

"I'll have to come down and see her then."

"That would be wonderful. She'd enjoy that."

Die Weisse Ratte was a cabaret popular with businessmen and rich speculators. Its dimly lit interior was furnished in opulent baroque style with small marble tables and deep plush chairs. The place reeked of cigar smoke and perfume. On the small stage four beautiful, nearly naked girls danced to the music of an excellent jazz band. Werner ordered champagne for Martin and a glass of seltzer water for himself. He paid with an English pound note, which so startled the waiter he nearly dropped his tray.

Werner held out another pound. "Tell the girls to outdo themselves tonight and they'll each get one of these."

The waiter stammered something unintelligible and scurried off.

Werner laughed. "Nothing like a little money to encourage true talent."

One million marks was not a little money, and in real value an English pound was worth much more than the official rate of exchange. The girls came on stage for their next number gazing fixedly, hungrily, in the direction of Werner's table. Then the lights dimmed and a pale blue spotlight bathed the group as they began to dance to the muted wail of a saxophone—to dance and to strip, until they wore nothing but their spike heels, dark stockings and flimsy garter belts. The audience roared its appreciation and men banged on the tables. The dance grew increasingly erotic, the girls touching one another, embracing, rubbing breast against breast. Two of the girls sank slowly to the floor and began to writhe in each other's arms, legs spread, feigning sexual ecstasy and the frenzy of orgasm as a drum rolled and the saxophone moaned a final note.

"Bravo!" Werner called out, clapping his hands. "Bravo!"

Martin's mouth felt dry and he sipped champagne. "Some show!"

"They were only faking, but I can take you to a place in Potsdamerplatz, a private club, where the girls make love on a round bed and pretend nothing."

The girls came for their money, transparent silk kimonos wrapped loosely around their bodies to artfully reveal naked breasts. Werner, laughing, held up four pound notes, teasing the girls before finally letting them flutter to the floor where the girls scrambled for them. One of the girls bumped heavily against the table, knocking the glass of champagne into Martin's lap. Werner removed a handkerchief from the inside pocket of his jacket and handed it across the table.

"Poor Martin. A cold shower." One of the girls, slipping her money into the top of her garter belt, bent over and whispered in his ear. "An invitation, Martin. A night with all four of them for whatever we care to give."

"No, thanks," Martin said, dabbing at his pants with the handkerchief. "But you do what you want."

"What I want," Werner said, getting to his feet, "is a breath of fresh air."

They walked toward Unter den Linden, the car trailing them. The streets still teemed with people, the rich and the poor. A legless war veteran sat on a little rolling cart in a doorway, selling nothing, staring into space. Young whores moved in constant patrol, some dressed in tight black or green leather and carrying thin, supple canes; others wearing demure schoolgirl smocks. Women for all tastes.

"We have become the nation of Sodom," Werner said. "And Berlin is our zoo."

Martin's smile was sardonic. "Don't be a hypocrite, Werner. You seemed to be enjoying yourself back there. Feeding time at the zoo—with pound notes."

Werner stared rigidly ahead for a moment and then paused in front of the frosted glass door of a restaurant. "I think I'll risk a Cognac and seltzer. Would you care for a nightcap?"

"I could use three fingers of scotch—make that four fingers."

It was an elegant, old-fashioned place—the only entertainment a string quartet playing Mozart. The restaurant was nearly deserted and they stood at the bar.

Werner splashed seltzer into a snifter of brandy. "I'm not unaware of the paradox, Martin. To be truthful, I'm both attracted and repelled by such women. What was unthinkable behavior before the war is now taken for granted. Those gaudy whores on the street— on Unter den Linden! And the police barely glancing at them. German womanhood rutting in an alley for the price of a meal. These are times when I feel I'm Dante strolling through hell."

"These are bad times, Werner, but they'll get better. Some kind of order will come out of this mess, you'll see."

"The eternal optimist." He drank a little of the brandy and seltzer and then placed a hand against his stomach. "Nice, but painful. They left me with a small, raw stomach. Those surgeons really gutted me, Martin. They even cut my rectum out. I shit through a hole in my side. Did you know that?"

Martin shook his head and took a drink of whiskey. "I'm sorry."

"No need to be. You didn't toss a grenade at my belly. When I was in hospital—that is to say, after I had been in hospital some time—a new surgeon was brought in to see me. A Dr. Kuebler. He told me he didn't believe in half measures. That if I wanted to live, he must do, in his words, some drastic pruning. I wasn't happy at the idea, but he was correct. He pruned away the rot—and I lived."

It had been an oddly disturbing evening and Martin was glad to be back at the hotel. He flopped wearily on the bed and studied the baroque designs on the ceiling, a bas-relief of cherubs, wood nymphs, and grape leaves. The cherubs and leaves spinning a bit as the whiskey went to his head. He sat up and then went into the bathroom and splashed cold water on his face. A bit drunk, he realized, but not sleepy. Thoughts whirled. Lieventhal's daughter's face . . . the writhings of the naked girls on the stage . . . Werner's thinly veiled despair. He groaned and dunked his head under the tap.

He dried himself off with a towel and then stripped. The suit was a mess, but the hotel valet could sponge and press it in the morning. He emptied the pockets, removing his cigar case, lighter, wallet, and a few coins. Werner's handkerchief was a damp wad; he unfolded it and spread it over the porcelain rim of the sink. Something was caught in the folds, a tiny dot of gold and enamel, a lapel pin of some sort stuck in the cloth. He plucked it out and held it between two fingers, staring at it. A well-crafted piece of jewelry, smaller than a shirt stud. A circle of plain yellow gold with an emblem in the center delicately enameled in red. He had seen the emblem before, but couldn't remember where. An ancient symbol, of course, old as time, and yet . . . where? The memory eluded him.

When he went into the bedroom to get his pajamas, he placed the pin on the dresser, the *hackenkreuz*, the tiny red swastika.

XIII

Paul was tired but elated. He celebrated by ordering a gargantuan lunch, washing it down with a bottle of superb Moselle.

"Five point two million," he chuckled, cutting into a thick slice of roast pork. "I tell you, Martin, there was no fight in them. I would have gone to eight—hell, *ten* million if it came to that." He chewed slowly, relishing it, then washed the mouthful down with wine. "Old Theodor made a long speech about corporate integrity and rambled on and on about the history of Rilkewerke and crap like that, but the others knew where the bread was buttered. Joining the cartel didn't bother them a bit." He gave Martin a puzzled look. "How come you're not eating?"

"I don't feel very hungry." He dabbed at his vegetable salad. "So it wasn't just a matter of buying patents."

"That was part of it. Own the patents, control the product. They jumped way ahead of us in the last year of the war in research on certain types of electron tubes, high-frequency alternators, generators, electric motors, and a host of other things. We may produce *more* in the States, but they produce *better* over here. So . . . I own the patents and they'll produce and then sell to me at a price I set. It's a good deal all around."

"No one's producing anything at the moment, Uncle Paul. Or haven't you noticed?"

Paul dismissed the remark with an airy wave of his fork. "To be successful in business, Martin, one ignores the present and eyes the future. I'm looking down the road."

"And seeing what?"

"A big, basically sound country. Germany may have lost two million men in the war, but they didn't dent or scratch one factory, one mine, or one inch of their soil. This inflation is mostly deliberate. It's a ploy to bring the Allies to their senses and ease the reparation demands. It's going to take Washington, London, and Paris to end this craziness—and they'll do it. You'll see." He downed the last of the wine, belched slightly, and took out a cigar. "I'm heading back to the States tomorrow—booked passage on the *Berengaria* from Cherboug. Would you like to spend a few days in Paris with me before I sail?"

"I'm going down to Bavaria with Werner."

"Oh? I was getting the impression you couldn't wait to get out of the fatherland."

"I'd rather be in England, but, as my old editor on the *Express* would have said, this is where the story is."

"Getting back into harness?"

"I think so. Once a reporter, always a reporter, I guess."

"For INA?"

"Possibly. But not as a bureau chief. I can't chain myself to a desk."

Paul lit his cigar and blew a satisfied stream of

smoke toward the ceiling. "I'll be seeing Kingsford in New York. Can I tell him you're back on the payroll?"

"Sure."

"I'll see to it you get a raise. Just leave it to your uncle Paul."

Stories abounded in the streets of Berlin, a cavalcade of arrogant wealth and harrowing poverty and despair. The mark now stood at two hundred and fifty thousand to the U.S. dollar—the current rate posted in front of every bank, written in chalk on a small blackboard so that the figures could be erased as they changed, almost hourly. A story in every face—the angry eyes of ex-soldiers, the bewildered gaze of the elderly, the wizened faces of the starving young. But he knew as an editor that no one cared to read about it.

He took a taxi to the INA office in Neu Konigstrasse on the other side of the river. Only the bureau chief was in, a tall, stoop-shouldered, gloomy-faced man by the name of Wolf von Dix who had taught German at the University of London in 1914 and had left England at the eleventh hour to report the war for the *Frankfurter Zeitung*. His dispatches on the horrors of the western front had been as heavily censored by the German military as Martin's had been by the Allied.

Dix swung his long legs off the top of the desk, polished his monocle with his tie, and then popped it back into place.

"Well, Martin, of all people. What brings you to Berlin? On a Cook's tour?"

"No, just slumming." He reached down into the chief's ever-open humidor of cigars and took one. "How are you, Dix?"

"Fine. Thanking God I'm working for a company that pays its salaries in dollars."

"Where are Kurt and Emil?"

"In the Ruhr. Trying to get through the French army blockades. That ass Poincaré. Thank the Lord the British and Americans viewed with alarm, as the saying goes, or this country would have exploded. Things are bad enough without having the French marching through Essen." He took a cigar for himself and clipped off the tip with a silver cutter.

"Why did you quit, Martin? I was stunned when I heard the news. Did Kingsford ride you too hard for stories of girls in bathing suits?"

"No, nothing like that. I just got sick of being cooped up in Fleet Street. But I'm back with the firm now, unofficially at the moment. A common, everyday, grind-out-the-wordage hack."

"Hardly that, old fellow. I read your Iraq story in the *Daily Post*. Very Beau Gestian. No wonder you couldn't lock yourself back into an office after dashing about in the desert like Rudolph Valentino. You're a romantic at heart, dear Martin. I suppose that's what makes you such a good journalist."

Martin reached into his pocket, took out the little lapel pin, and handed it to Dix.

"What can you tell me about this?"

The chief held it up to his monocled eye. "Nice bit of workmanship. Real gold. Swastika emblem."

"I've seen the design before, but I can't recall where."

"Common enough in Berlin during the Kapp putsch. Were you here then?"

"Sure . . . now I remember. The Ehrhardt Brigade."

"Most of the Freikorps troops who came down from Estonia had a swastika painted on the sides of their trucks. I never knew why and neither did they. Just something they picked up the way troops will, I guess. Never saw the design worked into an expensive piece of jewelry, though. Did you find it in a pawnshop?"

"No. A person I know had it in his pocket."

Dix handed the pin back. "This person—he wouldn't happen to come from Bavaria, would he? Munich or Nürnberg?"

"Munich—Bad Isar, to be precise."

Dix let his monocle fall into his palm and gave it another polish with his tie. "The Thule Society used the swastika as a symbol at one time, and so does the National Socialist German Workers' party. You may have seen their two-page rag being peddled on the streets—the *Volkischer Beobachter*. They bought it from the Thule Society as a house organ. It comes out once or twice a week and people buy it for toilet paper."

"What is this National Socialist whatever?"

Dix shrugged as he replaced his monocle. "I don't know for certain. All we get out of Bavaria is unconfirmed chaos. There must be a hundred political parties down there, all with impressive-sounding names. All I know about the National Socialists is that they have about three thousand members—give or take a couple of thousand—and that they must have some money, though God knows how they get it."

"Is there anything in the morgue I could read?"

"Maybe. I don't know. Anna keeps that in order, and only she knows how obscure items are filed." He glanced at the wall clock. "The girls will be back from lunch in a few minutes. Have a glass of schnapps and bide your time."

The female typists and clerks trooped in, chattering noisily, happy as only people could be who had the good fortune to be working for an American company. A middle-aged woman with iron-gray hair nodded respectfully to Martin as she headed for her desk.

"Anna," Dix called out. "Is there anything in the files on the National Socialist German Workers' party—in Bavaria?"

The woman paused by her desk, frowning. "We have copies of the *Volkischer Beobachter*, Herr Dix. And—I'm pretty sure—one or two items on the party leaders. I filed them under Eckart, D., and Hitler, A. Do you want them?"

"Do you?" Dix asked.

"If it's no bother," Martin said.

The Junkers monoplane rose swiftly from the old military airfield at Tempelhof, banked low over the Berlin slums, and then headed south, rising to five thousand feet. The sun glinted sharply off its silver and black metal wings.

"I love to fly," Werner said happily, shouting over the engine noise. "I wish to God I'd had sense enough to go into the flying service. So clean in the clouds. The great tonic of air!"

Martin looked through the window. A green and golden blanket of woods and fields far below. "It's a long way down."

"Shot down, you mean? By a Camel or Spad! What a glorious way to die! A ball of bright flame, scattering one's ashes in death! That's how gods die—in flaming chariots pulled by winged horses. For four years I was rooted in the mud where men die like crushed lizards. No—no—I wish I had left the infantry and flown in a squadron with Richthofen—Boelcke—Immelmann! I know Hermann Goering, by the way—last leader of the Richthofen circus, winner of the Pour le Mérite, the Blue Max. A wonderful fellow. He flew our first company plane for several months right after the war. Our pilot today, Rudi, he flew Gothas and made three trips over England. Never saw anything but cloud and couldn't find London—dropped all his bombs in the Channel. But he can tell some stories! That took guts, I can tell you."

It was too difficult to carry on a conversation against the hammering throb of the engine. The plane climbed, rocking on the thermals rising from the slopes of the Erzgebirge. And then they were soaring over the dark forests of northern Bavaria, the Danube, and then the river Isar flowing from the great barrier of the Alps and threading its way through the old city of Munich.

A car and driver were waiting at the airfield to take them southward in the gathering dusk, past the city and along a narrow road that climbed into fir-shrouded hills.

"Nearly home," Werner said, lowering the window and breathing deeply. "One could get drunk on this air."

Martin reached into his coat for a cigar, his fingers touching a small envelope which contained the lapel pin. He drew it out and handed it to Werner. "This was caught up in your handkerchief. A gold swastika."

"Oh, that." Werner took the envelope and slipped it into his pocket. "One of my party badges."

"Do you belong to many parties, Werner?"

"No—but I contribute money to several, both left and right wing. I can't afford not to do that—the pendulum has swung too many times during the past couple of years. It's cheap insurance to keep from being branded as an enemy of whatever faction comes out on top."

"The National Socialists—they're nothing but a hate group as far as I can see. Pure rabble-rousing with no political aim at all."

"It would seem that way—if one merely listened to the speeches or read their little paper. They direct their message to the middle class and the unemployed—anti-Jew, anticapitalist, anti-Republic, pro-army, and pro-Bavarian. But most of that is pure rhetoric. The people are so numbed by events, they need strong words to shake them out of their lethargy. I find Herr Hitler, the true head of the party, to be an interesting man with a pragmatic approach to life. He may scream in the beer halls about how the capitalists are joining with the Jews to ruin the country, but he comes to me, the biggest capitalist he has ever met, and asks for money. Rhetoric, Martin, pure rhetoric. Rabble-rousing is merely a means to a finer and more noble goal."

"Which is?"

"Why, what we *all* want. A strong and revitalized Germany."

"You seem to be very impressed by this man."

"I am, Martin. I am. Goering introduced me to him—brought him up to the villa last year. I'd heard of him, of course; everyone in Munich had heard of him even though he's virtually unknown outside Bavaria. I thought he would be just another swaggering ex-soldier trying to organize all the roaming Freikorps gangs into another private army, but I was wrong. He's a shy, soft-spoken man. Not well educated, but surprisingly well read. A genuine soldier, too. Iron Cross First Class. And merely a corporal, mind you, not one of those insufferable Junker officers. He earned his decoration the hard way with the List Regiment. Wounded on the Somme and again at Ypres. I recognized the type instantly—a good, faithful, reliable noncom who did his duty and never bitched about it. I had several like him in the grenadiers. We hit it off instantly."

"And you gave him enough money to buy the *Beobachter*."

"I have no idea what my money was used for then, nor what it is used for now. That's none of my business." He reached across the seat and patted Martin on the knee. "But enough political talk, Martin. Smell the pines. Inhale that zephyr of wine from the Tyrol. Tomorrow we'll drive to Starnberger See and go sailing."

Werner's villa in the pine forests above the gorge of the Isar was a small, baroque palace built by King Ludwig II in the misguided hope that Lola Montez would live there. She refused, and the place became only one of many ornate and expensive structures that the poor and mad king scattered across Bavaria to remain unoccupied until after his death.

It was not a happy home. The conclusion seemed obvious to Martin as he sipped a martini cocktail be-

fore dinner. Certainly all the elements for happiness
were present—the beautiful and gracious wife; the
two lovely sons, aged eight and six; the frolicking
dogs and doting servants—but the strain between Werner and Carin shadowed it all. It was as present and
real as the constant wind that came down from the
distant peaks and moaned in chill streams through the
pines.

"You seem to live separate lives," Martin remarked
as he sat in Werner's study late that evening. "Carin
has her section of the villa and you have yours. It's
none of my business, of course."

"You have a right to comment, and I appreciate
your concern," Werner said. "The truth of the matter is
that if I had not turned Catholic in order to marry
Carin, we would be divorced by now. So, we have an
arrangement of sorts. I split my life between Bavaria
and Berlin. It is better for the children to remain here
with their mother." He gazed into the crackling fire.
"But there is no need for that to mar your sojourn.
This is a heavenly place, Martin. Treat these woods
and mountains—the river—the lakes—as an oasis of order, tranquillity, and peace."

On the final night of his stay, Martin sat in bed in
his spacious but drafty room. His cigars and a crystal
decanter of whiskey on the table beside his bed. A
fire burned in the massive stone fireplace and the
wind sighed under the eaves beyond the tall, leaded-
glass windows. He was writing in his journal for the
first time in over a week.

* * *

Sunday night, May 24, 1923. Observations and reflections. Bad Isar, Bavaria.

Werner was quite wrong. There are no oases of tranquillity left. There are only places of great scenic beauty that impart an illusion of contentment on the viewer. Bavaria, like almost every other place I know, is haunted by the past and dismayed by the future. I have never felt the impact of the war as strongly as I did the other day when I drove with Carin and the children up to Garmisch. Those magnificent mountains . . . the meadows and wildflowers. When we stopped the car in the little village of Oberau, we could hear cowbells far off across meadows and the bleating of sheep.

The children, Max and Josef, held each other by the hand and ran off across the fields. Carin and I walked through the village, past the rococo church. In front of the church there stands a wooden display case with glass doors. In the case are the snapshots or class portraits of dozens of young men from the district who went to war and never came back. For some there were no photos, and in place of a picture, their names have been printed and pinned to the backing. And the sun falls on this depository of dead youth. And the wind blows and the cowbells clang softly in the valleys and sheep roam the high meadows, but the boys are dead and some of the warmth is gone from the sun.

Carin married Werner in the spring of 1915. They had known each other since they were children. Carin's father, Count Urfeld of Wurttemberg, owned the largest bank in south Germany and had financed many of the Rilke projects for Frederick Ernst. They were married in the Roman Catholic cathedral in Stuttgart and honeymooned in Innsbruck. Max was conceived then—Josef late in 1916 when Werner was given leave after the battle of the Somme. The night when little Josef was destined for the world was the last night Werner and Carin slept together—his decision, not hers.

Well, that is another tiny tragedy of the war, it seems to me. One that will never appear in any statistics regarding casualties. The war changed men, sometimes drastically. It warped and seared the soul as well as the body. Werner, when he finally got out of the hospital, felt that his body had betrayed him. His body, Carin told me, became an obscenity to him. The little excrement bag taped to his side. The terrible scars running from rib to crotch. When Carin wanted to go to bed with him, he sneered at her, saying that only a whore would sleep with a man who smelled of shit. And so a hand grenade tossed into a trench alters more than a soldier's life.

But the rift between Werner and Carin developed in other ways besides sex—or the lack of it—in their marriage. She does not like Werner's political meanderings, nor the assorted people who come to the villa in quest of backing. She especially does not like Hitler and the National Socialists. She does not like virulent anti-Semitism and made it quite clear to Hermann Goering one night at dinner that she would not permit such talk in her house. Goering, apparently, told this to

Hitler, and when he comes to the villa he never says a word about the Jews or tells one Jewish joke.

I find Adolf Hitler to be pretty much the way Werner described him. Shy, polite, constantly watching his manners, a bit awed by the signs of wealth he finds at the villa. Rather acting like a village postman who, for some unaccountable reason, has been invited to tea at the manor. They tell me he's a fiery, almost hypnotic speaker in front of a crowd; but at the dinner table, or after dinner in Werner's study, he talks in a monotone, skipping from one subject to the next, rambling on and on—a mélange of theoretical platitudes and patriotic fervor.

I found him interesting only when we discussed the war. Werner told him that I had been a war correspondent on the Somme, and he was interested in knowing what events I had covered there. He had been at Pozieres and Bazentin Wood, and both of us had witnessed a tank attack in September which the German artillery had smashed—"Thank God for our wonderful gunners," Hitler said with a laugh, "or we'd have been crushed like toads." He had then, and still retains, an admiration and respect for the Tommies, but his hatred of the French is intense. He can't speak of them without trembling with suppressed rage.

I can understand Carin's dislike—not so much for the man, but the quasi-military aspects of his party. It's unusual for a political movement—if indeed that's what it is—to gather about it so many martial trappings. I asked Hitler about that, and he told me that the vast number of ex-soldiers who had formed into Freikorps groups to fight the Communists felt more comfortable in a military atmosphere. These men had been welded into a common body, the Kampfbund, or into a sort of praetorian guard, the Sturmalteilung, formed to protect political meetings from interruption by Red Front rowdies. A vast store of military uniforms that had been destined for German troops in Tanganyika had been acquired. The pale brown shirts and forage hats gave the National Socialists a distinct air—that plus the swastika armbands. "It makes a man feel important to march with his fellows in a smart uniform and under a banner that is a symbol of a cause.

Hitler appears to be a fervid believer in symbols and slogans. On the swastika flags—the *hackenkrause* black on the flags, set in a white circle surrounded by red—he has emblazoned the words "Deutschland Erwach!" A noble and patriotic sentiment, but the only storm troopers I have seen were marching through the Hofgarten in Munich chanting, *"Death to the Jews!"*

Werner dismisses that as a sop to those virulent anti-Semitic Russian émigrés who contribute large sums to the party. Carin doesn't believe it and neither do I.

The wind blows. A soft rain falls. And high in the mountains, locked in a wooden box at Oberau, are the fair and pleasant faces of the dead.

* * *

He flew back to Berlin with Werner. Neither man felt like conducting a shouted conversation over the racket of the engine. They sat across from each other, staring out through opposite sides of the aircraft. When they landed at Tempelhof, they shook hands, Werner looking both somber and uncomfortable.

"I feel I owe you an apology, Martin."

"And why's that?"

"First of all, I should have told you about Carin and me before you flew down to discover it for yourself. And secondly, it was wrong to expose you to political friends of whom you most obviously do not approve."

"Look, Werner, there was no reason for you to tell me about Carin. If I'd lacked a reporter's eye and ear, I wouldn't have known anything was wrong between the two of you. And as for your politics . . . well, that's your business, not mine. I just don't like what Herr Hitler is selling. There's enough hatred in this country. It crackles through the air like electricity. Why add to it?"

Werner's smile was cryptic. "There's an old saying in the Tyrol: 'Only a storm can clear the air.'" He made a point of scowling at his wristwatch. "I'm late for an appointment in Lichtenberg, but I'll be glad to drop you off at the Bristol."

"No . . . no, go ahead. I'll take a taxi."

"Thank you, Martin, you are most thoughtful." He glanced toward his Benz, which was bumping across the field toward them. "You really should go back to England. This is not a land you will ever understand."

That was not quite true, Martin was thinking as the rattletrap taxi carried him toward the center of the city. He felt, in some ways, that he understood Germany better than Werner did. He had the advantage of objectivity, of standing off from a distance and observing dispassionately the varied elements in flux. The revolutionary struggle . . . brown shirts and red shirts . . . monarchists—Socialists—Communists—republican democracy. Weimar to Munich to Berlin. The struggle to meld a nation out of millions of fragments. He watched some women hurrying across Zimmerstrasse against the traffic, bulging shopping bags in their hands. Bags stuffed not with food but with marks to buy food. Tens of thousands of marks to perhaps buy some turnips and a little bread.

Messages had piled up since he'd been gone. He took the bundle from the desk clerk and sorted through them as he walked to the elevator. There was a note from Uncle Paul: *Martin. Cabled Kingsford in NY before I left. Told him you'd take the "Kingsford shilling" again, but only as roving correspondent at double what he was paying before. Leave things to your uncle.*

The cablegram had had its effect, because there was a cable from Scott Kingsford: *Dear Martin. Stop. Delighted by news from Paul Rilke. Stop. Roving correspondent it is. Stop. Salary will negotiate. Stop.* Martin smiled and shoved the message into his pocket.

There was a slim envelope of expensive cream-colored paper. He slit it open with a fingernail. The note it contained was heavily embossed with an address on the Charlottenburger. *My dear Martin Rilke. I regret the missed opportunity of talking with you at any length. I have returned to the city from Weimar and trust you will call on me at your earliest convenience.* The note was signed Erich Lieventhal.

Most of the other slips of paper were telephone

messages from stringers hoping to sell their stories, or their hot tips for stories, to the great Herr Rilke. But one message caught his eye and made him grin with pleasure: *A Herr Golden telephoned. He is staying at the Adlon Hotel.*

Seeing Jacob was a tonic. He flopped onto a sofa in Jacob's luxurious suite and lit a cigar.

"What in God's name brought you to Berlin?"

Jacob, looking pale and desolated, managed a wan smile. "Comfort, I suppose. You're the only chap I can talk to. I've had the most ghastly couple of weeks, so I just decided to chuck it all in and fly over for a rest."

"What happened? Circulation of the *Post* fall off to zero?"

"I rather wish it had, old boy. The fact is our little campaign for military unity had such a dramatic impact on readers and government that old Fenton was whisked from the burning sands practically by order of Parliament. In a nutshell, he's home, and my rather foredoomed affair with Winnie has come to a total and irrevocable end. I thought I could handle it with grace, maturity, and sophistication. After all, having love affairs has become somewhat of an international sport these days, hasn't it? Breaking one off shouldn't upset a man of the world like me, should it? An amusing dalliance, no more than that. Something to do on rainy afternoons.

"I wish to God I was that sort of chap. When I kissed Winnie for the last time—except perhaps for a kiss on the cheek one day—I thought the ground had dropped away and I was falling into a bottomless pit." He parted the white lace curtains and stared numbly at the ornate facade of the British Embassy on Wilhelmstrasse. "Talk about the proverbial someone being torn in different directions. I can't even explain how I felt when Fenton shook my hand. We had to have a cocktail party for him, you see—meeting the press. He's the *Daily Post's* colonel now. He thanked me for being such a good friend—and he was so bloody sincere when he said it. No sardonic Fenton smile. Just the handshake and those quiet words. His *friend!*"

Martin studied the ash on his cigar. "You *are* his friend, Jacob. You didn't seduce Winifred. You just fell in love with her. You knew it would have to end, and now it has. I don't know what to say or what to suggest."

"You might suggest we go out on the town and permit me to get disgustingly drunk. I expect you to remain halfway sober. And my treat, needless to say."

"Fine," Martin said. "I've heard of a club in the Potsdamerplatz where naked women cavort on a round bed."

Jacob eyed him sourly. "I would prefer, considering my present state of mind, to get drunk in a monastery."

Martin couldn't be sure when or where the envelope had been slipped into his pocket. It could have been anywhere during the night—at the Adlon Bar, the Excelsior, the cabaret Luna—a haze of places packed with people and blue smoke. He discovered it in the morning after the valet came to get his tuxedo and had dutifully gone through the pockets, leaving change, crushed cigar, lighter, pocket handkerchief, and the envelope on top of the dresser.

Martin eyed it blearily. A thin, narrow envelope of cheap gray paper. The note inside had been written in pencil on equally cheap paper. He walked over to the window and stood in a patch of sunlight to read it. It was written in English . . .

> *Herr Rilke:*
>
> *I am willing, for the modest enough sum of 50 English pounds, to provide you with information regarding a matter of some great importance and international significance. I am, sir, a man who served honorably in the war, but am now a pacifist. I have read your pacifist book—the French edition—and was most moved by its contents. For blessed are the peacemakers on earth—as the good King Lear states in your fine Shakespeare. If you, too, are willing, board the number 42 omnibus in front of the Hotel Excelsior in Kreuzberg at precisely noon tomorrow. Go to the top deck—alone—and I will contact you if I think it is safe.*
>
> *P.S. This matter is in regard to Minister Lieventhal.*

Martin stood in the shaft of light and reread the note, then placed it on a table and wove his way into the bathroom, taking off robe and pajamas as he went.

Jacob showed no effects of the night before. He sat across from Martin in a restaurant facing Leipziger-platz devouring lamb chops and fresh peas. The note was propped against a bottle of wine in front of him.

"Well?" Martin asked, toying with a cup of black coffee. "What do you make of it?"

"The quote is from *Henry VI*, by the way. I wonder if he really did read your book in French."

"The *contents*," Martin said irritably. "Genuine?"

Jacob chewed a slice of lamb and gazed for a moment at the chestnut trees seen through the windows. "Difficult to say. All it takes to find out is fifty pounds and a bus ticket. If you were a reporter working for me, I would say take the gamble. Fifty pounds—not such a modest sum when converted to marks. One pound sterling at this morning's rate, about one million, five hundred thousand marks—times fifty—no, not a modest sum at all. Lieventhal. At least he's specific about his information. Have you met Lieventhal, by the way?"

"Once in London, and once here, briefly."

"Charming fellow. A good friend of my father's. I spent two weeks one summer with him and his daughter—Amelia—sailing the Baltic on Father's yacht. That would have been, oh, nineteen twelve I imagine. Haven't seen him since."

"Or Amelia?"

"No. Horrid little brat."

Martin choked down a swig of black coffee, treating it as medicine for his splitting skull.

"She's changed—somewhat."

He had always shunned informers in the past, never having found the information worth the price. It smacked of the police beat, the money doled out on a regular basis to shoeshine boys, hackies, station-house sergeants, and ladies of the night. It paid off in crime stories, but rarely, if ever, in politics—at least not for fifty pounds, inflation or no inflation.

But he was sufficiently curious to wait at the bus station next to the ponderous, columned bulk of the Hotel Excelsior at noon. A number 42 bus arrived, trailing long plumes of smoke. He purchased a ticket and mounted the outside stairs to the top. It was nearly empty—a bus ticket was not a minor purchase in these times. He scrutinized his fellow passengers and took a seat in the back. People came on or got off at various stops, but no one approached him. As the bus crawled along Kochstrasse, Berlin's Fleet Street, a young man in a threadbare but neat suit swung onto the bus and climbed to the top deck. Unfolding the newspaper in his hand, he sat next to Martin. Neither spoke for several blocks, and then the young man lowered his paper.

"May I have the money, please?" he said in English.

Martin shook his head. "I pay on delivery. You'll have to trust me."

"But of course, Herr Rilke. I will not introduce myself by name, but I work on Auntie Voss—the *Vossische Zeitung*—as a clerk for one of the editors."

"That's a good paper."

"Yes, Herr Rilke, it is. During the war I was in the flying service—an observer. On my first flight over the lines in nineteen seventeen my pilot got lost, ran out of fuel, and came down on the wrong side of the trench line. I was a prisoner for the rest of the war. I studied both English and French to pass the time—also shorthand writing. I tell you this so you will know you are not talking to an unintelligent man."

Martin took a good look at him. He was in his middle twenties with the pale Nordic complexion and blue eyes of the north German, Mecklenburg or Schleswig-Holstein. His features were thin and pinched and there was a fragility about him, as though he were on the verge of malnutrition—which he probably was.

"You can come to the point now," Martin said.

"Yes." He took an envelope from the inside pocket of his jacket and held it tightly in his hand. "I have written down in greater detail what it is I shall now tell you. It is so. There is a secret society composed only of those men who were fliers or observers in the air service during the war. It is not a large group, and almost all of them were officers. They meet from time to time, not on a regular basis, at any of several bars and cafés in the city. Six members of this society—the Black Knights of the Sky—are plotting to assassinate Erich Lieventhal. Plans are now set. Only the exact time of the murder has not been finalized."

"Does your paper know about this?"

"Yes, Herr Rilke. So do the police. But you must understand that there have been at least twenty known plots to assassinate the minister in the past eight months alone. Freikorps bands openly boast of planning to kill him and the police do nothing—except place bodyguards at the minister's disposal. My own editor does not take the Black Knights of the Sky seriously."

"What makes you think I will?"

"Because," he said in a low, intense voice, "I know it to be true."

"Do you belong to the society?"

"No, Herr Rilke. I do not join *völkisch* organizations."

"Are they linked with the National Socialists?"

The man frowned. "The Nationalsozialisten in Bavaria? No. *Lumpenpack,* that group. These men are idealists—patriots—or so they believe. I know two or three of them—not the conspirators. That is a secret it would be impossible for me to penetrate—and live."

"I understand." Martin slipped a folded wad of ten-pound notes into the man's pocket and took the envelope. The man rose without a word, strolled casually down the stairs and off the bus into the flowing crowd.

Martin fixed himself a scotch and soda and drank it while Jacob read and reread the tightly jammed pages of handwriting before him.

"Extraordinary," Jacob finally said. "So Teutonic. Black Knights of the Sky! Blood oaths . . . suicide pacts . . . brotherhood to the death. Do you believe this?"

"I have no reason not to believe it."

"What are you going to do with it?"

"See Lieventhal first of all. Let him read it. Then—well, I'm not sure. I doubt if a Berlin paper would touch it. The mood is too shaky at the moment. I could send it out over the wires and let the British and American papers break the story. That might embarrass Weimar enough to make them act positively for a change and really crack down on these groups."

Jacob snorted. "Crack down on them with what? Half the regular army is in league with the Freikorps troops, and the police merely stand around wringing their hands."

"I'm open to suggestion."

"My advice, Martin, is to show this to Lieventhal

and then follow *his* suggestion. I don't think sending it out over the wire would be a good idea. This is totally unsubstantiated material at the moment. Leave us not forget our little codes of journalistic integrity. I sack reporters who send in a story beginning, 'Rumor has it . . .'."

The Lieventhal mansion on the edge of the Tiergarten had been built for Professor Sigmund Lieventhal as a gift from the nation. Kaiser Wilhelm had helped design it, and the great Thomas A. Edison had come to Germany for the dedication ceremonies. The three-story pile of marble and stone looked more like a temple or a public library than a house where people actually ate and slept, but the interior was surprisingly warm and comfortable. The minister received Martin and Jacob in his library on the second floor, a long room of polished mahogany, crammed bookshelves, soft leather chairs, and vibrant Oriental carpeting.

"It was good of you to come, Martin. And you also, Jacob." He gave Jacob a friendly pat on the cheek. "Your father's death distressed me greatly, but I could understand his reason. Such a strong, vital man. Like a Viking when he sailed his beautiful yachts. He sought out death with great dignity."

"He had no fear of it—only of wasting away."

Martin cleared his throat and removed a letter from his pocket. "Your Excellency, we have come on a matter of grave importance. I was given this document this afternoon. Please read it."

The elderly man took the papers and walked over to a desk to read them. When he was done, he removed his pince-nez, polished them with a handkerchief, and chuckled softly. "Given to you, you say? And what did you give in return? Some money?"

"A little money, yes," Martin said.

"I'm afraid, my dear Rilke, that you are the victim of a confidence trick."

Martin exchanged a quick glance with Jacob. "I'm afraid I don't follow you, sir."

The minister tossed the pages idly aside. "Assassination plots against me are so common, the newspapers no longer take the trouble to mention them. I receive a dozen letters a week signed by *this* secret organization or *that* society threatening me with death because—of any number of reasons. You are a well-known journalist, *and* an American—therefore considered gullible. A story is hatched—not a plot, a *story*—and offered for sale. An exclusive scoop. Is that the correct word, Martin? Scoop?"

"Yes, sir."

"And you pay good money for a fabrication. Thus the confidence trick."

In the sudden silence Martin could hear the twittering of birds in the garden below the windows.

"I think," he said slowly, "that this is genuine."

Lieventhal glanced back at the scattered pages. "Black Knights of the Sky! The mumbo jumbo of oaths and fraternity to the death! The type of nonsense undergraduates at a university fencing club might come up with."

He sighed and got to his feet. "The real death threats are the ones I get every day as I drive to the chancellery. Some ex-soldier who blames all of the Republican ministers for stabbing the Reichswehr in the back. These poor fellows will never believe they were defeated on the western front by force of arms. *Never.*

The Republican politicians are to blame . . . the Jews are to blame . . . the Communists are to blame. Everyone is to blame except tanks and guns and aeroplanes and a million American doughboys coming into battle at the eleventh hour. And I am a politician, and a Republican—and, ostensibly, a Jew. It hardly matters that I am not by birth a Jew. They know that. 'Jew' is simply a term, a label stamped onto anyone who favored an end to the war and an end to the Kaiser. And so I drive to my office in the morning, and I drive home in the evening, and the ex-soldiers shout at me—or simply raise a sign that I can see. And the words are always the same—'Kill the Jewish hog Lieventhal.' "

He reached down to his desk and crumpled the sheets of paper in his hand. "Do you think *this* nonsense frightens me? It is just one more absurdity—and a minor absurdity to boot."

Martin gave him a helpless look. "Please, sir, I still feel that—"

Lieventhal clapped his hands, pronouncing an end to the matter. "I appreciate your concern for my welfare, but I am quite used to this sort of thing. Now, let's indulge in more pleasant conversation in the drawing room over good, strong cups of English tea."

She was seated in the drawing room when they entered. No painter, Martin thought, could have posed her more carefully. She sat on a small divan of yellow silk, large windows behind her, the pale afternoon sun falling softly across her.

"Amelia," Lieventhal said, "you met Herr Rilke at Werner's party—and I'm sure you remember Jacob Golden."

She stood up—a tall, slender, beautiful woman.

"Good Lord," Jacob said. "You're not the Amelia I remember."

She smiled brightly as he walked toward her. "But you're the same Jacob. Do you still get irritated with young girls when they ask a lot of silly questions about ropes and sails?"

"No," he said, taking her hand. "I know now that young girls grow older."

Servants entered the room pushing wheeled trays piled with delicacies for tea.

"Amelia," her father said, "you pour."

The conversation was light, dominated by Jacob's account of a performance of *Romeo and Juliet* he had seen at Max Reinhardt's theater and a very good vaudeville act at the Winter Garden. Martin found it difficult to concentrate on what was being said. The room was warm, the tea hot, and yet he felt a cold chill along his spine every time he glanced at Lieventhal. Somewhere beyond the smiling man, beyond the French doors and the garden wall, perhaps at this very moment, young men were talking in a bar or café, whispering dark plans for death.

"Do Romeo and Juliet actually get into bed together on stage?" Amelia asked.

"Now, now, Amelia," Lieventhal said. "It is hardly proper to ask such questions."

"But, Father, it's only make-believe. Reinhardt theatrics. Do they, Jacob?"

"Well, as a matter of fact, they do. But it's handled with great delicacy."

Martin excused himself and went back into the library. The sheets of notepaper lay crumpled on the desk and he smoothed them out with his hand, then folded them carefully and slipped them into his pocket. When he returned to the drawing room, Jacob was still talking about the theater, but Lieventhal was taking peeks at his gold pocket watch.

"I think we'd better be going, Jacob," Martin said.

"Must you?" Amelia asked.

"I'm afraid so, yes."

She stepped over to him and held his hand. "Please come again."

Martin could only nod. It was like holding Ivy's hand. Like looking into Ivy's face.

They walked through the Tiergarten in the dusk, not saying anything until they reached the Brandenburg Gate and waited for the traffic to ease before crossing Pariserplatz.

"I know what you were thinking," Jacob said. "Amelia's resemblance to Ivy is quite extraordinary."

"Yes. But to me, the resemblance of any darkhaired, violet-eyed girl is extraordinary. It's disconcerting how many there are. But it wasn't so much that, Jacob. What struck me was how young and beautiful she is. Ivy was that young and that beautiful when she died. These Black Knights of the Sky. What if they go after Lieventhal when he least expects attack? Perhaps on his way to a restaurant . . . or a theater? What if they go for him when Amelia is by his side? Will they shoot carefully, or cut loose with a submachine gun?"

"You're totally convinced the plot is real, aren't you? In spite of what the old boy said?"

Martin put his hand in his pocket and touched the folded papers. "It's real, Jacob. Real as death."

XIV

Wolf von Dix read what Martin had placed before him and then tilted his chair back and swung his legs onto a corner of his desk.

"And you say you gave this to Lieventhal to read?"

"Yesterday afternoon."

"And what was his reaction to it?"

"A kind of weary contempt."

"That's understandable. Death threats are hardly news to him."

"Why so many directed against *him*, for Christ's sake?"

Dix shrugged and folded his hands behind his head. "Because he's not afraid to stick his neck out and allow the extreme right wing to chop at it. Approver of the peace—if not the terms—signer of the trade agreement with the Soviets—any number of things not popular with certain ingredients of our ideological stew—these Knights of the Black Sky among them."

"Black Knights of the Sky," Martin muttered.

"Yes. *Black* Knights."

"Have you ever heard of them?"

"No. But then, there are so many secret societies. The Black Knights, the Red Knights, the Sons of Siegfried . . . Whenever three embittered ex-army officers get together they form a society. One such group murdered poor Erzberger because he had followed orders and signed the armistice agreement. That was his only crime—helping to end the slaughter. Don't look for any degree of rationality among these self-righteous thugs, Martin."

Martin leaned forward in his chair and tapped his fingers on the edge of the desk. "I was hoping you might know something about this particular band. That perhaps Anna . . ." He paused, eyeing the lanky editor steadily. "I think both you and Anna knew a little more about Herr Hitler and the National Socialists than was contained in your files. Am I wrong about that, Dix?"

Dix yawned and stretched his long arms toward the ceiling fan above his head. "That's possible. But then you casually mentioned that the little gold swastika pin had come from a friend's pocket. Werner von Rilke's pocket, no doubt, of Bad Isar and Berlin, your kinsman. I purposefully held my tongue. As for the files in the morgue, may I remind you, dear Martin, that I am the bureau editor of an American news agency. I send Herr Kingsford only those items that he can sell, and he is not interested in reports of minor beer-hall brawlers and Jew baiters."

"What made you so sure it was Werner's pin?"

"Because, like you, I'm a good reporter. I may make my living sending out stories on Berlin night life, visiting celebrities, and rising theatrical stars, but in my off moments I keep my ear to the walls and my nose to the ground. Werner von Rilke is the primary financial backer of the budding Nationalsozialisten party—'Nazi,' for short."

"Is that hard evidence, Dix?"

"As hard as it comes." He swung his legs from the desk and leaned forward. "I have people who pass on information, all of it sound as holy gospel. I'll make some calls and see what I can find out about the Black Knights—but don't expect much. These little societies have raised secrecy to a fine art. And Berlin is a big city, Martin—and as tangled as a jungle."

Martin scanned faces on the street as the taxi inched its way toward the Unter den Linden, through traffic congealed by swarms of bicyclists, great horse-drawn wagons, rickety trucks, and worn-out cars that seemed to stall or break down completely every few yards. Streams of people, overflowing the sidewalks, wove through the stalled lanes of vehicles. Two young, fair-haired men wearing leather jackets crossed in front of the taxi, talking earnestly, and disappeared from view in the crowd. What were they talking about? Martin wondered. Their jobs—or lack of jobs? Their girls? Or were they perhaps discussing murder? He stared broodingly at the passing throngs, but there was no point in that kind of crazy speculation. Equally pointless, he felt sure, was the possibility of uncovering the names of six conspirators in this city of so many millions. And he doubted strongly that any of Dix's informants had the necessary qualifications to penetrate such a close-knit band. There was only one person who could, conceivably, have the proper connections to ferret them out. He leaned forward and tapped the driver on the shoulder.

"Take me to the Grunewald."

The von Rilkes' majordomo, splendid in velvet

jacket with brass buttons, was quite taken aback by Martin's arrival at the house in a wheezing, spluttering Berlin taxicab. It was not the custom for visitors to drop by unexpectedly. Every morning the majordomo was presented with a list of callers by Frederick von Rilke's secretary, with the approximate hour of their arrival. Martin Rilke's name was not on the list—but then, he was, to be sure, a relative. Still, it was hardly proper.

"Herr Werner?" The old man looked puzzled. "He is not here, Herr Rilke, neither is he expected."

"Today, you mean?" Martin asked.

"This is not his residence. His apartments are in Zelton Allee, Herr Rilke, number forty-seven, off the Charlottenburger Chaussee."

A spit and a holler from Lieventhal's home. He felt like an ass.

"Thank you," he said, backing away from the door. "Thank you very much."

Number 47 was one of a row of four-story stone buildings of baroque design set back from the street behind a screen of linden trees. Flags flew from the balconies of several, marking them as the residences of foreign ambassadors. Martin paid the taxi driver with an English crown. The man was so startled to have a solid silver coin pressed into his hand that he almost stripped the car's gears as he lurched away from the curb.

Werner had a twelve-room apartment on the ground floor. The upper floors had been turned into two huge apartments which he rented to a Chilean businessman and the Argentinian chargé d'affaires.

"This was Father's city house in the old days," Werner was saying as he took Martin on a tour of his apartment. "I decided to turn it into flats. I live like a cozy bachelor here with a cook and a valet." He indicated the spacious billiard room. "Would you care for a game of snooker?"

"Not just now," Martin said.

"A drink, then."

"Nothing, thank you. I'd just like to discuss something with you. Perhaps you might be able to help."

Werner read the papers carefully and then placed them on the coffee table that separated their two chairs in the drawing room.

"But it's too fantastic, Martin. Black Knights of the Sky! Why, that's the sort of name one would find in a boy's adventure story printed in a penny dreadful. This is not to be taken seriously, surely?"

"I take it seriously. Lieventhal doesn't, and neither, I've been led to believe, do the Berlin police."

"I tend to go along with their feelings on the matter."

"Do you? But such secret groups exist—and are potentially dangerous despite their penny-dreadful names. Wouldn't you say so?"

"Your question seems pointed. What exactly are you implying, Martin?"

"I'm not implying anything. I'm asking your opinion."

"Yes, they exist." Werner stood up and began a slow pacing of the room. "It's not difficult to understand their emotions. They are men who fought in the war. Spilled their blood from Tannenberg to the Marne. The army was not beaten. It never surrendered. And yet the war was lost. So many men feel it was lost because while they were at the front fighting nobly for Germany and the Kaiser, others—Bolsheviks and politicians—were stabbing them in the back. And so all the sacrifice came to nothing. Two million dead and the fatherland turned into a living grave. A Germany looted of its wealth—castrated by its enemies.

"Yes, Martin, such little groups of angry men do indeed exist. But it would be a mistake to lump them all in one basket. They are not all Freikorps rowdies and street toughs. Many of them are sincere men motivated by the highest ideals of patriotism. Their sole intent is to see that justice comes to the traitors among us."

Martin's mouth felt dry. "Do you place Erich Lieventhal in that category?"

Werner paced in silence for a moment, then stopped and fixed Martin with his intense and troubled gaze. "Erich is motivated by his own ideals and sense of patriotism. A traitor? Hardly that, but his policies are being proved terribly wrong and Germany suffers for it. He's too weak and *diplomatic* with the West. All of the ministers in this pathetic Republic act the same way. They are like men trying to keep a dog happy by offering their own hands for the beast to chew on."

"The funny name aside, what you're really saying is that an assassination plot against Lieventhal is not, to use your own words, so 'fantastic' after all."

"I must admit," Werner said, almost in a whisper, "it is not."

"That's more like it. I'll be blunt, Werner, and I hope you won't take offense. There's a group of young men somewhere in this city. Men with the highest of ideals and the ugliest of pistols. I believe you have the sort of contacts who could reach those men. I think you could not only find them but talk them out of this insanity."

Werner stiffened as though slapped in the face. "I'm afraid I do take offense, Martin. I have no such contacts. None at all."

"I find that very hard to believe."

"I am not a liar."

"I'm not saying you are. Maybe you honestly don't recognize the type of men to whom you give money. Herr Hitler's storm troopers are not so very different from the Black Knights!"

Werner turned his back on Martin and looked toward the windows at the flickering green linden trees. "You have no right to criticize who I back or do not back. Hitler is not an assassin. He wishes only to heal. You can't understand that, Martin, because you are one of the victors. I regret deeply having to say this, but I must ask you to leave my house."

The pages handed to him on the bus were now worn and limp, the cheap paper beginning to deteriorate, the writing barely legible. Martin knew each word by heart. The pages lay on top of the dresser where he could see them as he struggled to turn his black tie into an acceptable bow. Was he the victim of a confidence trick? He wished to God he were. It would have been fifty pounds well spent. But the tattered paper sent a chill through his body. What they contained was as real, and as deadly, as a coiled snake.

He took a taxi to the Adlon Hotel and picked up Jacob, who was standing in front of the awning.

"You're a bit late, old boy," Jacob said as he got into the cab. "Have trouble with your shirt studs?"

"Tie. I might just buy one of those ready-made ones attached to an elastic band."

"I'm afraid you'll never be a social success, Martin." He lit a cigarette and leaned back in the seat. "Any luck at all today?"

"No. One blank wall after the other."

"I'd stop worrying about it if I were you. No one else seems overly concerned. Just a sign of the times, as it were. Men of Lieventhal's stature learn to take it all in stride. They develop a strong sense of fatalism—a German characteristic to begin with. Being threatened with death nearly every day merely strengthens it. You have to admire the old boy. He doesn't deviate from his established routines. Never drives to the chancellery by different routes or leaves at different times. Regular as clockwork, there and back. It makes it easy for the Berlin police to keep an eye on him."

"Who told you all that?"

"Amelia. I took her to lunch today."

"Oh?"

"Yes." He sounded vaguely defensive. "She's a delightful girl."

"Woman, Jacob—woman."

"Is she? I hadn't noticed. Certainly a very *young* woman. I felt downright avuncular."

"That must have been a novel experience for you."

"As a matter of fact it was. It made me feel protective. I told her about your cloak-and-dagger incident on the bus—and the letter. She was very appreciative of your concern—and mine, of course."

"Of course."

"To cut the story of a long and pleasant afternoon short, Amelia is as fatalistic as her father. Concern, but not a shred of panic. She told me that the police know his routines. They can set their watches by him. Six days a week at seven-fifteen every morning he leaves the house, drives along Charlottenburger past the gate, then down Wilhelmstrasse to the chancellery. The police watch his progress—wary but unobtrusive. They do the same when he leaves his office at precisely six-thirty in the evening. His addiction to routine keeps him relatively safe. Any assassination group worth its salt must know that his car is always being tailed and that the two beefy guys puttering along in the Opel behind the limousine aren't out for an airing. They'd be taking a hell of a chance if they tried to get to him. The local bobbies may be hopeless at nipping conspiracies in the bud, but they know how to follow a car. Does that make you feel better?"

"I'm not sure."

"Well, it certainly made *me* feel better. Your informant may have been correct, but in all probability it's no more than one of scores of half-baked ideas hatched over brimming mugs of beer and quite forgotten in the morning. Still, you got your money's worth. Amelia's terribly grateful."

Martin glared at him in irritation. "What's that supposed to mean?"

Jacob leaned forward and stabbed his cigarette into an ashtray. "I honestly couldn't say, dear fellow. A question of semantics—my *girl* vis-à-vis your *woman*."

*   *   *

Erich Lieventhal loved the city of Berlin, and had been, before the war—and for a time during it—very much a part of its night life, a familiar figure at the opera, the theaters, and nightclubs. Such places still existed, of course, but he would not go to them. The vision of men in top hats and women in furs alighting from gleaming limousines in front of the Winter Garden or the opera house and strolling inside past hordes of restless poor was too painful for him. So was the thought of having a fine dinner in the comforting *Germütlichkeit* of an elegant restaurant while, perhaps only a few doors away, long, patient lines of ragged gray blobs lined up for a tin bowl of turnip soup at a Salvation Army kitchen. His entertaining was done at home. It was, at times, lavish—but beyond view of the hungry and the dispossessed.

A servant took their coats and another servant escorted them upstairs to the ballroom, from which came the melodic strains of a small orchestra playing "April Showers." Beautifully dressed couples were dancing under the shimmering glow of a crystal chandelier while others lined the great room enjoying cocktails and hors d'oeuves.

"Is my tie straight?" Martin asked before entering.

"Reasonably," Jacob said. "There's Amelia, dancing with a chap who looks like Siegfried."

Martin saw her, slender and lovely in a dress of the latest style, dancing with a tall blond man of her own age. He looked away and walked toward the long table where servants in white mess jackets were pouring champagne.

The orchestra swung into "A Pretty Girl Is Like a Melody" and Martin felt a touch on his shoulder. He turned, glass in hand, to face a smiling Amelia.

"Is it proper for a lady to ask a man to dance?"

"I'm not sure," he said. "You could ask and see what happens."

"Very well, I shall. May I have this dance, Herr Rilke?"

"Only if you call me Martin."

"Very well, *Martin.*"

He set his glass on the table and took her hand. "It will be a pleasure—at least for me. I have to warn you, I'm not as good a dancer as your last partner."

"Kurt? Oh, he's not very good. His lips move when he dances. He counts the cadence—one-two-three, one-two-three. I don't like to dance with Kurt at all— although all the girls are mad about him. He's very handsome, but he knows it. He's very conceited. Don't you hate conceited people, Herr—Martin?"

"Yes." He held her stiffly, unwilling to press her body against his own. She was aware of his reluctance.

"You can hold me closer. It's allowed these days."

"Sorry. I'm not used to dancing."

"You're doing very nicely. You simply need to relax more."

He found that difficult to do. He was thinking of the first time he had danced with Ivy—in London—Ivy in her nurse's uniform of blue and red. The music had been a tango and he had held her tightly, her body fitting so neatly against him. He had thought it miraculous at the time, as though God had made them for each other. Two pieces of the same entity.

"That's better," she said. "And you lied. You're very good."

"I think you're just being polite. How old are you, Amelia? Eighteen?"

"I'll be nineteen in a short while."

"Going to school?"

"I was at a finishing school in Zürich, but I hated it. All of the girls were snobs. What I really want to do is go to Heidelberg or the Sorbonne and study chemistry, but Father refuses to send me. He's terribly old-fashioned. To Father, a good education for a girl consists of learning to play the piano—but not *too* well—and learning to sew and embroider—*very* well."

The music ended and then swung into a fast two-step. Martin smiled at her in apology. "That's a bit more than I can manage."

"Then we shall sit this one out. I wanted the chance to talk to you anyway. Would you get me a glass of punch? We can talk on the balcony."

She was waiting on the balcony, leaning against the stone balustrade and gazing into the garden below. He handed her the glass of punch.

"Thank you very much." She looked at him somberly. "I was deeply touched by your concern for Father's safety. How brave of you to go on that adventure."

"It was hardly an adventure, Amelia. Merely a bus ride at high noon."

"I disagree. Anything could happen in Berlin these days."

"That's really my point, but your father doesn't see it quite the same way."

"But he's so used to threats. If he reacted strongly to every one of them, he would spend his days hiding in his room behind armed guards and machine guns."

"He could at least have bodyguards."

"How many of them? One or a hundred? Besides,

he feels that bodyguards would only give satisfaction
to his enemies by offering visible proof that he's
afraid of them. He's not afraid. He has only contempt
for those who consider him a traitor to the *Volk*. But
neither is he foolish. Leon, Father's driver, was a soldier and keeps a reolver under the front seat—and the
police follow Papa in Berlin and Weimar at a discreet
distance. What more can be done? There has been
violence in the past and no doubt there will be more
violence in the future, but one simply cannot wilt under it in fear."

He smiled gently and touched the side of her
cheek—the skin soft as down. "Spoken very bravely."

"I'm my father's daughter, that is why." She looked
away from him, at the moon-drenched garden below.
"How long will you be staying in Berlin?"

"I'm not sure. I have no specific plans at the moment, although I would like to get down to Essen."

"I understand that would be difficult. And Father
said it was dangerous. The French and Belgian soldiers are quick to start shooting."

"I know, but that's my job."

"It must be exciting to be a journalist. I might consider it as a profession. Much grander than being a
chemist. Perhaps I could talk Papa into letting me go
to Oxford. Do you think he would approve?"

"You'd have to ask him."

"He would only say no." She sighed. "We have
nightingales in the garden. I love hearing them sing.
Do you like birds?"

"Very much."

"Are you married?"

He laughed. "Your thoughts skip around like a dervish. No, I'm not married. I was. My wife was killed during the war."

"I'm very sorry."

"She was a nurse with the British Army. She died at Passchendaele."

Amelia turned her eyes to the moon-tipped trees. "That name is a chill on the heart. Here as in England. My cousin Helmuth was killed there, too. He was twenty. He taught me how to ski."

The orchestra was playing a fox-trot and she put her glass of punch on the balustrade and smiled at Martin. "May I have one more dance with you?"

She could have dozens, he was thinking as they moved briskly across the floor. But as soon as the tune ended and another began, a tall young man with dark hair asked politely if he might cut in and Martin had to force himself to be gracious about it.

The party ended before midnight, the guests streaming out into the night to the waiting lines of limousines and taxis. Martin caught a quick glimpse of Amelia, but as she was surrounded by young men he didn't say goodbye to her. He was in a solemn mood as he shared a taxi with Jacob back to the hotel.

Jacob, humming softly as they rode, removed a cigarette from a silver case. "Rather a nice gathering, don't you think?"

"Yes," Martin murmured.

"Care to stop off at the Adlon for a nightcap?"

"I don't think so. Not tonight."

Jacob lit his cigarette with a small lighter and blew a lazy stream of smoke. "We've been friends for a long time, Martin. I was watching you dance with Amelia. She isn't Ivy, dear chap, she only resembles her. I hope you're aware of the difference."

* * *

Martin ordered his nightcap from Room Service and sat on his bed to drink it—three fingers of neat scotch. He then lit a cigar, the last of Uncle Paul's superb ones, and made a brief entry in his journal in his neat, swift-flowing Pitman.

Hotel Bristol—Observations and reflections.

Jacob was quite right. There is very much a difference, but one can't be blamed for taking advantage of the opportunity to indulge, even for the briefest of time, in make-believe. Closing my eyes it *was* Ivy. Seeing Amelia from a distance was to see Ivy. Beautiful yet awful feeling. Milton would have understood. His poem to his dead wife . . . *Methought I saw my late espoused saint brought to me like Alcestis from the grave . . . But O as to embrace me she inclined, I waked, she fled, and day brought back my night.*

The city never slept, it simply paused for a few brief hours as though worn down by the events of the day before. Dawn brought it to life again in a rattle of streetcars and the plodding, iron-shod clop of horses hauling wagons across the Mühldamm, the river dark and oily in the half-light. By the first true light of the sun, trains rumbled into the Bahnhof Friedrichstrasse, disgorging their torrents of businessmen, clerks, and secretaries who could still afford the price of a ticket. There was hot coffee or a bowl of steaming pea soup to be bought at Aschinger's, and then a check of the day's value of the mark scrawled on the blackboards in front of the banks. An even three hundred thousand to the American dollar on this first day of June.

"My God!" a portly businessman cried out as he studied the figures in front of the Dresdener Bank. "We are all ruined!" His voice carried a tone of almost giddy excitement. The figures had lost all meaning. "Three hundred thousand marks—my God!"

The figures had a reality for the wasted shells of people inching painfully from the shelters where they had spent the night. The very young and the very old. Starved and bewildered. Hopeless. Lost.

Erich Lieventhal read his newspaper and drank his morning cup of coffee—good Brazilian coffee poured from a silver pot. He, too, read the figures, the exchange rate in dollars, pounds, francs. He drank his coffee slowly, as though savoring it for all those millions in Germany on that morning whose coffee was ground from acorns or brewed from turnips.

He read only the newspapers at breakfast. The other papers—the diplomatic correspondence and the reports from the other ministries, the cables from Paris, London, and Washington, the papers stamped *Secret*—a torrent of paper—would be waiting for him when he got to his office in the chancellery building.

The tone of the newspapers was bitter. But then, all Germany was bitter. It was understandable. He felt no anger toward their bitterness. They simply did not understand. How could they? Defeat was strange enough. Humiliation was beyond comprehension. Demands for money to pay the cost of the war. Demands for coal, timber, iron ore, barges, railroad locomotives and cars. And now the French and Belgians squatting in Essen, Düsseldorf, Krefeld . . . marching into the

Ruhr like so many bailiffs come to foreclose on a poor man's house. Bismarck and the great Moltke were rolling in their graves, pounding their tombs with blind fists of rage.

He drank some more coffee. He knew all that, and there was nothing on God's earth to be done about it. Not yet. One needed to be patient. *Passive resistance.* That was the order sent to the Ruhr. Even after the massacre of some eleven Krupp workers at Easter. *Passive* resistance. Not a bucket of coal to be dug. Not a tree cut down. Not a wheel to turn.

Three hundred thousand marks to the dollar bill. One million, five hundred thousand to the English pound. The savings of every worker in the reich wiped out. Gone. One egg worth more than the nest egg of a lifetime's work. But it was the price that must be paid. The Allies must be made to see—to realize— that the Treaty of Versailles had not been carved in stone. That it was no more than a scrap of paper and that every word on it was an iron nail in the German heart.

All this he knew as he sipped the last of his coffee, dabbed his lips with a crisp linen napkin, and stood up from the table. He removed a gold watch from a faultlessly tailored waistcoat, snapped open the cover with a thumbnail, and glanced at the time: 7:13

He walked serenely through the marble hall to the foyer and then down the three broad marble steps to the drive, where his car stood waiting, Leon Hofer opening the left rear door.

One needed to remain calm and have faith. Prosperity would return when the trade routes were open— when German goods moved into open markets. Good money would replace the worthless. The war indemnities could then be paid—if the Allies still insisted that they be paid—over a more reasonable length of time. They could be paid in coin and not in the swollen bellies of starving children. Time. It was the key to it all.

The sun tinted the Quadriga atop the Brandenburg Tor. There was traffic on Wilhelmstrasse and the Linden, but less every day as fuel became an increasing problem. Some cars and trucks were running on coal gas and carried a huge rubberized balloon on their roofs. In the Tiergarten, children gathered twigs for fuel and the police chased them away before they could damage the trees.

7:20

Time. Well, they would have to give them time. President Harding, Prime Minister Baldwin . . . the rapacious Poincaré . . . Mussolini in Italy. They would have to find the time or Europe would be dragged under by the weight of starved corpses. Vengeful politicians, generals, and sea lords had hammered the fatherland to the cross of Versailles. Now the businessmen must plan the resurrection.

7:23

"*Schwachkopf!*" The chauffeur swore as the lone driver of a six-passenger touring Benz with an open top cut in front of him.

Blame? There was no one to blame. The Kaiser, perhaps. The old regime, paying for the war by printing more money instead of increasing taxes. That might have worked if they had won. But they had not won. The *Volk* had cried out for war in 1914 and they had got one without paying a pfennig for it. They were paying for it now.

"Idiot!" Leon Hofer cried out as the car in front suddenly, for no reason he could see, stopped. He had to slam his foot on the brakes to keep from crashing into it. His forehead struck the windshield—not very hard, just hard enough to knock off his cap.

The sudden stop sent Lieventhal sprawling from the seat. Neither he nor his chauffeur saw the car with four young men in it come streaking out of Behrenstrasse and skid into a broadside collision with the Opel that always trailed them. The did not even hear the splatter of pistol shots as the two policemen in the Opel died. Erich Lieventhal knew nothing as he started to pick himself up from the floor. He did not hear the rapid footsteps of running men, nor see the hand at the open window on the driver's side toss in the grenade with the wooden handle. The grenade landed on the back seat beside him and he could only stare at it in that split second before it exploded in his face.

It was exactly 7:25.

The telephone woke him. It was Wolf von Dix.

"Martin? Your information was terribly correct. They killed Lieventhal—twenty minutes ago on Wilhelmstrasse."

He felt numb. The true horror would sink in later. Now he could merely mumble a few meaningless words before hanging up the receiver.

Wilhelmstrasse was cordoned off from the rear of the Adlon Hotel to the steps of the Ministry of Justice. A handful of overworked police were holding back the crowds and trying to shove the curious along. More police and army troops were arriving in trucks or double-timing in squad strength down the side streets. Martin, hastily dressed and unshaven, reached the barricade, where a young policeman refused to even look at his press card. He had to browbeat the man, acting more like a Junker officer than a journalist, in order to be let through the lines.

The effect of the grenade inside the closed car had been catastrophic. The bodies had been removed, but the blood-splattered evidence of violent death remained on ripped metal and shattered glass. The sight chilled and paralyzed with its mute horror. Martin could do no more than stare at it in a daze. Then, slowly, he took out notepad and pen. It was a story and it had to be written.

He was telephoning Dix from the lobby of the Adlon when he saw Jacob enter the hotel with one of the AP correspondents and head for the bar. He finished telling Dix what he had seen and followed them.

"Well," Jacob said, his face grim, "I guess the local bobbies believe in the Black Knights of the Sky now." He stirred the ice in his drink with his finger. "The bastards even dropped a note at the scene. Said they'd done it for the fatherland and the honor of the Second Reich."

Martin signaled the bartender. "Did you see the note?"

"Briefly. I was damn near the first person on the scene. That bloody bomb went off practically below my window. Didn't realize it was Lieventhal, of course, until I got down there and saw them take what was left of him out of the car." He took a big swallow of whiskey. "Anyway, one of the local bobbies had the note in his hand and I got a glimpse of it before a detective whisked it from further view."

The AP man shook his head. "It's going to be like the war from here on in. You'll see. Total government control—official communiqués and censorship." He downed his drink and stepped away from the bar. "This country's having a nervous breakdown. It's like covering events in some loony bin."

Martin watched the bartender fix his scotch and soda. Out of the corner of his eye he could see Jacob playing with the ice, turning it around and around in his glass.

"Ben has a point. Of all the people to kill. No sense to it. No sense at all."

"I know," Jacob said. "It's the insanity that frightens me. I'm worried about Amelia. Those thugs had no political motive. They weren't trying to foment a putsch or anything like that. They were simply out to *punish*. There could be another group who feels this bunch didn't go far enough—that the daughter needs punishing, too. That's pagan philosophy, isn't it? Slaughter thine enemy and the family of thine enemy—down to the last child!"

"I think that's an unreasonable fear, Jacob."

"Reason? How in the name of God does *reason* enter into this? That word no longer exists here."

"Have you had a chance to see her yet?"

"No. I tried to get to the house, but it's surrounded by troops and police. I'm sorry I went. Some of the men guarding the place were laughing and joking. I'll bet half of them feel that the late Erich Lieventhal got exactly what he deserved."

"A traitor to this country," Martin said softly. He was thinking of Werner pacing the room—the painfully hidden rage. "And traitors must die."

The AP correspondent had been wrong in one respect—the government had no ability to control the news; it was totally out of their hands. All during the long day reporters and foreign correspondents raced through the city following leads and hunches, solving the crime long before the police had done so. The killing had been so brazen, the eyewitnesses so numerous, that by the evening of the following day everyone in Germany who could read a newspaper knew that a secret, mystically patriotic society called the Black Knights of the Sky had murdered Lieventhal. An eyewitness had recognized one of the gunmen as a man he often drove in his taxi to the Mutter Engel, a café on Wilmersdorfer popular with ex-fliers. The eyewitness had mentioned that fact to a room full of reporters and there had been a mad stampede to the café. No exclusive story was possible, so they had pooled every scrap of information they had found.

It was considerable. The face and name of the one known killer was in every paper. The photograph taken from the man's apartment was disconcerting. It showed a slender, handsome young man dressed in a leather flying coat standing beside a Fokker. Pinned to his uniform was the Iron Cross, First Class. A blond youth with a steady gaze. A hero who had risked his life time and time again over the fields of France. Leader of a *Jagdgeschwader* who had shot down twenty French and English planes in honest combat in the skies. A hero but a killer. For some papers it was a delicate line to tread.

HOW DEEP DOES THIS CONSPIRACY GO? ran the headline in the democratic *Berliner Tageblatt*. They began their story by praising the flier's war record and then bemoaning the fact that he had been

led astray by extremists and reactionaries who sought
to cripple the Republic by meaningless acts of terror.

A hastily printed special edition of the *Volkischer
Beobachter* viewed the gallant flier in a different
light. They blamed Erich Lieventhal himself for forcing the man to take such a drastic step—"an action
motivated by the highest degree of patriotism. It is a
well-known fact that Erich Lieventhal was a member
of a small group of international bankers and financiers, mostly Jewish, who were seeking—with the aid
of Jewish bolshevism—to control the world. Herr Lieventhal has paid a terrible price for his arrogance and
deceit, but we, the National Socialist Movement of
Greater Germany, cannot weep for him!"

And rumor swept the city. In the western districts,
red flags hung from the tenement windows of the
workers. They saw in Lieventhal another victim of
Freikorps terror and elevated this man, who had been
neither the workers' friend nor enemy, to that same
pantheon of the martyred slain where rested Karl
Liebknecht and Rosa Luxemburg. The old *Spartakist*
banners were unfurled and two hundred thousand
people marched in a slow procession through the
streets to crowd into the Schlossplatz and listen to
hours of oratory while sullen-faced army troops
looked on. There were few incidents, but here and
there Red Front and Freikorps toughs clashed, and
one or two men were kicked to death before Lieventhal's sealed coffin had been carried into the Reichstag
to lie in state.

GERMANY, BE CALM! cried the sane and sensible *Vossische Zeitung*. THERE IS NO CONSPIR-
ACY AGAINST THE GOVERNMENT.

They were right and the rumors began to fade. A twenty-four-hour holiday was proclaimed by President Ebert—"A day of mourning for a man who gave his all for the Republic."

The funeral service began in the Reichstag—eulogy following eulogy. Black bunting. An orchestra playing the *Coriolanus* Overture followed by the funeral march for Siegfried from *Götterdämmerung*. The cortege wended its way slowly, to the sad rolling of muffled drums, to the Brandenburg Gate and on through the Tiergarten to the Lieventhal family plot.

If a great man had died, so had a father. Amelia, veiled in black, sat in a carriage between an elderly uncle and aunt. She sat stiffly and shed no public tears.

"It was good of you to come," Bernhard Lieventhal repeated as a select group of mourners entered the mansion on Charlottenburger. He was the elder of Sigmund Lieventhal's sons, but had left business and politics to his brilliant brother. He was a professor of chemistry at the University of Heidelberg and had been for over thirty years. "So good of you to come. Yes, so good of you. . . ."

Champagne and little cakes were served in the marble rooms. Muted conversation. The awkwardness of paying respect and showing sympathy to the living— "Words cannot express . . ."

"I'm sorry, Amelia. Sorry I was too late." Martin held her hand tightly and then let go of it.

She smiled wanly, the veil raised from her face and draped across her hat. "You did everything it was possible to do, Martin. I shall never forget your concern."

"If only I could have done more."

"So, Martin, you mustn't think that way." She

looked past him, down the long line of dark-clothed people waiting to offer their condolences. "Did Jacob come?"

"Of course, Amelia."

"I thought he might have returned to England."

"He's going back tomorrow. So am I."

A shadow of dismay crossed her face as she scanned the crowd. Martin looked at her for a moment, then moved on.

The von Rilkes were there—not Frederick Ernst, but his brother Theodor—and Werner. Werner stood pale and stony-faced next to Carin, apart from the crowd. Martin walked up to them and Carin hugged him fiercely.

"It's so ghastly," she said, her voice trembling. "What must the world think of us?"

"I hope they feel a sense of shame. Lieventhal once said they couldn't squeeze blood from a stone, but he was wrong."

Carin stepped back and dug out a handkerchief from her small black beaded purse. "Dear Christ," she murmured, dabbing at her eyes, "will it never stop?"

"I don't know," Martin said, looking at Werner. "Will it?"

Werner stared back, coolly unperturbed. "It will stop when a sense of order and direction returns. Not a moment before then. You know that as well as I."

"There have been over three hundred assassinations since the Republic was founded. That can hardly lead to order."

"A nation's destiny is often forged in chaos. Perhaps this is the final act—the final brutality. God grant it be so."

Jacob waited patiently so as to be the last in line.

When he stepped up to Amelia he took her by the arm and led her gently to the library where they could be alone.

"I haven't had a moment's sleep since this happened, Amelia."

"It was not unexpected," she said. "I knew they would kill him if they wished to do so."

"It's you I'm concerned about. I don't want any of the hate to touch your life."

"It won't."

"There's no guarantee of that. I'd feel a great deal happier and at ease if you left the country—at least for a while. I talked to your uncle about it. He agrees. He mentioned Zurich. You could enter the university there. I would prefer England. I'm sure you could get into a college at Oxford."

She was as tall as he and her eyes met his in a steady gaze. "But why England, Jacob?"

"Because—well—because I'm very *fond* of you. I would like you to be near. I'm not very fond of Switzerland, by the way. Not overly fond of mountains."

She nodded solemnly. "I think I understand. Very well, I will talk to Uncle Bernhard about it."

"Yes," he said with relief. "Please do that—as soon as you can."

As he turned toward the door, she held out her hands and touched his face, then bent forward and kissed him softly on the lips.

"Thank you, Jacob. Thank you very much."

The Deutscher Aero Lloyd Fokker with five passengers aboard roared down the packed-earth runway at Tempelhof, soared into the bright June morning, and headed for Paris. Martin and Jacob sat across from each other, and neither man said a word even when the plane landed in Frankfurt for refueling. Martin felt too worn out by events to do anything but doze. Jacob's reflective silence was his own affair.

They landed on the outskirts of Paris in the afternoon and walked stiffly toward the terminal buildings and hangars.

"Do you want to stay overnight and fly out tomorrow?" Martin asked.

Jacob stopped walking and set down his leather suitcase. "No. I'm going back to Berlin, Martin."

"When did you decide to do that?"

"Just this second. I've been agonizing over it all day."

"Amelia?"

Jacob nodded. "I've had this—*feeling* about her ever since the day I took her to lunch. Concern . . . protection. I can't explain it, Martin. She's so—*young*—vulnerable. Marbe it's no more than a kind of brotherly concern. I can't sort it out. Do you understand, or am I talking crazily?"

"I understand, Jacob. And you won't find any answers standing here. If you hurry, you might catch the plane for Frankfurt."

"Yes—yes, I'll do that." He picked up his suitcase and started back toward the tarmac. "Odd how things work out, isn't it? So damn odd."

Martin watched him run toward another Aero Lloyd plane that was loading its passengers. He felt a pang of regret—even, he thought dimly, a touch of envy. Then he turned and walked quickly toward the terminal building and the waiting taxis.

XV

Summer had lingered on into a hazy, golden October that was, Lord Stanmore thought, quite un-English. He was grateful for the warmth, however, dreading—after five months in California—the inevitable sleet and cold. The hot sun of that semiarid land had tanned his face and thinned his blood. Leaning back against his shooting stick, he closed his eyes to the sun. Pleasant enough, but there was no real heat to it. Yuma, Arizona, in September. Now *that* had been a sun! He had stepped off the train for a few minutes and had seen a Mexican gandy dancer expectorate on a rail. The spittle had turned to steam with a sharp pop—the way a drop of water reacts when dropped on a red-hot skillet.

"Would you like to time him, Father?"

He was startled out of his reverie of Yuma, the barren yellow wastes and the burning rails. Opening his eyes he turned his head and looked at William striding toward him through the tall grass at the edge of the track.

"No, Willie. He's your bloody horse. You have the pleasure. How far are you running the poor beast?"

"Seven furlongs." Holding the stopwatch in his

hand, he pointed off. "From Handley's Corner, up the rise, and down to the wire."

There was no wire at the moment, only two flags on poles stuck into the ground where the wire would be. Another ten days before the Sullington races began. Workmen swarming about, painting and repairing, mowing the grass, unloading and stacking a mountain of hay. There were several horses cantering about the grassy oval or being walked from the stables to the track. He spotted Baconian, his light chestnut coat gleaming like a polished penny. Young Ralston up, William's girl friend—or whatever she was—walking alongside with Martin, the two of them talking a blue streak, Dulcie Felicia Gower waving an arm in animated self-expression.

"What's Martin and—the redhead discussing, you think?"

"Dulcie," William said, frowning at the stopwatch. "You know her name as well as I do. I don't know what they're talking about. The life of Jesus, the Communist Manifesto—who knows?"

"Trouble with the watch?"

"The sweep's gone bonkers all of a sudden."

"Rubbishy clockwork these days." He plucked a silver beauty from his waistcoat. "Take mine, lad. It'll bring you luck."

Not that much was required. The earl didn't need a watch to judge the speed of a horse. Baconian, two-year-old son of Buckminster out of Pearly Pride, soared through seven furlongs like a horse possessed. It took all of young Ralston's strength and skill to slow the animal down.

"He'll do ten furlongs in two minutes six and bleak fractions—and on *this* turf! That's an Ascot winner if I ever saw one. There won't be a horse to touch him when he reaches three. And what a stud he'll make!"

Martin, lounging back in the grass and studying the cloud patterns, had not paid much attention to the workout. He found horses to be pleasant creatures to look at, but that was about it. "Willie thinks he's got this—cup—or whatever—in the bag."

"Yes," the earl said. "King George's Cup. I feel he does, too. It'll be quite a boost up for the Biscuit Tin. Of course, he's got one or two good horses to beat and Ralston will be going against some shrewd jockeys. But it'll take more than luck and jockey tricks to beat Baconian. That ruddy horse could race the wind."

It was pleasant to lie in the grass on a balmy day. The South Downs of Sussex. Low, rolling hills. Distant woods in yellow leaf. Indian summer they called it in Chicago and the Midwest. Martin wondered idly if the English called it anything but *decent weather for a change.*

The earl plucked his stick from the soft ground and folded the small canvas seat. "Well, Martin, it's back to Abingdon for me. Are you going stay and drive up later with Willie?"

"I don't think so. I've had enough of horses for one day. I'll keep you company."

"Splendid."

The earl drove the Rolls himself—with more skill and speed than his chauffeur would have done.

"That girl . . . Dulcie. What do you think of her?"

"Highly intelligent," Martin said. "A bit impassioned on certain subjects."

"Daughter of an Anglican bishop. First time I met her she launched into a lecture on free love! Quite set me back on my heels, I must say. Doesn't believe in marriage, but she's faithful as a saint to Willie. I've no real objection, I suppose. Sleeping with a nice girl isn't the worst of crimes, is it? And she's handy around the horses. You should see her up in Derbyshire, in old hip boots, mucking out the stables!"

"They'll get married. It's just the marriage vows she objects to at the moment. The honor and obey part. She feels it smacks of slavery."

"Today's youth! Minds of their own. Even more evident in America. *Flaming* youth, as the moving pictures call them. But I like America, although it is filled with the most curious customs. Take having a drink as an example. You go into a place, say the Coronado Hotel, sit in a splendid lounge. Waiter chap comes up to you and asks what you'd like. Pot of tea, you say—and then you give him a wink. If you don't give him a wink, you get a pot of tea. If you do wink, you get gin! Quite curious, but one soon gets the hang of it."

"I gather Alex is happy there."

"Why shouldn't she be? Little Colin racing around on the beach all day, brown as an Indian. And the new baby . . . and the new house in La Jolla with the most breathtaking view of cliffs and the sea . . . and James's business growing by leaps and bounds. Happy? That's a bit of an understatement. But she deserves it. Plucky girl, my Alex."

Martin had come to look on Abingdon Pryory as a retreat. If it had been Lord Stanmore's design to create a sanctuary from the turmoils of the second decade of the twentieth century, he had succeeded. The harsher realities of the world were screened out by the gates. In the great, rambling house, in the stables and gardens, orchards and lawns, it was Edwardian England at the zenith of its opulence and grace. It was not the best place for a news correspondent to spend much time. The temptation to pluck lotus from the trees was too great. He came for an occasional weekend, or to rest up after some particularly grueling assignment. He had come back from two months in Greece and the Balkans, had seen Zankov's murder squads gunning down the Communists in Sofia, and had watched the Italian fleet bombard Corfu and land troops in a fishing village filled with dead Greeks. All in all, a harrowing summer. And here at the Pryory the leaves fell soundlessly in the woods, and sheep inched across the lawns near the tennis court, keeping the grass clipped, and the horses trotted from the stables into the dawn pastures. There was peace, harmony—and honey still for tea.

"I wish you'd stay another week, Martin," the earl said as he turned the car into the gravel road leading to the house. "We so enjoy having you."

"Not half as much as I enjoy being here, Tony. But things are piling up in London, and Kingsford arrives Monday from New York."

"This chap Kingsford. A go-getter, I understand. Fellow I met at a golf club in San Diego advised me to buy a few hundred shares in his company. Not the news agency, the other one—CBC Radio. I bought five hundred shares and the ruddy things went up a dollar a share a week later. Seems to have the touch."

"I wouldn't say *touch*. Scott Kingsford knows just what to *grab* and how to squeeze the hell out of it."

* * *

He had bought Jacob's old flat—a ninety-nine-year lease. The neighborhood was becoming seamier as more and more clubs and restaurants crowded into Soho, but he felt comfortable in the place and appreciated the convenience of being so close to the center of things. It took him a day and a night to get used to the ceaseless rumble of traffic along Regent Street after the stillness of Abingdon. Finding sleep to be impossible, he pored over the accumulated dispatches from INA field reporters and the tips and leads from scores of stringers, looking for a story he could cover in depth. He decided on Turkey—the withdrawal of the Allies' Army of the Orient, the imminent proclamation of Mustapha Kemal as first president of the new republic. . . .

"Germany," Kingsford said, cutting into a double-thick mutton chop at the Savoy Grill. "I want you to go back to Germany at the end of the month."

Martin played with his own food, moving a grilled lamb kidney from one side of his plate to the other. "Why there?"

Kingsford chewed thoughtfully, then downed the mouthful with a swallow of Guinness. "Number of factors. First of all, as of this afternoon, the mark dropped to—are you ready for this?—twenty-five billion, two hundred sixty million, one hundred eighty thousand and no cents to the *buck*. And they bitch in New York because hot dogs went up a nickel." He sliced off another chunk of meat. "The German monetary system no longer exists. The zeroes are fantasies. They could print a ten-trillion-mark note and it wouldn't buy an English sixpence. That's one reason you're going—or, rather, living up to our agreement, why I would *like* you to go. It's your decision."

"I'm open-minded about it, Scott. But I've written about the inflation. It's yesterday's news."

Kingsford waved his fork at Martin's nose. "I'm not talking about *writing*. You won't be writing a line in Berlin. You'll be talking—on the radio."

Martin gaped at him. "Radio?"

"Radio Berlin. They have a honey of a station. Telefunken equipment—a damn near two-thousand-kilowatt arc converter, the works."

Martin took a slurp of burgundy. "I've never talked into a microphone. I wouldn't know how to go about it."

"Simple. You open your mouth and move your lips."

"No point in being facetious."

Kingsford's grin was huge. "I love, admire, and respect you, Marty, but you're an old-fashioned sonofagun. It's a wonder you don't wear celluloid collars and high-button shoes. Radio is the future, and that future is right here, alive and kicking." He waved his fork like a baton. "It's a new kind of journalism. The news coming into a million living rooms—hell, ten million living rooms. Fresh, immediate—while it's happening. Can you imagine reporting a *war* over the radio—the sound of guns in the background, screams and yells? Reality. There is nothing more real than the sound of the human voice. There's greater impact in that *sound* than in a newspaper headline a foot high printed in red."

"I imagine you're right."

"Of course I'm right. I haven't pumped millions into CBC because I think radio's a toy."

"I still don't see how you can make money. Everything you broadcast is free."

"You've been away from the States too long, Marty.

Sure, it's free—free music, baseball games, news. People getting something for nothing every time they turn on their sets. But America isn't Europe. The government doesn't own the radio stations. We can sell air time to companies who have a product they want to move. A short message over the radio can sell a lot of toothpaste or long winter underwear. There isn't too much of that yet, but it's growing steadily. It'll take some time to pay off, but don't worry your head about my going broke."

"That's the least of my worries. This broadcast from Berlin—"

"Two broadcasts—*two*. One in German at about six P.M. Berlin time; the other at midnight, in English, for transmission to New York."

"You can do that?"

"You bet. If I showed you the radio tower I just built at Sandy Hook, you wouldn't believe your eyes. This is going to be a historic broadcast, and an important one." He leaned closer toward Martin and lowered his voice. "A lot of things are taking place in Washington these days. I'm not one to speak ill of the dead, but it was a blessing for progress when Harding dropped dead. Coolidge may look like a sour apple, but he's a smart, honest guy and not afraid to ask for advice. He wants stability in Germany and he wants it now. So do the financiers in America and here. They want to invest in Germany and do business, but not with the mark sliding like a pig on ice. There's a plan being worked out between Washington, the Bank of England, and the new German finance ministers. I don't know the details yet, no one does, but you'll be told the whole story when you get to Berlin in November."

"When is the broadcast to take place?"

"Saturday, November third."

"Will you be there?"

"I'd like nothing better, but I have to be back in New York by the first." A wistful look came into his eyes. "Berlin won't be the same when the inflation's over, will it? You know, Marty, I once spent over two hundred *million* for a piece of ass."

The waning days of October brought a warning of winter in bitter winds and low, sullen clouds. It was too dangerous to fly. He took the channel steamer to Rotterdam and then traveled by train to Berlin. Dix met him at the station with his car and drove him to the Hotel Bristol, through a city bleak and cold, but crowded with people. There was an air of delirium in the rushing throngs. Those who had jobs were being paid daily, or even twice daily, and then hurried to the shops with thick bundles of marks, hoping to buy something, anything, before the money turned useless in their hands. The mark, on this first day of November, had plummeted to one hundred and thirty *billion* to the dollar. Kingsford's two hundred million wouldn't have bought much of a woman now.

"Did you find Herr Kingsford in good spirits?" Dix asked.

"Happy as a fed tiger," Martin said gloomily. "Are you up to date on what this broadcast is all about?"

"Reasonably. Herr Schacht will be sending me more data tomorrow."

"I'm not familiar with the name."

"You soon will be. Hjalmar Horace Greeley Schacht. Head of the Darmstadt National Bank. He's giving advice to the finance minister, Hans Luther, on a plan to go into effect on the fifteenth of the month. It's simple but brilliant. There'll be a new currency called the rentenmark, backed by a supposed mortgage on what gold there is left and on *all* of Germany's land and assets. It'll be pegged at the prewar rate of the old mark, four point two to the dollar. The rumor is that the Bank of England will participate in underwriting the new marks and that the Americans will rework the reparation agreements to be more realistic and less punishing. Thank God this madness is coming to an end. Democracy never stood a chance while a postage stamp cost a year's salary."

"And the broadcast, Dix. What am I to talk about?"

"On the German broadcast you'll interview Schacht and Luther, starting off by saying that America is deeply concerned about the deteriorating financial condition of the country. Schacht and the minister will then go into details on their plan. All very dry and formal. The midnight beaming to New York will be what you do best, a kind of verbal article about what inflation means in human terms. Pull out all stops, as Kingsford would say. Pluck a few heartstrings. The Yanks may have talked about hanging the Kaiser and General Ludendorff, but they don't like to hear of women and children starving to death because they can't afford the price of bread. It's a public-relations broadcast, Martin, to pave the way for whatever conciliatory plan President Coolidge is working on."

"It sounds simple enough—if I don't get stage fright at the last minute."

"You won't. Forget about the microphone. Simply pretend you're in your own living room talking to friends." He pulled up in front of the Bristol and a uniformed doorman hurried to the side of the car. "I'll drop by later if you'd like—we could go to the Romanische for a taste of the low life."

"I had enough low life in London with Kingsford."

Dix laughed. "I know what you mean. He told me once, quite seriously, that he required two women a day—for health reasons!"

Hotel Bristol, Berlin. Sunday, November 4, 1923
Observations and reflections.

Talking over the radio is like jumping into a chilly lake. The idea of going into the water is repellent, even terrifying, but once in—well, the water's fine. I couldn't hear myself, naturally, but Dix and a dozen or more people came into the studio after the broadcast and patted me on the back. They all said my voice sounded deep and resonant—a voice of *authority!*

Hello, America. This is Martin Rilke speaking to you from Berlin, Germany . . .

I can't for the life of me understand why I started out that way. It just seemed like a natural thing to say, like talking to a friend. Hello, John . . . Hello, America. Well, it's over—and I hope that was the last time. Not as unpleasant an experience as I thought it would be, but I still prefer shorthand, the typewriter, and the cable office. Scott Kingsford was right. I'm old-fashioned.

Hjalmar Horace Greeley Schacht. Extraordinary name for an extraordinary man. Prickly, brilliant, a chain smoker; not much for small talk, but sure of what he's after and what he intends to get—which is financial health for Germany. He expects the mark to tumble to four trillion by the middle of the month. When it does, he will permit it to drop to exactly four point two trillion and then wipe out twelve zeros. A theatrical touch. He's in his early forties, but likes to be referred to as the Old Wizard. After the broadcast he handed me one of the new rentenmarks as a souvenir. It's still nothing but printed paper—but nicely printed paper, he told me with a wink.

And so it will end soon. Order and stability, the matrix of any nation, will return. But how much damage has been done? Can the scars ever be erased? Stability, even if it comes tomorrow, will be too late for millions of people. The once solid middle class has been wiped out, the young have pinched faces and rickety legs, and the vaunted Lutheran morality of the old days is now a painted whore's face along the Kurfürstendamm.

His eyes were getting tired and he put pen and notebook away, poured a glass of Cognac, and sat in bed to drink it. Wind drove a thin, cold rain against the windows. He sipped the brandy, listened to the wind, and thought of ragged people huddled on the subway steps of Spittelmarkt, and of men curled under their wagons in the leafless Tiergarten while their unsheltered horses nuzzled the freezing grass.

When he came down to the lobby in the morning, he found that he had become, if not famous, at least better known. A smiling desk clerk presented him with a sheaf of cablegrams.

"The telegraph office says there are more to deliver, Herr Rilke."

They were addressed care of Radio Berlin, but there was one from Kingsford that had come directly to the Bristol and was in his mail slot.

> *All thrilled. Stop. Reception faint but perfect. Stop. Hello America catchy as twenty-three skidoo. Write yourself a fat raise. Stop.*

Wolf von Dix read the cablegram with amusement and then handed it back across his desk to Martin.

"I've seen him get carried away before. I wouldn't write too many checks on that raise or they'll bounce like rubber balls."

"I think he's sincere this time. Anyway, raise or no raise, I'm inviting you and the staff for dinner tomorrow night—at Resi's."

"Ah, Resi's. I'll have to sponge and press my dinner jacket." Dix swung his chair to face the window and rested his feet on the sill. "When are you planning to go back to England?"

"Tuesday."

"I think it would be better if you went down to Munich."

"Why?"

"Because I believe, from information received from various sources, that a good story is brewing down there."

"So? Send Kurt or Emil."

"Emil's been in Munich for the past ten days. You'll find him at the Sternhotel in Goethestrasse."

"Come on, Dix, I'm not a backup reporter. What's this about?"

"A contemplated revolt in Bavaria against the Republic. Nothing new in that, I'm sorry to say. Withdrawing from the reich is a Bavarian preoccupation. State Commissioner Kahr is toying with the delicious idea of becoming either a kingmaker and helping the Wittelsbachs regain the throne, or an Oliver Cromwell. He's hardly suited for either role. The point is, he's beginning to act as though a separate Bavaria is a fait accompli, which it isn't. Hitler and the Nazis are about as anxious to see a king on the throne as they would be to see Lenin. A God-awful stew is brewing down there, and your kinsman is salting the pot."

"Werner?"

Dix popped his monocle out and held it to the light, squinting at the glass. "Herr Hitler and the National Socialists have made big strides since you were here in the spring. Enrollment has shot up to nearly thirty-five thousand and they have a private army of considerable size. The Storm Troops—well equipped with everything from steel helmets and machine guns to trucks. Supplying an army, paying and feeding the men, that takes money; but then, Werner von Rilke has the money, so there is little problem on that score."

"Is that proven fact, Dix?"

"He's quite open about it. *Recklessly* open, I would say. Friday's edition of the *Munchener Zeitung* is a case in point. He wrote a long article which you will find revealing. You can read it on the train."

Martin helped himself to one of the editor's cigars and toyed with the ornate band. "There's hardly a state in Germany that doesn't have putsch fever. When the mark's stabilized, most of the intrigues will blow over."

"Not this one. Emil was able to get through on the telephone this morning. He said that things are heating up, not cooling down. The thinking among all the factions in Munich—the Nazis as well as the royalists—is that they'd better do something before the rentenmark turns from theory to fact. Strike while the iron's hot. The mark slumped a great deal overnight. It reached a *trillion* to the American dollar."

"They breed in chaos, these people, don't they?"

"Yes, Martin. Turmoil is their life's blood."

The train rumbled out of Berlin in the dusk on the long run to the south. An old engine and dilapidated carriages, the overhead light so weak that Martin could barely read the newspaper Dix had handed to him. He didn't have to read all of Werner's article. The opening words set a strident, almost hysterical tone: *Deutschland Erwache!* . . . .

Germany Awake had been written on the swastika flags. The article called for the people of Bavaria to throw their loyalty to Herr Hitler, who had the vision—and the will—to lead Germany to greatness and power.

He folded the paper into a ball and shoved it under the seat. Through the frosted window he could see the blistered slums of the city, unlighted windows and broken glass. It would be a harsh winter.

He thought of Werner as the train rattled and swayed across Brandenburg toward Leipzig and the mountains beyond. Was he going to Munich because Dix had assured him it was a good story, or was he going with some notion that he could stop Werner from plunging any deeper into the politics of discord? A combination of both, he decided, thinking not only of Werner but of Carin and the two little boys. Blood was thicker than water. And yet he knew in his heart there was nothing he could say to Werner that would alter his fervid beliefs. Drawing his overcoat tighter around his body, he curled up on the seat and closed his eyes.

Emil Zeitzler had received a telegram from the Berlin office and was waiting at the station when Martin arrived. He had been waiting for hours and looked drawn and cold, but he could still manage a smile as he watched Martin walk wearily through the frigid station toward him.

"A terrible trip, Herr Rilke?"

Martin gave the young man a baleful look. "Grim is the word, Emil. I never thought we'd get here. It was nice of you to meet me, but I could have found my way to the hotel."

He took Martin's suitcase and led him toward a side exit into a narrow street choked with wagons and trucks. It was bitterly cold with a fine sleet swirling in the wind.

"I left the Sternhotel quickly this morning, Herr Rilke. I believe I was being watched."

"By whom?"

"I can't say for sure. Two men. I think they were possibly separatists from Dr. Kahr's faction. The rumor I heard was that—but let's find a taxi and go someplace warm. I know a quiet little restaurant in Schwabing where we can talk in peace. A Chinese artist owns the place and the customers have no interest in politics."

They ate rice and tiny rolls of chicken wrapped in

paper and dipped in a sauce of soy and sherry. There were only a few other people in the restaurant, a group of artists arguing loudly over the merits of Dadaism.

"Kahr, General Lossow, and Hans Seisser of the Bavarian State Police have called a mass meeting for tomorrow night at the Bürgerbräukeller, on the other side of the river. I'm sure they intend to declare Bavarian independence—or at least the need for independence. Whether they'll propose restoring the monarchy is anyone's guess. Anyway, they're so touchy about it that there's talk of them placing foreign journalists under house arrest until after the meeting. And by 'foreign' I mean any journalist not on a Munich paper."

"Does Hitler go along with this plan?"

Emil shook his head and lifted a chopstick of rice. "God, no. He has more ambition than that. If Kahr succeeds, the Nazis are finished here. And the one thing Hitler would hate to see is an idiot like Crown Prince Rupprecht mounting the throne. He wants Bavaria to move forward, not backward. That's one of the things the Storm Troops have been shouting in the streets for the past week: Forward! Forward! The great example of boldness they keep referring to is Mussolini's march on Rome last October."

"Do you get the impression Hitler's thinking of stealing a page from the fascists and marching on Berlin?"

"I do—crazy as it sounds."

"The army would have to fall into line behind him in order for that to succeed. What can you tell me about that possibility?"

"Remote to impossible. General Lossow can't even guarantee army support for Kahr, let alone for Hitler. He doesn't even have command of the army in Bavaria any longer. Another general's been sent down. I don't know his name. It's almost impossible to get any confirmed information in this city, Herr Rilke."

"Well, Emil, we'll just have to use our own eyes. Do you know of a place we can spend the night? I don't want to risk missing that meeting tomorrow night."

"I met a girl, Herr Rilke. She has a large apartment on the Shellingstrasse. Her parents are in Stuttgart and she can find plenty of room for us."

Before going there, Martin placed a call from a kiosk to Bad Isar and finally, after many delays, was connected to Werner's villa. The servant who answered said, no, Herr Rilke was not at home. And, no, Frau Rilke was not at home either—she had left with the children for Salzburg.

He was grateful for that.

November 8 was a cold, wet day. Looking down from the apartment at the avenue below, Martin could sense nothing out of the ordinary. People went about their business. Traffic moved in a normal fashion in spite of the slippery streets. There were no demonstrations of any kind in view. Later in the afternoon, walking through the Odeonplatz, he was struck by the same sense of calm, unhurried behavior that was the stamp of this southern city. He saw no more than the usual number of police and none of Hitler's khaki-clad storm troopers with their swastika brassards.

"I get the feeling that absolutely nothing is taking place," Martin said as he met Emil for supper in a café near the river.

"Which in itself is out of the ordinary, Herr Rilke. There have been demonstrations of one kind or another almost every day since I've been here."

"Maybe they've burned themselves out."

Emil scowled and stirred his coffee. "Or are preparing to pounce, Herr Rilke."

There were at least three thousand people jammed into the cavernous beer hall by 7:30 that evening, almost all of them men. Emil had made contact with a waiter who had agreed, for three American dollars, to sneak them inside. He led them to a small table in the very back of the room near one of the urinals, a busy place on that night with the beer flowing. The acrid ammonia smell of urine was almost overwhelming.

"You should have given him more money," Martin said.

"It was the best he could do for us," Emil said, breathing through his mouth.

Martin noticed several men turning in their seats to look at him. My clothes, he thought, the English cut and cloth. Emil was aware of the attention also.

"We'd best order some beer, Herr Rilke. We'll be too conspicuous if we don't."

The beer came in heavy stone mugs, and Martin, making sure that everyone in the immediate vicinity could hear him, complained bitterly in faultless German at having to pay two billion marks for two mugs of watery brew.

"You tell him!" a man shouted, leaning across his table toward Martin. "It's an outrage!"

There were speeches, difficult to hear. The clang of beer mugs; muted, rumbling conversation nearby; the very pall of tobacco smoke hanging in wreaths, obscured the droning words. Martin had not brought a notebook, as anyone seen jotting down things in a notebook at a political rally was more likely to be taken for a police spy than a reporter and run the risk of a well-aimed beer stein hurled at his head.

Gustav Ritter von Kahr was standing on the low stage, making a speech. The state commissioner for Bavaria spoke in such a toneless voice and rambled on for so long that his very banality brought a hush to the crowd, his phrases reducing even his most ardent supporters to a semistupor. Waiters scurried between the rows of benches and tables bringing mugs of beer; the smoke thickened below the rafters; and a river of men flowed back and forth between their seats and the urinals. After one hour, Kahr showed no sign of drawing his speech to a close. The atmosphere of boredom deepened. Martin looked at his watch: 8:35. The evening, he felt sure, was a total bust.

He sensed their presence before he saw them—a vague shuffling in the corridor behind him. At first he thought it was a scuffle in the urinal between drunken men, but the sound persisted. A steady thumping. Glancing over his shoulder he saw, through the smoke and haze, men in brown shirts and ski caps, heavy boots, swastika emblems around their left arms, hurrying into the hall in single file and spreading out around the walls.

Commissioner Kahr droned on, oblivious to the rising disturbance coming from the fringes of the huge hall. Martin stared at the storm troopers hurrying past him. A few old soldier faces, but most of them young, grim-faced, and pale. Four men, sweating heavily, carried in a machine gun and clamped it to a tripod in the passageway. A command was shouted and from all points of the Bürgerbräukeller came an ominous chanting, drowning the pathetic words of Gustav Ritter von Kahr forever . . .

Heil Hitler! Heil Hitler! Heil Hitler! Heil . . .

His primary obligation was to INA. To delay meant yesterday's news. He wrote the story quickly in the spacious lobby of the Kaiserhof Hotel, overlooking the Englischer Garten. Six hundred words. The hard core of facts. When he was finished, he handed the pages to Emil who raced off with them to the telegraph office.

And that was that. He felt deathly weary after so many hours without sleep, but was too keyed up to go in search of a bed. He drank some coffee, lit a cigar, and watched the crowd moving in and out of the hotel—mostly officers in the. *Reichswehr* in rain-blackened field gray, or high-ranking officials of the state police in green uniforms. A squad of steel-helmeted regular army troops carried dismantled machine guns from the upper floor, their jack-booted progress down the red-carpeted stairway viewed with dismay by a frock-coated desk clerk.

Images pestered the brain, whirled like snowflakes in a glass ball. Six hundred words of fact, but nothing about the young Jew dragged from his room in his underwear and booted along Briennerstrasse until the storm troopers tired of the fun. And nothing of the old man in the Königsplatz buttoning up his Prussian blue uniform jacket with the faded sergeant's stripes on the sleeves and crying, tears running down his face, "Thank God Germany is saved!"

Nothing of that. Or the sound of the brass band or the sight of the swastika flags waving in the thin rain . . .

Munich. November 9, 1923
Observations and reflections.

The waiter assured me the coffee was real, but I'm sure they keep the genuine grind for the guests and not for unpaying squatters in the lobby. It is hot, but tastes faintly of dried acorns and chicory.

The images blend and it is difficult to sort them out and place them in the proper order. Not that order is that important. The event itself lacked structure and cohesiveness. Ignorant armies clashing by night. The frenzy in the beer hall when Hitler made his entrance, the chanting of the Storm Troops, the howls of derision from the beer drinkers. The howls turning to angry shouts and mocking laughter when Hitler climbed onto a chair and shouted for quiet.

He looked, frankly, too absurd to be taken with any degree of seriousness. A pasty-faced man in a badly tailored cutaway coat—like a maître d' or a Charlie Chaplin imitator. He was being howled down until he fired his pistol at the ceiling. There was silence then—shocked, incredible silence as the pathetic man on the chair holding the small pistol in a pale hand proclaimed that the national revolution had begun. A beefy man seated near me hurled his beer stein—a gesture; it hit the floor without breaking and rolled under a bench. "We've *had* a revolution, you son of a bitch! We dumped the pig Kaiser!"

That brought laughter—a release of tension. Catcalls and booing as Hitler and others pushed on toward the platform where Kahr was standing, thunderstruck.

Others. Only one I knew—Werner, a soft felt hat pulled low, the wide brim obscuring his face. But it was Werner—seen from a distance, taut-faced, walking stiffly. A thousand people separated us—but the distance between us was far greater than that.

Hitler's speech when he climbed onto the platform difficult to hear at first, but the opening sentence must have struck a chord, because silence spread, slowly, moving back like a wave until there was nothing heard in the enormous room but the sound of Hitler's voice—firm, impassioned, almost hypnotic. He did not denounce the commissioner for Bavaria; he told that sea of faces staring up at him only that Dr. Kahr was wrong in wanting to separate Bavaria from the rest of Germany. It was, Hitler cried out, the duty of Bavaria to lead the way to a new Germany, a greater Germany. It was Bavaria's duty to organize a march on Berlin to save the German people.

And that is the fact reported—Adolf Hitler made a speech before three thousand Bavarian separatists at the Bürgerbräukeller in Munich at 8:45 P.M., November 8. The speech was successful and he won the crowd over to his cause. There is nothing in the report of the hysterical euphoria that swept the hall, the tears and the shouting, the banging of beer mugs on the tables, the raucous singing of "Deutschland uber Alles," the hundreds of ex-soldiers standing on their chairs whistling or humming the old marching tunes—"Heir dir im Siegerkranz" and "Die Wacht am Rhein."

Nothing of that.

The crowds spilling out into the night, into the cold wind and the flecks of snow. Storm Troops everywhere. Fixed bayonets glistening under the streetlamps. Trucks packed with Brownshirts rumbling over the Ludwig Bridge. The fever spreading into the center of the city. Byron's stanzas coming to mind—*And there was mounting in hot haste: the steed,/The mustering squadron, and the clattering car,/Went pouring forward with impetuous speed,/And swiftly forming in the ranks of war* . . .

Rather more mindless riot than war. Wildly singing ranks under Nazi banners serpentining through the narrow streets. A broken shop window here, a manhandled Jew there; the wanton, gleeful wrecking of a socialist newspaper's office and shop—spilled type and smashed presses. No, hardly a war.

It burned itself out. The frenzy was missing at dawn in the cold, the wind, and the soft, wet snow. The Storm Troops looked bleary-eyed and self-conscious. They stood about in the streets under the soggy flags hanging from lampposts. They were waiting for someone to tell them what to do. The fire was gone. One man kicked the side of a parked car, rhythmic, sullen, the heavy boot thudding against the metal. A man hurried past on his way to work, fearful, eyes downcast.

"Dirty Jew!"

"I am not a Jew!" the man cried out, starting to walk faster—starting to run. "I am not a Jew!"

And there were rumors. The rumors of the state police and the army setting up machine guns in the Odeonplatz and of the Storm detachment under Captain Röhm under siege at the police headquarters. There was nothing to eat. Nothing hot to drink. No one had any money for cigarettes.

Nothing of that is in the report.

Hitler came. Only a glimpse of him in the Marienplatz. A glimpse of Werner walking behind him. Some of the excitement of the night before returning, but the bands were gone. There were crowds singing marching songs and there was the clomp of storm trooper boots on the paving stones, but no one knew where they were going. No one knew what they were supposed to do.

"We march on Berlin!" a Brownshirt cried, waving a banner. "We march on Berlin!"

But they were marching into the narrow Residenzstrasse toward the Feldherrnhalle, following Hitler, and General Ludendorff in his brown overcoat, and Werner and a dozen others who led the way.

And that is in the report. And the quick rattle of gunfire and the wild stampede away from the cracking rifles. The ranks of the Storm Troops tearing apart like wet paper as the men bolted and ran. Steel helmets and rifles being thrown away. Swastika armbands torn off and shoved into pockets or dropped in the street. It was over. The putsch had died in an alley along with sixteen men.

And that is in the report. But not what the blood looked like on the stones; the dirty scarlet puddles; a clot of spilled brains on the pavement. The pale, sweaty face of a young policeman vomiting next to a machine gun. None of that is in the report because it is irrelevant. Only pertinent information goes over the wires.

Fact. Hitler was injured in a dive to the pavement when the guns went off. A reliable observer saw him get into a car, in obvious pain, and be driven away. The police are searching for him.

Fact. General Ludendorff marched straight into the fire and was not touched. He is under arrest for treason.

Fact. Goering was shot in the leg. The police have told me that Werner von Rilke helped him away. They were seen getting into a Mercedes parked in Maximilianstrasse. Warrants have been issued for both of them.

"Hitler is finished," a Munich city official told me. "All the National Socialist scum are finished. You can tell that to the world."

But it is not fact and is not in the report. On a wall in the Löwenbräukeller where two thousand storm troopers spent the night waiting for Hitler to cross the river, there is a painted prophecy. White paint against a brown wall—SOON BURN THE RED JEWS AND LIBERAL FILTH.

And that is not in the report either. It is not, as Scott Kingsford would say, significantly germane to the story.

Book Four

GOD REST YE MERRY, GENTLEMEN

Christmas 1923

XVI

It began to snow a week before Christmas, a gentle fall that merely dusted the hills and villages and turned the landscape phosphorescent under the pale sun.

"I do hope we get more of it by Christmas Day," the vicar remarked. "The children do love it so."

His wish was granted. There was a heavy fall the day before Christmas Eve, deep enough in some places to block the less traveled roads. But there was no wind and little bite to the cold. Snowmen appeared with lump coal eyes and children sledded on Burgate Hill.

Martin came down from London by train and Charles met him at the station, Banes being laid up with bronchitis.

"Quite a fake cough, I believe," Charles said as he walked with Martin to the car. "Poor old fellow, he lives in dread of icy roads."

"You're certainly looking well, Charles."

"I feel splendid—although somewhat depressed. I understand from Mother you're going back to Chicago."

"Wrong by a few miles. New York."

"And for how long?"

Martin shrugged. "I'm not sure. Scott Kingsford wants me to organize and run a news division for his CBC radio group. Easier said than done, I expect, but I'll give it a try—and the salary is princely."

"Sounds rather challenging, old boy."

"I'll find out soon enough if an old dog can learn new tricks."

"I'm glad for you, Martin, but I'll miss your long weekends at the Pryory."

"So will I."

And that was certainly true, Martin was thinking as Charles put the Rolls into gear. He had accepted Kingsford's cabled offer without really giving it much thought. He had been soul-weary after returning from Germany and any change had seemed welcome. Now he had misgivings. Europe had been home for nearly ten years, and this spot, Abingdon, was where the heart lay.

Lord Stanmore smiled slightly to himself as he came down the stairs into the great hall. Coatsworth was standing at the bottom, a picture of martyrdom.

"If you would be so kind as to speak to the children, m'lord. They're quite possessed, I'm afraid."

"I'll try, Coatsworth, I'll try. But you know, they are children and it is Christmas."

"I'm aware of both those facts, m'lord, but I hardly find it reason for destruction."

"Destruction" turned out to be a small pane of glass in one of the ballroom's French doors—cracked in a game of blindman's buff. The house was filled with children of all ages. There were twelve boys and girls from the school, children who for one reason or another could not go home for the holidays. And then there were the Wood-Lacy twins, six-year-old Jennifer and Victoria, who had so much energy they always appeared to be in two places at the same time. And there was Winifred's new child, Kate, but she was only a baby and no bother at all—even to Coatsworth.

A broken window was a small price to pay for children's laughter. The earl's only regret was that Colin was not part of the happy noise and that Alexandra did not have her baby, John Anthony, upstairs in the nursery. Hanna shared his regret. It was the only thing that marred an otherwise perfect Christmas. But next year would be different, if James could manage to get away. Or perhaps they could go to California. That would be a novel experience, Christmas under palm trees.

"Mind if I pop in for a minute?"

Martin glanced over his open suitcase. "Of course not, Willie."

William strolled into the bedroom and plopped down in a chair. "Lord, Christmas! Soppy sort of holiday. I should be in Derbyshire looking after the horses."

Martin smiled as he unpacked his evening clothes. "Just a cowboy at heart, aren't you?"

"Something on that order. I say, that's a dreadfully wrinkled suit. I'll send Eagles up to press it."

Martin dabbed at it. "It'll hang out."

"By the way, a word of warning. Christmas being what it is, a time of cheer and all that sort of thing— not to mention roast goose, mulled wine, and mistletoe. In other words, the type of atmosphere Mother finds heaven-sent. She invited a youngish sort of woman she hopes you'll find attractive."

"Good God!"

"My words exactly. But you know how Mother is. Bachelors bring out her sporting instincts."

"I'll have to tell her that there happen to be women in New York. I don't need to export one from Abingdon."

"New York! What a marvelous life you lead, Martin. Will you be back in England next June? For Ascot? I'll be entering Baconian in the Prince of Wales—mile and a quarter. He'll win hands down."

Martin hung his suit on a hanger and eyed it dubiously. "Maybe you'd better get Eagles up here after all. June? Sorry. The Republican party convention is in June. I'm sure I'll be covering it, but put five pounds on the nose for me."

"Righto, and you bet the dark horse for me."

The woman that Hanna had invited turned out to be sweet, quite pretty, and dull. So as not to insult his aunt in any way, Martin devoted most of the evening to her—even kissing her under the mistletoe. The woman was flustered and Martin unmoved by the experience. Fortunately, she complained of a splitting headache and went up to bed early. Her headache coincided with William's playing the latest jazz tunes on the phonograph.

"May I have the honor of this dance?" Winifred asked. "Or is the man supposed to ask that question?"

"It hardly matters," Martin said. "These are modern times."

They moved briskly across the ballroom floor to the syncopated rhythms of Dusty Swan and his State Street Five.

"I never realized how tall you are, Winnie."

"*Junoesque* is the correct word. By the way, if you're wondering why Fenton has said so few words to you this evening, it's because I warned him, under pain of disfigurement, not to take you aside for an interminable chat on the condition of the world. You can do that tomorrow. Boxing Day is ideal for that sort of thing. Christmas is for unsullied happiness and joy."

"I couldn't agree more. Do you think he'd shoot me if I led you under the mistletoe?"

"He's more liable to shoot you if you don't."

He kissed her beneath an arch, under a dangling sprig of green. She drew her head back and smiled at him, her hand pressing his.

"You've been a wonderful friend, Martin."

"I've been blessed with people to have as friends."

Her smile was tender. "You know so much and keep such silent counsel. Jacob's getting married. Did he tell you?"

"Not yet—but he'll get around to it one day."

"He called yesterday. I wished him and his Amelia well."

"And meant it."

"Yes, of course."

He kissed her again, lightly on the cheek. "You'll see him before I will. Tell him that I knew all along it wasn't brotherly concern."

* * *

It was cold on the terrace. The clean, crisp cold of snow, a star-filled sky. There was no moon, but the stars sent down their own pale light. Turning up his coat collar, he walked slowly along the terrace, the sound of the phonograph fading behind him—*Dance time . . . dance time . . .*

He hummed the Charleston tune and strolled on, hands in his pockets, past the yellow rectangles of light cast through the ballroom's tall windows. Christmas night. And all is still—all is bright.

He took out a cigar, found a lone match in a pocket crease and lit it, holding the cigar to the tiny flame until it nearly touched his finger.

He'd be at sea in two days. The gray channel, England and the Continent slipping away beyond the curving wake. So much left behind. All the happiness he had ever known buried forever in a Flanders grave.

He blew a thin stream of smoke and watched it drift beyond the stone balustrade into the dark gardens. He could see lights far off across the snow-covered lawns, winking through the trees that flanked the drive; could hear the faint sound of many voices singing. He thought of Munich and the cold, wet snow, the lanterns and the flags. Thought of marching men singing of blood, terror, and death. Leaning against a carved granite post, he watched the oncoming procession wend its way closer to the house—people from Abingdon, singing, their strong voices carrying in the still air . . .

> *God rest ye merry, gentlemen!*
> *Let nothing you dismay. . . .*

He walked slowly toward the front steps and the approaching carolers, toward the marching ranks and the lanterns swinging blotches of light on the dark ground, and he whispered: God. Oh, God . . . let the marching always be to glad song—to tidings of comfort and joy

A cold-hearted bargain...
An all-consuming love...

THE TIGER'S WOMAN

by Celeste De Blasis
bestselling author of *The Proud Breed*

Mary Smith made a bargain with Jason Drake, the man they called The Tiger: his protection for her love, his strength to protect her secret. It was a bargain she swore to keep...until she learned what it really meant to be The Tiger's Woman.

A Dell Book $3.95   11820-4

Once you've tasted joy and passion, do you dare dream of

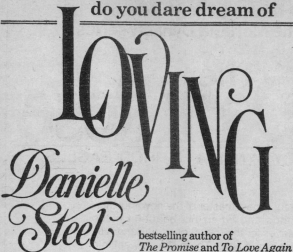

LOVING

Danielle Steel

bestselling author of
The Promise and *To Love Again*

Bettina Daniels lived in a gilded world—pampered, adored, adoring. She had youth, beauty and a glamorous life that circled the globe—everything her father's love, fame and money could buy. Suddenly, Justin Daniels was gone. Bettina stood alone before a mountain of debts and a world of strangers—men who promised her many things, who tempted her with words of love. But Bettina had to live her own life, seize her own dreams and take her own chances. But could she pay the bittersweet price?

A Dell Book ================================ $3.50 **(14684-4)**